LOCKER
ROOM
LOVE

FUTURE GOALS

GENEVIVE CHAMBLEE

HOT TREE PUBLISHING

Locker Room Love

FUTURE GOALS

LOCKER ROOM LOVE
BOOK 5

GENEVIVE CHAMBLEE

HOT TREE PUBLISHING

For information, contact the publisher, Hot Tree Publishing.

WWW.HOTTREEPUBLISHING.COM

EDITING: HOT TREE EDITING

COVER DESIGNER: BOOKSMITH DESIGN

E-BOOK ISBN: 978-1-922359-81-0

PAPERBACK ISBN: 978-1-922359-82-7

This book is not dedicated to any petty, rude, trifling, or spiteful people. Instead, it is dedicated to decent folks, aka the rest of humankind. Life is a playground. Enjoy it while you can. Stereotypes are not genuine definitions, and everything is possible.

To CKMC, I would like to say that it's true. Mommy knows best.

Finally, to my precious Leah. You are so missed.

FOREWORD

Although *Future Goals* is part of the *Locker Room Love* series, it can be read as a standalone novel. However, readers should be aware that there are some plot points and/or storylines that overarch across all books in the series. As a result, not all plot points or storylines in *Future Goals* may have a finite resolution at this time.

Additionally, this story is about breaking down barriers and busting stereotypes. It may tackle topics that are difficult to discuss.

The story is set in South Louisiana. Some of the terms, phrases, and sentence structures used are common regional expressions and may at first glance seem like a typo or grammatical error. For example, "What did you say?" may be expressed as "What you said?" "Why do you care?" may be expressed as "What care you?" Instead of "buying groceries" or "putting up groceries," it is common to say "making groceries" or "saving groceries" or "make a bill." There may be times when verbs are intentionally omitted. For example, the question "Who is that?" is famously expressed as "Who dat?" Furthermore, characters may speak using proper grammar in a professional setting but revert to their regional dialect when relaxed or in informal environments.

TEAM ROSTERS

Lafayette Ice Water Moccasins
(Minor League)
Dalek "Taz" Tazandlakova
Ian Whittaker
Kaden Blanc
Eric Chapel
Donavan Sawyer
Stavos Pokrefrke
Sartor Tzotzolas
Dustin Ames
Chandler
Pernell (coach)

Rebels
(Minor League)
Oliver Nash
Wayne
Barlow
Peters
Rich
Hyatt
Kitchens
Kelly

Wolves
Beau Doucet
Brody Simmons
Thad Clark
Gagon
Pittman

Owls
Timothée Croneau (former)
Aidan Lefèvre (former)
Giles Wayne
Nowak

Northcove Mutineers
Timothée Croneau
Benoit
Walsh
Andrew Calhern
Gerrick Polak
Pierre Tremblay
Joe Hales
Carter (trainer)
Bert Addison (coach)

Saint Anne Civets
Christophe Fortenot
Aidan Lefèvre
Gatien Glesseau
Brighton Rabalais
Semien Metoyèr
Nicco Bale
Vadium Stepanov
Francis Gillory
Jasper Jordan
Ludvig Enok
Rory Cathey (coach)
Carlton Varner (general manger)
Michael Darbonne (owner)
Harold Whittle (owner)
Shaw (owner)

ULSA Minotaurs (College)
Corrigan Ellery
Bowen "Bo" Nguyen
Ramsey "Rams" Theriot
Shade Franley
Roland Cardenas
Shelby Kavanaugh
Thad Hansford
Reid Larousse
Miles Posey
Hen Sweeten
Marshall Girid
Owen Massey (Coach)
Paul DeSevren (Asst. Coach)

LOCKER
ROOM
LOVE

1

CORRIGAN

TICK, TICK, TICK.

"Which way is it?" Corrigan wondered aloud, turning his smartphone to rotate the digital campus map and hoping something would look remotely familiar, or at least less Southern plantation. Rows of antebellum buildings—the very definition of grandeur and prestige—situated on tidy squares of impeccably manicured lawns adorned with hydrangeas, azaleas, and camellias surrounded him. Pretty for a tourist. Not so much for someone with a scheduled practice. When he'd toured the campus three months ago, it hadn't seemed as overwhelming or daunting. Then again, perhaps having a personal tour guide and being chauffeured in a snazzy Cushman Hauler had cast an illusion of simplicity.

He'd caught himself paying attention to the names boldly etched across the fronts of buildings, but it did little to help him presently.

The tree-killer map he held in his other hand listed the buildings by numbers, and the legend arranged them in alphabetical and not numerical order. And with all the construction, the phone's GPS Walking Directions feature kept steering him to a labyrinth of tall scaffolding, orange barricades, chain-link fences encircling heavy equipment, and impassible stacks of steel girders. The results: he was lost as fuck.

Dammit, he wasn't aspiring to rival or reincarnate Lewis and fucking Clark in expedition. The world had been mapped, and as far as he knew, it wasn't flat. But it sure as hell felt as if he was about to fall off the face of the Earth. Okay, perhaps that was a tad of an exaggeration. He only needed to get to Prograis Athletic Centre, the PAC for short, which a reasonable person would assume to be located near the athletic dorms. But no! Of course not. Not on this campus. Just like the financial aid office didn't grace the same hemisphere as the registrar's office, and the office for student affairs didn't issue student identification cards. To add to the crap pile, he'd been bumped from his flight due to over-booking. Because fuck his life!

His stomach lurched at the thought of being late. The coach had been clear. Tardiness would not be tolerated unless a limb was being amputated, and even in that instance, it depended on which limb and the credentials of the surgeon.

I can do this, he told himself with little certitude as he arbitrarily chose a direction. More precisely, he *had* to do it. As cliché as it sounded—and oh, how he detested being cliché, not that he ever was—he had no turning back option. Well… he could, but the consequences of doing so would suck, and he'd had enough suckage in his life. How would he look his parents in the eye when they had been so proud? Eh, maybe not so much *proud* as relieved, and perhaps even relieved was too strong of a word. Maybe it should be called laissez-faire, as said in this region, with a splash of reduced burden. Not that his parents would call him that to his face—at least, not these days. They wouldn't, not because it wasn't true, but because his father couldn't remember, and his mother lacked the energy to recall.

I really can, he continued convincing himself, something he'd been doing all morning. He belonged here. He'd worked for it. He'd earned it. For years, he'd sweated and trained despite the badgering and disparagement from peers, friends, and relatives who only visited on holidays. Even many of his teachers—the very people expected to support and encourage betterment—had joined the naysaying group. However, that was the past, and at present, he had no time for reflection. He was smack-dab in the middle of his own not-so-remarkable White Rabbit moment—minus the waistcoat and gloves—and getting upset wasn't going to improve the situation.

You got into college. Use your head. Technically, sports and not brains had gotten him into college, but he wouldn't argue semantics with himself at the moment. He was here now. Besides, a shortage of smarts had not been the reason for his dismal academic performance. Other circumstances attributed to his academic challenges. But his coach wouldn't give a shit about circumstances if Corrigan didn't haul his ass into practice on time. Bottom line. Fact.

He tilted his chin up defiantly toward the sky, recalling the one day of Youth Brigade Camp, a Boy Scouts of America knockoff group, he'd attended in grammar school before it was disbanded for low interest. "The sun rises east and sets west." It wasn't a groundbreaking revelation, but it gave Corrigan a starting point. Although the buildings blocked much of the sky, the small piece that peeked between the trees appeared brighter to his left. According to the map, his destination was located on the east side of campus. Maybe.

With nothing to lose, he turned left at the large octagonal building that seemed out of place among the rest. He rotated his map again as he rounded the building. *Finally!*

As the stadium came into sight, he suppressed the excitement of relief in case it was a mirage or angst-conjured hallucination. Two years ago at camp, he'd been tricked into consuming pizza with shrooms sprinkled atop. His so-called teammates thought it would be hilarious to witness him scampering through the dorm hallways with his jockstrap perched on his head. Fortunately, he'd experienced minimal effects and disappointed his teammates, but he'd heard habitual users claim that flashbacks could occur years later. Could now be it? He had no time to ponder the thought. He still wasn't where he needed to be, but the stadium was within view. If his memory served correctly, two miles on the other side of the stadium sat the arena.

Picking up the pace, he hurried across a parking lot and down a steep hill that he would bet his last dollar wasn't meant for foot traffic. Well, lawn maintenance would have to get over it, because there was absolutely no way he'd be on time following the sidewalk. However, cutting through the stadium would shave off at minimum a half mile. As luck would have it—and he could stand a bit of luck at the moment—one of the stadium gates was open for workers hauling in buckets of paint, industrial cleaner, and new chairbacks. No one noticed—or if they did, no one cared, which was more likely the case—as Corrigan slipped inside the ninety-thou-sand-seater.

Swiping the sweat from his forehead with his arm, he eyed crew workers meticulously painting the Astroturf as he trudged across Robichaux Field. He got it. Football was the omnipotent sport of gods. Nothing reigned more supreme in the South, and every aspect of the university was arranged for the utmost convenience of the pigskin Olympians of Beauvais Hall. But could the hockey arena have been situated any farther off the main campus? Another foot and it would plunge into the abyss of Minotaur athletics.

He supposed he shouldn't complain. The exercise would help loosen his muscles for practice. But damn if his weighty backpack didn't feel as if it gained five pounds with each step like a waterlogged boot camp torture exercise. Who gave homework and reading assignments before the first day of classes? Yet, honestly, the mound of newly purchased textbooks wasn't the problem—although, he much would have appreciated an e-book option. No, the humidity was the culprit threatening to drag him to his knees. How did people breathe in such heat? The Bronx got hot but nothing close to this Louisiana stratosphere of suffocation and misery. He willed himself not to think about it.

As he reached the end zone, it dawned on him that he hadn't considered if a second gate would be open for him to exit. If not, he'd be royally screwed. It was fair to say strategic planning wasn't his strongest suit, but if he intended on completing college, it was a skill he needed improving.

Fortunately, he had his pick of outlets as a flurry of workers scurried to unload crates from two eighteen-wheelers in preparation for the season opener in three weeks. *What it must feel like to have ninety thousand screaming fans.*

He continued onward, exiting to a flat concrete path leading to a bell tower. *Hot damn!* The tower he remembered from his orientation tour. He was certain he was headed in the right direction now.

After eight additional minutes of jogging—

huffing and puffing at this point—the PAC appeared ahead of him, and the air seemed to sweeten. In two additional minutes, he found himself on the front steps. A burst of cool air hit him the second he pulled open the tinted glass door. *Ahh, heaven.* However, as welcomed as escaping the unrelenting July sun was, he had no time to relish it. He still needed to find the locker room.

Rounding a corner, Corrigan nearly smashed into a wall of chest adorned in an ULSA T-shirt, a shiny whistle dangling on a lanyard, and a badge.

Shit! Coach.

Assistant Coach Paul DeSevren folded his muscle-swollen arms. "You're late," he snapped, his gruff voice oozing with irritation.

"Sorry, Coach. I got lost. It won't happen again."

"It better not." DeSevren's gaze scanned Corrigan slowly from head to toe, and his expression relaxed a notch. "Did you walk here from the dorm?"

Corrigan nodded. "Yes, sir."

"May I ask why you didn't take the shuttle?"

Shuttle? There's a shuttle?

Corrigan's expression must have given the coach his answer, because he shook his head before Corrigan could respond. "I've been telling Owen those campus tours are shit." Making a tsking noise, he scribbled something on his clipboard and then jerked his head toward the corridor on his left. "Hurry it up. Everyone else has signed in."

That's it? Corrigan's entire body practically jittered with relief. This was his hall pass, likely the only one he'd ever receive, and he wouldn't take it for granted. As expressed in the antiquated idiom dictated by a thousand old wives, never stare a gift horse in the mouth even if it's wearing wooden dentures—or something to that nature. All he knew was he was appreciative of the assistant coach not chewing him out.

"Yes, sir," Corrigan responded, thankful for the reprieve.

His gaze floated to the numerous framed professional jerseys of former ULSA players who had advanced to the professional league, the most recent two being Semien Metoyèr and Brighton Rabalais, both playing for the Saint Anne Civets. One day, Corrigan's professional jersey could be hanging there beside them. True, less than 2 percent of college players made pro, but it could happen. So when the NHL trumpet sounded its recruiting call, Corrigan would have to make sure he got in that number. The thought played in his head to the tune of "When the Saints Go Marching In," indicating that Louisiana was already beginning to rub off on the part of him that hadn't sweated onto the pavement.

"Go on. Git!" DeSevren ordered, snapping Corrigan from his fantasy.

"Right."

Music overlayed with chanting, laughing, and clapping drifted from down the corridor, and a charge rippled through his bloodstream and warmed his skin. A new realization swept over him. For months, he'd been waiting for this moment, and now it was about to happen. His gut churned with nervous excitement, and the anticipation of meeting his new teammates for the first time—his brethren for the next four years—distorted his face with a goofy expression, resembling a person straining to hold in flatulence. Or... maybe it wasn't anxiety he felt.

Holy mother of shit! That bowl of porridge with apples and raisins, sourdough biscuit, and skinny latte probably wasn't the best breakfast option. His stomach rumbled again, and he inwardly grimaced. *Planning.* He must do better.

Blowing out a shaky breath, he followed the clamor down the corridor. With each step, his heart thumped hard and quick, then stilled once he reached the locker room door. Above the head, a bronzed inscribed hockey stick read *"Les rêves deviennent réalité un changement à la fois."* Corrigan didn't speak French, but he'd seen the team motto written enough times to know it translated to "Dreams come true one shift at a time." Yes, he was about to step into his dream, which would make it a reality. All the exasperation from earlier dwindled as the elation of this moment preempted everything else. When he opened the door, the applauding, whistling, and cheering crescendoed.

"Percolator," someone yelled.

A few seconds later, someone called, "Charlie Brown."

Half-dressed men gathered in a circle cheered and recorded on their cell phones as several men in the center appeared to be having an old-school dance-off.

"The Carlton," another player who looked every inch of a young Billy Idol but with freckles and braces announced.

A guy with bulky arms resembling Popeye the Sailor Man pointed at him. "Dude, if I throw my back out doing this crazy shit, I'm going to kick your ass."

A burst of laughter erupted from the group but

immediately began fading at the sound of the door closing behind Corrigan. As more team members stared in his direction, voices quieted and smiles ebbed. Lips pressed in taut lines and curled downward as faces scrunched as if odors of rotting vermin and waste in the sewers had seeped through the facility's vents. The music abruptly stopped, and the room filled with a deafening silence. Corrigan suppressed a shudder at the iciness that now consumed the space. Suddenly, the room felt much smaller.

"You lost, jungle monkey?" Bulky Arms snarled.

A flurry of emotions raced through Corrigan, and he balled his fists at his side, yet the shock robbed him of his speech. Pooling tears stung the backs of his charcoal-colored eyes, but he blinked them away, avoiding providing evidence of his humiliation and pain as his absurd unbridled optimism plunged into a black hole. Only by the grace of God did his feet remain in place, preventing his fist from streaking into Bulky Arms' condescending mug and dragging him over the river and through the woods to Grandma's house.

A player who appeared to be of Asian descent shoved the guy in the arm. "Hey, man, not cool."

"Clamp it, Nguyen," Bulky Arms hissed.

"Um… the basketball pavilion is next door," a tall redhead with his hair twisted in a man bun added, his voice laced with a mixture of empathy and bewilderment.

Corrigan's muscles coiled tighter.

"When I call a practice," a deep voice boomed from the opposite side of the room, "at 10:00 a.m., that does not mean 10:01 a.m. or 10:06 a.m., or whatever hell time you decide to show up, Ellery. This is not a garden party where your presence is optional or a red-carpet event for you to make a dramatic entrance in a stunning ensemble. You will be on time or not bother being on this team. Do I make myself clear?"

Corrigan turned, along with the rest of the team, to face Head Coach Owen Massey at the end of the long row of benches.

"Yes, sir," Corrigan replied, responding to his surname.

"As for the rest of you," Coach Massey continued, "you should already be warmed up on the ice and not in here waving your pricks around and acting like a group of prepubescent clowns." He cast a warning glare at Bulky Arms. "Theriot, as captain, I expect you to make sure each member of this team is where he is supposed to be when he is supposed to be there. You are *all* your brothers' keeper."

Captain? Corrigan's frown deepened. This asswipe was Ramsey Theriot, the center he'd heard nothing but how amazing and upstanding of a player he was?

Nodding, Theriot replied with the assertiveness of a military private. "Sure thing, Coach."

"Now, everyone, dress out and be on the ice in three minutes," he commanded, turning to leave. "Not four. Not three and a half. Three."

There was a collective "Yes, Coach," as players scrambled to tug on jerseys, pads, and skates.

Theriot peered over his shoulder at Corrigan with a blunted countenance, but an edge remained in his voice. "Freshmen stalls are by the toilets."

Welcome to ULSA.

2

SACHA

So, this is what being banished feels like, Sacha wondered as he stood on the steps of Weymouth Law Center and overlooked the ULSA campus. One fuckup and no redemption. Weymouths weren't supposed to lose.

Thirty years. Wow! He ran his fingers through his sun-streaked auburn hair. He still couldn't fathom that his client had gotten thirty years. Honestly, he'd feel worse had his client been innocent, but for defense attorneys, innocence was an optional luxury. Losing the case maimed his ego, but the sentence had sealed his fate to academia hell and decimated his career trajectory goals. He should be in a courtroom and not some damn classroom as a teacher's assistant babysitting pre-adults. Hell, he hadn't liked school when he'd been *in* school. However, this was what happened with failure at his firm… with his family. They might as well condemn him to the guillotine or airdrop him into Siberia with three days' rations and no shoes.

He slumped against a cast stone column, his sleek tailored suit easily differentiating him from the main student body despite his baby face, and sighed. It wasn't his fault his client lied on the stand. *Pshaw*, his client had lied to him—repeatedly. And convincingly. Over and over, his client had insisted there were no foreign bank accounts. Sacha had even had his people—some of the best in the business—investigate to validate the existence of no such accounts, and they'd come up with zilch. But the prosecution had managed to find not one. Not two. Not even three. But *four* accounts. Four fucking offshore accounts with hundreds of thousands in each. And why had they found them? Because despite Sacha warning his client not to talk to anyone, his client couldn't keep his trap shut—or dick soft—and ended up drunk blabbering to an undercover agent in a micromini and with blow-up tits. His intoxicated ramblings relayed enough details that the prosecution had been able to hunt down all they needed at the eleventh hour.

But even the discovery of this incriminating information hadn't been enough to bake their uncooked chicken. No, it had been the lying. Since Sacha's client had been caught perjuring himself during cross-examination, the judge allowed the prosecution to bring it all in as evidence—evidence that Sacha previously, and masterfully, if he said so himself, had gotten suppressed. Talk about an epic clusterfuck. In eight short minutes, the entire case he'd built for weeks before the jury had been decimated to shit. All that effort for what? Nothing. Absolutely nothing. *Beep, beep, bitch! Off to jail you go.*

"Hey," Paxton called, exiting the frosty glass doors. "What are you doing?"

Sacha sighed again. "Nothing. Just needed some air."

Paxton's molten silver eyes softened knowingly at his younger sibling. "It's going to be okay. It's not half as bad as you think."

"Don't serve me that bucket of fish heads. This is your jam. You're here by choice and can still practice."

"You can still practice, geez. No one stripped you of your license."

Sacha's pained expression didn't change.

"Think of it as a refresher, a getting back to basics."

Uh-huh. Being a lackey. "Maybe I should join a monastery. Leave Saint Anne altogether." If he wasn't in a courtroom, what was the point of even having a law degree? Trials were his power source—his big bang and sonic boom all rolled into one.

"Now you're talking gibberish. You haven't even given this a chance. You're assuming instead of basing your summation on facts."

This elicited a weak smile from Sacha. "Clever."

"Here, why don't you take this over to the PAC?" Paxton shoved a large, overstuffed manila envelope toward Sacha.

"What is it?"

"Some contracts that need to get signed. The names and instructions are on the top."

So, the gophering starts now. Sacha screwed up his face.

"I know it's nothing exciting or revolutionary that will have you marching the stairs of the Supreme Court, but it'll get you away from here for a while, and you seem like you could use the break."

True. As far away from this place—the constant reminder of his failure—he could get, the better. Each time he crossed the threshold, he felt a piece of his soul rip out of his body. But if he was ever to regain his position, he would have to claw his way back up the corporate ladder, starting at the bottom rung and playing the game as the rules had been set.

"Fine." He accepted the envelope.

"Good." Paxton smiled.

Sacha returned the smile with less enthusiasm. Despite being six years younger, he and Paxton could pass for twins with the same lean build, plump lips, deep-set eyes, Nordic nose, and square jaw. But the similarities stopped there. Personality-wise, they were opposites, with Sacha being what his friends referred to as careful and tight-assed and Paxton as dynamic and cavalier.

"Now that's settled, why don't you come over tonight for supper? The kids are at camp, and Gretchen would love to see you."

Sacha inwardly cringed—not that he didn't like his sister-in-law. On the contrary, he thought the world of her, not to mention her cooking, being a chef and all. He wasn't one to turn down a free meal. However, he always felt out of place, like a third wheel, around the two of them. Their love radiated off each other like some cosmic event. Sacha had never experienced anything close to what the two of them seemed to have, and, at times, he doubted he ever would. For as much as he dated, he never became enthused by the women he found himself meeting. They were always *meh*. And knowing his brother the way he did, this wasn't a random invitation for a tasty meal. Sacha could smell another setup a mile away. No surprise there. It had been months since Paxton last arranged him a blind date. Sacha presumed it was Paxton's turn in the family who-fixes-Sacha-up roulette. A few weeks ago, it had been his sister and the prior month his mother. He probably held the record for the most dead-end setups. What was worse was that he wasn't even getting his dick wet. He'd all but resolved himself to being in an exclusive relationship with his right hand. Well, truthfully, he was ambidextrous, and if he got creative and contorted himself in the correct position, he could use his—

He interrupted his self-deprecating thought before it could go any further.

"I'm sure your wife would prefer to spend the evening alone with her husband."

"We spend plenty of time together."

"Uh-huh. Who is she?"

Paxton grinned. "One of the sous-chefs at the new restaurant."

Sacha groaned. "Pax, we've talked about this."

"It's one meal, not a blood sacrifice. It won't kill you." He looked in the opposite direction and lowered his voice. "And it's not like you have plans or anything."

"Right, because my life is so pathetic." Which wasn't far from the truth if Sacha was counting all the things going right in his life at the moment. "Thanks for reminding me."

"That's not what I meant."

"Sure it isn't." Shoving one hand in his pocket, he started down the steps. "Why do you do this to me?"

"Because you are entitled to and shall receive the same bullshit the rest of us must. I didn't get a memo saying you were exempt."

"What time?"

"Six."

Oh, goodie. Plenty of time to fill the day with suckage. Beginning with occupying his afternoon meeting with a gaggle—well, nearly a gaggle—of banal, pompous, unappreciative, obtuse jocks.

3

CORRIGAN

THE SOUND OF THE VULCANIZED RUBBER SMACKING against the ice followed by the thwack of it against a stick resumed after a brief recess that had lasted long enough for Coach Massey to reorder the line... again... and bark out new instructions... again. The play called for the center, Theriot, to pass the puck to the right-winger. Simple enough—or so Corrigan would have thought.

Everything went south from the start when Corrigan lost his footing at the drop. Call him peculiar, but the ice felt different from that at his old rink, and he hadn't adjusted. Yet his tripping hadn't been what mucked up the sequence. Shelby Kavanaugh pitchforked the puck to center ice, and

Miles Posey picked it up. Posey turned at the line with Hen Sweeten in front. Corrigan attempted to get past Sweeten, but Shade Franley, defenseman for the opposing line, closed him off. Swooping in, Theriot stole the puck from Posey. However, after looking to his left and spotting Corrigan as his left-winger and clearly the open man and sensible choice, Theriot passed right, overshooting his unexpected right-winger, Roland Cardenas, and sending it onto the stick of Franley. Nothing about this sequence had been executed well.

Conceivably, Corrigan could rationalize—to make himself feel more accepted and convince himself that Theriot was less of a jerk—that the captain had made his choice due to his left side weakness. The assessment wouldn't have been completely inaccurate. Most left-handed shooters—and Theriot fell into that category—favored passing to the right due to their dominant hand being positioned at the top of their stick. If the theory held true with Theriot, then what happened on the ice wasn't personal but rather Theriot covering a handicap or, at the very least, reacting instinctually.

Yes, Corrigan *could* think that. But he wouldn't. Why should he make excuses for someone else's shitty behavior? He may not be able to present irrefutable proof, but he sensed why Theriot had neglected to pass the puck to him. What he couldn't do was blame his shock on the captain. This was hockey. This was the South. It was something Corrigan probably should have expected—not because he deserved it but because it wasn't something unusual. He'd heard a lot. Read a lot in history books. Watched plenty of documentaries. The element of surprise should have been removed from the table.

A high-pitched shrill of a whistle pierced and echoed throughout the rink.

"Is this what we're doing?" Coach Massey shouted. "Everyone designing their own plays now like Tennessee Williams? Or were you expecting some Georges Méliès special effects to make that wreckage work? Or maybe we're in the Land of Make Believe, and a miniature trolly's about to pop around the corner and transport us all to a magic castle with unicorns and hockey goals that jump in front of pucks. Explain to me what was going on out there."

"Ellery wasn't in position," Theriot blurted. "He's too slow to keep up."

Asshole!

Although Corrigan wanted to protest that he

had been in position, the second half of Theriot's statement had been true, at least partially. Corrigan had kept up with his teammates but just barely. Until two years ago, he'd played defense. Then he'd caught mononucleosis—from where or whom remained a mystery. As a result, he'd lost twenty-two pounds, and he'd struggled to regain any of it. His former coach declared him too small at one hundred and sixty-two pounds and six feet in height to continue being a defenseman and switched him to right-wing before settling on left. Over the two years, Corrigan had increased his speed, but he remained slower than many of the other forwards—just one more struggle he had to face daily. Determination had kept him a spot on his old team and won him a place on this new one. While he might not have the speed, he was a banger at assists. He wouldn't permit some bigot to destroy his dreams on the first day of practice by allowing anyone to see how they'd gotten under his skin. *Restraint.*

"That may be," Coach Massey agreed, making eye contact with Corrigan. "So, what would you suggest we do about it?"

Theriot parted his lips to respond.

"Iron crosses," the coach answered for him.

"Excellent idea. Everyone line up at the goal. Iron cross to the other end and back. Let's go."

A sea of groans spilled from the team, and DeSevren skated onto the ice from the bench.

"What's that, ladies?" Coach Massey chirped, cupping his hand to his ear and glancing at his assistant. "Did someone insist they be allowed to do ten sets followed by suicides, Paul?"

DeSevren mock-laughed. "Sure did."

"Well, if you ladies insist, I wouldn't dare stop you," Coach Massey stated, crossing his arms against his chest.

More groans rumbled from the players. Although it had been Theriot's action and ultimately his mouth that had sentenced the team to the punishment, Corrigan received the stink eye from his teammates as everyone skated to the goal.

How was this his fault? He'd been guilty of many things gone wrong today during drills. Nerves. But this? No.

DeSevren said something to Coach Massey that the rest of the team couldn't hear.

"Everyone get ready except Ellery. You're needed in the lyceum."

Why? Am I being cut? Corrigan's innards lurched.

Players cast more seething glares in his direction

as he skated past them to the chute. *Great. Now they all think I'm being absolved from punishment.* He stepped off the ice and plodded down the chute on his walk of... what? Shame? He had no idea why he'd been summoned to the lyceum, but dragging his heels—or rather skates—wouldn't amend his having to be there.

Without bothering to change, Corrigan roamed the corridor until he came to a frosted glass door with Lyceum written in scripted, etched lettering. Had this been a television game show, he may have been granted an option to choose a door or walk away with what he had. Under those circumstances, he knew what his choice would have been. Instead, he sighed and entered.

Corrigan opened the door and was taken aback for a second. *Holy mother of South Sea pearl! What an undeniable mesmerizing male specimen*—not that he should be having such thoughts. He had enough complications without adding an out-of-his-league crush to the pile. Attitudes were changing in hockey, but not that much. Corrigan had just witnessed firsthand a few hours ago how little had changed with hockey traditionalists' mindsets. Or maybe the lack of progression was due to it being the South. Or maybe both factors—traditionalists and region—were the culprits. Or maybe it was neither.

It didn't matter the reason. At the end of the day, his closet door needed to remain deadbolted. But his hike across the universe and workout in Satan's den had left him too exhausted for this type of fool-la-la today. Ninety-eight percent of his body screamed for a hot tub and liniment oil while the remainder annoyingly twitched against his jock cup at the sight of Adonis reincarnated. And here he was standing before this exquisite demigod and looking like a garbage boat—not to mention the fetid odor wafting from his pits that could stop a Roman legion dead in their tracks.

"Mr. Ellery," the handsome man seated at the long conference table greeted as he rose and extended his hand to shake. His smile appeared cordial but didn't seem to reach his eyes, and his demeanor screamed that he'd rather be someplace else—not stuck-up but distracted. Honestly, Corrigan wouldn't have been shocked to learn the man was indeed a snob. He had the bone structure for it. Everything about him looked expensive. Hell, he even smelled expensive. The man oozed vacations in the Hamptons, private jet weekend getaways, and black credit cards with offshore accounts. Even his chiseled features and creamy skin looked as if he'd descended from a line of nobility. And Corrigan probably would have found this well-put-together man intimidating had it not been for his liquid mercury eyes with a dash of melancholy watching him... waiting.

Waiting! Oh. Corrigan tuned in.

"I'm Sacha Weymouth of Ananke Legal Associates," he continued. "I represent the Croneau Foundation."

An attorney? What the hell had he done that required an attorney? Was being late that serious? Or maybe it had been his traipsing across the lawn. Or, heaven forbid, his shortcut through the stadium.

He swallowed hard as he forced his feet to move toward the man at the table. Corrigan nodded as if the company name meant something to him. It didn't, but he'd go along with whatever was happening here. He shook Sacha's hand.

"This shouldn't take long. Have a seat." Sacha motioned to the chair across from him.

Corrigan did as requested and waited while Sacha sat and shuffled papers.

"I'm pleased to inform you that you've been awarded a Croneau Foundation scholarship."

"Scholarship?" News to him, but again... gift horse.

"Yes. Since the NCAA limits the number of university athletic scholarships that can be awarded, ULSA stretches those funds by awarding mostly partial scholarships. Each year, the Croneau Foundation offers up to four gap scholarships to athletes whose athletic scholarships do not cover the full cost of attendance. This will cover the cost of textbooks and necessary class materials such as computer software, lab equipment, art supplies, and so on. Priority always goes to students on the hockey team for the obvious reason. Your coach reached out to us and explained your financial situation."

Corrigan's expression flickered between surprise, enthusiasm, and frustration. While he could use the money since he barely had enough to scrape by for the semester, it didn't thrill him to learn that others were discussing his *situation.* He wasn't destitute—at least, not yet—and he wasn't too proud to find a part-time job. Plenty of students worked. He'd never accepted charity and wouldn't begin now. He'd rather wallow in hot coals in too-tight underwear or have his toenails peeled off with a dirty paring knife first.

Except scholarships weren't exactly charity. He

would at least listen to what this dazzling human with the sexy voice and Cajun accent had to say.

"We just need to finalize everything."

Sacha's smile broadened, and Corrigan could have sworn all the oxygen dissipated from the room. The way his chest constricted, he'd gamble that better breathing conditions could be found in a diamond mine. And the way Sacha's eyes sparkled in the overhead lighting caused Corrigan's libido to run amuck. Was he an asshole for ogling and objectifying this man? Probably. But the eyes liked what the eyes liked. However, Corrigan preferred to call it appreciation.

Sacha's lips moved and then stopped.

Oh. I'm supposed to answer.

Collecting his brain cells from wherever they'd fled, Corrigan tuned back in to the present. "Sorry," he replied, flushing a splotchy red. "I'm still wrapping my head around winning a scholarship. Could you repeat the last part?"

"I asked what your major is."

Corrigan's dark brows pinched. "I'm listed as general studies."

Sighing, Sacha placed his fountain pen on the table and interlocked his fingers. "General studies?"

"My advisor suggested it because I wasn't sure."

"Honestly, these advisors need to step up their game." He smiled... kind of. "This scholarship has conditions, one of which is the recipient must have a declared major. While general studies is technically a major, it's, shall we say, wanting of distinction. Is there anything you're leaning toward?"

"I'm interested in linguistics, but I don't want to teach or be an editor, so it seems pointless."

"Is there anything else?"

Corrigan shrugged. "Architecture, but I suck at math and can't draw worth shit." His cheeks flooded with color. "Sorry. I didn't mean to cuss."

"You're perfectly fine. I can't draw worth shit either." Sacha winked.

Corrigan nearly wet himself and emitted some gasping-gurgling sound. "Egads."

Calm it down, Ellery. Be cool.

Sacha's brows arched. "You okay?"

"Yeah. My advisor said lots of players get degrees in general studies."

"Only the players who don't give serious concern to preparing a contingency plan if they don't make pro. General studies is good shoptalk for the university because, face it, you're here to play hockey. That's money in their pocket for the next four years, but not if players are flunking out. Their investment in players is a free education in exchange for their athletic ability. No pass, no play. Then they'd go in the red. It's Accounting 101. General studies typically has easy classes, minimal effort to pass, and tenured professors counting down to retirement who don't give a rip one way or the other. And it's easier dealing with those professors than ones who insist all students do the work. Fifteen years ago, the university didn't even have general studies as a major. Then the university saw the benefits, and here we are."

"So you're saying it's a trash degree."

"Not at all." Sacha shook his head. "It has merits in a whitewashed type of way. It's more tedious obtaining a job with a degree that falls into the vague and elusive abyss of 'jack of all trades and master of none.' That's not especially valuable when you need a plumber or physician—someone who knows the ins and outs of a specific trade. You don't want just anyone fumbling around with your pipes. You want someone who knows what he's doing."

You can fool around with my pipes anytime. Dammit. Uh-uh. Not going there. Concentrate! "What's wrong with being well-rounded?"

"Nothing for ordinary people who won't have assumptions made about being promoted solely for the benefit of the university." He picked up the pen and tapped it against the table. "Besides, that's why tutors exist. All athletes are required to have a study hour. The team regularly provides tutors, but if that's not enough, the scholarship covers private tutoring."

"Really?"

Sacha nodded. "Moreover, all the clichés are true. You won't know what you can and can't do unless you try. Nothing worth having comes easy. Not trying is guaranteed failure. You can do anything you put your mind to. Shall I keep going?"

"No, I get it."

"I'm going to list architecture as your major on this form, but you'll have to get that switched at the registrar's office. And I'll also need a copy of your class schedule." He slid a form toward Corrigan and pointed at a blank line. "Sign here."

Corrigan quickly scanned the document and then signed.

"These," Sacha stated, removing another form from the folder, "are the conditions of the scholarship. They are nonnegotiable. You must maintain a minimum 3.2 GPA, have regular attendance in class, not have disciplinary actions taken against you by the university, maintain a position on an athletic team, and attend at least three Croneau Foundation-sponsored events during the academic year."

Corrigan watched Sacha's rosy lips move but didn't hear anything after 3.2 GPA. The number ricocheted in his brain. *Damn!* He'd be lucky to get a 2.0 considering.

"This is especially important."

Important. Right. Corrigan refocused.

"Keep your receipts. Anytime you use scholarship funds, the purchase will need to be verified as a legitimate expense."

"So no drugs or hookers."

Corrigan didn't expect the laugh that tumbled from the lawyer. Instead of being silky smooth, it was deep and rough.

"Exactly." Sacha leaned back in his chair. "If you need something and think it's not covered, call or make a pass by the law center on campus. Someone there can answer any questions you may have."

"Make a pass?"

"Sorry. I forgot you're not from around here. It means to come by." He waited until Corrigan signed the document before continuing. "And there's one more thing."

Sacha rolled his succulent lips as he thumbed through more papers, and the tiny hairs on Corrigan's neck sprang up while his satiric meter rose another degree.

"The Croneau Foundation is a multifaceted organization that's highly visible and prominent in the community, and scholarship recipients should be a reflection of that."

Uh-oh. What shoe is about to drop now?

"And what better way to do that than by being a member of a Panhellenic fraternal group?" Sacha continued.

Fraternity? Every *National Lampoon's Animal House*, *Revenge of the Nerds*, *Alpha House*, and *National Lampoon's Van Wilder* stereotypic frat guy cliché instantaneously popped into Corrigan's mind. What the hell would he look like running around draped in a sheet with a bunch of weeds stuck in his raven hair? Wasn't the world over the whole macho guzzle from a keg and puke and whack on the ass with a wooden paddle scene?

"Rush? I have to pledge?" *Say it isn't so.* Corrigan's jaw dropped. That was so not what he expected to hear.

"I believe it's called intake now."

"Aren't fraternities expensive?"

"The foundation covers the monthly dues."

Sure, Corrigan needed the scholarship, but

joining a fraternity? He needed that as much as he did a brain bleed. No way. The idea reeked of body funk and bad decisions. This gift horse was rapidly transforming into a donkey.

"I don't think I'm the fraternity type."

"And what type is that?" Sacha asked with an edge.

Arrogant. Shallow. Materialistic. Rich. Non-inclusive. "I don't know," Corrigan answered, shaking his head and not wanting to admit his true thoughts.

"You shouldn't stereotype. There are nineteen chapters on campus. I'm positive you'll connect with some house."

"Really?" Some people required being connected to a ventilator, but Corrigan didn't fancy that idea either.

Sacha shifted in his chair and nodded as if he understood. Something in the gleam in his eyes changed as if viewing Corrigan for the first time. For a moment, Corrigan thought he detected a flicker of non-lawyerly interest but questioned if his imagination had galloped deep into the land of lunacy.

"I could write you a recommendation to my fraternity if you like."

"And say what? You don't know me."

"I know you're here. That's something."

"I'm sure none of them would be interested in me. Isn't there something else I could join? An intramural club maybe?" *Something less segregated?*

"It's nonnegotiable, Mr. Ellery." Sacha studied him for a moment before continuing. "Certain stipulations have been added to ensure that the NCAA doesn't consider the foundation scholarships to be duplicitous bribes from boosters. In short, it allows the university to have credible deniability of wrongdoing by allowing the university to argue that these are Panhellenic stipends and sponsorships should anything be questioned. It's a safeguard for the university and the recipients."

Corrigan dropped his gaze to the floor.

"What is it?" Sacha inquired.

Corrigan shrugged. "This isn't exactly how I imagined things would be."

Sacha nodded slightly. "It never is."

After a longer pause than necessary, Corrigan exhaled. "So, that's it?"

"Yes." Reaching inside his suitcoat pocket, Sacha retrieved a glossy metal case, opened it, and removed a foil business card. "Here's my card. You can call or text me anytime." He stood and extended his hand.

Corrigan stood as well, took the business card, and reluctantly accepted the handshake—not because he felt any animosity or slight toward Sacha but, rather, he was strangely disappointed that their time had come to an end.

4

SACHA

"I DON'T GET IT," XYLA GRIPED, SPOONING Hollandaise sauce on her roasted asparagus. "How can you be indifferent regarding if your client is innocent or not?"

"Because it's irrelevant. Innocence and guilt are a sliding scale," Sacha responded.

"Right and wrong are absolute."

"Oh, really? Miss me with that." Sacha darted a raised eyebrow at his *date* and wondered how this conversation had arrived at where it was. He certainly hadn't brought up his job or anything close to it. The last thing he wanted to engage in was a tête-à-tête defending his profession after his fall from grace without a prospect of redemption in sight. A unanimous executive order from the firm partners had already handed off the appeal of his last case to one of his colleagues, and he'd been designated to the academia hell of preparing course syllabi for the fall semester and acting as a carrier pigeon.

The only half-decent part of his day had been meeting with Corrigan Ellery. Sacha had gone to the PAC with the expectation to get the necessary paperwork signed and nothing more, but, instead, he'd seen something in Corrigan's eyes—something that had made him pause. Most of Sacha's clients strolled arrogantly into a room, even when they were steeped chin-deep in up-the-creek situations. When he was in college, jocks had been some of the most egotistical people he'd had the misfortune of encountering. But something about Corrigan seemed different. His intense, dark eyes seemed weighted and lost—sentiments not unfamiliar to Sacha. On the other hand, what did he know? It wasn't like they'd deep-dived into a riveting, life-altering conversation. Yet Sacha had found his mind drifting back to the hockey player throughout the day and growing curious when he shouldn't have been.

"Yes," Xyla continued, her lips turning downward. "Anyone who says otherwise has questionable morals."

"Anyone who believes that is unlucky in thinking," Sacha refuted.

Gretchen placed a platter of yeast rolls on the table and plastered on one of her famous charming smiles she reserved for terse situations with patrons. "Fresh out the oven," she stated, the intention to change the conversation not disguised in her tone.

Sacha didn't bite at the out.

"Two people have a telephone conversation. Person A calls Person B and discloses an elaborate plan he's developed to murder Person C and dispose of the body. Person A has taken active steps to put his plan in motion, including purchasing a weapon, disguise, and chemicals to clean up. Person B is a known pathological liar who knows no one will believe him and tapes the conversation without Person A's knowledge in a state that requires two-party consent."

"Come on, Sacha," Paxton interrupted. "This is supper, not Intro to Criminal Justice."

Sacha ignored his brother. "Before executing his plan, Person A becomes aware of the recording, aborts the plan, and destroys all the materials he'd purchased.

There are no other corroborating witnesses to Person's A intention. Person A then goes to the police to press charges. So, should Person B be prosecuted for illegal wiretapping despite the recording being what prevented a murder? And because the only evidence of the crime is illegally obtained, is Person A criminally guilty of plotting to commit murder?"

Xyla's bottom lip jutted out in a pout. "That's different."

"No it's not. Either way, I would be defending a person who is guilty, technically speaking. And that's the thing about the law. It's not always about innocent or guilt. It is about justice and due process, which are not the same. Just because a person has good intention does not necessitate that it will reflect positively in their favor."

"Wine?" Gretchen asked.

Xyla scoffed. "Well, that's an irrational and ludicrous disservice to the people and a mockery of this country's principles."

Sacha raised an eyebrow. "You're calling my job cretinous and me iniquitous?"

"Aw, look at you using those dictionary words." Paxton passed a serving bowl of mushroom risotto to Sacha, practically shoving it beneath his nose.

"*Mais* talk about, she isn't," he refuted, the tension in his jaw obvious.

"So, you defend anyone, no matter how evil, as long as they can pay?" Xyla asked. "That doesn't sound scrupulous in the flimsiest sense."

"Sometimes Lucifer has to make his rounds in the underworld," Sacha replied.

"Oh, Jesus," Paxton muttered.

"No, I haven't gotten to Him yet."

"Anyone care for garlic butter?" Gretchen asked. "It's hand churned."

Sacha continued. "You're naive about how the law works. It's 'justice for *all*.'"

Xyla's eyes widened, clearly stunned.

"And speaking of justice," Gretchen interjected before anyone responded, "Justine Casey asked that we cater the Le Debut des Jeunes Femmes de la Sainte Anne."

Paxton smiled at her. "That's great, honey. It's the perfect opportunity to showcase your new menu."

Gretchen nodded. "Yes, and also for Xyla. She makes the most amazing champagne sabayon steak carpaccio with Ossetra caviar."

"It's raw," Sacha emphasized.

Gretchen's frown returned, and Paxton kicked Sacha beneath the table.

Oof!

"I mean, sounds delicious," Sacha reluctantly added. "Who doesn't love a good case of salmonella and *fwa?*"

Paxton kicked him again.

Fuck, dude! He rubbed his shin.

"He's joking," Paxton said with a nervous laugh. "His sense of humor is a little... discoloring."

Sacha brought his wineglass to his lips. "Some would call it *bruising.*"

"It's fine." Xyla smiled. "Not everyone has a sophisticated palate that appreciates food delicacies."

"That's me. Rudimentary and unrefined." He swiveled swiftly in his chair, dodging a third blow from his brother. *Ha!* Only to be kicked in his other shin by his sister-in-law. *Ow! Damn!*

"Actually, Sacha is taking a sabbatical from criminal law to help us at the university," Paxton stated tersely.

"Well, that's one way to put it," Sacha muttered into his wineglass, doing little to mask his scowl. If his fate was to be damned to a classroom, at least it could have been defense, civil, or hell, even corporate. But no. He was reprimanded with contract law, the most boring of all fields of law in his opinion. It had been the only class he'd struggled in—not because he found the work difficult but because he barely managed to get through the required readings without falling asleep. If it hadn't been for Paxton's excellent note-taking and the OCD packrat's need to hang on to every scrap of paper he'd ever scribbled on, Sacha may have never completed the course.

Of course, Sacha knew Paxton lending him his notes hadn't been completely selfless and without motive. His intent had been to tempt Sacha into specializing in contract law alongside him. For Sacha, it had been the means to an end. He'd rather have his nose hairs plucked than ever read another tort. Just thinking about having to do so broke him out in pure meat sweats. Stubbing his pinky toe on a table leg held more appeal. While he couldn't comprehend his brother's fascination with the work, he could respect his passion for it. After all, Sacha felt the same when in front of a jury. Besides, there had been no ill will in Paxton having given Sacha a small nudge in a direction if his younger brother had seemed a smidgen lost in the sauce. That's what Sacha had done today with Corrigan… kind of.

Okay, so it had been more of a shove than a nudge, and Sacha didn't know for sure if Corrigan was bewildered about an appropriate career path. What he did know, from what he'd read on the application in the file, was that a major in general studies didn't appear to be in Corrigan's best interest. True, the application didn't tell the whole story —likely because it had been completed by Coach Massey—but it told enough to give Sacha some insight. A hockey college freshman at twenty who hadn't played in the juniors had to have some kind of story, right?

Plus, there were plenty of hockey schools in the Northeast. There had to be a reason Corrigan had selected one so far away. Then again, maybe not everyone appreciated being a homebody like Sacha. Some people enjoyed traveling. Sacha enjoyed traveling, just not alone, which was what occurred the majority of the time. It wasn't drawing the odd stares when eating in restaurants alone or being seated next to strangers on bus tours that created a pit of loneliness in him. It was seeing something amazing and having no one to share the moment. It was feeling profound and having no one to tell. It was waking up alone in a strange place. Even misery loved company.

He shrugged at his thoughts and cut into his salmon.

"Right?" Paxton asked, and Sacha realized the question was directed at him.

"*Fo sha*," he said, zoning back in and hoping like hell he hadn't agreed to something he'd regret. He shoveled a forkful of salmon into his mouth and chewed slowly. He rationalized he wouldn't be expected to speak with his jaws crammed full.

The conversation continued around him, and he attempted to focus. Honestly, he tried. Something about a science fiction movie premiere. Something else about getting stains out of tablecloths. And maybe something about mattresses. Or perhaps they had said waitresses. Or maybe it was paintbrushes. Hell, he didn't know.

He glanced at Gretchen, who still brandished an uneasy expression. Thus he didn't need to look at Paxton to know his brother was harboring a deep frown. If there was one thing Sacha knew for certain, it was when Gretchen wasn't happy, neither was Paxton, and someone would be made miserable for it. He'd prefer not to be that someone.

Plastering on his best smile, Sacha turned his attention to Xyla.

"I like scallops seared in black truffles," he blurted. It was random, out of place, and off-topic at this point, and Sacha had no idea where he was going with it. But fuck, what did it matter if it got him off thin ice with Paxton and Gretchen?

And speaking of ice, maybe he should take in a hockey game or two at the university since he'd be spending his days on campus.

He enjoyed hockey. Watching skilled athletes synthesizing catlike agility and grueling speed while maneuvering on razor-sharp blades of steel *and* remaining upright on a rectangular hunk of ice despite being intermittently bludgeoned by human cannonballs at speeds upward of thirty miles per hour warmed Sacha's blood. He considered it a brutal ballet with chest protectors and shin guards instead of tutus. In court, he played a mental hockey of chasing justice through precedents and summations rather than a puck.

It had been a while since he'd attended a live game. Well, in all truthfulness, he'd technically never seen a game in person when he thought about it. The first time he'd *attended*, Kian had been so disgustingly intoxicated that he'd puked in the parking lot, and they'd never made it inside. The second time he'd purchased tickets, his date wasn't into the whole sports scene. She'd complained so much that they'd left the arena before the National Anthem. The third and final time he'd planned on going to a game, Gretchen had gone into labor, and he'd rushed to the hospital for the birth of his first niece to ensure he'd be her favorite uncle—at least in his head that was how he saw it.

Why he'd never gotten back around to attending a game, he wasn't sure. It certainly wasn't because he couldn't get tickets. He had an excellent connection to see any Civets game, and Paxton went all the time. He supposed it was one of those things that had slipped through his social life cracks.

Yes, he definitely should catch a hockey game now that he had more free time. And it had absolutely nothing to do with a Croneau Foundation scholarship recipient who had pecked at his curiosity. Well, almost nothing. In any case, that was how Sacha was going to convince himself.

Faking paying attention, he smiled at his dinner companions discussing ganache fillings—or something of the sort—while counting the minutes until the meal ended.

Why couldn't he have an uncomplicated supper like the rest of the world?

5

CORRIGAN

ASSIGNED SEATS? THEY WERE GROWN-ASS MEN. WHO thought assigned seats were a good idea?

The dining hall was packed, and most of the diners were already seated, not because Corrigan was late but rather because he'd gotten in the wrong serving line. When the coach had finally dismissed them from afternoon practice for dinner and Corrigan had seen the multiple serving lines, he thought it was a "pick a line, any line" situation and randomly chose one. Lunch had been brown bag at the PAC, so it never dawned on him that the team's nutritionist had placed him on dietary restrictions. But when he made it to the serving bar and was asked his name, he was promptly, and unceremoniously, rerouted to the end of another line. Apparently, he was deficient in vitamin D and calcium, and the coach wanted him to bulk up. While he was too light for defense, he wasn't heavy enough for offense. Again, fuck his life. So, to the special diet line he went, where his tray was prepared for him like an infant. And now he couldn't even select where he wanted to sit and eat his baked, skinless chicken, cottage cheese, yogurt, and a clump of something that masqueraded as dessert. If he weren't so damned hungry, he'd throw his tray in the trash and head to bed. After the day he'd had, he'd have no problem crashing. But his rumbling stomach was screaming, "Feed me," like Seymour in *Little Shop of Horrors*. The irony that he was chin-deep in his self-created shop of horrors didn't elude him.

Corrigan inhaled and kept walking past plates heaped with hunks of fried chicken and mounds of mashed potatoes with flowing gravy. Restraint was something he possessed. He'd developed maturity well beyond his years. He'd had no choice. He wasn't some naive eighteen-year-old to be discounted. At almost twenty-one, he carried the burdens of a forty-year-old and had done so since he was twelve. But just because he'd become well versed in the art of refrainment didn't mean it was easy or he wasn't tempted. He had to dig deep.

Bright recessed LED lighting illuminated the cafeteria like a stadium. Oddly, Corrigan found the harsh glow soothing—familiar, reminiscent of the one in the Upstate Medical Arena at the Oncenter War Memorial. And what an arena that was. Often, he daydreamed of playing professionally there one day before advancing to the big time, racing up the ice alongside his idols with thousands of fans chanting his name and waving those annoying cheap pompoms the arena armed the crowd with for free. But then he reminded himself of the less than one-in-one-thousand chance of that happening to ground himself and remember how important this opportunity he had was. *Baby steps.* The odds of his dream developing into a reality improved by being on a college team, where scouts came to recruit and had connections with coaches. Therefore, his remaining on the coach's good side held the utmost importance.

He wasn't sure how the alumni situation worked, but it couldn't hurt to have current players on professional rosters pulling to have players from their alma mater succeed them. Plus, when he was informed that he'd been awarded the Croneau Foundation scholarship, he hadn't stopped to think what it meant. Although he'd never heard of the scholarship or the foundation, he had heard of hockey great and billionaire Timothée Croneau. Corrigan wasn't 100 percent certain that Timothée was associated with the scholarship, but surely the name wasn't a coincidence, especially given that Timothée was a Louisiana native.

Two walls were painted with murals of football players and the third with basketball, soccer, volleyball, baseball, track, and hockey players. *Nice to see such an even distribution of recognition of various sports,* he thought as he navigated his way through the maze of bodies, especially since more ULSA basketball, soccer, and hockey players had made pro teams than the football players. And if Corrigan was being honest—no bias in his opinion, of course—the football team's overall stats weren't that impressive with a 662-527-93 win-loss-tie record. In the school's history, the team had only won eleven of its twenty-four bowl games and boasted one national championship. But just to piss on that golden crown, that championship had been won before penicillin was invented. In contrast, the hockey team had over nine hundred wins, forty-five playoff appearances, and six national championships despite not being established at the school for nearly two decades later. Incontestably, the hockey team had the best record, next to gymnastics, than any other school sport. That, in Corrigan's opinion, should have elevated the hockey team to more than a scrunched parchment of wall. Again, he reminded himself where he was and dismissed the thought.

Although classes wouldn't begin for another two weeks, the majority of the university's athletic teams were holding camp. With one glance around the room, Corrigan could practically predict who belonged to what sports group. On his way into the dining hall, he'd passed the soccer team having a leisurely dinner on the knoll beside the three-tiered marble fountain with a granite statue of the school mascot towering on top. The baseball team was the closest to the entrance doors, and all wore their caps backward, and the wrestlers all donned buzzed haircuts and T-shirts with the sleeves ripped off as they gathered closest to the dessert buffet. The basketball players sat at tables located on top of the split level that were elevated higher than the others in the room to accommodate their height. Damp hair and flip-flops, not to mention the scent of chlorine, made the swimmers easy to identify. However, he couldn't differentiate between the golfers and tennis players. They both modeled striped or checkered polos and matching shorts. Of course, the gods of the university, the football players, were the easiest of all to spot in their jerseys and their premier seats in the center of the cafeteria. They were also the loudest group.

Carrying his dinner tray, Corrigan weaved through the tables of the athletic dining hall. According to his lunch card, he was assigned to table thirty-two, which turned out to be beside the glassed patio and farthest away from the drink fountains and return tray windows. Blackout curtains had been lowered to block the view of the outside world. And if the day couldn't get any worse, already seated at his assigned table were Shade Franley, Reid Larousse, and king asshole himself, Ramsey Theriot among other players.

With his eyes averted, Corrigan headed for a vacant seat at the end of the long table.

"Hey, man, where are you going?" Bowen Nguyen asked, snagging the hem of Corrigan's shirt as he passed. His smile was wide, bright, and… inviting, as opposed to the others at the table, who either looked baffled or horrified but said nothing. "Grab a piece of furniture." He jerked his head toward the chair on his right.

"I don't want to interrupt."

"Nah," Nguyen continued. "We're bitching about the first day of camp."

Larousse, goalie, dragged his hand through his coiffed haircut, pushing it away from his face. "Surely Coach can't keep this up all season. My glutes feel like I've been bashing against a hedgehog."

"Dude, tell your girl to shave," Franley heckled, bringing a round of laughs. His hair looked more orange than red beneath the lights.

"Bite me," Larousse heckled back.

"What we talking about?" Billy Idol's doppelgänger, Roland Cardenas, asked, approaching the table.

"Larousse's ass," Theriot replied.

"We're not talking about my ass."

"I stand corrected. His girl's beaver."

Another round of laughs exploded from the table.

Cardenas smirked, his braces glinting between his lips. "Y'all stupid. Larousse doesn't have a girl. An inflate-a-fuck maybe."

"I can't stand any of you," Larousse replied, feigning anger and doing his best to stifle a grin.

"Have a seat before your yogurt melts," Nguyen insisted, nudging the chair beside him from beneath the table with his foot.

Corrigan looked at the dairy cup on his tray and wondered if Nguyen knew something he didn't. After all, it was regular yogurt and not frozen. Nothing should be melting.

As much as he didn't want to accept the invitation, he equally did not want to offend the one teammate who behaved affably toward him.

I can do this. With an inward sigh, he set his tray on the table and sat.

The table grew quiet with awkwardness.

Focus on eating. Corrigan poked at the dessert blob with his spoon and watched it jiggle. Against his better judgment, he sniffed it and screwed up his face. It smelled of mint and mothballs—like the sticky candy he'd find stuck to the inside bottom of his granny's purse.

"Why do you look so miserable?" Cardenas—the one person who seemed oblivious to the mood—asked, unwrapping his silverware from the napkin and breaking the silence.

Larousse grunted. "I'd be miserable, too, if I had to eat that." He motioned toward Corrigan's tray.

"I'm not," Corrigan denied.

"You know," Theriot said, twisting his fork in his half-eaten mashed potatoes, "if Ellery could keep up, your ass wouldn't be feeling like a pincushion."

"If you would skate the plays as laid out instead of doing your own thing and being all over the ice with your head up your ass, I would be in position."

Theriot shook his head and twisted his face as if he'd bitten into something rancid. "Naw, you're just slow as fuck."

Skating speed wasn't a fixed attribute and could be improved with dedication, persistence, determination, and hard work. Being an asshole wasn't as easily overhauled.

"Theriot, chill, bro. It's the first day," Nguyen interjected. "He hasn't had time to get used to us."

Unlike football where players huddled between plays to determine their next move, nearly everything about hockey was on the fly, and teammates needed to share a brainwave. The pace and intensity didn't allow time for hesitation. Corrigan shouldn't have to guess what any of his linemates were doing; he should be able to read their body language and follow. Yes, it was only the first day, and he hadn't had much time to learn the other players' instincts and defaults, but when the coach dictated the play to skate, it eliminated all guesswork. Again, simple.

And yes, he understood he would have to step up his skate game. Yet he also knew that practice was not at the high speed of an actual game to allow the team to develop new skills and play patterns and to get used to working together as a *team*. Novel concept. So no matter how anyone wanted to contort it, Theriot's problem with him had nothing to do with hockey.

"Why are you taking up for this—"

"This what?" Corrigan snapped, the anger that had never quite subsided from earlier attempting to boil to the forefront. "Say it."

Theriot snarled, his eyes never leaving Corrigan. He clipped his sentence and stood, taking his tray. "Fucking quotas," he grumbled, heading for the exit.

Chairs scraped across the floor as most of the others at the table team followed the captain.

Cardenas glanced over his shoulder at his departing teammates and cut into his meatloaf. "Don't worry about Theriot," he reassured. "He can be a bit of a dick sometimes. He doesn't mean anything by it."

Corrigan's scowl deepened. People like Theriot he could appreciate on a certain level. At least it was upfront and allowed Corrigan to know what he was dealing with. However, people like Cardenas perpetuated the behavior by minimizing or not acknowledging it for what it was. Of course Theriot had meant something by it. The message had been loud and clear and had been cosigned by the majority of the team.

Quota. That stung, because as much as he didn't want to admit it, Corrigan had to suck down the possibility that it may have been partially true. The team had six players graduate in the spring, two to transfer, one recovering from elbow surgery, two out indefinitely on academic probation, and one to enter the draft. ULSA was certifiably in a rebuilding situation and had lots of room on the roster to fill. Corrigan had convinced himself that Coach Massey had recruited him because he was a top-notch player. But suppose he'd just needed warm bodies, and Corrigan was filling a slot until someone better came along?

And that was the kind of thought that, when it crept in, would get him booted from the team—the type that people like Theriot provoked and, if allowed, would root deep in one's subconscious and spread like cancer. If anyone thought Corrigan would sit idly by to be a placeholder, the joke was on them. He intended to be a starter despite that being a longshot for a freshman. That meant doing whatever it took, beginning with….

A final sigh escaped his lips before he scooped his spoon into the pile of cottage cheese. If that was what the coach wanted, then he'd hold his breath and swallow.

"So, you got a girl?" Nguyen asked, his smile still wide.

Momentarily, Corrigan's chest constricted with panic as his pulse thumped in his ears. Thankful to have his mouth full, he shook his head. There was no chance in hell he'd be able to swallow.

"Well, don't worry. There are plenty of honeys here."

Nope, nope, and nope. The school had zero tolerance for discrimination by students, professors, or other university staff. Yeah, well, Corrigan had seen how well that policy was taken seriously and enforced. While Nguyen appeared cool with the race thing, bringing in sexuality was entirely next level. Race was apparent. Anyone looking at Corrigan immediately recognized him to be African American. He had to do nothing and say nothing. One couldn't look at a person and know that person's sexuality. They may guess or speculate, but there was no way to know for certain unless the person confessed. A built-in gaydar was a myth, especially considering sexuality was on a spectrum and not black-and-white.

Corrigan was comfortable being a gay man, in

general, but not in the world of hockey. Not on this team. Not with these teammates who would likely become all types of weird about showering and undressing in the same room as him, fearing he'd check them out or, heaven forbid, hit on them. Hockey players were notorious for regarding themselves as an irresistible gift of manna from the heavens. Even if they weren't homophobic, their ego wouldn't allow them to dream it to be conceivably plausible that a gay man wouldn't be interested. Because, of course, gay men from the beginning of creation were desperate for dick and survived solely to flip straight guys—not.

Besides, there was no rule demanding he tell anyone. Hockey would one day, hopefully, be his profession. And everyone knew it was a good business practice to have definite boundaries between one's personal and professional life. He was simply protecting his future professional portfolio—or at least that was what he was convincing himself today. When he was younger, coming to terms with his feelings, he'd wished he was straight because he knew it would have made his life easier. He didn't intend to hide it, but he didn't intend to discuss it either. Instead, he chewed his *scrumptious* cottage cud... uh, cheese... slowly.

Additionally, there was something about "coming out" that Corrigan found repulsive and resentful. Quote-unquote straight people didn't find themselves in positions of having to announce to the world their "straightness." Their sexuality was assumed and accepted. But why should anything be *assumed*, and why wasn't all accepted? Why were only members of the LGBTQIA+ community required to rent a billboard to proclaim a part of their lives which should be private? Why must he explain or defend who he was? Corrigan felt like a Billie Holiday song: "Ain't Nobody's Business If I Do." That being said, he knew there were members of the gay community who felt everyone needed to be out regardless of whether the individual wanted to be or not, and they made it a mission to out others on the regular. A person needed to live their truth, they argued. But the truth was the world was an ugly place with an even uglier past. There were consequences, and not everything was fair.

"Mm." Larousse nodded. "Just be sure to wrap it up. Double wrap if you must. Most chase after the pigskins or the screech courts, but there's a fair share of puck bunnies scheming how to latch on and deplete your paycheck once you go pro. They're pretty sly too."

"I'm here to play and not looking to hook up or anything."

Larousse crooked his brow but didn't look up from his meal. "You training to be a priest or something? Four years is a long time to go without nooky."

"Nooky?" Stirring his tea, Nguyen grinned. "What, are you ten and never built your vocabulary? And not everyone's a manwhore like you. Besides, he didn't mean four years of being sexually comatose."

But that was exactly what Corrigan meant when it came to women.

"Only that it isn't a top priority at the moment." Nguyen gave Corrigan a reassuring nod as if to say, *I got your back.*

Cardenas twisted his face in mock scorn. "I'm disappointed in you. Slut-shaming is so 1980."

"Yes, and you know because you were born decades later. Okay." Nguyen turned back to Corrigan. "Don't worry. If you find a honey who seems sketch and none of the guys on the team already knows, Gils, the athlete trainer, keeps a list—Ditch-A-Bitch—in his office. These are babes known to have made the rounds and who attempted to pull fast ones, regardless of sport. But be careful when asking him. He snitches regularly to Coach, and

Coach thinks girlfriends are a distraction and bumping uglies on game weeks drains your energy."

"Truth. He's a stickler on curfew," Larousse added. "On away games, he posts hall monitors by the elevator to ensure no one is entering or leaving rooms."

"Don't worry about that either. You'll find there are a few ways around it."

As Nguyen continued relaying information on the dating scene, Corrigan began regretting that he hadn't gone along with the idea of him having a girl back home and being a faithful boyfriend, as it was obvious he was expected to get laid regularly—not that he would have any issues with a roll in the hay. Hell, he could use one currently to burn off some steam and relax. On the other hand, he was bored of meaningless hookups—not that he was looking to settle down.

The matter was as complicated as a fucking SAT problem. Hookups were fine. They served a purpose. They allowed him to get his jollies and move on. However, they denied him the ability to be his full self and have a support system that he wouldn't have with others. They weren't interested in having profound conversations.

But having a steady meant outing himself, something he had already determined he wasn't ready to do. In the past, he'd lost friends. In fact, he'd lost his best friend of eleven years because of it. He'd had camp coaches who'd merely suspected he wasn't straight to bench him or send him home early. Although he had an awesome family, he couldn't saddle them with any of his shit when there were flare-ups.

Now, far from New York, where no one knew him, he had a fresh start. Yes, he felt it was yet another copout, but when compared to the alternatives, it was the lesser of the evils.

Looking at his two teammates, his spirit sagged. While Larousse was a coin toss for friendship, Nguyen had seemed like a guy he could gel with and be himself around. However, after this conversation, his confidence in that had faded. His mood dipped even more when he realized just how much he wanted a friend.

Corrigan nodded again at whatever Nguyen had said and kept eating to speak as little as possible. Saying nothing wasn't a lie—not exactly the truth, but also not an overt falsehood. After all, it wasn't his fault if people made erroneous assumptions.

6

SACHA

WHAT A DISASTER. SACHA SWIRLED HIS DRINK IN HIS glass as he sank farther into the cushy Chesterfield chair. Thank God supper had concluded and he'd been able to escape to Paxton's mancave for refuge.

"That went well," Paxton stated with a broad grin.

Where? Sacha's scowl deepened. "On what planet?"

Paxton stared at him wide-eyed, his grin instantly transformed into a taut line. "You don't think so? She was totally into you, even with your grumpy, constitutional framer impersonation."

Sacha groaned. Many women were into him... for his bank account and social status. By all means, he was a "good catch," as some would put it, blessed with a pleasant appearance and an above-average

IQ. And for those reasons, many women tended to overlook his crappy attitude in lieu of a country club membership. Yes, he was well aware his disposition wasn't always skyrocketing sunshine rays out his anus, but he also didn't always recognize when he'd fallen into that vault of foulness. That was why he needed people like his brother to shake him back to reality from time to time.

"Fine." Paxton threw his hands in the air. "What's wrong with this one?"

"Nothing."

"Then what's the problem?"

"That *is* the problem. Nothing's wrong with her, but nothing's right about her either."

"I'm not understanding."

"Do you think she's the type of woman Mother and Father would approve of me bringing home?"

Paxton's face grew red. "Don't you dare tell me you're judging because she's not some socialite."

Sacha stiffened, knowing he needed to stifle his brother's defensiveness before the conversation went south and turned into a brawl.

"You know I'm not like that. What I mean is I should be with someone who at minimum checks one box."

"Huh?"

"You know how Grandmother Esmée said after Grandfather Percival died that she stopped looking for a man who would check off all the qualities she wanted in a husband and settled for one who could meet at least one of the criteria so she would, at minimum, have a companion acceptable to others."

"Whoa!" Paxton held up his hand. "First, Grandmother Esmée swallows her tobacco. Those brain cells aren't firing like they used to. Second, why would you consider that?"

"I know it's foreign to you because you've found your soul mate. But if I'm not going to have that kind of thing, then I should choose someone everyone else finds acceptable, right?"

"You're making me think you don't have all the french fries in your kid's meal. That's the dumbest shit I've ever heard you utter, and you've said some pretty stupid shit over the years."

"Is it?"

"Listen, when Grandmother Esmée lost Grandfather Percival, she wasn't ever interested in finding another great love. He was her everything, and her heart never healed. I think she thought remarrying would seem like she was trying to replace him, and that's why she settled for something less. But that's not you. You haven't had that grand love yet, and it's wrong for you to give up. And if you're trying to find a woman only to appease Mother and Father, you're going to make yourself miserable. Trust me. I went down that path, and it's like crawling on shards of glass. Besides, in the end, they came around to accept Gretchen."

Yeah, because her brother is— Let it go. He took a swig of his whiskey and sighed. "Yeah."

"Perhaps you should focus on what you want in a relationship." Paxton plopped into the chair across from Sacha. "So, what is it that you want?"

"I don't know. Someone who makes me feel less dead."

"You feel dead?"

"Yeah, unless I'm in a courtroom, which I'm not anymore. There I have a purpose and feel energetic and challenged. It's like I walk in and start connecting with people—the jury, witnesses, the judge, and even the prosecuting attorneys. They listen, and what I say matters." He shrugged. "Well, most of the time. And while no day is ever the same, there's a predictability about it." Wincing, he finished his drink. "I know it doesn't make sense."

"No, it's starting to, but…." He hesitated while contemplating. "You're saying you've never dated anyone who's mentally challenged you? C'mon.

What about that drop-dead-gorgeous neurosurgeon? What was her name?" Paxton snapped his fingers. "Michelle?"

"Micaela," Sacha corrected. "She was brilliant."

"But?"

Sacha hunched his shoulders. "Something was missing."

"Like what?"

"I don't know. Something. I tried to make it work." And honestly, he had.

"Well, things seemed to have been working fine between y'all until Miami. What happened?"

"More like what *didn't* happen. She thought if I went with her to the medical convention, we could elevate the relationship to the next level. But things started falling apart the first night there. Our flight wasn't until 8:00 p.m., but a thunderstorm delayed takeoff. We sat on the tarmac for a couple hours while it passed. Then there was an issue at check-in. By the time we got to the room, I was exhausted. She wanted to fool around, but I'd already worked a full day. All I wanted was some food because they didn't serve supper on the flight, and I'd missed lunch, a hot bath, and sleep."

Paxton nodded. "Understandable."

"Not to her, it wasn't, and it got worse. Before

takeoff, we had developed a plan—I would hang out while she attended her lectures, and then we'd meet up later to do stuff. I suggested jet skiing, aquarium, botanical gardens, museums. Her only interest was sex."

"Not many men would complain about that."

"Only when it's good."

Paxton snorted. "Bruh, it's always good, even when it's bad."

"If you say so."

"I hate to ask this, but what made it... not good?"

"It just wasn't. A similar thing happened with Stacey and Brie. And Kendra. The conversation was popping, but the deed was flopping."

"Hmm." Paxton rolled his lips and remained quiet for several seconds. "Has this always been the case?"

Sacha contemplated for a moment before nodding. "Pretty much."

"So, you don't enjoy sex?"

"I do. I mean, I would," he stammered. "I want to."

"But you haven't?"

"Not with another person." As the confession left his lips, his dignity plunged into the toilet. "Frankly, there's been a few times when I couldn't... you know... finish properly. I've seen doctors, and they say there's nothing wrong with me physically, that perhaps I was overly fatigued or had consumed too many adult libations."

"Sacha...." Paxton set his glass on an end table and leaned forward. "Have you ever considered that you're not into women?"

What! Holy shit, Sacha hadn't seen that coming, and it took another moment before he was able to translate the thought into verbal speech. "What?" His voice hitched. "Of course I'm into women." Wasn't he? Sure. Stupid question.

Right?

"It's okay if you're not."

"What the absolute fuck?" Wouldn't he already know this? Wasn't he a little old to be discovering his sexuality? Wasn't there like some cutoff or expiration date or timestamp for sexual epiphanies?

His throat dried as doubt seeped in.

"I'm just asking."

Well, you don't need to. "Why would you jump to the conclusion that because I've never had a mind-blowing sexual experience"—*oh shit!*—"that I don't like women?" As he concluded the sentence, his confidence dropped even further.

"Well, clearly something's going on."

Put that way, yeah. Sacha stared over his glass with his mouth hanging open at his brother. Speechless. He placed his hand on his abdomen to soothe the trepidation clawing in his gut, threatening to bring up his honey-glazed salmon. *What's happening?* "But that? Why?"

Paxton's expression softened to one of pity.

Oh geez, not that look.

"Honestly?" Paxton asked.

Sacha nodded despite not wanting to hear the answer.

"Kian."

"Oh, because Kian is gay, I must be too?"

"Now you're overreacting." Paxton rose and went to the bar. "That's not what I said, nor what I meant." After retrieving the bottle of Little Book Chapter 5, he returned to his chair and refreshed both their drinks. "But you have to admit you were happier when you two were together."

"We weren't *together*." Sacha scoffed, his voice cracking in strange ways that it hadn't since adolescence. "He's my friend."

"You spent all your time with him."

"We hung out the way *friends* do because, you know, we're *friends*."

"Don't get defensive."

"I'm not defensive," he rebutted in a tone that

convinced no one ever. Every muscle in his body clenched.

"I never saw you more depressed than when he moved with his boyfriend to Seattle."

Sacha's bottom lip drooped in a pout. "How would you feel if your best friend moved across the country? I wouldn't imagine you'd be flipping cartwheels."

"Fair enough, but let me ask you something. You don't have to answer me, but be honest with yourself. If he had tried, would you have kissed him?"

"No." Sacha froze at his automatic response because something about it wasn't ringing one hundred with him. *Would I have?*

"You don't sound convinced." Paxton covered his brother's hand with his. "I remember one afternoon arriving home for spring break during my first year of law school. You were a senior and had friends over out by the pool. The music was blaring, and people were laughing and splashing around. But not you. You were focused on Kian and his then-boyfriend making out. Your cheeks were flushed, and you kept shifting as if you couldn't get comfortable."

"I don't remember that." *Ten Hail Marys for that whopper* as the image of the live boy-on-boy action flooded his memory. Damn if his cheeks weren't currently staining with color, causing him to want to dissolve into the floorboards.

"Then Sera Magee asked you to rub tanning lotion on her back, and you took her to your bedroom."

"To get the tan—"

"My bedroom was next to yours, remember?" Paxton interrupted. "I heard y'all. You oiled her up all right."

Ah! A reprieve. Yes, he could chalk it up to immaturity and hormones. "We were a couple of horny teenagers. Big deal. And," he drew out, "she was a girl, which doesn't support your theory."

"It does if watching Kian is what started your motor running."

As quickly as he thought he'd gained some ground, his buoyancy deflated. He swallowed past the lump in his throat. "He's my friend." *Lame rebuttal, but worth a try.*

"And if he wasn't?"

Sacha took a long sip, rubbed the throbbing center of his forehead, and sagged in the chair, afraid of the thoughts formulating. Was his brother right? His breath pulsated in his ears like thunder. Paxton's theory shouldn't be making as much sense as it did.

Oddly, the fact that he might not be sexually attracted to women wasn't what troubled him. Rather, it was his not realizing it was a possibility that shook him to his core. How could he have not known this about himself? It was like waking up and not knowing his eye color or favorite food. Sexuality was an integral part of human nature, and he just what? Got in the default line by mistake? And what was the exchange policy on this type of thing?

This wasn't how it was supposed to work. Other people didn't inform a person what that person's sexuality was. Seriously, how could Sacha not know every nook and cranny about this part of his life? After all, he was an overall observant guy, paying attention to the smallest details. It was what made him a great trial lawyer—well, until prior to the current debacle. He'd graduated in the top 1 percent of his law class. He figured out the twist ending of movies long before they occurred. He solved riddles that stumped all his friends at trivia. Yet he didn't know if he'd had a thing for guys, let alone for his quiche bestie? No, not quiche. Quiche would mean.... *Double shit!* Thoughts whirled in his mind too swiftly for him to latch on to any.

"Okay," Paxton continued, "suppose it was some other guy. How would you feel then?"

Not fair. Sacha parted his lips to speak the obvious, or rather the traditional, but then hesitated as he gave it genuine consideration. "I wouldn't be completely—" His voice shook as he fought to continue. "—opposed to it." Did he actually say that aloud? "But I'm not g-gay. I… I…."

"Don't have to figure it out right this second," Paxton soothed. "Breathe."

"But I'm not," Sacha continued. *And I doth protest too much.*

"Okay. So maybe you're not a zero on the Kinsey scale. There's nothing wrong with that. It simply gives you more options in finding your soul mate."

Great! Just what I needed to add to this flaming pile of crap day. I should have stayed at home and eaten a TV dinner.

7

CORRIGAN

CORRIGAN SKATED ONTO THE ICE WITH MINOTAUR veteran Shelby Kavanaugh and Thad Hansford, a college freshman after having aged out in juniors. Together, the three comprised the fourth offensive line. Ordinarily, this would have been a bruise to Corrigan's ego. He hadn't traveled all this way to be delegated to the fourth line. Then again, his line was far from sloppy. Kavanaugh may not have had the best form Corrigan had ever seen, but he knew how to hustle. He made plays where none were to be had. And Hansford possessed mad stickwork skills that surely were taking him places. But on the other hand, if his skills were that impressive, why hadn't the pros plucked him from the juniors? And if the coach thought Hansford was only fourth-line material with the skills he brought, what did that mean for Corrigan?

He didn't know what to make of it and shrugged off the thought as he took his position. Now wasn't the time for him to attempt to psychoanalyze his coach.

At the whistle, Theriot immediately took control of the puck and broke away across the line.

Damn, he's fast!

Corrigan chased Theriot but was checked by Sweeten, allowing Theriot to take a shot on goal before Corrigan could scramble back to his feet. Fortunately, Abe Barnes made a pad save and knocked the puck to Corrigan, who rifled past Theriot and won the race to the dot. His shot from the far circle went wide and was picked up by Hansford, who played it around the net. Corrigan took a cross-ice pass from Hansford off the left boards and snaked past Franley playing the opposing defense before lifting a shot over Larousse's left shoulder from the low slot and into the back of the net.

Yaaas!

Wham!

Ow!

For a second, Corrigan saw a flash of white light followed by darkness before focusing on fuzzy teammates. A sharp surge of what felt like a combination of scorching and constricting overtook his face.

"Jesus!" DeSevren yelled, rushing to Corrigan. "Someone fetch me a towel and some ice." He looked him over. "Are you all right?"

"Yeah," Corrigan answered as an automatic response. Although he'd heard the question, he couldn't process the meaning. His legs quivered as he skated toward the bench, and DeSevren grasped his upper arm to steady him. Corrigan's vision cleared further but was impaired by his fogged visor speckled with… blood. *What the hell?* Blood streamed from Corrigan's nose down his chin and onto his practice jersey.

"Theriot, what were you thinking?" DeSevren snapped.

"Sorry, Coach, it was an accident." Theriot's tone was 100 percent horse manure.

"Accidents like that better not happen in a game, let alone in practice against your teammate. Everyone, twenty laps, and each better be under fifteen seconds." He blew his whistle.

He hit me. The realization sank into Corrigan. Theriot had elbowed him in the face. His visor had caught the brunt of the impact but not all, not enough to prevent Theriot from bloodying Corrigan's nose.

That son of a—

Corrigan's lips pulled into a thin line, and he jerked to take off after Theriot but was held in place by DeSevren and blinded by a wadded towel pressed against his face.

"Cool your skates," Coach Massey ordered. "Theriot said it was an accident."

Uh-huh. How does one's elbow accidentally end up in another person's face beneath a protective visor?

"And you're on scholarship," Coach continued.

The latter kept Corrigan moving toward the bench. The conditions of his scholarship specified no university disciplinary actions. Fighting would most definitely fall under that category.

He clutched the towel and held it to his nose. "I got it, Coach."

Oh, and how he got it on every level. The golden boy, Theriot, was off-limits.

IF CORRIGAN HAD THOUGHT THE BEATING RAYS OF THE Louisiana summer sun on the rear of his neck were Dante's ninth circle of hell, this blustery blanket of trapped humidity beneath the stacking clouds was the tenth. He sucked in the thick air as he trudged up a hill and back to the athletic dorm from the arena since the shuttles had limited hours during the summer. He could have taken his chances and waited at the stop, but the angry clouds in the west threatened to burst at any second. Lightning skidded across the sky in the distance. His teammates had all piled into cars with no room for an additional passenger, of course. But so what? Hiking built character, right? At least today he didn't have a mound of textbooks strapped to his back. Maybe there was hope for his spine yet. Then again, what would it matter if he drowned in a flash flood and his body was washed into the Civil War trenches on either side of the road?

Okay, maybe calling the decline a trench was a bit of a stretch—or not. They were steep enough to be trenches, and several Civil War battles had been fought in the area. Plenty of statues and plaques strung across campus commemorated the events. One of the buildings—Corrigan wasn't sure which one—had been used as a war hospital for Confederate soldiers. During his campus visit, the guide had boasted about how the converted hospital had an innovative sewage system courtesy of the university engineering department. Corrigan stared at the long ditches again and frowned. Great. He'd be buried in a literal cesspool. Yet he had to admit, there was a poetic symmetry to ending a shitty day in a shithole. At least he'd have the university's chapel bells that rang in the distance to keep him company as his body lay decomposing.

A gust of warm wind, bringing with it a strong scent of wild onions, slapped against his face and tousled his hair. He squinted to shield his eyes from particles of blowing dust, because all he needed was a scratched cornea to go along with his black eye and swollen nose.

From nowhere, shimmering lights appeared far down the road and advanced. A four-door Mercedes slowed and eased to a stop on the semi-isolated *Rocky Horror Picture Show*-ish road. *Shit! The "Black people always die first in slasher films" cliché.*

This could play out several ways, with the majority of options not being favorable, especially since Corrigan hadn't taken any recent photos that wouldn't pixelate into a blurry blob when blown up for the back of a milk carton, provided that someone thought him worthy enough to be declared missing.

Wait. Are milk carton pictures still a thing since most of mainstream America seemed lactose intolerant?

Corrigan tensed as the tented passenger window —surely too dark to meet visible light transmission percentages regulations—lowered.

When Sacha leaned toward the window, Corrigan relaxed for a brief moment and then tensed again for an entirely different reason. *Fuck my life! Of course he'd roll up on a day my face imitates Kung Fu Panda.* The "killed by a madman on the side of a remote university side street" scenario he'd concocted in his mind was replaced with "kidnapped by a gorgeous demigod to be a sex slave." Actually, the second option didn't seem half bad, and Corrigan perked up marginally at the impure thought.

"Hey. Where you heading?" Sacha asked.

"To my dorm."

"Hm." He peered out his front windshield at the clouds and squeezed the steering wheel before looking back at Corrigan. "There's about to come a monsoon. You'll never make it in time. Hop in."

Corrigan shifted indecisively. Sure, his legs would thank him, and his eyes would be more than grateful to have Sacha as a view, but he despised accepting things from people. It put him in their debt and lessened who he was as a person. He was raised never to take handouts, and here, once again,

Sacha was offering him a handout. Yes, the scholar-ship was different but still a type of handout all the same. *He must think I'm pathetic.*

"I think I can make it."

"*Sha*, there's no way." Sacha pushed open the passenger door. "It's best to mow the lawn and cut up the snakes."

What?

Corrigan poised himself to decline again when a bolt of lightning streaked from the sky to the ground, followed by a vociferous boom. Although the lightning had been miles away, the heat had warmed his skin. In an instant, his mind was made up. Never mess with Mother Nature trumped snubbing handouts for the sake of pride. Respect.

"Thanks," he replied, stepping toward the car.

"*Pshaw.*" Sacha removed his neatly folded suit jacket from the passenger seat and tossed it over his shoulder onto the back seat without looking, then set a bottle of unopened Rhys Horseshoe Hillside pinot noir on the floorboard. "Looks like I happened along at the right time." A kind smile slid across his face.

"Yeah." As Corrigan fastened his seat belt, an awareness came over him, and his head snapped toward the radio. He couldn't suppress giggling like an adolescent.

Sacha studied him, brows furrowed, and tilted his head. "What's funny?"

"Nothing." Then he nodded toward the radio. "You're listening to 'Hotel California.'"

"The Eagles are humorous?"

Sacha listening to a band like the Eagles definitely shocked Corrigan. He'd expected him to be more of an opera or symphony music lover—smooth jazz at best—and not throwback classic rock.

"It's not that. You're on this back road... in a Mercedes...." Corrigan felt his face growing warm. "Church bells ringing...." He nodded toward his feet. "Wine."

"Ah!" Sacha grinned, accelerating. "Well, I guess you'll need to decide if you're in heaven or hell and if I'm twisted."

"This car is heaven, but this campus is definitely purgatory."

"Tough time adjusting?"

"I don't think adjusting is my problem. Some things suck no matter where you are."

Sacha nodded. "Now, that's true. Anything I can do to help?"

His offer seemed genuine, and Corrigan smiled. "Naw. I'll work it out, but thanks."

The music was interrupted by a phone ringing and the word "Incoming" appearing on the radio display. With his thumb, Sacha pressed a button on the steering wheel to accept the call. "*Quoi ça dit?*"

"Father called. He and Mother are still in Lake Charles, and the alarm is going off at the house. Security has already checked it out, and everything is fine. But someone needs to reset the alarm."

Sacha frowned. "And I suppose that *someone* is me."

"You're closer."

"You don't know that."

"*Mais*, I do. I called work, and they said you'd just left. It's on your way."

"Only if I go eighteen miles out of the way," Sacha refuted. "Do I look like the kid who ate the glue at school?"

"Come on. I'm at home with the kids. You wouldn't want me to have to drag your nieces out in this weather, would you? Say hello to your uncle, girls."

"*Salut, Nonc,*" two small voices said in unison.

"*Salut, mes belles.*"

"Go wash your hands for supper," Paxton

instructed, followed by the sound of scuttling feet across a wood floor.

"Really, Pax? You're going to guilt me with your kids?"

"Is it working?"

"No."

Corrigan could tell by Sacha's expression that it totally had worked, and something inside him warmed at how quickly Sacha melted from staunch affirmation to gooey fondness.

"I'll bring you one of Gretchen's deluxe cinnamon rolls tomorrow."

Sacha licked his lips at the bribe. "With extra icing."

"Fine. You drive a hard bargain."

"Sure." Sacha disconnected and glanced at Corrigan. "I feel like a cheap pastry whore."

"Nothing about you looks cheap."

"It's the cuff links," he responded nonchalantly. "If you ever want to fool someone into thinking you have money, invest in a good pair. The eyes always find the smallest details and give them the most creditability. You can be wearing a ten-dollar suit with rummage store shoes, and people see custom cuff links and assume you're hiding your wealth. But see someone wearing a five-thousand-dollar suit and designer shoes but with dollar store cuff links, and everyone will assume that person is faking the funk."

Corrigan laughed. "Nice to know, but it isn't solely the clothes."

"Oh?" Sacha's eyebrows flew up, and he glanced from the road to Corrigan.

"It's your entire demeanor—the way you speak and move."

"Move?"

"Yes. Kinda like you're gliding, flawless."

"While I don't trip over my feet most mornings, I'm definitely not flawless, but it's entertaining that someone thinks I might be." He chuckled to himself.

"Well, you certainly don't thump around the way hockey players do."

Sacha pulled to a four-way stop and clicked his blinker. *"Humph.* You've never seen me without contacts."

"I didn't realize." There was a pause. "Are they colored?"

"What? My contacts?"

Corrigan nodded.

"No," Sacha answered.

"That's good." *Oh no, you didn't say that aloud. Goof!*

"Why is that good?" Small smile creases formed at the corners of his eyes.

"They're pretty." *Shit! Open mouth, insert foot. Save yourself.* Heat crept up Corrigan's neck. "R-Rare," he stuttered, the heat climbing into his cheeks. "They're pretty rare. Less than 3 percent of people have gray eyes."

"And you know this because…?"

"I wrote a paper about eye color for biology class last year."

"Well, heck. I thought you may be one of those people who walked around with random statistics and weird facts in their heads. I got excited for a second and was going to invite you to be my partner for the next trivia night."

Excited? Ga-geez! Pull your mind out of the gutter. "I'm not that great at trivia."

"Eh." Sacha shrugged. Fat drops of rain began pelting the windshield, and he flipped on the wipers. "You'd probably be bored with all us geriatric folks anyway."

"You're not old."

Sacha grunted. "When I was twenty, I thought thirty was ancient."

"I'll be twenty-one soon." *But for you, my throat will turn forty, open up, and say ah tonight!*

"And I'll still be thirty-two and basic AF. Do you even know what it's like to be in bed and asleep by ten? I've already found my first gray hair."

Sacha sounded so dejected that Corrigan laughed. "Gray hair makes a man look distin-guished." *What the hell just fell out my mouth?* Next, he'd be declaring a daddy fetish.

Careful. This man oversees your scholarship. He blinked hard.

"Silver. Gray is trite. But silver…." Sacha wagged his finger. "Silver has charm and is on the stock exchange." He pulled the Mercedes into the parking lot of the athletic dorm and stopped at the front doors.

"Thanks for the ride." Corrigan lifted his gym bag into his lap and opened the door. "And it wouldn't matter gray or silver. You'd wear them both well."

Run.

He dashed to the building before Sacha could respond or he could swallow his entire leg.

8
―――――

SACHA

Sacha stretched out on the sectional in his parents' sitting room with his warmed kibbeh and toed off his shoes while he waited for the rain to slack. After passing several wrecks and hydroplaned cars off the side of the road, he'd preferred not to venture out among the *couyons* who couldn't conclude that it was wise to slow down in zero-visibility slanting rain. He especially wasn't motivated to leave when his parents' fridge and cupboards were stocked, and he was surviving off canned soup at his place until he made a grocery bill. Why adult when he could camp out here as long as his parents were away? Besides, he doubted his house had power if the storm-tracking radar was reliable. It showed his neighborhood on the grid for being in the thick of straight-line winds. Pine trees were known to snap if anyone sneezed too hard, and his gated subdivision was overrun with them—hence the name Pine Grove Estates.

Steam escaped the croquette when he cut into it with his fork, and he set it aside on a sofa table to cool. In the meantime, he scrolled through top newsfeeds on the internet before he found himself searching eye color.

If gray eyes were rare, black were rarer. He couldn't even find a percent for people with black eyes. Not brown or dark. Black. He'd inspected Corrigan's closely today, and they were indeed noir without a speck of brown. And no, he didn't mean the purple-and-black party happening on Corrigan's face... which piqued Sacha's curiosity. However, he figured inquiring would be rude, especially after Corrigan's purgatory comment. Something was definitely going on with Corrigan, but Sacha didn't know him well enough to start asking personal questions. He also didn't want to give the impression of being an ambulance chaser. Perhaps, if the ride had been longer, he would have felt more comfort-able prying. Maybe their paths would randomly cross again soon. Yet he couldn't shake the feeling that his seeing Corrigan today had been purely coincidental.

He rarely drove the back road, and the only reason he'd taken that route today was to avoid driving by campus police. They had been after him to get a faculty decal for his car. But once he did that, it would mean admitting what his life had become. It meant accepting being in a classroom and not a courtroom. He couldn't. He just couldn't. Not yet anyway. So he'd taken the long way around, where he'd been certain to bump into no one. But then there was Corrigan. Who walked from there to the main campus? Had to be fate.

But okay, if it was fate, exactly what was it saying? There was a moment—a couple, actually—that Sacha thought Corrigan may have been flirting with him. However, that didn't make sense. First, no way would Corrigan be interested in anyone his age. Second, did gay hockey players exist? In theory and the rest of the world, maybe. But in Bible Belt athletics, absolutely not. Well... he'd heard parlor room rumblings about some of the players on the Saint Anne Civets, but nothing official. In fact, he was fairly certain about two, but until either made an announcement, he wouldn't assume. All that aside, third, he wasn't gay. At least, he didn't think so. Or was he? *No, not that question again.* Ever since Paxton had broached the subject, Sacha couldn't shake the idea. And the more he thought about it, the more things stacked in that direction. For example, tonight, when he'd thought Corrigan had been flirting with him, he'd enjoyed it. And he'd be lying if he denied his eyes had lingered on Corrigan's ass longer than necessary or that he'd delighted in Corrigan's fresh soap scent. Labels didn't bother him. Well, they did when he didn't know which were appropriate.

His phone rang. Glancing at the screen, he saw it was his father and elected to let the call go to voice mail. Just because he was in his father's house and eating his food didn't mean he had to take his phone calls. As an employee, he knew he should answer, but as a son, he refused. His father had grounded him, so to speak, and Sacha wasn't above behaving like a sulking child. How long he could continue avoiding phone calls was another matter. Eventually, he would need to work his way back into his father's good graces.

As the screen went dark, an epiphany struck him. He needed a second opinion. Grabbing his phone, he clicked on Kian's number in the contact list.

Kian cheerily answered on the first ring. "My dude, what's going on?"

"Have you ever thought of me as being sexually ambiguous?"

"What?" There was a loud crash as if dishes were dropped in a sink.

"You know. Have you ever thought I might not be straight?"

Kian burst into a fit of laughter. "Are you drunk?"

"I'm serious."

"Who is he?"

"Who is who?"

"The guy who has your dick all tight?"

Sacha frowned. "There's no guy." *At least not yet, anyway.*

"Don't feed me that bullshit."

"It's not—"

"Okay, then why are you asking?"

"Why are you evading?"

Kian released a long sigh. "I'm tired of this *Dragnet* conversation. Tell me what's going on."

"It's something Pax said."

"Well, it took him long enough to notice."

Sacha set erect on the couch. "What's that supposed to mean?"

"That you've always acted a bit… fluid."

"Fluid?"

"Ah, Sacha, relax. You are what you call yourself."

"I want to be who I am." The tendons in his neck constricted. Perhaps calling Kian wasn't such a good idea after all.

"Listen, I wouldn't be honest if I said I haven't ever wondered, but you never said anything, so why should I?"

"Because you're my best friend."

"Yes, and best friends don't out each other, not even to themselves." Although Sacha couldn't see him, Kian's compassionate smile could be heard in his voice. "I think you fell into a comfort zone of what was expected of you and ignored everything else."

Sacha arched his brow. "Everything else like what?"

"My gay friends would hit on you all the time, and you would flirt back subconsciously but never go all in. Flynn Pelletteri worked himself up for a month to ask you to prom, and you told him if you found a date, you'd be happy to double. You crushed him."

"That never happened. He...." Sacha abandoned his sentence as he reflected on the memory of that day with Flynn at the stables. He'd been brushing down his horse when Flynn had approached him, acting fidgety and with a flushed face. It had been brisk out, and Sacha assumed Flynn's shuffling had everything to do with the chill in the air and not…. *Oh!* He *had* asked him out, and Sacha had been too oblivious to understand. *I'm an idiot.* "I—"

"Your family laid out a road map for you, and you unquestioningly followed because you want to be a people pleaser. You may pretend not to care, but you do. The fact that you're not in a courtroom isn't what's really eating you. It's wanting to get back in there for a do-over to win back your father's graces. And you've tried to love people who others said you should love instead of trusting your instincts. So, I'll ask again. Who is he?"

Ugh! Even thousands of miles away, Kian could call him out.

"This is going to sound weird, but there's this guy… a client, kinda." *Enter ethical complications.* "I was supposed to get him to sign some papers, but something about him…. He's not what I expected."

"What did you expect?"

"Some typical know-it-all muscle brain who thinks he's the center of the universe. I mean, he may be. We haven't interacted much. But from what I've seen thus far, he seems to be a decent person."

"And someone you wouldn't mind getting to know better?"

Sacha nodded as if Kian could see. "Something like that." The saying that birds of a feather flock together came to Sacha's mind. Corrigan seemed just as lost as he was. Sacha couldn't put his finger on it, but there was something—an *umph*—about Corrigan that he connected with. When he looked into Corrigan's eyes, a tenderness stirred on his insides. It didn't make sense.

"Then take your shot."

Leave it to Kian to make such an elementary proclamation.

"It's not that simple."

"It is if you want it to be."

Sacha rolled in his lips. Was that what he wanted?

"Thing is, I don't know if he would appreciate me doing so. He's a hockey player."

"And?"

"It's not something hockey players do."

"What medieval, intergalactic, heteronormative gender roles fantasy world do you live in?"

"I know how that sounds, but it doesn't make it any less true. Remember how it was for you on the lacrosse team?"

"What I remember is having people like you who

always had my back no matter what. I remember you standing up to bullies twice your size to defend your gay friend and being the champion of those who needed it."

"Funny, I remember getting my ass kicked."

"And that never stopped you. You've never been afraid to get in there and scrap. Plus, I recall you winning your fair share of fights. You have an uncanny, innate gravitation to those who need defending whether you know it or not. Whether *they* know it or not. It's why you're so good at your job."

"Obviously not good enough."

"When are you going to stop beating yourself up about something that's not your fault? You can offer advice. You can't force people to take it."

Sacha sliced into his kibbeh again. Less steam escaped. "I guess."

"There's no guessing about it. It's fact." Kian sighed. "Listen, stop trying to be perfect."

Sacha opened his mouth to argue, but Kian cut him off.

"You go out of the way to please everyone except yourself and have suppressed parts of yourself because they don't fit a mold."

"Did you get a new job channeling Sigmund Freud?"

"Well, speaking of jobs, I hate to cut this short, but I need to bounce. The station has me covering this state welfare audit that claims $94 million have been misappropriated. Seems it's linked to an investment firm in Nevada. The governor is holding a press conference. Call you later?"

"Sure thing."

Setting the phone down and twirling his fork in his food, Sacha thought over the conversation. He wasn't sure if he had gained clarity or muddied the waters more. However, one thing had been made clear: evidently, he'd been emitting some kind of vibes for years that wasn't hitting on the straight bar. He pondered if he would have gone out with Flynn if he had realized Flynn's invitation. He liked to think he would have. But if Kian was correct in his assessment, Sacha probably would have been too concerned with his parents' opinion to have accepted. And if the latter was the case, it made him chickenshit. Only, Weymouths weren't chickenshit. They led charges and carved new paths.

Maybe I'm adopted. Ugh!

He popped a forkful of kibbeh in his mouth and leaned back against the sectional.

A social media notification appeared on his phone, and he swiped to open it. It was an advertisement for a psychic reading. Considering, he arched a brow and slowed chewing. There wasn't a limit to the number of opinions one could get, now was there?

He scrolled to the bottom of the advertisement.

Then again, $1.99 a minute sounded exactly like his limit.

9

CORRIGAN

A SECRETARY LED CORRIGAN DOWN A LONG HALL adorned with oil portraits and into a room painted a soft yellow ochre trimmed in a rich gingerbread before closing the door behind him. He glanced at the nameplate on the door—Maxwell Weymouth—as it clicked shut. Stepping forward, he took in his surroundings. As expected, it was posh with a winter white velvet-tufted sofa and two ivory fauteuil chairs to the left. A mixture of sandalwood and black coffee fragranced the air, and Corrigan almost forgot where he was or why he'd come. But the shuffling to his right dragged him back from the land of awe.

Catty-cornered across the room, a large mahogany desk occupied the space. Behind it, Sacha rose in all his handsome glory, and a chill of excitement skidded across Corrigan's skin. He hadn't expected to see him based on the name on the door.

"Corrigan." Sacha extended his hand as he stepped around the desk, his crisp pale blue shirt with white collar and cuffs fitting his torso like a second skin. His tie was silvery white with tiny blue and gold polka dots and styled with an Eldredge knot. He completed the look with navy suit pants with a sharp crease.

Always so neat and tidy.

Immediately as Corrigan's palm slid against Sacha's, a familiar jolt of electricity sparked in him. It was becoming ridiculous how easily this man punched all his stimulation buttons in the right way.

Gesturing to the sitting area, Sacha asked, "What can I do you for?"

Corrigan strode across the room and lowered himself into one of the chairs. Unzipping his backpack, he retrieved a pink sheet of paper. "My schedule, Mr. Weymouth."

"No, no." Sacha shook his head as he sat in the chair beside Corrigan. "There are far too many of those around here. I'm Sacha." As he extended his hand to accept the paper, his fingers skimmed across Corrigan's, and Corrigan sucked in his breath.

Sacha's gaze flew up from the paper, and the two locked in a stare.

Sounds from a grandfather clock tucked in a corner filled the room as the background noise to their inhaling and exhaling. How were they that close—mere inches apart? Corrigan had an urge to reach out and trace Sacha's strong jawline to his glistening lips. *Whoa! Simmer down.* Instead, when Sacha's gaze turned inquisitive, Corrigan straightened, stiffened, and inched back. *Space.* Yes, that was what he needed. However, he could will his body back no farther than he'd moved, and the two remained close. So, if he wouldn't—*couldn't*—move, he needed to speak.

"I discussed changing my major to architecture with my advisor," Corrigan said, his voice shaky. "She advised against it."

"Well, of course she did."

"It's a five-year program."

"And you plan on being pro by then," Sacha said with a pert smile.

"Hopefully. You say it as if it's a bad thing."

Sacha shifted in his chair. "Not if that's what you want, but I don't see where one thing has to do with the other."

Cocking his head, Corrigan asked, "You don't?"

"Sure, it may be tough, but plenty of people work full-time and attend college. You may have to take summer courses each year or night classes. And there's always online or remote classes."

"But on whose dime? If I don't make pro, I can't afford—"

"If you commit to the major, you can apply for an extension. We can set up an appointment, and I'll help you complete the paperwork. All you'll need is your curriculum check sheet that proves the program is designed by the university to be five years. Or another other-case scenario is if your coach decides you require more growth and development and thereby redshirts you—in which case you'd obviously remain on the team for an additional year of eligibility—that would meet the criteria for an extension as well."

Redshirted? Corrigan went pale. He'd never considered being benched his first year as an option, but it could happen.

"Are you okay?" Sacha placed his smooth hand on Corrigan's calloused one, which should have been innocent enough but wasn't.

Corrigan's stare flew to their hands and stuck while a swarm of butterflies fluttered in his stomach. *Calm yourself. Play it off. He means nothing by it. He's talking business. You can't afford to blow this opportunity, and he doesn't want you hitting on him.*

However, his self-talk went ignored by his entire limbic system, and yearning gushed through his veins like viscous lava scorching a path. He parted his lips to respond, pressed them together, and then tried again cagily.

"I'm... I'm fine." He wasn't, but for the sake of his college career, he needed to be.

Sacha

WHAT WAS WITH HIM? SERIOUSLY, WHAT WAS HIS freaking problem? He had never been touchy-feely, especially not in a professional situation. A firm handshake sufficed in most situations, and occasionally, a reassuring, quick pat on the shoulder was appropriate. But a handhold or whatever he was doing? Nothing about this was appropriate. Yet something about Corrigan compelled Sacha to make physical contact. And the most puzzling thing about his action was he wasn't making an effort to withdraw—at least, not until his stomach unceremoniously rumbled through every section of his intestinal tract. *Sexy... not.*

Hold on. Since when had he become concerned about appearing sexy? Probably about the same time a scholarship extension required a meeting and paperwork. He could download the curriculum check sheet from the university website, and technically, the paperwork required checking a box on the current application. Admittedly, he could complete all that was needed in a few minutes as they currently spoke. However, there was only one reason Sacha would have fabricated a need for another meeting. He wanted an excuse to see Corrigan again. Why? He didn't know other than he was intrigued. While their conversations hadn't been intense, they had been more kindred than any other he'd had with people not related to him. It didn't make sense. Then again, multiverse time travel didn't resonate with him, either, yet millions of people hopped on that futurology train with full understanding.

Snap out of it. He's too young. Young but legal. He's a client. But not really. Technically, it's the Croneau Foundation that Father represents. I wouldn't be brought to the ethics council, although Father might skewer me up over a spit with a Granny Smith shoved in my mouth. But hasn't he already done that? He'd do it again. Get out of your head.

The door burst open. "Sacha, I need—" Paxton halted at the doorway with a stack of thick books pressed against his chest, and the words died on his lips. His eyes zoomed in on Sacha's and Corrigan's hands clasped on the table and then darted between the two men, his brows pulling together before arching.

Oh no. Sacha recognized that look. The recovery was quick, but not before Sacha noticed.

"I thought you were alone."

And he recognized that tone—not judging but judging. If his older brother thought for a second that Sacha would be acknowledging the elephant that had just stampeded into the room, he'd be thoroughly disappointed. *Not a chance. Divert.*

Sacha leaned back in his chair, breaking hand contact with Corrigan. He nodded toward the books, his lips tugging downward at the corners. "That better not be what I think it is." He knew it was.

"I need you to go through these and select a few cases—"

"No."

"It won't take you that long."

Sacha snorted and crossed his arms over his chest. "It'll take hours, and you know it. That's why you don't want to do it."

"I would, but Gretchen and I have plans with the Sterlings, and I can't cancel again because we canceled last week when the kids were sick and the week before that because Gretchen had a catering gig. And Cherry Sterling is on the Lisieux Academy school board, and if we ever stand a chance of getting the kids in—"

"All right already," Sacha griped, swiping his hand in the air. "Take a breath. My CPR certification has expired."

Paxton strolled across the room and set the books on the desk with a thump before turning to Corrigan with a peculiar smile. "Hi, I'm Paxton."

"Pax, this is Corrigan Ellery," Sacha introduced begrudgingly, shooting his brother a warning stare.

"Nice to meet you," Corrigan replied to which Sacha grunted under his breath.

"Well, I'll let you two get back at it." Paxton hesitated a moment as if he had more to say but left without adding anything.

Looking over his shoulder at the closed door, Corrigan asked, "Are you two twins?"

"No. People always ask that, but I have no idea

why," he deadpanned. He walked in his brother's shadow in more ways than one. "He's adopted."

Corrigan's mouth gaped, and his eyes grew as wide as plates. "No shit?"

Sacha chuckled. "No one ever falls for that. Do you have siblings?" There was a place on the scholarship application for family information, but most of it had been left blank. Sacha assumed that was because Corrigan's coach had completed it and didn't know. However, it also could have been omitted purposefully.

"Two sisters and a brother, all younger."

"Was it hard leaving them?"

Corrigan winced. "It had to happen sometime." He stood abruptly and rubbed his hand across his low fade. "I'm due at the dining hall."

Okay, family may be a touchy subject.

Sacha stood as well. "I can give you a lift."

"No," he rushed, clutching his backpack as if his life depended on it. Several emotions flashed across his face before settling on apprehensive. "Thanks, but Coach worked us out pretty hard." He patted his thighs. "I need to walk to prevent cramping up."

Sacha doubted that was the reason but had nothing to dispute it. "Okay," he replied, squashing the disappointment from his voice. "I'll see you when you're ready to apply for the extension, then?" *Oh, dear heavens. Do I sound desperate?*

"Yeah. Sure." With that, Corrigan bolted for the door and disappeared into the hallway.

Way to scare him off. Sighing, Sacha walked to the desk, sat, and opened one of the books Paxton had left there. *Guess it's me and DoorDash tonight.*

HE'D BEEN READING THROUGH MIND-NUMBING contract cases for Paxton's class when there was a quick rap on the door and one of his mentors and double first cousin, Mace Gardner, appeared in the threshold. Mace was eighteen months younger than Sacha but had been so gifted that he'd graduated high school by age fifteen and completed law school by age twenty-one. Although Mace denied it, Sacha was certain he was a card-carrying member of Mensa.

Sacha's face brightened. "Hey, I didn't know you were in town."

"I was supposed to meet with your father." He unbuttoned his suit jacket, hitched his perfectly pressed trousers, gracefully slid into the chair opposite the desk, and positioned his hands one atop the other upon his lap.

"He and Mother got stuck in Lake Charles unexpectedly. I'm filling in until he returns, but I didn't see your name on the schedule. Anything I can help you with?"

"It was a last-minute add, and probably not." Mace shook his head, his prematurely gray hair barely moving out of place. "He referred a case to me, and something about it isn't sitting right. The client isn't completely forthcoming—although, I truly believe he's innocent—and potential witnesses are nowhere to be found."

"How do you think Father can help?"

"He's known my client's family for ages. I was hoping he could provide me some insight." He crossed his ankle over his knee. "But I don't want to talk about work anymore. How you are?" he asked, relaxing and reverting to his easy Cajun dialect.

"The flu has been more pleasant."

Mace smiled slightly. "Any word on how long Max is planning on keeping you here?"

"Likely until I become as withered as a mummy's dick."

"Glad to hear you're optimistic." His smile

widened, but his eyes grew serious. "I believe most events happen for a reason and that we all have connections to each other and the universe that we don't understand or recognize. It's all a matter of paying attention and asking the right questions when the desirable combination of people comes together."

"Like seven degrees?"

"That and deeper," Mace agreed. "It's not invisible, though, but it requires time, patience, and a keen eye to notice. Eventually, something shakes loose that reveals the bond, and everything begins to make sense. There's this *aha* moment of clarity where the pieces fall into place. Little tidbits become important. People we didn't pay attention to play significant roles. We realize it's one journey but that we took all the side roads instead of the interstate."

"So you're saying this is a blip detour in my career?"

"I'm saying maybe it's more than just your career. Perhaps it's a nudge to reevaluate your entire life. I mean, is law genuinely what you want to do, or is it what you were expected to do?"

Sacha's face contorted. "Not you too."

"What?"

"Paxton and Kian said something similar."

"Then perhaps you should start paying attention."

"But I like practicing law."

"It's all you saw."

Sacha leaned back in his seat and crossed his arms over his chest. "You're one to talk, kettle."

Mace held up his hands in surrender. "I know, I know. I don't have much room here."

"Any room," Sacha corrected.

"Well, I guess not if you're going to be a hardass about it, but I do have a private life. Can you say the same?"

"Yes?" He bit his bottom lip.

"Uh-huh. Exactly." Mace rose. "Will you be at Mitzi's *fais do-do* Saturday?"

"I would attempt skipping, but I think she may have snuck into my bedroom while I was asleep and implanted a tracker beneath my skin."

Mace's laugh billowed in the room. "Leave it to you to think that, but you may be on to something. I'll see you Saturday."

Sacha didn't move for several moments after Mace's departure and reflected on the conversation. Maybe his cousin was right and he was missing the bigger picture.

10

CORRIGAN

"I SHOULDN'T HAVE TO TELL YOU THIS," COACH Massey announced, "but hockey is more than being on the ice. It's mentally preparing yourself and getting in the correct headspace to play. It's training your body to have stamina and endurance and learning your opponents. It includes feeding your body proper nutrition." He glanced at his assistant coach, who nodded in agreement. "If you think hockey is only about making goals, you have a narrow view of the sport overall, and that is not what this is about. You'll be sorely disappointed with such a narrow view. Some of the most dynamic aspects of hockey take place off-ice. Championships are won when teams comprehend and bring all aspects of the game together. Do you hear me?"

A unanimous "Yes, Coach" resounded from the team.

"I expect each of you to do the work—all the work—to earn a place on this team," Coach Massey continued. "You're here now, but that doesn't mean that will be the case once the season starts." He turned to DeSevren. "Have them skate it again."

DeSevren waited until everyone was in place before dropping the puck in the defensive zone. Hansford covered a lot of ice and created a good lane in the middle of the rink. Franley pinched, and Hansford cut hard at his tip, collecting a bank pass. He passed left to Corrigan, who took the shot, and Larousse batted it down with a wide grin. DeSevren blew his whistle.

"Ellery, you have to get your hands away from your body," DeSevren chastised. "Transfer your weight to your inside leg and get that outer leg up so you can put your weight into your low hand and push the puck out in front of you. Then, snap down on the puck. That shot had no power behind it whatsoever. Larousse could have blinked it away."

"You really are lousy," Theriot muttered under his breath as he skated past Corrigan to take Hansford's position to run the play with his line.

"Or maybe Larousse is good."

Theriot parted his lips to rebut but glanced at Larousse, whose eyes narrowed daringly. The captain appeared to reconsider whatever he was going to say and skated in a circle, getting the feel for the ice before stopping at the dot for the drop. He took command of the puck the second the rubber slapped against the ice and barreled straight for the goal with lightning speed. His pass to Cardenas was smooth, and the winger scooped it up effortlessly. Cardenas sent the puck out in front of him as he approached Larousse but then dragged it back with the toe of his stick. Misreading Cardenas's intention, Larousse dove forward, allowing Cardenas to sink the puck over his shoulder and into the rear of the net with flawless execution.

Theriot pumped his fist in the air and shot a smug smirk over his shoulder at Corrigan. "Now that's how you do it."

Although Corrigan wanted to slap the smile off the captain's face, he couldn't be mad that the play had gone as designed. After all, it wasn't Theriot's fault that Corrigan hadn't made the shot, and the only thing he could do was improve his game. But damn if his ego didn't sting… a lot.

He cupped the rear of his neck with his gloved hand and tilted his head back. Squinting at the bright overhead lights, he emitted a groan. He despised being subpar. Inhaling deeply, he attempted to mentally travel to his Zen safe place—not that he'd formally been trained in Zen techniques—and envisioned an optimistic future. *It's only four years.*

"You know, he's skated this drill hundreds of times," Nguyen stated, stopping beside Corrigan. "Don't worry. You'll have plenty of time to get it. It's one of Coach's go-tos. Plus, Ram's line has worked together for a year."

"Yeah, I get that," he replied, focusing on his teammates practicing the drill. But that wasn't the root of the problem. "Hey, Nguyen, where are you from?"

"Natchitoches."

Knack-o-what? Corrigan had no idea how to repeat it, spell it, or where to locate it on a map? "Where's that?"

"It's about a three-hour drive from here."

"Oh. So, have you've always been one of the boys?"

"What do you mean?"

"Fit in. It's not like there's much diversity on the team."

An awareness overtook Nguyen's expression.

"Maybe not this year, but that hasn't always been the case. It has more to do with football."

"How so?"

"If you hadn't noticed, football is all the shit here, and other athletic programs kind of fall by the wayside. A lot of hockey players would rather play for schools that spread the athletic love a little more. Well, that and the rumor that the rink is built atop a voodoo cemetery."

Corrigan's eyes bulged. "Holy shit! Is it?"

"Naw. At least, I don't think so." He shifted his weight. "There was a burial ground somewhere on campus, but the bodies were said to be excavated before any buildings were erected."

"Said to be?"

"Developers can be shady and cut corners. Several years ago, deputies busted a crematorium not too far from here for dumping bodies out back because their incinerator broke. They'd been sending fireplace and incinerated trash ashes to the families. When the hurricane hit, all the corpses washed up from the shallow graves and floated down the city square like a damn Mardi Gras parade. That's how they got caught. Of course, they tried denying it by saying it was an oversight."

Get the eff outta here.

"But most people aren't like that," Nguyen added.

"Let's hope not."

"Anyway, I suspect if the school hadn't relocated the burial grounds, the corpses would have popped through the ice by now. Wouldn't that be something? In the middle of a game and zombie heads springing up like Whack-A-Mole. That would totally violate regulations. Probably a game misconduct."

It took Corrigan a minute to regroup and remember why he'd begun this conversation. "So, I'm not the first Black guy on this team?"

"Far from it. However, you may be the first New Yorker." Nguyen flashed a weak smile. "I know you won't believe me when I say that most people here are good, but the stereotypes from the past over-shadow any progress made. Of course, that's not to say that all is perfect or there isn't room for much improvement."

Nguyen's explanation left Corrigan with more questions than answers.

WHEN CORRIGAN SIGNED UP FOR HOCKEY CAMP AND Coach Massey said hockey was more than being on the ice, he had no idea it meant this. He flipped open the spiral notebook handed to him by the class instructor and uncapped his highlighter to take notes. Who would have thought he'd have a seminar class about how to interview with reporters? The presenter had demonstrated acceptable standing positions and what to do with one's hands. Each member of the class then had to model each position while answering questions in a mock interview. What's more, they were being graded, and the head coach had expressed that any person not passing would be in jeopardy of not playing.

Nguyen, seated beside Corrigan, leaned over. "A couple years ago, some football players got into a scuffle at a bar, and it made the news. They said some pretty stupid stuff and embarrassed the university. The place has been on lockdown ever since. Goodbye freedom of speech."

Franley, who had his chin resting on his fist with his eyes closed and who Corrigan thought was asleep on his other side, perked up. "Because of those dumbasses, the athletic department got fined. The money earmarked for new seating in the arena got taken away."

Corrigan recalled his shortcut across the football field. "But they're installing new seats in the stadium."

Kavanaugh reared back from the seat in front of them. "Their mistake, our bill. Everyone else always ends up paying for those bozos."

"Coach is determined to make us an exemplary team in every way possible. Get ready to have every aspect of your life micromanaged," Franley added. "If it's not what the coach deems is up to par...." He drew a slash across his neck with his index finger.

Nguyen leaned in closer. "I heard all the coaches and trainers are getting together and forming a prototype media line to promote."

"What's that?" Corrigan asked.

"They're selecting a few players who they think will be the best representation of the team—who play a good game but who are also socially acceptable."

Corrigan's eyes clouded with confusion. "Meaning?"

"Damn, you're dumb," Theriot chimed in from beside Kavanaugh. "They want players who have all the Bs—brains, beauty, breeding, and bank—to parade in front of the world as the college hockey Harvard of the South."

Thoughts began ticking in Corrigan's head—the first being slamming Theriot's face into the desk and sending him to Jesus same-day shipping. However, the second centered on the captain's words. "But if they do that, only put effort in highlighting certain players, agents and scouts will only look at them."

Theriot nodded. "Maybe you're not so dumb."

The thought of smashing Theriot's face reemerged. "The two places I refuse to go to today are back and forth with you."

"I don't see how that's possible," Franley disagreed. "If scouts come to the games, they'll see everyone playing."

"And who do you think will be given the most ice time?" Kavanaugh thumped Franley on the head. "Who do you think the coaches will push for scouts to meet with?"

"Like old Hollywood," Corrigan muttered.

Nguyen scratched his chin. "Huh?"

"Back in the day, movie studio executives would pluck an ordinary person off the street, give them some plastic surgery and dental work, change their name, create a backstory, and boom, they had their new star. Branding."

"Exactly," Kavanaugh agreed. "They write the narrative for everyone to follow. Instead of the audience deciding who should be a star, the studio executives did it for them."

"Now we have committees watching our social

media accounts and scripts written to recite to the press." Theriot swiveled in his chair and faced forward. "Big Brother 1984 has returned."

Corrigan attempted to look indignant, but the conversation disturbed him. He was aware that going pro was equal parts talent and luck. He even knew politics played a role. However, he'd had no clue he'd be starting this soon. Despite all the hype he'd heard surrounding college application, his high school guidance counselor in his sophomore year had conveyed to him a guarded secret regarding the process and saved him a multitude of time and wasted effort. She'd informed him that most colleges only cared about standardized test scores. Persons with perfect grade point averages but low standard test scores were usually denied but not the other way around. Students with high scores and a low GPA frequently found acceptance somewhere, even if it was on probation. It was why standardized test coaching was a multimillion-dollar business and susceptible to buying scores. All the hullabaloo about extracurriculars didn't mean a damn thing unless aiming for an athletic scholarship. And once again, the athletics had been about another set of numbers—the statistics. Stats couldn't be made by bench-warming. Now all that was being flipped on its head with the insertion of another critical factor: aside from numbers, it all boiled down to who a person knew and nepotism.

People grew up with connections, cliques. And outsiders didn't waltz into a clique. They had to receive an invitation. To be invited required being noticed—but not *just* noticed. One had to stand out as being extraordinary, as having that added *oomph*.

"Cuff links."

"What?" both Nguyen and Franley asked in unison.

Corrigan flattened his lips, shook his head, and flipped a page in his notebook.

11

SACHA

Mitzi had plans to fix him up tonight at her dinner party. Sacha could feel it in his bones. In fact, he'd been feeling it all week. The early morning phone call that had woken him from a lovely dream to ensure his presence solidified his suspicion of his sister concocting a scheme. After Xara... Xia... whatever the hell her name was, Sacha didn't have the energy to ride another merry-go-round of disaster, especially not without strong coffee.

He scraped the last grains of coffee from the canister, hoping like hell it would be enough for one cup. After fiddling with the coffeemaker, he sighed. There was no way he could postpone making groceries any longer. Food, he could live without. Coffee, he could maybe survive a couple hours. He didn't need a list because he basically needed every-thing, but he sat at his breakfast counter where he kept a notepad to make one anyway. So much for sleeping in and basking in a lazy day at home. He hadn't had one of those in a while, and it looked as if that streak would continue into the unforeseeable future.

Before his demotion, his weekends used to be crammed full of meetings with private investigators and mulling over ways to combat prosecutorial evidence. His spirit would be invigorated with how to read a jury and play to their sympathies. Friends called him a workaholic, but his work was also his fun. Now he had a void—or rather a second one. He'd always been able to fill the holes in his personal life with work. But not anymore. Both glared at him with red bulging eyes and a persistence that refused to be ignored.

When he became an attorney, it had given his life a new kind of definition. He'd become important for the first time in his life and stepped outside his fami-ly's shadow. Yes, he was still an attorney like the rest of them, but he'd gone into criminal law—fighting for the everyday man and not billion-dollar conglomerate corporations. Okay, so his clients weren't the average Joe Blow on the streets. Millionaires needed defending too. But that wasn't the point. His work mattered. People depended on him, although his parents disagreed on some level.

Sacha's great-grandfather, a probate attorney, opened the practice with his twin brother, who specialized in contracts. After several years of success, they decided to expand the practice into a firm by merging with two other family-run law practices, Calais and Gardner. These included criminal and corporate law. However, the Weymouths through the generations stuck with civil and contract law while the descendants of the other families continued in their families' footsteps. Then Mace, a hybrid of the Weymouth and Gardner families, elected criminal law and gave Sacha the courage to do the same. But perhaps Sacha should have known better than following in his genius cousin's footsteps, because failure was easier to accomplish in criminal law than it was in probate, and Weymouths were not allowed to fail. The thought depressed him nearly as much as the thought of the one lonely egg sitting in his refrigerator.

Since he was up, he decided to check his messages. He skimmed over several texts from his parents—yeah, he was going to have to quit avoiding them—and a few messages from colleagues wanting to play golf. Truth be told, he despised golf and only went because his father had dragged him kicking and screaming. But in actuality, he'd witnessed more business deals than he could count come together by the eighteenth hole. From a business perspective, his playing made sense. He just found the sport to be so incredibly dull. Hit the ball. Walk. Hit the ball again. Walk some more. If you fancy, ride in a one-cylinder wagon with a tarp that could get up to the whomping speed of fourteen miles per hour. And for some really over-the-top excitement when he went buck wild on the course, he could shake the sand out of shoes. Woohoo!

But hockey. People hit pucks. People hit people. People—

A text from an unknown number snagged his attention.

There's no hole to fit it in. How do I link over the button? the message read.

Perplexed, Sacha stared at the message and pondered if it was a wrong number or spam, but not before his mind sank straight into the gutter. The area code didn't register as familiar. None of his clients had his private number, and all his family and friends were programmed into his contact list. The message didn't read as if it came from a business, and he couldn't recall visiting any porn sites. As he decided to swipe Ignore, the phone buzzed in his hand with a second message.

Or do I rip the buttons off?

Could this be someone his mother had passed along his number to for a fix-up? Sacha may not have known who the sender was, but ripping anything didn't sound like a good idea.

That may be a bit rash, he typed in response. **But to be sure, what are we talking about?**

There was a delay before his phone indicated another text. This time, instead of a message, he received a photo of a shirt sleeve and a pair of brassy-colored ball return cuff links that looked one step up from coming out of a drugstore jewelry case.

Huh? He stared at the screen, attempting to figure out the meaning. Who would send him a picture of cuff links and why?

Then it hit him—*Corrigan*—and his belly flipped.

"That's not going to work," he replied at the phone before it dawned on him that he needed to respond via text.

That's a barrel, he typed and clicked Send.

A barrel of what?

A genuine laugh burst from him. Instead of

texting back, he swiped the green phone icon for voice calls. Corrigan answered on the first ring.

"You need a French cuff," Sacha replied as a greeting. "Links can't be used with barrel cuffs."

"Oh."

There was a beat of no response, and Sacha waited for the question he knew would come next. It wasn't rocket science what Corrigan was thinking, but Sacha always enjoyed anticipating a person's next move or statement. It was what he did in law all the time. However, when the silence extended longer than Sacha thought it should, he asked, "What are you doing?"

"Searching French cuffs on Google."

Or you could have asked me since I'm on the phone with you. "I take it you've not been to many formal events."

"I went to prom."

And boom! Sacha was reminded of how young Corrigan was. He could barely remember his senior prom, and honestly, he didn't want to. He'd wanted to ask Frances Borchardt, an outspoken theater student. However, his parents pushed for him to pursue Didi O'Brien, whose conservative beliefs and demure demeanor had been more acceptable in social circles. It had been another disaster in his life, and he'd spent most of the night with Kian and his date.

No wonder Sacha had actively suppressed the memory.

"I wore... barrel cuffs?" Corrigan continued.

Sacha smiled at the phone. "So I also take it you've never worn links before."

"I bought them yesterday. The salesclerk didn't say anything about needing a special shirt. None of the sites I looked at for how to put them on listed anything either."

So I'm the last resort for information. "What's the occasion?"

"I have to take a mandatory interviewing class, and part of the course is mock interviews and... socializing?"

"You don't sound so certain about that last part."

"I don't guess I am." He sighed heavily. "I don't know what I'm doing. I suppose I am one of those naive people who thought hockey was only about hitting a puck around after all. The instructor started talking about meeting boosters and having to speak at fundraisers."

"As much as hockey is a game, on this level, it's a business first. If you continue in it, it's only going to grow bigger. If you think small, you'll be small. The people you're dealing with are looking at the universe and planning how to carve out their portion."

"I'm not sure I'm ready for all this next level."

Something in Corrigan's voice touched Sacha and made him want to help. "I can't assist with the physical stuff, but I do know a little something about prepping witnesses for the stand and media." *Even if they don't follow my advice.* "I was headed into Le Quartier Jardin." He wasn't. The grocery store where he shopped was miles away from Le Quartier Jardin, but he could make a detour. "How about I swing by and take you to The Hub."

"What's that?"

"From what you've told me, it's a place you need to be."

Corrigan

CORRIGAN'S LEGS QUAKED LIKE JELLY COME ALIVE AND clawing its way from the inside out. At 5:00 a.m., Coach DeSevren had awakened the team by running down the dorm hallway banging clash cymbals. Players had little time to toss on clothes and shoes before he ousted them outside for sets of push-ups, squat jumps, and lateral lunges. And since that hadn't stamped the life out of them, he had them sprint to the arena and perform sets of mountain climber burpees, backpedal sprints, and box jumps. Then they'd sprinted back to the dorm for a shower and breakfast. By eight o'clock, Corrigan's every muscle wrenched with pain. However, since it was the weekend, DeSevren said he would go easy on them. Therefore, he had them lift weights until noon, skate drills until two, and gave them the afternoon off until six.

Sacha had agreed—no, insisted—to meet him at the PAC after practice. Corrigan lacked the energy for shopping but doubted he could muster the stamina to drag his tired body up the hills and back to the dorm to pass out. He was thankful for a ride. Plus, he could use Sacha's expertise. A morsel of eye candy to go along with it never hurt either. A naughty tutelage session fantasy popped in his mind as the Mercedes rolled to a stop.

On weekends, most people Corrigan knew looked chill and comfortable. However, Sacha's casual look was put-together and neat in his three-quarter-sleeve navy Mandarin collar polo, bleached sand flat-front chino pants, and navy moccasin driving shoes. A pair of Cartier sunshades with lenses so dark that they completely obscured Sacha's eyes from view perfected his ensemble. Already, Corrigan felt inferior outfitted in worn jeans, a faded graphic T-shirt, and dingy sneakers.

"Thanks for coming, but you didn't have to do this," he said, sliding into the car's cool interior and shutting the door behind him. "I could have figured it out."

Sacha's smile warmed his face. "So you've informed me multiple times. And like I told you, I know I didn't." He waited for Corrigan to buckle his seat belt before he pulled away from the curb.

"Coach only gave us a few hours off."

"That should be enough time. I've already called Truman and made an appointment."

Corrigan's brows shot up. "Appointment? To shop?"

"If you want a custom fit, yes."

"Whoa!" Corrigan raised his hand. "Custom fit sounds like expensive custom price."

"Depends on how you look at it. If you view it as an investment in a few key pieces, it pays for itself."

"Yeah, but paying right now is the issue."

"No worries. I got you."

Jerking back toward the door, Corrigan clenched

his jaw. His chest constricted so tightly that breathing became demanding. "I don't want you paying for me."

His sharp tone had Sacha's head snapping from focusing on the road to him, and Corrigan promptly regretted making the statement.

"I may hold the checkbook, but it's not my money. It's a school expense and therefore covered by your scholarship."

"Clothing?" The skepticism was obvious in his voice.

"If it were a lab coat or safety goggles, would we be having this discussion?"

"That's different."

"Earlier when we spoke on the phone, you said you're required to wear a suit."

"Only on game day."

"And you said the coach suggested you own at minimum three."

"A recommendation, not a mandate. I have one."

"Which means your scholarship will pay for two."

Corrigan expelled a long breath. "I appreciate the offer, but I don't want to waste funds on frivolous items."

They came to a stop at an intersection, and Sacha glanced from the road back to his companion. "I don't think you understand. When this scholarship was created, it was with the intention that the recipient would become a professional athlete—ergo, designed to meet all the needs that encompasses." He turned back to stare out the windshield and kneaded the leather steering wheel firmly. "For recipients falling short of this goal, the idea was that they would be successful in their endeavors and give back by helping create opportunities for future athletes. So you see, this isn't free money. It's a pay-it-forward."

"But—"

"You'll use the suits now for game day. Keep them in good shape and you can use them when you go pro. If you don't, you can wear them for job interviews or on the job. You can wear them at work functions. Think of them as an extension of your uniform. The team provides you with your game and practice uniforms, and the scholarship will provide you with your travel uniform."

Corrigan opened his mouth to speak but then decided against it. He would have never thought of a suit being a uniform. "Sorry."

"No need to apologize. But for the record, not every helping hand is a handout."

Casting his gaze down, he inspected his sneakers.

"I'm used to paying my way is all, never owing anyone. Strings are messy."

"Not when the terms are clearly defined, transparent, and reasonable."

"That rarely happens, even with the smallest of things."

"Why do you believe that?"

Shrugging, Corrigan clasped his hands together. "One time, my aunt from Rhode Island came for a visit. It was her first time visiting the city, and my mom was so excited to have her. She planned for weeks how she would entertain her, starting with us kids drawing a big welcome banner to greet her at the airport. My aunt's reaction to the sign should have been the first indication that the visit wouldn't go smoothly."

"She didn't like the sign?"

"She took one look at it and turned all ruddy. She practically ran past us." He looked over at Sacha, who was scanning a parking lot for a vacant spot. "The plan was to go back to our house, but my aunt wanted to go shopping. My mom tried to explain about the traffic, but my aunt dismissed her and said it wouldn't matter. Long story short, we ended up getting stuck in the evening rush hour."

"That must have sucked."

"It did, but here's the messed-up part. My mom had planned to cook a big dinner, but my aunt complained that she couldn't wait. Every time we passed a restaurant, she whined to stop. My mom is perhaps the most benevolent person you'll ever meet. She didn't have any money because she hadn't planned on staying in the city, and she'd spent a fortune on buying things that would make my aunt comfortable during her visit like new pillows, her favorite soda, fancy soap. But my aunt's whining started turning dark and angry, and she insisted on buying pizza for everyone. My mother acquiesced because my aunt feigned fainting from hunger. Several years later, my mother and aunt had a huge disagreement because my mother had visited my aunt many times, but my aunt always declined to visit us. I'll never forget the look of hurt on my mother's face when my aunt said she refused because on her only visit, she had to buy all of us pizza due to my mother refusing to feed her. It was an outright lie, and she had been spewing that lie to other family members for years without my mother knowing. Then my dad scolded my mom because he said she should have known my aunt would twist the situation."

Sacha pulled into a vacant space and killed the engine. "That's shitty."

It was a shitty story, and Corrigan didn't know why he'd shared it. He'd never conveyed it to anyone. Although it was something that happened to his mother, it had always felt like a family shame. Additionally, speaking the words aloud reminded him how deeply the event affected him. His aunt's words hadn't only hurt his mother, but they had cut him tremendously. He had been a mouth to feed—a reason for his parents' lack of money and his aunt purchasing more than one pizza. He'd been content that day to wait for his mother to prepare her delicious paprika twice-baked chicken but also had been excited to be fed pizza in its stead. When his aunt had turned to him and inquired if he wanted pizza, his face had lit up, and he'd smiled brightly with an eager positive response. He'd eaten the pizza heartily without thought, adding to his aunt's ammunition against his mother. In hindsight, his actions felt like a betrayal to his family, especially toward his mother. And no action he could take would undo it. But no one needed to know about the incident, except obviously he felt Sacha should for some reason.

"My mom has never gotten over it. From that day

forth, none of us kids were allowed to accept anything from anyone, not even after—" He clipped his words.

"After what?"

"Nothing." He turned his focus ahead. "Is this the place?" he asked, despite the store name being displayed in big, bold letters across the front of the building. He'd said more than enough.

Shopping wasn't something Sacha enjoyed, but it was a skill in his wheelhouse. He staged his clients for juries consistently. He had an eye for what worked and what didn't. However, Corrigan was a special case. A lot of the clothes worked on him if Sacha wished to transform him into a typical college athlete in a suit without an ounce of personality but rather a look-at-me vibe.

"Take it off," Sacha instructed, waving his hand. "You look like you're playing dress-up." He turned to the store clerk. "I'm looking for classic elegance that's not going to age him fifty years."

Corrigan removed the jacket and handed it to a second assistant. His eyes scrutinized Sacha as if unsure. "Coach is trying to bulk me up."

"We'll leave some room," he said, searching through the racks. "Unless baggy is what you're going for—a hip-hop look." He froze and looked up from the clothing, realizing he'd not asked an important question before beginning the search. "What is it that you want for your brand?"

Corrigan shrugged but seemed to consider. "To not look crazy."

"Now there's a word open for interpretation. But what I mean is, what aesthetic expresses you?"

"I don't think I have one. I just put on what's clean. I spend most of my time at practice, so there's no need for more than sweats and a tee."

"Point taken." Sacha leaned against the rack. "Let's look at it from a different perspective. Of the people you know or have seen on television, what styles attract you?"

"I guess sporty that's not all stiff and crunchy."

"Crunchy? Like a taco?"

Corrigan smiled and rested his hands on the back of a nearby chair. "You know. The kind of clothing that makes a lot of noise when you move."

"Ah," he responded, feeling a smidgeon older for not knowing the lingo but happy that Corrigan hadn't pointed it out. "So you're talking stretch cotton or wool."

"I guess." Corrigan hunched his shoulders in a way Sacha found adorable. "Is that bad?"

"Not at all. Not only can cotton be fashionable, but it's also cool and easier to clean. Wool's a might much for this time of year and even in most of the winter, if we're being honest."

"But it's not too… common?"

"It's all about styling—the right fit and color." Sacha moved to the opposite side of the rack to search. "You said sporty. I'm thinking plaid."

"Not just that. I want to look sexy like you."

Sexy? Wait a damn minute.

Sacha's head popped up like a hound catching a scent, his lips curling slightly at the corners before schooling themselves to a more generic expression. His brain wouldn't allow him to graze over a comment like that. Had Corrigan called him sexy? Or had he meant the suit was sexy? Or him in the suit sexy? Was there a difference? *Uh.*

He peered at Corrigan with a thousand rampant thoughts, and the gleam he discovered in the man's eyes shook him. Was Corrigan flirting with him? *Get it right this time.* But that would mean….

He's a hockey player.

Sacha squashed the thought. Instead, he rationalized that Corrigan's comfortability with expressing casual appreciation for someone of the same gender was a generational thing. After all, Corrigan had made the hair comment when Sacha dropped him off at his dorm that could be interpreted as a generalized statement to apply to all men.

Whatever Corrigan had intended, Sacha knew he needed to eradicate the bewildered expression currently on his face that surely would make the situation awkward, especially if he was way off base.

Quit gawking.

"Cornflower blue," Sacha said, finding his voice. "As a color choice." *Really? That's the best you could come up with? Couyon.*

The gleam in Corrigan's eyes dulled, and he stared aimlessly at the pile of disregarded jackets. "I'm not up on color names outside the primary ones."

"I can teach you."

That and a whole lot more.

Suits, ties, and socks purchased, Sacha had Corrigan tag along for his adventures in grocery shopping. As he pushed the buggy down the aisle, he couldn't prevent himself from glancing at Corrigan periodically. The tumble of thoughts and emotions occurring within him made him want to fall prostrate and scream into the linoleum. He wouldn't, of course, because there was no imagining what bacterium and fungi customers had tracked across the floor. However, the what-ifs were churning in his intestinal walls. Was he once again being blind to a man seeking his attention? Or was he a victim of an overactive imagination? Did he even want it to be true? Was he attracted to Corrigan?

The last two questions he had answers for. Yes, he fancied Corrigan's interest. If that was wise was another can of worms, wigglers, and whatnots. And most definitely he found Corrigan attractive. He'd been downplaying his dick twitching ever since receiving Corrigan's text message. It wasn't a full-raging hard-on, but it was enough to make its presence known and caused Sacha to walk bowlegged.

He added a bag of rutabagas to his buggy. He had no clue what he'd do with them, but he'd figure it out later.

Corrigan eyed the selection suspiciously.

"You don't like bagas?"

Corrigan's eyes softened when he smiled. "I don't even know what those things are, let alone what they taste like."

"They're a vegetable, and you'll have to make a pass by the house so I can cook them for you."

What the hell? Did I ask him out?

Corrigan's face lit up. "I don't know when I'll be free, but okay."

Holy cannoli. He accepted. What did I just do?

"The coach keeping you busy, huh?"

"I think he's trying to murder us. I've attended some intense training camps before, but none like this."

"Funding."

"What?"

Sacha debated whether he should continue and decided most of the information was already in the public domain, thus he wasn't divulging any confidential university secrets. However, technically, he didn't work for the university and owed them no allegiance.

"More budget cuts are coming down the pike. It's slated to be a 30 percent slash. Massey is trying to spare his program by winning trophies. Championship teams don't get cut. Losing as many players as he did last year, especially Rabalais as netminder, has a lot of sports analysts ranking y'all in the bargain basement this season. But predictions are little more than spitting in the wind—someone is going to get wet, but who? Playoffs are a long, mangled road brimming with potholes from start to finish. Yet they're enough to spook boosters. If the season goes sour, they won't hesitate in seeking a new bench boss."

Astonishment crossed Corrigan's features. "You follow hockey?"

Sacha chuckled. "Don't look so surprised."

"I took you for more of a golf person."

"God, no." Sacha shuddered. "Why would you assume that? You think all attorneys golf?"

"No. You seem like a tremendously busy person who would want a low-key activity to burn off stress in your downtime."

Sacha considered for a moment. "Makes sense." He was about to continue when his cell phone rang. He removed it from his pocket, read the name on the screen, and rolled his eyes. "Yes, I'll be there tonight, Mitzi," he answered without preamble.

"How do you know that's what I called to ask?"

"Because it's what you wanted the first two times you called me today. I'm not going to back out. We'll dance, drink, make merry, and have a blooming good time. I love you, but I have to go. Bye." He disconnected before she responded. "Sorry about that."

"No problem," Corrigan answered, rolling a cantaloupe in his hand with his back to Sacha. "Hot date?"

Hot seat, maybe. He snort-snickered. "Wine party. But knowing Mitzi, I'm sure she's got something *special* planned for me."

"Oh."

Was that disappointment Sacha detected in Corrigan's voice? He sensed something had changed. His gut screamed it, and he didn't like it. *What's happened?* However, he feared that asking would make the tension that had cropped up weirder. Yet he couldn't allow it to persist and decided to ask a noninvasive question.

"How'd you become interested in playing hockey?"

Corrigan replaced the melon on the pile and stared aimlessly around the store with a look of despondency. "It's not an interesting story."

"Try me. I find lots of things interesting."

"My father was a crane operator. When I was eight, he fell off and fractured his spine. It paralyzed him and left him with a severe TBI, virtually wiping his short-term memory. Most of the time, he doesn't recognize us."

"Damn. I'm so sorry."

Corrigan nodded. "It was a long time ago." He attempted to deliver the comment nonchalantly; however, Sacha sensed the pain.

And my nosy ass just had to ask. Guilt raged through him. "Still, that must be difficult to deal with."

"After a while, it becomes part of everyday life. You get used to it. Anyway, at the time, my mom was working as a prop master for a soap opera, but then soap operas lost favor with television audiences. Production relocated her soap to LA to reduce cost, so my mom had to take up odd jobs. One was a private event whodunit company."

"Whodunit?"

"Yeah, like the game Clue or an Agatha Christie novel. My mom decorated the various theme rooms and hid the clues."

"I see."

"A combination of her work hours being insane, inability to afford a babysitter, and my dad not being able to care for me, my mom took me with her. Only I couldn't go on the job with her, so I waited at the ice-skating rink across the street. She'd pop in and have her coworkers check on me during her breaks. Then one day, I was sitting where I usually sat, and one of the new coaches thought I was there for team tryouts but had chickened out. He made me do the drills. When my mom got there and he realized his mistake, he offered to let me join the team for free."

"And it stuck."

"Eventually. My mom didn't want me at home too much. We had moved to a not-so-great neighborhood. Hockey kept me out of the house. Then, when I got a little older and began helping around the house, it—" He stopped abruptly, shoved his hands in his pockets, and walked down the aisle with distress etched on his face.

Don't pry. It's not your business. "Finish what you were going to say." *Way to go, mouth.*

"It was my escape." He hung his head, clearly defeated.

Sacha approached him and placed a hand on his shoulder. "Why is that a bad thing?"

"Because it was selfish to run off when they needed me. I could have taken more shifts busing tables or stayed home to help my siblings with their homework. Instead, I was at practice or on road trips."

The raw emotion in Corrigan's voice ripped through Sacha. "It's not wrong to do something for yourself."

"Yeah, well, I owe it to them to make it to be able

to help out so my sisters and brother won't have to go through what I did."

Don't dare ask. "What was that?" Obviously, his mouth was going to do what his mouth was going to do, brain functioning be damned.

"Getting held back because of the school closing due to insufficient education and its failure to meet state minimal standard regulations. I'll do whatever it takes to move them someplace better."

Ah, that explains why he's a freshman at twenty.

The gravity of Corrigan's statement slapped Sacha square in the face with a reality he hadn't considered. On a subconscious level, he'd always thought jocks to be about partying, getting laid, not interested in grades, and overall reckless individuals. But Corrigan's explanation snuffed out that stereotype. Going to school, playing hockey, and working was a lot of pressure for anyone, especially someone as young as him. He wasn't a typical twenty-year-old. Corrigan's ambition to improve his family's situation garnered Sacha's respect and admiration.

Then another realization struck, and Sacha felt like a wad of chewed tobacco. All his life, he'd been privileged—prestigious private schools' education, a home most would deem a mini-Versailles, and an abled-bodied, healthy family. He'd not wanted for anything, and yet he'd not been as appreciative as he now realized he should have been.

His phone buzzed in his pocket, reminding him of the time. Corrigan had to be back on campus soon. Sacha would be sure not to make him late. Hurrying down the aisle, he plucked what he needed from the shelves and filled his buggy.

13

CORRIGAN

STUPID. CORRIGAN COULD KICK HIMSELF FOR BEING such an optimistic dumbass. When was he going to learn? He dropped his guard for a nanosecond and instantly got dropkicked in the teeth.

For a brief moment in time, he thought Sacha had been flirting with him, or at least receptive to being flirted with. It could have all been in his imagination, but he didn't think so. Sacha hadn't balked when Corrigan called him sexy. In fact, he thought he'd witnessed a shy smile. Or had Sacha been mocking him for being so forward? But later, he thought when Sacha offered to cook for him, it would be a date... kind of. Apparently not. The man had a girlfriend. Of course he did. How could Corrigan expect prime real estate like Sacha to still be on the singles' market? He'd have been gobbled up the first day.

Dumbass.

Besides, what would an ultrasophisticated man like Sacha want with him?

Yet….

Corrigan worked the puck inside-outside, back-hand-forehand in a figure eight through the cone maze Coach Massey had formed on the ice. He needed to focus on the drill and not on Sacha having some hypnotic truth serum effect over him. Each time he was around Sacha, Corrigan found himself spilling his guts. He had to stop doing that. However, he didn't want to. Talking to Sacha was easy, easier than with any other person he'd ever encountered.

Picking up his speed, he rounded the cone for the final time and dashed to the opposite end of the ice to await instructions for the next drill.

"Hey," Nguyen said, elbowing him in the side, "later, a group of us are going to pass a good time at a frat party. You should come. It'll be lit."

Corrigan used the sleeve of his practice jersey to dry the sweat from his face. "You think Coach is going to approve that?"

"Actually, yes. Ticket sales."

"I don't get it."

"Think of the Greek system as the machines in *The Matrix*. Unknown to most, they silently control everything. Members—and there are thousands of them—are expected to perform hours of community service which enhances their visibility, thereby raising their public profile both on campus and in the community. Members are also expected to support other members, which equates to butts in seats at games. But it's not solely members in their organization but other Greek houses as well. Basically, it's grassroots door-to-door advertising."

"Damn, does everything has an angle?"

"What can I say? It's college athletics, and we compete on every level. So, are you in?"

Corrigan parted his lips to refuse but remembered the conditions of his scholarship as well as the conversation he'd had with his teammates in the interview seminar. Already dog-tired, he didn't know how he'd get through a party of any sort. However, he could use it as an excuse to text Sacha again and ask him for advice. But how desperate and cringy would that be? Sacha was preparing for a date, for Pete's sake. He wouldn't want to be bothered. *Leave him alone.* Then again, he did tell Corrigan he could call him anytime.

"Sure, if you're certain Coach will be okay with it."

"Trust, he'll have spies there."

Corrigan wanted to ask who the spies were, but the whistle blew for the next drill. Taking his position at the line, he handled his stick to the front and then to the side before pulling back and sliding the puck through his feet. Although he'd practiced this drill with his old team, he struggled with how Coach Massey had modified it with a direction transition after every pull-through, and his thoughts lingering on Sacha didn't help his coordination.

Spinning for the direction change, Corrigan momentarily lost sight of his puck in his blind spot before it came back into view. He extended his stick and dragged it toward him but immediately realized it wasn't his puck. The freakish sequence of events that followed was anyone's guess, but Corrigan's stick lodged in the top of the captain's boot.

Plunk!

"Yow!" Theriot yelled, crashing to the ice with a thud. He spun on his belly across the ice while Corrigan's stick helicoptered through the air and landed in the bleachers.

The shrill of DeSevren's whistle pierced through the arena. For a split second, the entire team stood slack-jawed and wide-eyed before bursting into hysterics.

"What in tarnation was that?" DeSevren questioned, scratching the bristles on his jaw.

"You did that on purpose," Theriot accused, scrambling to his feet, his face scarlet.

It would have been hilarious had it been, but Corrigan couldn't have orchestrated that masterful debacle had he tried.

He shrugged. "Umm… karma?"

"Well, whatever it was, don't do it again," DeSevren ordered.

Shaking his head, Coach Massey scowled with an expression somewhere between disgust and disbelief. "I think they've had enough," he said to his assistant. "Wrap 'em up." He shook his head again and skated off the ice.

"Okay, Minotaurs, let's bring it in for the chant."

Well, hell, if Corrigan knew that was how to end practice, he would have aimed to do it hours ago.

As he crossed the Gamma fraternity house threshold, the scents of stale cigarettes, booze, and tawdry perfume descended on him. Following his teammates, he hedged from the entry hallway through the dense crowd to a large gathering room with a vaulted ceiling, floor-to-ceiling windows, and a stone fireplace. For a place that housed dozens, the space felt impersonal with its sleek and modern design but still held a marked male influence. It wasn't what he'd imagined the inside of a frat house to look like, but it wasn't what he hadn't imagined either. From the exterior, the mansion resembled a relic of *Gone with the Wind*—as did all the other fraternities on Fraternity Row, as well as the sorority houses on Sorority Row—but the interior was in stark contrast. The jitteriness of uncertainty Corrigan had been feeling intensified.

He'd expected to witness a sloppy drunk fest, and within thirty seconds, his expectations had been met. Gathered in clumps, cliques communicated with grand gestures and exaggerated expressions while hugging each other to remain upright. Initially, he'd thought no fraternity members were present at their own party because he couldn't distinguish members from nonmembers. However, he later learned that chapter rules dictated that no member could be seen—or perceived as being—intoxicated while representing the organization. Thus, members were not allowed to wear their letters anywhere alcohol was served. Although small, it was another detail the movies Corrigan had seen featuring Greek life had gotten wrong but he'd assumed was true.

K-pop spilled from a sound system that pumped music throughout the house, but it was mostly inaudible due to uproarious chatter and boisterous laughter. It wasn't his favorite type of music, but he could get into it.

"Let's grab some brews," Nguyen suggested.

While downing a cold one sounded ideal to calm his nerves, Corrigan remembered Coach Massey's spies. Getting busted for underage drinking the first week wouldn't sit well with anyone and could derail all his plans. Besides, he didn't trust any of his present company enough not to have his wits about him at all times.

"I'll stick with soda," he replied.

"Soda, ha-ha," Kavanaugh called over his shoulder, heading to a makeshift bar. "Pussy."

Larousse started to follow Kavanaugh but was highjacked by a raven-haired beauty who stepped in his path and superciliously folded her arms across her voluptuous bosom. "And where do you think you're going?"

Larousse wiggled his brows. "Obviously with you

and any place you take me." He swung his arm around her shoulders. "Lead the way."

With a giggle, the coed clamped her hand over his, and the two disappeared into the crowd.

"Yo, Bo," called a thin guy with hair that looked stiff with product. "How's it going, man?"

"Hoyt," Nguyen greeted in return with a fist bump. "It's all good."

"I see you got paroled from the ice prison." Hoyt laughed. "I didn't expect to see you until spring. Word in these streets is y'all not getting any conjugal visits until after playoffs—if you make playoffs."

"We will."

"Yeah? Team any good? Y'all lost a lot of good players last season."

"And gained some good ones." Nguyen turned to Corrigan. "Hoyt, meet Corrigan Ellery, one of our new wingers. Corrigan, this is Hoyt Lemelle, rabble-rouser and vice president of this here shanty."

Hoyt's hooded eyes appeared to conceal a smile as he extended his hand to shake. "I haven't seen you around campus."

"It's the first flipping week," Nguyen replied.

Corrigan shook Hoyt's hand. "As you said, practice keeps us busy."

"Well, I'll be waiting to see if it pays off. I'm going

to be pissed if I drop a couple hundreds on you guys and you turn out to be shit."

A surge of pride struck Corrigan. "Your money will be well invested."

"Ah, big talk." Hoyt nodded. "Confidence. I like that. I like big returns better. I'm in finance. What's your major?"

"Gen—" He caught himself. "Architecture."

"Impressive." Hoyt grinned, placed his hand on his own shoulder, and tapped his fingers.

"Oh, brother," Nguyen mumbled beneath his breath.

"Difficult major. You must be super smart to tackle it and hockey."

"I don't know about smart, but I intend to work hard at both," Corrigan replied. "I'm used to juggling hockey with other things."

A guy who Hoyt introduced as Alton joined them. "Alton's majoring in environmental design. He can tell you a lot about the department."

Corrigan spent the next several moments engaged in conversation with both Hoyt and Alton before a guy named Bullard joined them and Hoyt disappeared. At some point, Alton left, too, and Corrigan chatted with a guy named Omari, and finally with a guy nicknamed Pelahatchie. Other than them each having an odd habit of tapping their shoulders, Corrigan thought they all seemed pretty chill.

After Pelahatchie wandered back into the crowd, Corrigan realized Nguyen was gone as well. He searched the room and didn't see any of his teammates. He deduced that they'd probably ditched him to return to the dorms, leaving him to navigate his way back in the dark, which wouldn't be fun.

As he made his way toward the front door, an inebriated coed crashed into him. Her ankle twisted awkwardly in her stiletto, and Corrigan caught her before she slammed to the floor. Her drink splashed in his face as she puked down the side of his leg.

"Shit fire!" Corrigan yelled, gagging and struggling to not see his meal again as he felt the puke soaking through his pants. The force of her falling body pushed him back, and he collided with a brawny guy who had him outmatched by weight and height.

"Watch it," the guy growled.

"Sorry, man. It was an accident."

The guy's stony gaze sharpened and then narrowed with a flash of dark emotion, his displeasure displaying in the taut restraint of his lips. His burly chest bowed outward as the robust muscles in his biceps flexed beneath his gabardine Henley with the sleeves hoisted up to his elbows. "Stupid bitch," he added, shoving Corrigan in the shoulder as the group he was with turned their attention to Corrigan as well.

"Don't put your hands on me," Corrigan stated firmly but maintained his composure.

"Or what, bitch boy?"

"Or we kick your ass," a voice behind Corrigan responded.

I know that voice. He turned to find Theriot standing behind him, the lines in his face hard and ready for battle. *Wait. Theriot's my avenging angel? What the fuck?*

"Sit your punk ass down," the guy spat, stepping forward as if he was going to do something.

Theriot stepped up to meet him. "Why don't you backstroke to the deepest pit of your ratchet, dilapidated lair and take all your kowtowing minions with you? Swerve, bitch."

The guy's jaw tightened, and he attempted to push past Corrigan. However, Corrigan pressed his palm against the guy's chest, holding him in place. "I wouldn't."

"Oh, you wouldn't?" the guy mocked in an insidious whisper, his lips curling back like a wolf baring its fangs, and slapped Corrigan's hand away. "I'll snatch your trachea out of your throat." He faked to turn but instead threw a sucker punch at Corrigan and landed a snap jab to Corrigan's rib cage, knocking the breath out of him. While doubled over, the guy snatched Corrigan's hair to pull him upright. Corrigan retaliated with a knee to the crotch, and the big guy went down to his knees.

As a second guy jumped in, Theriot lunged forward, knocking them all backward and into furniture. Bodies scattered in all directions, and more joined the skirmish. Corrigan wasn't sure who he was fighting, but he connected his fist to the flesh of anyone he didn't recognize. *Fucking insane.*

Within minutes, someone yelled that campus police were on the way, and Corrigan knew this was not a place he needed to be found. It was all about to hit the fan.

Nguyen grabbed him by the collar. "Come on. We have to get out of here."

Corrigan didn't argue and followed Nguyen outside to where Kavanaugh, Theriot, and Larousse were gathered on the porch.

"Okay, everyone knows the drill," Theriot commanded.

"What's the drill?" Corrigan asked as everyone else nodded.

Theriot released a frustrated breath. "Split up and get an alibi, moron."

"What the hell is your deal?" Corrigan snapped. "Seconds ago, you were ride-or-die, and now you've reverted to complete asshole."

Theriot's lips spread in what Corrigan thought might almost be amusement. "I can say things like that to you. He can't."

"That's all kinds of fucked-up."

"A discussion for a later time," Larousse stated. "Right now, we gotta disappear."

"Right," Nguyen agreed. "See you guys back at curfew."

And just like that, within seconds his teammates had dashed in opposite directions.

In the distance, he heard the campus police sirens. He hurried down the steps and turned in the direction opposite the sirens. Unsure of where to head, he hurried down Fraternity Row toward where he thought he'd seen a path leading to the main campus. However, he soon found himself in the backyard of another fraternity house where there was a party in full swing. In the center of the yard, a long table was covered with newspaper. Atop the newspaper was a heap of boiled potatoes, peeled onions, short corn on the cob, and crawfish.

"Oh, dude, what happened?" a guy dressed in a plain T-shirt with the sleeves folded, Levi's, snakeskin cowboy boots, and a pinched front cowboy hat asked. He gestured toward Corrigan's soiled pants.

"Some girl—"

The guy raised his hand. "Say no more. Come inside, and we'll get you cleaned up. I'm Leo, by the way."

"Corrigan."

"Yeah, I know. I recognized you from your recruiting photo in the *Minotaur Advocate*, the school newspaper," He opened a patio door to a laundry room. "Think you'll be starting?"

"That's up to Coach."

"But he has favorites, right? Players who he's paying close attention to during practice?"

Yes, but I'm not telling you. "He looks at all of us and at whose style best complements the others on the ice with him."

The answer seemed to satisfy Leo, and he handed Corrigan a towel and a spray bottle. "Emergency stash," he explained. "It's vinegar and water. You'll smell like Italian salad dressing for the rest of the night, but it'll take out the stain and cover the stench."

"Thanks," Corrigan said, accepting the items. "I take it this has happened before."

Leo grinned. "A time or two."

They continued to chat while Corrigan cleaned himself up, and then the two returned to the backyard. At Leo's insistence, Corrigan prepared himself a plate of food and chitchatted about hockey, majors, and hobbies with Leo and a few of his friends who were making their way through the party. Strangely, Leo had the same habit as the Gamma house guys of tapping his shoulder.

By the time Corrigan decided to return to the dorm, he'd found his night hadn't been as dreadful as he'd expected and that most people he'd met had behaved decently.

14

SACHA

I'M GROWN, SACHA REMINDED HIMSELF. HE'D BEEN AN
adult and independent for quite some time. So why
was he cowering away in a corner of a dark room in
his sister's house? Good thing he wasn't afraid of the
dark.

Was his life really this pathetic?

He sipped his wine and looked out the large
window over the lake. It was a beautiful view. But he
had a beautiful view from his home too. So why
didn't he go home? Well, he knew why. While he'd
been able to sneak off through the house, Mitzi had
stationed her cronies at the doors. Okay, they were
service workers for hat check and valet, but they
diligently reported all comings and goings of guests
to his sister. If he dared try to escape, they'd have the

bat signal or the dark mark in the sky before he fastened his seat belt. But as long as she knew he was looming somewhere, he was safe—well, safe enough. She would assume he was engaged in some mindless conversation with any one of the strings of women she'd invited on his behalf and had practically betrothed to him.

Normally he would entertain the thought of playing the game and dancing the waltz—do the "small talk and exchange digits" thing. However, tonight, he couldn't stomach pretending. After a few minutes of schmoozing through the guests, he knew no one there piqued his interest, and his mind kept drifting to earlier in the afternoon with Corrigan and how a comfort had seated itself in him during their time together. He'd not felt compelled to carefully construct his statements to avoid disclosing his private thoughts. Corrigan would listen without judgment. Sacha felt it.

Besides, if Paxton, Kian, and Mace were correct, Sacha owed it to himself to be authentic. And if that meant exploring his sexuality, then so be it. Maybe he was one of those people who could get turned on by the fantasy but chicken out when it came to the follow-through. Or maybe he was a person who wanted what he couldn't have. Was Corrigan even available to him? Was he attracted to Corrigan because unavailable people were safe and would give him an excuse not to answer the questions Paxton had raised?

Shit. He was driving himself crazy. At least if he still had criminal law in his life, he would have a distraction.

Closing his eyes, he leaned against the wall.

A courtroom would allow him to remain in his comfort zone and within the expectations of others. The only problem with remaining in his comfort zone was that a part of him was itching to know the unexplored.

He couldn't shake the thoughts of Corrigan from his mind.

In typical Sacha fashion, he'd created a mental list of all the cons of being with Corrigan. Most were relevantly weak and fear based. The only strong, legit concern—well, there were two, assuming he was indeed gay—was the age gap. How much would they have in common? Wouldn't Corrigan want to have a full college experience? Play the field? Swing from chandeliers? Streak buck naked across the stadium? Okay, maybe not the last one, but Sacha wouldn't judge.

He had dated—a lot. He was tired of the scene

and desired something steady, and this led directly to his second legit concern. Corrigan was so young. He wouldn't want to be tied down and settled. If Sacha allowed himself to fall for him, he very well could end up nursing a broken heart, which would probably be worse than being alone. Again, this assumed that Corrigan was both interested and gay.

Sacha knew investigators and had an entire catalog of them in his contacts. He could always give one a call and have them snoop into Corrigan's private life. However, that felt like a violation— borderline cringy slash stalkerish—especially when Sacha hadn't bothered (aka manned up) to ask Corrigan about it. How was he to figure it out? He considered for another moment and decided, *Screw it.* He slipped his phone from his pocket and typed a text.

Hope you made it to practice on time. I know we cut it short, and it has me worried. I wouldn't want to be the reason you're skating laps or anything. Lies. All lies. Sacha had dropped Corrigan off at the PAC for practice with time to spare. But since this was the angle he was taking, he needed it to sound convincing. **I also didn't want to text too soon and interrupt.** *Or appear desperate*—which he probably did.

All good came the reply minutes later.

That's it? That's all he's going to give me? Disappointment swept over Sacha. He didn't know why he'd expected that to open a dialogue, but he had. He sucked at flirting.

Great. I'll be able to sleep better knowing.

He was about to slide his phone into his pocket when it vibrated again.

You're in bed? Sounds cozy.

Ah! There was his opening. Sacha debated how to proceed and decided to go all in. **It would be if I were and weren't alone.** *Let's see what he does with that.*

What happened to your wine date?

I'm sipping a glass while attempting to construct a plausible exit strategy. My fallback used to be having to meet a client at the jailhouse for an interrogation. It takes more effort to fabricate a contract emergency.

I'll call you if they haul me down to the campus police station.

Sacha's brows bunched, and concern crept into his eyes. **Why would you be taken there?**

Fraternity brawl.

You're joking, right?

Unfortunately, I have the upchuck on my pants as evidence.

Should I even ask? **What happened?** *I guess so.*

A drunk chick must have thought her body was on fire and decided to stop, drop, and roll right into me. Are you certain the nonnegotiable is nonnegotiable?

Irrefutably, but if you would like to discuss it, we can. I can even arrange an emergency consult tonight.

Wow. You must be desperate to get out of where you are.

Yep. Sacha scowled. Although true, he wanted to retain some form of dignity. However, he was willing to make the sacrifice if it meant spending the rest of the evening with Corrigan.

Wait. Did he honestly feel that way? He considered the thought and came to the conclusion that he did.

All in, right?

I enjoy your company.

He held his breath as he awaited the response. *Was that too much? Too weird? Inappropriate?* Why he worried about being inappropriate when he'd already referenced sleeping alone? A case—a weak one, granted—could be argued for sexual harassment. Well, whatever it was, it was too late because he'd already hit Send. *Kee-yaw!*

Admit it. You like me because I don't mind getting cans from the bottom shelves at the grocery store so you don't have to stoop low.

Sacha laughed aloud. *That's not the reason.* It wasn't the cans on the bottom shelves that he'd wanted. Rather, he enjoyed the scenery—Corrigan bent over with his ass—

"There you are," Mitzi huffed, entering the room. "I've been looking for you for half an hour."

Sacha jumped, startled. *Ah, crackers! Busted.* He'd swear his sister was part bloodhound.

His smile faded as he turned to face Mitzi. "I haven't been gone that long."

"Right. It's been longer, but that's when I missed you."

"I needed air."

"You promised."

"Yes, to come, and I'm here, aren't I?"

"You said you'd try."

He held up his phone. "I have—"

"No, don't you dare say you have to leave. Harvey took over your caseload."

"Fine." Sacha slipped his phone into his pants and groaned. The thought of returning to the others brought bile to the base of his throat. He took a step and then stopped. Suddenly, he felt like a fraud lying to his sister. "No, it's not fine." Reaching for Mitzi's elbow, he pulled her toward him. "Mitz, I think I'm gay."

"What?" Her eyes glossed with a glaze Sacha couldn't identify, and her energetic demeanor crumbled.

He braced himself for a reaction of mortification, disgust, and condemnation to hell—a typical response from his family when something occurred outside of what was deemed respectable. After all, they were Weymouths, the epitome of tradition and conservatism. Articulating the words had made his soul quake, and he wasn't sure he didn't regret his spontaneous confession. Was he ready for this? Losing the affection of his sister would slice deep, especially since he still had so many questions for himself.

For what seemed like an eternity but couldn't have been longer than a few seconds, a deafening silence filled the room. "Well, that changes things," she finally murmured, her lips puckering the way they always did when she was deep in thought. "You should have said something sooner so I could have planned better. I may have time to change the seating chart. George's cousin is here, and I think he's gay. Rumor has it that Hunter is bi, but it's nothing solid." She scrunched her nose. "I don't think you'd want to get involved with him, though. He harbors enough pettiness to choke a mean girl."

"Seriously? I come out to you, and all you have to say is that I screwed up your seating arrangements?"

"What do you want me to do? I could leave it as is if you prefer, but how are you going to chat comfortably with these men if you're at the opposite end of the table?"

Speechless, he studied his sister's determined glare. "You're unbelievable."

"Why? Because I want you to be happy?"

"Who says I'm not happy?"

Mitzi crossed her arms, her tone nonchalant and assessing. "You're alone. Even misery doesn't always dine alone."

"I'm *single*. There's a difference. Lots of people are single."

"Lots of people like anchovies too."

He paused, his words once again lost. "That makes no sense as a rebuttal."

"You want to know what makes no sense?" Her jaw clenched in a stubborn line. "That you would wait this long to share this with me. I'm your sister."

"I'm just now figuring it out myself, so it would be appreciated if you didn't go blaring it to the nation yet."

Mitzi's eyes glinted with sadness as if she might cry. "I don't want you keeping secrets from me."

His face softened as he drew her to him in an embrace. "I would never."

"Trevor Lampley recently broke up with his boyfriend," she mumbled into his chest.

And while he wouldn't keep secrets from her, that didn't mean she wouldn't continue to meddle in his life. He was certain, the minute they left the room, she'd begin pimping him out to any man in the vicinity with a dubious sexual reputation.

Poo-yi.

15

CORRIGAN

IF CORRIGAN HAD LEARNED ANYTHING DURING THE past week, it was that Coach Massey indeed had spies and plenty of them. After returning to the dorm for curfew on Saturday, he and the rest of the team had been met in the lobby by the assistant coach, who spent ten minutes chewing them out and another thirty minutes having the team perform push-ups and squats as punishment for the frat house scrimmage. But the discipline hadn't stopped there. Coach Massey had lengthened practices and doubled down on drills to the point that Corrigan's muscles were too sore to be sore. The situation had become so dire that even Theriot forgot to be an asshole on most days.

Likely the practices violated NCAA regulations,

but who paid attention to the rules during the off-season? Besides, conditioning and weight lifting weren't technically considered *practice*, which gave Coach Massey a vast loophole, not to mention when workouts were labeled as *student-led* and, thus, exempt from being monitored. The logistics of the rights and wrongs of the hockey program being run could be argued to the moon and back. However, nothing would be done because the system was too well oiled. The people who counted knew the precise language to use and how to skirt the lines of acceptability. So this was the price Corrigan would pay.

When his body wasn't being physically pushed to its limits, his mind was being challenged in classroom seminars on interviewing, nutrition, tactical sessions, and game mentality preparation. With both his body and mind drained, all he wanted was to crash, decompress, and relax. If he could find a reason to smile or laugh a little, even better. So, when Coach Massey cut them loose at six o'clock on Friday and said they could have Saturday off with no curfew to attend the dedication of the new Student Aquatic Center, Corrigan was elated. That was until Nguyen charged into the dorm room Corrigan shared with Marshall Girid, a rookie defenseman from Livonia, Louisiana, without knocking.

Girid never said much to anyone; thus, the room was mostly quiet—*mostly* being the opportune word. When awake, Girid usually wore noise-canceling headphones while he streamed or listened to music. But when asleep, he snored like a tractor, leaving Corrigan with more restless nights than not. Having a free Friday evening for Corrigan translated to being able to catch some z's before Girid crawled under the sheets and cranked the bulldozer. His evening had been looking better when Girid hadn't returned from practice. But now Nguyen was looming in the middle of his room with a forlorn expression.

"Problem?" Corrigan asked, his hands crossed behind his head on his pillow.

"It will be for you if you don't get out that bed."

Corrigan's brow arched. "And why is that?"

"A little birdie told me Coach has planned another room raid, and anyone found here is going to catch it all weekend."

"But he gave us time off."

"A farce for us to let our guards down. He's coming, and he's coming hard. I hear it's a trip out into the woods to a deserted Army Reserve obstacle course. I suggest you pack a bag and find a place to lie low for the next thirty-six hours unless you want to play G.I. Joe."

Corrigan sat upright, concern etched on his face. "I guess I can get a cheap hotel room."

Nguyen shook his head and snorted. "That's the first place he'll look. You don't think he has goonies stashed at the front desks who will call to snitch the instant you check in?"

"Where is everyone else going?"

"Different places. Friends. The ones who live nearby are rolling home."

"What about you?"

"I'm busting a nut at this chick I met's studio apartment. She's like six feet tall with triple Ds. I figure it'll take twenty-four hours to satisfy her and another twelve for me to recover." He chuckled, wiggling his eyebrow. "I thought I'd give you a heads-up before heading out. If you're going to go, you better move fast. Roundup begins in about twenty minutes."

"Twenty? Shit!" Corrigan sprang from his bed and snatched his athletic bag from a chair.

As Nguyen turned to leave, he paused by Corrigan's desk and lifted several colorful index card-size envelopes. "What's all this?"

Corrigan shrugged as he opened drawers and crammed clothes into his bag. "They were taped to the door when I returned."

Nguyen flipped the envelopes in his hands. "Looks like someone's being recruited."

"What?"

"These are dirty invites. Frats pass them out to people they're interested in recruiting." He opened one of the envelopes and pulled the card from inside. "Chi Delta Upsilon. Interesting. I didn't know you were pledging."

Corrigan shook his head. "I'm not. I mean... I completed an intake application, but I had to as a condition of my scholarship. And what do you mean by dirty?"

"Technically, they're not supposed to make contact with any PNMs until recruitment officially begins."

"PNMs?"

"Potential new members. It's supposed to keep recruiting fair by balancing bids because some houses are more popular than others. But when a house finds a person they like, they stoop to dirty recruiting by sending out invites before the other houses have an opportunity to meet the PNM." He waved the envelopes. "Seems like you've caught a couple eyes."

"I don't know how. I've only been to that one fraternity...well, aside from when I accidentally walked up the drive of another. A guy there let me get cleaned up."

"So you cleaned up and left?"

"I got some food."

"Mm-hm. Didn't talk to anyone?"

Corrigan rummaged through a crate beside his bed where he stored his hygiene products. "A couple guys as they stopped for a few minutes on their way to the food table."

"Let me guess. They mysteriously appeared after the person you were talking to developed an itch on his cheek or chin that had to be scratched."

Looking up from the crate, Corrigan frowned. "What?"

"You didn't notice any of them do anything weird?"

"No. Well...." He reflected for a moment. "Except they tapped their shoulders a lot."

Nguyen glanced down and shook his head. "You're so naive. That's code for another member to come in to help scope PNMs." He tossed the envelopes back on the desk. "You're on their radar.

Anyways, I've got to boogie if I want to avoid Coach's henchmen. You'd better do the same."

"On it," Corrigan replied, haphazardly flinging toiletries in his bag. His mind whirled as he scanned the room for any other items he may need while in hiding.

Dear God, this is like some black ops thing.

Seeing nothing else necessary, he stuffed his feet into his shoes, grabbed his wallet, and rushed out of his room and down the side stairs, where a few of his teammates scurried with apparently the same intentions. Once outside with no plan of where to go, he picked a random direction and began speed walking.

At some point during Corrigan's walk, he'd decided to head to the library. Who would think to look for a jock in a library, right? He figured it wasn't the safest place to hide since it was bound to have spies, but it also had plenty of dark cubbyholes and would get him out of the open.

"Where's the fire?"

Startled, Corrigan jerked his head in the direction of the voice. Between two vehicles in a parking area, Sacha was leaning against an SUV with a pretty —*exceptionally pretty*—woman in a stylish suit beside him.

"Oh, hey," Corrigan responded, coming to a halt and taking a second to find his voice. His eyes floated up the beauty, from her long legs crossed in front of her to her cinched waist accented by a designer belt to her draped blouse covering a generous bosom to her oval face with high cheekbones and sculpted nose. Beautiful and exactly what he imagined would be Sacha's type. Something about her looked familiar, yet Corrigan knew he didn't know her. "All around, apparently."

"That sounds cryptically alarming."

"I don't mean to be. It's just—" He cut his sentence short and glanced nervously over his shoulder with his heart thumping against his rib cage as a convertible with the top down sped past. Not recognizing any of the passengers, Corrigan sighed a breath of relief before tensing again. Coach's spies could be anyone, including students in a ragtop.

To some, this would appear as a petty overreaction. Sure, his situation wasn't on the same level as being hunted by international terrorists or drug lords, but he had to remind himself that this was hockey culture. While he'd never experienced anything to this level on his previous team, he'd heard stories and had a comprehensive understanding of how it worked. Much like a military hell week, some athletic programs were designed to test endurance by physically and mentally taxing players to the edge to eradicate the *weak*. The merit of that philosophy could be debated, but the fact remained that those serious about going pro accepted the challenge without pushback or questions. Those who failed to comply with the draconian training conditions and code of silence didn't advance. All he'd experienced the past week was nothing compared to what he imagined the coach had planned for the weekend. Being hidden away in secluded woods created an ideal no-holds-barred condition. While whistleblowing might be an option if someone was willing to listen, no player ever wanted to be labeled as the one who distracted focus from the team's goal of winning games. And that was exactly what Coach Massey would ticket this weekend as.

"I have to go," Corrigan finally replied.

"Wait," Sacha called after him. Turning to his companion, he pecked her on the cheek and informed her that they would talk later. He jogged across the parking lot to catch up to Corrigan, whose long strides had taken him several paces in a few seconds. "Wait," he requested again, clutching Corrigan's elbow. "What's going on?"

Corrigan came to a full stop at the firm grip. "I need to get to the library."

"Sure. I'll give you a ride."

"No—"

"My car is right over there." He jerked his head toward the building. At Corrigan's hesitation, he added, "I have to pass there on my way home."

Corrigan bit his bottom lip as another car motored down the street, and his anxiety rose another notch. He was certain—well, mostly—that a van wouldn't roll up beside him, have people dressed as ninjas jump out, shove a sack over his head, and drag him inside. However, if he were located and refused to go, he couldn't imagine good results. His body needed the rest.

"Thanks."

The two walked to Sacha's car and climbed inside. Initially, neither spoke as they began the short drive to the campus library. However, Sacha broke the silence.

"You seem a bit on edge."

"Yeah, I guess I am." Corrigan attempted a smile but failed. "I'll settle down once I get to the library."

"Is there some special event happening?"

"No. I'm going to hang out for a while."

"In the library?" Sacha's brows bunched.

"I get it. Jock and library equal an oxymoron."

"Not at all, but it's Friday. The library closed half an hour ago."

"Shit!" *Think.* He considered places to go. *The mall? Is that too obvious? Maybe the movie theater where it's dark.*

"You seem a bit scattered. What's going on?"

"I need a place to hide for a few days."

"Why? Are you in trouble?"

"Not the way you think." Quickly, he rambled through his dilemma.

"Well, that's simple enough. Come to my place."

The hideaway was perfect, but... "No, I couldn't."

"Why not? No one will look for you there. My house is safe. I have haint paint and everything."

"What paint?"

"It keeps the Lutin at bay. Trust, I'm too old to have spirits running amuck in my attic, especially if they aren't paying rent or doing laundry. Do you have any idea what exorcisms cost?"

Exo...? What the...? Gah! Let it go. Do not fall down this rabbit hole.

"Besides," Sacha continued, "even if someone did

come searching, they wouldn't make it past gate security. So, why not stay?"

Because being around you causes me to spring a boner? No, Corrigan definitely couldn't answer with the truth, but he could think of no other excuse. So, against the better judgment of his raging libido, he agreed.

16

SACHA

WHY WAS SACHA NERVOUS? HE'D HAD HOUSEGUESTS before, although none had ever stayed overnight. He valued his privacy, but mostly, a situation had never arisen that a friend or colleague had needed to crash at his place. If they'd had problems with their significant others or spouses, they rented a hotel room or returned to their condos where they'd never terminated the leases. And women... well, that was an entirely different story. Awkward morning-afters had never been his jam. He preferred to do his business—preferably not in his house—and go.

Again, he questioned if his actions were ethical. Technically, Corrigan wasn't his client, and neither was ULSA. But would the bar and ethics committee see it that way? Would his legal peers? Would this smear the Weymouth name... further? Sacha was already in deep enough shit with his father without adding to it. Pissing him off even more wouldn't help him get back to practicing defense law again.

Sacha selected a bottle of wine from the cabinet in his kitchen but then remembered Corrigan was underage. Deciding sweet tea would be a better option to go with their meal of apricot orange glaze butter steak, zucchini fries, and roasted chickpea salad, he returned the bottle. Yes, he was going out of his way to impress Corrigan with his cooking skills.

Okay, if he was forced to come clean about the meal, the food had been frozen leftovers from Mitzi's party. The benefit of being the single sibling was that at the end of any family event, his family ensured he was loaded with leftovers as if he would starve without them. It was a phenomenon he didn't understand, but certainly not one he'd complain about. And unless Corrigan insisted on knowing, not one Sacha felt compelled to confess. After all, he'd warmed and plated it. That counted for something, right? Besides, it wasn't as if he'd had advanced notice to plan a proper... what? Did this count as a date? Damn. Why did he feel so incognizant and inept?

He strolled into the living room where he'd left Corrigan to have some privacy as he video-chatted with his mother, who'd called. He found Corrigan seated on the sofa, fumbling through his athletic bag and muttering.

"Everything okay?"

"Yeah. My phone died, and I can't find my charger. I threw everything in so fast. I think I grabbed it, but I'm not sure."

"I probably have one that fits." Sacha walked to the wall shelving unit and opened a drawer. He returned to Corrigan with a storage case of a neatly twined assortment of extension cables, port heads, and power plugs.

"Whoa. Are there any adapters left at Best Buy?"

"I use a lot of different devices."

"Apparently."

"Supper's ready in the dining room."

The dining room felt date-like. Sacha rarely used it, usually eating in the kitchen or at his breakfast nook. Or on the patio or in the living room. In his bed. Hell, anywhere other than the dining room. He led the way.

"Thanks again for allowing me to hang out," Corrigan said, situating himself at the table. "I'm pretty sure all this seems weird to you."

Sacha smiled. "Not especially. I've had a few clients to go on the lam before."

"It must be interesting being a lawyer—lots of compelling cases."

"It can be."

"Was there ever a time that you considered doing anything else?"

Sacha paused with his fork suspended midair as he pondered the question. He thought hard. He remembered his classmates from grammar school on career day stating they wanted to be astronauts and firemen, but not him. Attorney had always not only topped his list but been his entire list. There had been no plan B.

And that brought him to a question both his brother and cousin had stirred in him. Was he an attorney because he wanted it for himself or because his parents had mapped it out for him? Had he simply followed the path like a good little foot soldier? But if he wasn't an attorney, what would he be?

"I suppose not," he finally answered.

"Must be nice knowing your dream and not having to depend on chance."

"What do you mean?"

"Hockey's a coin toss. As a lawyer, you could go

anywhere and set up a practice. You could even do it virtually if you wanted. You don't need agents or get stressed out about being picked for a team. Age and injury aren't issues."

"Law is more competitive than you think."

"I'm not implying that it isn't, but there are so many more options. There are over two hundred law schools in the US"—according to the poster in the law center lobby that boasted ULSA as being ranked the ninth top law school in the nation—"so unless a person is a complete idiot, I'm sure they'd manage to get into one. And there's no limit to how many lawyers there are. Compare that to thirty-two NHL teams with a roster limit of twenty-three. Of course, there's also the AHL and ECHL that add roughly another sixty teams, but that's still not half of law schools." He dug into his salad. "And attorneys don't wake up one morning and find that they've been traded to another team."

Sacha nodded. "Valid points. You make a good argument. Maybe you should consider law. You'd make a damn convincing prosecutor."

"Nah, I get stage fright."

"No way."

"Public speaking has always been a dread. I get tongue-tied every time. I have it all perfectly planned in my head, and then out of my mouth comes utter gibberish."

"Didn't you say you were taking an interview course?" Sacha asked.

"Don't remind me. It's horrible. I either freeze up or repeat myself a gazillion times."

"Well, I'm sure you'll get better with time."

Corrigan shook his head. "Time isn't something I have on my side. Nguyen, he's one of my teammates, says only players who ace everything are going to make the starting line."

"Sounds like maybe your coach is looking for character."

"If that's what you want to call it."

"Well, what would you call it?"

Corrigan shrugged. "I don't know. Me complaining?" He took several more bites of food before speaking again. "So, is your girlfriend going to be ticked that my coming over wrecked your plans for tonight?"

Sacha looked up from sipping his tea. "What girlfriend?"

"The beauty you were with tonight?"

A pit formed in Sacha's stomach. "You think she's beautiful?" What was he saying? Of course Mitzi was beautiful. "She's married." *What in the wide world?*

That was not an appropriate response for a rational person. However, it was quite fitting for a jealous one.

Damn, he would go for Mitzi. What hot-blooded male wouldn't?

Wide-eyed, Corrigan stuttered, "O-Okay."

"No, that's not what I meant." He waved his hand. "I mean, she is married, if you're interested."

"Why would I be interested in your girl... lover...?"

"Gads, no! Mitzi's my sister."

"Oh, well, that's good to know."

"It is?"

"I mean...." Corrigan's cheeks reddened. "It's good that you're not involved."

Sacha's eyebrows lifted.

"I mean, with someone who's married... not to you."

"Oh. I see." Sacha stared down at his plate, not knowing how he felt about this exchange. A part of him was relieved that Corrigan wasn't interested in Mitzi—at least, he didn't think he was. Then there had been a glimmer of hope that Corrigan could be interested in him... maybe. But then he'd added the whole "not to you." What the whole hell did that dangling participle or whatever part of speech it was mean? Was Corrigan saying he was relieved that Sacha wasn't having an affair with a married woman? Or did he mean he wasn't attracted to Sacha?

Shit! He was more confused now than he had been seconds ago. One of the first rules in defense law was not to ask questions he didn't already know the answer to, but fuck this.

"So, to be clear, you're not interested in Mitzi."

Corrigan raised his hands in surrender. "Simmer down, overprotective brother. I'm not going to try to hit on your sister. Yeah, she's pretty, but she's not my type."

"What is your type?"

Yep, that fell out of his mouth. His mouth was officially disconnected from his brain. He'd likely regret asking in a minute judging by the stare Corrigan was giving him. Granted, the question was forward and a bit rude. Okay, a lot rude.

I've lost my ever-loving mind. He had no clue what he was doing. Was it creepy to have offered Corrigan a safe haven for the night and then to hit on him? If Kian's lifestyle was that of a typical—if there was any such thing as *typical*—gay man, boldness wasn't a recessive trait. But he wasn't Kian, and Corrigan wouldn't be a hookup.

Well….

Shit!

Corrigan

HAD HE HEARD CORRECTLY? SACHA WANTED TO KNOW his type? And why? Was he emitting some type of vibes? And what about the vibes he was sensing from Sacha? Call him crazy, but he detected something a little more than the overprotectiveness of a sister. It was almost as if….

If he gauged the situation wrong, this would make for a completely thorny and uncomfortable weekend or worse. Sacha could ask him to leave. But Corrigan was taking huge leaps when he needed to take baby steps. Was Sacha someone he could trust to disclose his sexuality?

Corrigan straightened in his chair and studied him. Yes, he believed Sacha was trustworthy. Lawyers knew how to be discreet. They took oaths of confidentiality.

Next question. Was he a homophobe? He didn't appear to be, but that didn't make him gay. Nothing about Sacha screamed queer, except maybe his fashion sense. But that, too, was an antiquated stereotype. Plenty of straight men dressed well and had high-décor homes. Of course, they probably weren't discussing throw pillows and placemats regularly, but that didn't translate to a thrift store sofa with a hodgepodge of accessories in a room. Besides, Sacha likely had a professional interior decorator design his home. Undoubtedly, he entertained wealthy friends and clients. He wouldn't live like a hobo.

Finally, and the biggest question, if he came clean, what were his prospects of landing a catch like Sacha? As much as Corrigan would like to believe himself not to have an ego, he did. Rejection would be a hard pill for him to swallow.

"I'm sorry," Sacha said.

Corrigan realized a considerable—more than socially acceptable—amount of time had elapsed since he'd been asked the question. He'd sat stunned with a dumbfounded expression. He took a deep breath and exhaled slowly. He couldn't fathom he was about to say what he was about to say.

"Men," he finally replied. "I like men." Another lapse of silence passed before Corrigan asked, "What about you? What's your type?"

"I'm still figuring it out," Sacha admitted, "but I'm willing to explore."

"Curious, huh?"

"No, it's more than that." He folded his hands in his lap and interlocked his fingers. "I've had feelings for years that I've never owned up to or acted on. The attraction to men exists."

"But?"

"Some people have fantasies, but they never live them."

"Why?"

"Fear, most likely."

"Of what?"

"Judgment."

Corrigan smiled sweetly. "That's kind of ironic, isn't it? A lawyer afraid of being judged?"

"It is. But it's also if I try it and don't like it, then what? Where does that leave me? The fantasy would be blown."

"So you'd rather not know?"

"No, I'm not saying that. It just makes proceeding a little more complicated for me."

"What makes you think you wouldn't like it?"

"Well, I haven't liked it much with women." Sacha covered his mouth, as though he hadn't meant to say that aloud.

That was some confession, and Corrigan was unsure how to respond. "I'm sorry?"

Lowering his hand, Sacha refocused on his food. "It's not your issue."

"No, but maybe I could help."

17

___

SACHA

HELP? WHAT DID THAT ENTAIL? HERE IT WAS—THE moment he thought he'd been waiting for, and the *yellow-belliness* sprouted in him. He had no one to blame but himself. He'd opened this can of worms by asking the question. He'd bared a part of himself that was intimate and personal. It had all sounded easier in his head. But once the words were out, it was something entirely different. Now he was unsure how to proceed. In a courtroom, he always felt in control, familiar, and safe. At present, however, he felt vulnerable and exposed in uncharted territory. Normally, if he felt his cross wasn't going as planned, he'd ask for a brief recess to regroup.

Ducking his head and swallowing, he attempted

to suppress his unruly emotions. "I need to check on dessert." He pushed away from the table and stood on unsteady legs. *One foot in front of the other*, he ordered himself, making his way to the kitchen without bursting into a sprint. *You like him, and he seems to like you. Stop being a candy-ass.* Opening the oven, he checked on the peach cobbler inside—his easy go-to dessert when he needed a sugar fix in a hurry. The timer indicated thirty seconds remaining, and he determined that was close enough, as the cobble's crust was nice and golden. All it needed was time to cool—sort of like him. Grabbing a pair of oven mitts, he removed the dessert and set it on the stovetop.

Pivoting to return the mitts to the drawer, he came face-to-face with Corrigan and froze. He was close. Tremendously close. So close that Sacha could see the subtle shift in darkness around Corrigan's irises and feel the soft puff of his breath. And that look as Corrigan's stare dipped to Sacha's mouth… he recognized that stare. It was one of someone about to kiss him.

Oh God. Am I ready?

A lump formed and lodged in his throat.

"Um… it, uh, needs to cool," Sacha stammered.

"Oh," Corrigan replied with a nod, an expression

of uncertainty crossing his features. "Cool." His voice wavered. Taking a step back, he leaned against the island. "It looks… delicious."

"Mm." Rolling his lips in, Sacha stuffed the potholders inside a drawer. *Chicken liver!*

———

WHAT WAS HIS PROBLEM? WHY DIDN'T HE TRUST himself? Corrigan had been right there… willing. And how had he responded? Made some idiotic comment about a peach cobbler.

Sacha flipped from his stomach to his back and stared at the ceiling as he replayed the kitchen scene in his head on loop, dissecting every second and regretting not having the courage to allow events to unfold naturally. What could have been a romantic dinner had transformed into a PTO luncheon— polite, dull, and gauche.

As he adjusted the pillow beneath his head, an alarming thought occurred to him. Perhaps in the past, he'd been aware of his sexuality and run from it. But was sexuality something a person could outrun?

His fault. All his fault. He'd created this situation, and the most frustrating part was he didn't know why he'd done it. All he'd had to do was allow Corrigan's plush lips to meet his.

Closing his eyes, he allowed himself to sink deeper into that thought, which quickly transformed into a wanton fantasy of Corrigan's lips all over him. How would he feel? Taste? Groaning, he screwed his eyes tighter, as if the act would block the heated images in his mind in the same manner it did the moonlight streaming through the window. Before he realized it, his lips parted to the air, and wistful moans floated from his throat. His palm resting on his stomach drifted slowly toward his groin. He presumed Corrigan would have a firm grip and agile fingers and that his hands would be rough, raking over his skin. As the images in his mind grew more vivid, the twitching between his thighs intensified.

"Oh, Corrigan," he sighed, clasping his semi. Since it had been a while since he'd pleasured himself, he reckoned rubbing out a quick one might help. Maybe that was his problem—he'd gone too long and had become too wound up to process information clearly. According to some experts, sex improved memory. At the very least, relieving himself would facilitate sleep. A hearty orgasm always knocked him out for a couple hours.

"You called?"

Sacha's eyes flew open as his head simultaneously snapped toward the voice coming from the doorway —his wide-open door that he'd not thought to shut. *Fuck!* Living alone, he didn't have a need to close doors for privacy. He snatched his hand from his crotch and sat erect in the bed—though that wasn't the only thing erect. Heat threatened to set his face aflame.

"Don't stop on account of me." Corrigan approached the bed. "I didn't mean to interrupt."

"Did you need something?" Sacha managed, his voice quite shaky.

"I found this." Corrigan held up an object.

Sacha squinted, attempting to make out the form. "What is it?"

"Sorry, I forgot you wear contacts," Corrigan answered, stepping closer. "It's your watch. It was in the bed."

"It must have fallen off when I was changing sheets."

"Must have." Corrigan now stood beside the bed and stared down at Sacha. "I'll leave it here." He placed the smartwatch on the nightstand.

"Thank you."

Silence ensued for a beat.

"It's late. I should get some sleep," Corrigan said

after several moments.

"Okay," Sacha answered, almost inaudible. "Don't let the boo hag ride you."

Gazes locked, neither moved, and another silence filled the space. Sacha could hear his own heartbeat in his ears. He didn't know what to do next. Or did he? Assuming he didn't, he knew the two of them couldn't remain as they were.

Corrigan broke the silence.

"May I ask a question?"

Sacha nodded, uncertain if he could muster an even tone. Did he want to answer questions? "S-Sure."

"Were you thinking about me just then... when you were touching yourself?"

"What would you say if I were?"

"I'd ask if I could watch."

Oh, hell!

Instead of verbally responding, Sacha relaxed his head against the pillow and pushed a few fingers under the waistband of his sleep pants. Even with Corrigan so close, without his glasses and nothing but the dull glow of moonlight as the sole light source, it was difficult for Sacha to see Corrigan's reaction. However, he could palpably feel Corrigan's eyes gawking at his hard-on.

"Lower," Corrigan urged at Sacha's hesitation to continue. He sat beside him on the mattress.

Curling his fingers around his shaft firmly, Sacha slowly stroked upward and hissed as his hand returned to the base. He smeared a trickle of precum across his crest and down his length, relishing the friction of flesh on pulsating flesh. In a matter of seconds, he'd grown to his full length. The idea of being watched had Sacha turned on, but Corrigan directing what to do kicked it up another notch. In all his previous sexual exploits, Sacha had been in charge. To his surprise, he didn't find playing a less dominant role objectionable. However, this was likely due to it being Corrigan. Had it been any other person, Sacha wouldn't have been as trusting. While being with Corrigan did make Sacha nervous, it simultaneously made him comfortable.

A strange type of fear ebbed in him. Venturing into the unknown offered no comfort, but the exploration of something new roused enthusiasm. In his head, things were safe. What he was engaging in now was undeniably not safe. Yes, Sacha was a ball of contradictions tonight that he couldn't explain.

"Does it feel good?"

"Mm." Where were his words? Why could he no longer put together a coherent sentence? His mind sifted through more than a dozen protests he should have been making. Instead, he continued to gaze into Corrigan's ebony eyes as he massaged his cock.

"Let me see. Pull yourself out."

Sacha obeyed and pushed his pajamas and underwear beneath his balls. Something about being partially clothed made him feel more exposed than being completely naked.

Corrigan rested one hand beside Sacha's thigh while the other hand found the hem of Sacha's T-shirt and grazed the velvety skin beneath, coercing another moan from Sacha.

"Do you have any lube?"

"In the nightstand drawer beside you."

The drawer was as neatly arranged as his electronic cords had been. Corrigan discovered not one but three tubes of lubricant. He read the labels and paused before grinning uncontrollably. "These are all flavored." Opening the one labeled mint chocolate chip, he sniffed it. "Do they taste the way they smell?"

"They're pretty accurate."

"Pistachio," he read aloud. "Better hope no one has an allergy to *nuts*."

"If they did, they wouldn't be in my stash."

"Here, then." Corrigan squirted a glob of gel in

Sacha's hand. "Rub it around good. Make it nice and wet."

The dirty talk was something new for Sacha too. Rarely was he vocal in bed, but when he was, he'd been careful not to offend the genteel nature of his female partners. None of them had been into that sort of thing—not that he'd tried often. But he was finding it to be a turn-on, and he obeyed the command, slathering the lube from the swollen, almost purple head of his cock to his sac.

"Good," Corrigan continued. "Now stroke faster."

Sacha's eyes began to close as he increased his pace.

"No," Corrigan ordered. "Look at me. I want to see you when you come."

Mewling softly, he reopened his eyes with a mixed expression of concentration and desire and focused on Corrigan's face.

Corrigan returned his hand to the exposed part of Sacha's abdomen and tenderly traced the light line of auburn hair that ran from his belly button to his patch, charring a path of electric sensations as he went. He leaned in close to Sacha's ear, blowing on his lobe, and whispered, "Faster."

Sacha thrust harder into his fist, and his breathing reduced to panting. "*Kee-yaw*."

"Look how tight your balls are. It won't be long now, will it?"

Well, it probably would have been had Corrigan not said anything, but his husky voice combined with his combing fingers and warm breath tossed Sacha off the cliff of no return. Grunting, Sacha was overtaken by a throbbing release that hurled him into spasms of ecstatic pleasure and delight. Semen pulsated from his slit in long streams in quick succession. He struggled to keep his eyes open.

And just when Sacha thought he'd finished, Corrigan said, "That was fire." Then, to Sacha's amazement, Corrigan raised his hand to his mouth and licked off the semen that had landed on his hand, sparking another spurt from Sacha's dick.

"Oh, *mon Dieu!*" Sacha exclaimed, blinking.

"So, do you think you're ready now to explore what it's like being with a man?"

He nodded as he regained his breath. "I think so."

"Good. Let's start here." Leaning forward, Corrigan sucked Sacha's bottom lip between his teeth and gently nipped it before licking the seam of his mouth.

Sacha responded by opening on a gasp, and Corrigan slipped his tongue inside. Their tongues tangled together in a wild and raw dance, and the faint scruff on Corrigan's cheek abraded Sacha's jaw. The kiss wasn't how Sacha had expected; although, he wasn't exactly sure what it was he *had* expected. But he had no complaints and was disappointed when Corrigan pulled back and stood.

"Good night, Sacha."

"What you said? Why are you leaving?"

"Baby steps."

Baby steps my foot! Sacha had gotten a taste and wanted more. Now.

Hopping out of bed, he stood in front of Corrigan, his clothing still disheveled. "Look, I don't know how this works, but I'm pretty sure it's rude and not proper etiquette for me to show you mine and you not show me yours."

Corrigan laughed. "You want to see?"

"Oh, I more than want to see. *Je voudrais* to taste."

18

CORRIGAN

"ARE YOU SURE ABOUT THAT?" CORRIGAN ASKED, licking his lips and closing the space between them. He wanted more as well, but he also didn't want to push Sacha too far too fast. Unlike a popular gay stereotype, Corrigan had no problems with taking things slow. While he had no qualms with promiscuity, random hookups, and quickies, not all gay men were about that life. It was also a lifestyle that didn't coordinate with his plans. Multiple partners were fine… until they ran their mouths.

"Positively," Sacha answered, his voice saturated with lust.

Corrigan placed his hand on Sacha's shoulder and gently pressed down. Understanding, Sacha dropped to his knees and looked up through his lashes, to which Corrigan almost lost all control.

What a visual.

Rushing his hands up Corrigan's muscular thighs, Sacha dragged Corrigan's shorts and boxers down his legs to his ankles. Corrigan's cock sprang up and rested on the flat of his abdomen.

"Holy hell," Sacha muttered, smacking his lips.

"It's all yours. Don't be shy now."

The briefest moment of hesitation flicked in Sacha's eyes before he swiped his tongue across the slit to lick away the salty precum, circled beneath the rim, and then closed his mouth over the crown with a slurp. Normally, Sacha maneuvered with polished, graceful movements and seamless effort, but now, Corrigan watched as he clumsily fumbled with inexperience. Sacha appeared to have no inkling of what he was doing, but the gleam in his eyes indicated that he was determined to compensate in enthusiasm for what he lacked in skill. Corrigan observed intently, his eyes blurring with bliss, as Sacha took as much as he could in his mouth, which was about half, and wrapped his hand around the exposed shaft. Pulling his hand toward the base, the saliva allowing for an easy slide, Sacha squeezed and sucked hard before pulling off the tip only to take him in again.

"Geez!" Corrigan cried, his thighs jackknifing forward reflexively. He plunged deep into Sacha's mouth and hit the back of his throat.

Sacha made a choking sound.

"Sorry."

He wasn't. Although he hadn't meant to hurt him, hearing Sacha make that sound perversely heightened Corrigan's arousal even more. Additionally, Sacha hadn't seemed to mind because he hadn't stopped. On the contrary, he continued bobbing up and down and rolling Corrigan's member around in his mouth like candy. With each tug and pull, Sacha's suction grew tighter, and his pace increased. Obviously his learning curve was short, and it encouraged Corrigan to thrust in earnest.

"That's so good," Corrigan whimpered shamelessly. It had been too long since he'd been touched this way. As a result, his desperate pent-up longing caused him to lose control of his body. His hips jutted and grinded in Sacha's mouth as if on autopilot. Everything within him began to tighten. To maintain balance, he dug the pads of his fingers into Sacha's shoulders. "That's it."

He attempted to roll and pull out of Sacha's

mouth but was too late. A deep, thunderous wave of a glorious orgasm rumbled through him, and he watched as his seed seeped from the corners of Sacha's mouth. And although he'd just come, the sight had him stiffening again.

Sacha rocked back on his heels. Red splotches stained his cheeks as evidence of the effort he'd put forward. "That was... was...," he stammered, his voice hoarse.

Corrigan nodded, his senses calming as the rapturous pulsations of his climax subsided. "Yeah, it was."

CORRIGAN HADN'T EXPECTED SACHA TO BE A cuddler. Yet here he was with his body slightly curled, his head pressed against Corrigan's chest— his long lashes brushing against his skin—and an arm draped across Corrigan's midsection as they lay in Sacha's bed. Due to Sacha's stillness, Corrigan assumed he'd fallen asleep, but when Corrigan shifted to slide out, Sacha's arm tightened around his waist.

"Where are you going?"

"To get water, but it can wait." He peered down at Sacha's silhouette. "How are you feeling?"

Sacha glanced up at him. "What do you mean?"

"It was your first gay experience. Are you okay?"

"You don't have to treat me with kid gloves. Geez!" He rolled onto his back. "It's not like you deflowered me or anything. Besides, I'm ten years older than you."

Corrigan's brows bunched. "What does age have to do with anything?"

"I'm the elder. I should be teaching you, not the other way around."

Chuckling, Corrigan caressed Sacha's biceps. "I don't know if that statement's ageist, but it's something not right." He allowed his hand to trail up Sacha's shoulder to the rear of his neck and tangle in his hair. "I'm only asking because at dinner you seemed unsure."

"That was dinner, not what we did." A defensive tone had entered his voice.

"I don't mean to offend you. I just don't want you to have regrets."

"Do you? Regret it?"

"Of course not. Actually…." He shifted and kneaded Sacha's pectorals with his free hand. "I was hoping for an encore."

Sacha's eyes widened. "You mean I didn't suck at it?"

"Oh, you definitely *sucked*. You were like a freaking car vac." He hummed with a broad smile. "And your tongue... so wicked."

"But I gagged. I didn't take all of you."

"I don't think anyone is able to deepthroat on the first go. It takes practice. But if it makes you feel any better, I'm willing to let you practice on me anytime."

Sacha grinned. "How generous of you."

"Yeah, I'm a nice guy."

"You are." Tilting his head back, he raised his chin toward Corrigan.

Responding, Corrigan leaned forward and pressed a lingering kiss on Sacha's lips. It wasn't something he typically did with his lovers—not that he'd had many in the past or that he could call Sacha a lover. Well, maybe. Calling him a hookup felt wrong. Sure, they hadn't known each other long, but it already felt like more than a hookup. Corrigan felt a connection. But he couldn't ignore that Sacha was new at this. Undoubtedly, he'd want to explore... experiment... with other people. Besides, how was Corrigan supposed to balance dating—gay dating at that—with being on a conservative—overly conservative—hockey team? If, that was, Sacha even wanted to date. He hadn't said anything about wanting to date. In fact, Sacha hadn't said anything about anything. For all Corrigan knew, Sacha might have decided this was a one-and-done, that he'd satisfied his curiosity and moved on. Maybe being with men wasn't something Sacha wanted to continue.

Corrigan allowed the kiss to end. *Fuck. Things just got complicated.*

Not wanting to pressure Sacha but also not willing to continue playing out scenarios in his head that could probably win an Academy Award, Corrigan decided to pry. "So, did you get anything figured out? Cure any curiosity?" he asked.

"As a label, I'm pretty sure I'm queer."

"Pretty sure?"

"Well, yeah. It's hard to explain. I've never not liked women. I've just not enjoyed them sexually. But could I fall in love with a woman?" He shrugged. "Hypothetically, I suppose so. That would mean maybe I'm asexual or aromantic. But I've never been content in a relationship with a woman. It's why they've always ended. I've grown accustomed to being alone, but I wouldn't call it being content. So, that blows that theory. But what we did…." Sacha smiled. "I really liked it. Does it mean I'm gay?" He shrugged. "I swear I'm too old to be trying to figure this stuff out."

Corrigan chuckled. "You're never too old."

"When did you know?"

"Maybe always, but junior high for sure. One weekend, some friends and I went to an anime expo. We got separated, and as I wandered around looking for them, I stumbled across a comic book booth. What drew my attention were the number of colorful flags draped around the display table." He shook his head. "At the time, I had no idea they were pride flags and thought they represented foreign countries. I mean, I'd only ever seen the one rainbow flag. I didn't know there are over fifty flags that represent all the different groups in the LGBT+ community. I even asked one of the workers if the comics were in English. I guess he figured out what was going on in my head, because he laughed and assured me that they were. Anyway, he asked me what type I liked—shojo, kodomomuke, and so on."

"That's English?"

Corrigan chuckled again and combed his fingers through Sacha's hair. "It's Japanese and refers to the drawing style. Anyway, after chatting with him for a while, I purchased a few that sounded interesting. Halfway through the first comic, it dawned on me that the two main characters, both men, had an interest in being more than friends. And then I realized how much I was rooting for them to get together. When I flipped the last page and saw the two of them lip-locked, I literally fist-pumped the air. It was odd because all my so-called friends constantly made homophobic jokes and talked about how gross it was for two men to be together. And I never said anything about it."

"You were young."

"Odd how people always find reasons to excuse deplorable behavior. It was wrong, no getting around it. Yet my friends somehow made me feel that what they were saying was natural. Reading how that comic book relationship unfolded did something for me, though. Until then, I'd always had a feeling deep down that I didn't belong, that I was different from my friends. They were starting to get into girls, and I wasn't. I tried faking it for a while, but it all blew up when one of my friends had his first boy-girl party, and they decided to play a kissing game. I had to kiss one of the most popular girls in school. It was awful—not because I was inexperienced but because nothing about her appearance or personality appealed to me." He shivered at the memory. "Later that night, I signed into a comic book's fan video chat group. I'd become a part of that online community. And that's when it hit me, I mean really hit me, how close I'd gotten to some of the members. There was this one guy who I thought about all the time. And like the comic book characters, I wanted to be more than friends with him."

"Were you?"

"We sexted some, but that was the extent of it. He lived in San Diego. With the time differences and both of us having our own stuff going on, it was never going to work."

"Hm." His body tensed slightly.

"What?"

"Sexting. Do you do that often?"

"No. Do you?"

"Never."

Corrigan's eyes widened. "As in ever?"

"As in, why would I want to?"

"It can be fun."

Sacha merely grunted in retort.

While the response shouldn't have bothered Corrigan, it had. Perhaps Sacha did have a low libido after all. Corrigan wasn't sure how he felt about that. Could he be involved with someone who didn't desire sex? All his relationships involved sex. Sometimes they were exclusively restricted to sex.

Cripes, I sound like a sex fiend.

"I'm going to get that water now," he said, slipping out of bed. "Do you want one?"

"No, thanks."

He took his time making his way to the kitchen. He needed time alone to think and consider what came next. Were these red flags Sacha was throwing, or was this a matter of him crawling into his head and misreading the situation? He'd come to ULSA to play hockey, not to get wrapped up in an unsustainable relationship with a sugar daddy.

Yikes! Did I just refer to Sacha as a sugar daddy? No, that was not what he meant. Though someone with Sacha's means would be able to toss money at any given situation or feel they could purchase anything or anyone. But Corrigan wasn't there for handouts. He hadn't fooled around with Sacha as some strange obligation of gratitude for allowing him to stay the night. Had he? No, of course not. Corrigan shook the thought from his head.

Reaching the kitchen, he removed a bottle of water from the refrigerator and sat in the dark at the counter. *Stop this,* he warned himself. His thoughts ping-ponged from one extreme to the next. On one hand, Sacha remained uncertain about his sexuality, meaning he may not want to be involved with Corrigan. On the other hand, what if Sacha did want to take this thing between them further? How would Corrigan keep it a secret from his teammates with his coach apparently having spies all over the fucking place?

It's one night. It means nothing. But it did mean something. Though *what* it meant, he wasn't sure.

After finishing his water, Corrigan returned upstairs. His first thought was to go to the guest bedroom and pretend none of this had happened. If it didn't happen, he didn't have to sort through it. However, he walked to Sacha's room.

On his stomach, Sacha sprawled across the bed, his knee bent and hands stuffed beneath the pillow. The steady rise and fall of his chest indicated he was asleep. For a moment, Corrigan watched him from the doorway before quietly making his way across the room and slipping beneath the top sheet.

19

SACHA

SACHA STARED AT THE SHAPE OF HIS MOUTH IN THE foggy mirror as he brushed his teeth. Giddy was how he'd describe himself. His mouth had kissed another man, wrapped around a cock, and swallowed semen. He'd only hesitated due to performance anxiety, not because he hadn't wanted to. But now, the morning after, standing in his bathroom with nothing but a damp towel slung low around his hips and shaving cream slathered across his face to soften his overnight growth, he wondered about his giddiness. Was it the man who made him feel renewed? Or was it the feeling of having performed an act so unlike himself? Or maybe he was having some sort of pre-midlife crisis. Instead of buying sports cars, he was fooling around with a guy ten years his junior. Well, more than that, but ten was a depressing enough gap without mathematically calculating any further.

What was it about Corrigan Ellery that made Sacha lower his inhibitions? No, he wasn't fooling himself. He knew how prudish he could be—not about others but rather the standard to which he held himself. He wouldn't have done what he did with just anyone. If he was certain of nothing else, it was that.

But was this thing—whatever it was—even viable? Corrigan had plans to go off and play hockey. Why start something with someone who would be leaving eventually? And Sacha had his busy career to consider. Would he have time to see where this would lead?

Well, yes, now that he thought about it, remembering his career was in the toilet.

He spat toothpaste in the sink, rinsed, and returned his toothbrush to its holder. Because he felt like being a rebel, he skipped flossing. Why the hell not? He padded his way to his walk-in and selected clothes for the day. Normally he reserved Saturdays at home as days to lounge around in his most comfortable boxers and bathrobe while writing closing arguments. But having a houseguest, he wanted to make an effort to look decent. He didn't want to scare Corrigan off; although, he feared he may have already.

A weird kind of tension had cropped up between them. Sacha could feel it when Corrigan got out of bed to get water last night and again this morning when he'd returned to the guest bedroom to work on a hockey assignment. Sacha supposed it could be true. He'd no reason to believe Corrigan would lie to him. But who the hell worked on the weekend? Well….

Sacha sighed, wandered back to the bathroom, and retrieved his razor. He did, that's who. He used to be the guy who worked on weekends. That was why he'd gone all out designing his home office—a room he utilized more than any other in his house. At least he used to. But now look at him. He frowned in disgust as he scraped the razor across his stubble. What use was that home office now? Fuck up and this was what happened. That was the price of being a Weymouth. He'd give anything to have his old position back.

But wait. Was he replacing his job with an affair? Was Corrigan a placeholder or a gap fill-in for being ousted from the firm practice? Maybe not completely ousted but close enough in his opinion.

Dammit!

Rinsing the razor, Sacha continued staring at himself. Why was he still so confused? At present he couldn't even get his morning routine together, aimlessly roaming about his closet and bathroom. Being angsty wasn't like him. In courtrooms, he knew all his moves and his opponents' moves before they occurred. Yet in his home, in his personal life, he was baffled by nearly every fucking thing.

Pull it together.

He finished his shave and trudged back into his walk-in. Plopping on a plush ottoman, he pulled his knee close to his chest and studied his neatly clipped nails. He'd been annoyed that the nail salon hadn't had his usual jojoba foot soak and had substituted with rosemary and tarragon. Pretentious? He was pissing himself off.

He could have a far worse life. He'd made the grades and gotten the LSAT score, but truthfully, his father's check and donation had probably held more weight with the admissions council. He hadn't had to compete for a position in the prestigious law firm; his surname had guaranteed him an in. And even his being booted hadn't left him jobless or destitute. Yet here he was whining and feeling sorry for himself—agitated because his father had snatched his job from beneath him and his last night's lover had pulled away. Ticked because he'd taken the first step and not gotten what he wanted. Spoiled. Entitled. How dare his life be messy.

His vision flooded red, and impulse overtook him. Multiple conflicting and opposing emotions warred within him. Retrieving a nearby shoe, he hurled it across the room. It crashed into the wall with a loud thud, bowling over several hats on mannequin heads, and shattered one of the glass doors to his suits' enclosure. The sound shook him back to reality, and he stared at the destruction as if caused by someone else.

Great. Now I have to clean that up.

Seconds later, Corrigan, wide-eyed, appeared in the doorway. "Geez!" His gaze darted from Sacha to the broken glass and back again. "Are you okay? What happened?"

Sacha flushed with embarrassment. "Stupidity and existential neuroticism." He stood and moved toward the debris.

Corrigan grasped Sacha's upper arm and held him still. "You'll cut your feet."

Sacha nodded and blew out a bitter laugh. "I do bleed like everyone else."

"Huh?"

Shrugging, he met Corrigan's concerned eyes.

"Nothing. I got this. You should go back to doing what you were doing." He tilted his head. "What are you working on, anyway?"

Corrigan shuffled and groaned. "Right now, training is mostly about conditioning and technique development and not so much execution of plays. Coach is seeing who works well together, how players play off each other's strengths. So I have to make a list of all my strengths and weaknesses."

"That doesn't sound too tough."

"I also have to do it for every member on the team—at least five things listed in each category. Plus, I have to write a plan of correction for all the weaknesses, i.e., what can be done to improve them. Whatever I write will be implemented during the fall. So, if I say I need to increase my speed and that running five miles daily will help do that, then that's what I'll have to do all semester."

"Still, that doesn't sound bad. You want to be your best, and you're working toward that currently. So what's the problem?"

"It's not just what I list. Everyone's opinion is being taken into consideration. So if the majority thinks I need to go rock climbing every week, rock climbing it is."

"Someone would really suggest rock climbing?"

"I don't know. Maybe."

"I take it you wouldn't be thrilled if it was."

"Do you like it?"

"I've never been, but my brother's brother-in-law loves it. He's climbed K2 and Annapurna. But I get what you're saying. Your teammates could hang you out there if they want, and you'll have no say."

"That and the fact that I'll have to read aloud everything I list about everyone. It'll be as pretty as popping a zit."

"Criticism can be harsh, but if it's constructive, it'll only help you improve. And that's the ultimate goal, right?"

Sacha reflected on his own words. Perhaps his father's point had been valid. Maybe there was more Sacha could have done to prevent what happened with his client from happening. Maybe he deserved the demotion.

"I know. Doesn't make it any easier, though."

"No, it doesn't."

Corrigan's eyes scanned down Sacha's torso to the towel. With his knuckles, he skimmed from Sacha's hip to his navel. "For a lawyer, you have some decent abs."

"Racquetball," he answered, attempting to squash the quake in his voice stemming from the simultaneous shiver and heat skittering across his skin at Corrigan's touch. "I play a couple days a month." He neglected to disclose his doing so was solely to justify paying the outrageous fees for his country club membership his mother insisted he keep. "Maybe you and I could—" Sacha stopped abruptly. No, they couldn't.

Weymouths were generational members, practically a mandatory staple. His children's children's children were already welcomed, but Corrigan wouldn't be. Only now did Sacha realize how little he cared for the place and why. How had he allowed himself to be a part of an organization with such fucked-up restrictions without noticing?

Note to self: cancel membership on Monday.

"On second thought, I don't enjoy racquetball all that much."

"Then why do you play?"

Sacha hunched his shoulders. "Because my brother does."

Corrigan smirked.

"What?" Sacha asked.

"Nothing," Corrigan replied, shaking his head, his grin widening. "Well, maybe. Do you ever say no to your brother and hold to it?"

"Certainly." *Well, not always. Sometimes. Okay, no.* "What makes you think I don't?"

"From the way you talk, like about attending your sister's party or going to your parents' house for your brother."

"That's what family does." He didn't want to discuss his family, and Corrigan appeared to pick up on that.

"Okay." Corrigan inched his knuckles closer to where the towel was tucked in. "There seems to be something protruding beneath your towel."

"Maybe you should examine it. You know... for scientific purposes."

Corrigan chuckled and inhaled deeply, seemingly savoring Sacha's scent of fresh soap and shampoo. Leaning close so his lips were only a hair away from Sacha's ear, he asked, "Science?" He hooked his index finger in the towel.

The warm tickle of Corrigan's breath on Sacha's earlobe combined with the delicious tease of his touch propelled frissons of desire through Sacha's body. He should be getting dressed, cleaning up the mess he'd made. Returning phone calls. Anything but this. Hadn't he just demolished his damn closet door because he was spiraling? But instead of pulling his shit together and using any type of judgment, all he could think and feel was how much he wanted this man.

"Back in my day, all majors required a science course."

"Uh-huh." Corrigan plucked at the soft cotton, and the towel plunged to Sacha's feet. "Oops."

20

CORRIGAN

STARING AT THE TOWEL CRUMPLED ON THE FLOOR, Corrigan released a dithering hiss. Hadn't he convinced himself that he wouldn't do this? That he wouldn't involve himself with someone who was playing sexual orientation bingo? And that he would allow Sacha space to sort through his doubts and feelings? But more importantly, to protect himself from being crushed if Sacha reverted to his heterosexual lifestyle? Sure, perhaps it was a hypocritical stance for Corrigan to take since he wasn't scaling the Empire State Building, waving a rainbow flag, and screaming his favorite color was glitter. Yet he wasn't crouched in a dusty, cobwebbed closet either. He knew how he identified and was comfortable with it. The fact that he lived in a world where he didn't feel free to openly express it was another matter entirely.

On the contrary, Sacha couldn't admit to himself how he felt because he didn't know.

Corrigan knew the pain well of a person who was unsure of himself. He'd watched his father struggle with it daily for years after his accident. Each day, he didn't know the father he would wake up to. Would he be kind and joking, making the most of his situation? Or would he be cranky and insolent, incensed that he could no longer perform the mental or physical tasks he once could? Indeed, part of his father's issue was the result of brain injury, but not all of it. He took his frustration of uncertainty out on those around him, and that wasn't something Corrigan wanted to experience with Sacha.

On the other hand, Corrigan wanted Sacha with every fiber of his being. The very thing that repelled him from wanting to take things further with Sacha was the exact thing that drew him in. He couldn't help feeling drawn to him on both a physical and emotional level. There was something about him that fired up parts of him that no one else did and made him want to ignore all the red flags to run. If Sacha wanted to explore, Corrigan wanted to go along on the expedition and be his tour guide of pleasure. As an overall picture, it didn't make sense. Then again, weren't athletes stereotyped as not smart?

He glanced at the shattered shards of mirror on the floor. "Are you sure you don't want to talk about why you're destroying your closet?"

"It's just a mirror."

"It brings bad luck."

"Hockey players are always superstitious, aren't they?" He shrugged. "I had a moment—a stupid one —but it's gone now that you're here. You don't have to worry. I'm usually not reckless. In fact, everyone says I'm exactly the opposite, that I'm always careful and never do anything out of the ordinary."

"Oh, I have to disagree with that last part... unless having a 'physics lesson' in the buff is what you consider ordinary."

"Well, if it's okay with you, I'd rather pretend it never happened and proceed with other *teachable* moments."

"It's okay with me."

Corrigan dragged his fingers across Sacha's hip to the small of his back and tugged him forward, closing the gap, but not close enough that their bodies met. There was no resistance in Sacha, and a small, tortured sound escaped him that caused Corrigan's full, sultry lips to quirk at one side. No amount of prudence would stop him from diving into this jumbled mess. The animalistic urge to ravage the attorney was too great.

"C'mere," Corrigan growled, crushing his mouth against Sacha's, and melted. His tongue delved into the warmth of Sacha's mouth. Nudging Sacha's knees apart, Corrigan stood between them with his erection pressed firmly against Sacha's thigh. All the emotions he'd been harboring—confusion, hesitation, frustration, and irritation—evaporated in a moment. This felt right. "I need to collect data," he uttered.

If scientific proof was what Corrigan sought, he found it in physics. Newton's third law of motion theorized that for every action, there was an equal and opposite reaction. Corrigan's greedy kisses were matched with Sacha's hungry ones. His moving back and forth against Sacha was equaled with Sacha's hips grinding against the rigid muscles of Corrigan's thigh. Their tongues teased each other with maddeningly dawdling strokes while their hands groped and fondled each other.

"How far do you want to take this?" Corrigan managed.

"As far as you're willing to go."

"Are you sure?" Corrigan's hand rushed up Sacha's torso and cupped his throat with enough pressure to cause Sacha to tremble, startled. Being the stronger and more dominating of the two, Corrigan could overpower Sacha, rendering him helpless in minutes if he squeezed harder. However, Sacha's eyes glinted with excitement and awe, indicating he was ready and willing for anything Corrigan decided to offer. Although Sacha nodded, Corrigan already had his answer.

"Never more positive."

With a slight shove from Corrigan, Sacha landed in a reclined position on his elbows on a chaise lounge. Taking a step forward, Corrigan tugged his shirt over his head and heard Sacha's breath hitch. It gave Corrigan pause only for a second before he toed off his shoes and unbuckled his jeans.

"Gravity," he said, allowing the denim to fall to the floor. "That's more science."

"It certainly is."

Never breaking eye contact, Corrigan reached into his boxers and stroked his hardened shaft. "Would you call this antigravitational pull, then?"

"I'd call it still too many clothes."

"Oh, in that case…." Corrigan pushed down the underwear and stepped out. "Better?"

"Much."

Straddling Sacha, Corrigan gazed at their swollen cockheads and the fat veins that lined their shafts. The sight was almost enough to make him lose it, and his entire body vibrated at the contact. However, he contained himself. Wrapping both his palms around their shafts to form a sheath and using their leaking precum as a lubricant, Corrigan rubbed them together as if they were one. At the same time, he rotated his hips, pressing their balls together and simulating penetration. The growl that tore from Sacha's chest sent Corrigan into a frenzy of thrusting.

"Not this soon," Sacha begged in vain as he pushed against Corrigan's shoulder. "You've got… you have to slow down or…." He gasped for breath between each word. "*Mon Dieu*, you're going to make me come."

"I know. Eventually."

Sacha's expression of panic, lust, and exhilaration thrilled Corrigan but didn't worry him. He'd always possessed a canny ability to sense how much he could tease his lovers before cascading them over the brink. Sacha wasn't there yet; therefore, he pumped them together several more times before abruptly standing.

"What's the matter?" Sacha whispered.

"I have a taste for strawberry."

Grasping Sacha's hand, Corrigan led him from the walk-in to the bedroom. With a salacious grin, he retrieved a packet of strawberry lubricant and a condom from the nightstand. Instead of applying the lube directly to Sacha's groin, he squirted a generous amount above his navel and watched it slowly slide to Sacha's auburn thatch. Sacha moved his hand to massage it in, but Corrigan slapped it away.

"Don't you dare."

"You're teasing," Sacha hissed after releasing a dramatically long breath.

"Guilty as charged, counselor," he replied, squeezing on more lube. "Get used to the slow burn your body will feel." He licked a line along Sacha's jawbone to his ear. "I'm going to do all sorts of naughty things to make your dick twitch," he cooed in Sacha's ear before nipping his lobe. "And you're going to beg for all the pleasure." That was if he didn't find himself begging first. Corrigan monitored Sacha's reaction to the statement for any reluctance, again not wanting to push him too far too fast. Sacha's dilated pupils indicated he was into it and spurred Corrigan to continue. "You're about to be schooled."

"Do I need a safe word or something?"

Corrigan's eyebrows arched. "What do you know about safe words?" Not that he thought Sacha was virginal, but he'd always pegged him as a vanilla kind of guy.

"Just that some couples have them."

Couples? Corrigan was too invested in his own lust to analyze Sacha's use of the word, but it wasn't completely lost on him.

"Sure, we can have a safe word. What do you want it to be?"

Sacha shrugged. "Jalapeño?"

"Jalapeño?" Corrigan chuckled. "Why?"

"You know." Shuffling, Sacha hooked his arms around Corrigan's neck. "For when things get too hot."

"But you don't mind spicy, right?"

"Call me cha-cha." He emitted a hissing sound.

Thank fuck. Corrigan questioned if he'd be able to temper his urges to mild.

Pressing his body against Sacha, Corrigan gyrated his hips to spread the lubricant between them while digging his fingers into Sacha's ass enough to leave a mark. "Jalapeño it is."

Sinking to his knees, Corrigan ripped open the foil packet with his teeth and inserted the tip of his finger into the reserve. Being sure not to break eye contact, he placed his finger between his lips and teeth, positioning the condom in place. He then lowered his head over Sacha's penis and in one swift motion used his lips to carefully smooth the latex over the supple mushroom crest and down the shaft.

"Oh my fucking word!" Sacha squeaked, his breath erupting in a thick gush.

"Let's get you ready to go." Corrigan smacked both palms against Sacha's ass and drew him forward. Interlocking his fingers behind his back and taking his hands out of the equation, Corrigan swirled his tongue hungrily over the head, causing Sacha to hum with pleasure. With the momentum of his upper body, he bobbed his head, sucking deeply and controlling the rhythm and depth despite Sacha's hip thrusts. Slow and firm. Back and forth. Corrigan allowed himself to relish each pull and the feel of Sacha's smooth, rigid flesh. When Sacha teetered on the brink of release again, Corrigan pulled off and stood.

"Wh-What?" Sacha questioned with a dizzy gloss in his eyes.

Taking more of the lube, Corrigan smeared it

across his own rear before slicking it over Sacha's fingers. He bent across the footboard, wiggled his ass, and looked over his shoulder at Sacha. "You need to prep me."

For a moment, Sacha looked like a deer in head-lights before something seemed to click, and he moved forward. Timidly, he pressed the tip of his forefinger against Corrigan's puckered hole. However, Corrigan reached around, grabbed Sacha by the wrist, and bucked back so that Sacha's finger aggressively plunged in up to the knuckle.

"You won't hurt me," he assured, rocking across Sacha's digit.

The reassurance worked, and Sacha inserted a second finger and then a third, shoving them in and out with quick, hard strokes. A tingle began building inside Corrigan as Sacha's fingers brushed across the outer nerves. It didn't take long for him to be completely relaxed.

"I'm ready," he panted, looking in the dresser mirror for a full view. "Go hard. I like it hard."

Placing his hands on Corrigan's hipbones, Sacha breached Corrigan's hole—the first ring of muscles giving away to the pressure and burn of being stretched. Corrigan's lungs ignited in his chest, and his forehead beaded with a sheen of perspiration. He couldn't describe what he felt. All he knew was he wanted it to continue. He needed it to continue. He needed deeper. He needed faster.

"Move," he demanded, rocking back as far as he could and not waiting to adjust to Sacha's size. "Take my ass. Own it."

Although Corrigan instructed Sacha to up the pace, it was Corrigan who controlled the movements. He pumped hard against him, sliding all the way to the tip and then bucking back to have Sacha's balls slap against his ass.

Yes, yes.

Sacha grunted and swore behind him. At least, Corrigan thought Sacha may have been swearing. The few words that were in English were incomprehensible, not that they needed words in this moment.

"I... I...." Sacha's grip tightened on Corrigan's hips. "Ooh," he drew out.

Corrigan felt Sacha's jerky movements behind him and watched in the mirror Sacha throw his head back with a hoarse cry, an expression of delight and agony on his face. Corrigan allowed Sacha no time to collect himself before he moved off and pivoted around to face him. He shoved him onto the bed and kneeled over him. Wrapping his big fist around his girth, Corrigan pumped himself furiously until he saw a white-hot oblivion of fireworks, and his ejaculation exploded from his prick onto Sacha's chest.

As the haze of euphoria faded, Corrigan stared down at Sacha. "You're going to need another shower."

21

SACHA

MONDAY MORNINGS IN THE LAW CENTER USUALLY blew chunks in every direction except the right one. However, after the weekend Sacha had, his tolerance for the day was better than normal, though he wasn't sure why. He'd eaten good food and slept soundly. He'd streamed several entertaining movies and even had delightful conversations with Corrigan. But they hadn't discussed their... situation. After their Saturday morning romp, they'd avoided the topic altogether. Corrigan had returned to the guest bedroom to work on his class assignment while Sacha had piddle-paddled around the house, cleaning and ordering shit off the internet he didn't need—although, the retro gauge kettle and toaster set he had coming were going to look bomb in his kitchen. Of course, for the ridiculous purchase price, the appliances should also take out his trash, wash his windows, polish his silverware, and mow his lawn.

The "morning after" awkwardness that had developed between him and Corrigan surrounding the topic not discussed was a problem sure enough, but not enough to prevent Sacha from enjoying Corrigan's company. It merely dampened it, and Sacha remained without answers.

And perhaps that was why he hedged away from answering questions—because he knew if Corrigan asked certain ones, he couldn't provide a valid answer. What he did know for sure was he felt something for Corrigan, something deeper than anything he'd ever felt for a woman. In the past, if he'd developed some type of emotional attachment to a woman, he hadn't been too broken up about it if his feelings hadn't been reciprocated. He wouldn't classify any of his splits as emotional but rather inconveniences at times. Other times, they came as a relief. He'd been more bothered by being not both-ered—so unbothered that deep down, he'd begun to wonder if he was a sociopath unable to connect with people. But there existed a difference between

unable and incapable. He did form meaningful relationships, just not romantic ones.

Besides, what was the point of drudging up his
shit when he and Corrigan had completely different
trajectory paths? The young buck was trying to get
to the pros. He had a college degree to obtain and
wild oats to sow. He didn't need some dude
barreling toward midlife holding him back or suffocating him.

At what age does midlife start, anyway?

Yet it didn't diminish or negate what Sacha felt—
his want and need to be with Corrigan. But obviously, Corrigan was comfortable with random
hookups. He'd demonstrated that by the ease with
which he'd walked away. Twice.

Sacha exhaled. Maybe it wasn't important to have
all the answers and all that was needed was to live in
the moment. Only, it felt important to him.

His thoughts were interrupted by his ringing cell.
From the tone, he knew it was Kian.

"You're up early," Sacha greeted, acknowledging
the two-hour time difference.

"Yeah," he sighed. "I'm still working that crazy
missing welfare money story. It's actually why I'm
calling."

"Ah, and here I thought it was my sexy telephone voice that allured you."

Kian chuckled. "Phone sex is passé. I'd be more interested in your dexterous texting fingers."

"Oh, you talk so *puurrty*. Speak to me, Daddy."

Kian laughed again. "You're a nut. But speaking of nuts, how are yours?"

"Attached."

"You liberated those suckers recently?"

"We weren't discussing my sac."

"Doesn't mean we can't."

"And it doesn't mean we should."

"Did you know the most frequent cause of death for men under forty is an excessive buildup of cum?"

"Stop making up shit."

"I'm an investigative journalist. I research these things."

Sacha rolled his eyes despite Kian not being able to see him.

"I'm telling you," Kian continued, "not getting laid is unhealthy."

"Well, in that case, I should pass a physical." He heard a thud on his best friend's end followed by a brief silence.

"You're shitting me. You legit got laid? As in, had

sex? With someone else? Besides yourself? And not a doll?"

"You asshole." Sacha attempted to sound annoyed but failed.

"Who was she?" Kian sang. "Anyone I know? Someone from the office? You know, office romances never work out."

"Geez, I miss you."

"You're deflecting."

He was.

"Come on. Who was she?"

"*He* is someone you don't know."

"Oh shit!"

This time Sacha heard a loud crash, as if several objects had fallen.

"Are you for real? A guy?"

"Yes, yes, already. Don't act so surprised. I told you it was a possibility."

"No, you said you had thoughts, and I never thought you would act on them. Wait. Is this the hockey player? How was it? Tell me everything. I need details."

"Those you're not getting."

"But I'm your best friend. I'd tell you."

"And?"

"Sacha Yves Weymouth, don't make me blow my

frequent flyer miles just to come and shake the snot out of you. You know I'm that bitch. Now spill it."

"Oh *mon Dieu*, you're so dramatic. You didn't have to use my entire government name." Sacha cradled his phone between his ear and shoulder as he poured a fresh cup of coffee from the pot he'd made in some fancy-schmancy contraption with a gazillion buttons. No way was he drinking the sludge Paxton had left. *What happened to machines where you just pour in water?* "Yes, it was the hockey player, and we fooled around a little."

"Uh-huh." Kian sounded skeptical. "Define *fooled around*."

"You know. Did stuff."

"Dammit, no I don't know. That's why I'm asking."

"We may have kissed and touched some."

Kian gasped loudly. "You fucked him."

"Kian—"

"You did. Fess up."

Nope. Not going there. "Didn't you call for a reason?"

"I did, but this conversation is long from over."

No shit. When Kian wanted information, he was like a dog with a bone and refused to let go.

"So, I've been working on this piece about

welfare funds that are thought to have been misap-propriated."

"What do you mean, *thought?*"

"It's the strangest thing. There's extra money on the books, but no one knows who put it there or where it came from. It's been allotted and assigned to various welfare programs, but those programs never received the funds. It's like ghost money."

"That is odd."

"It gets weirder. Before the money vanishes, it looks like it was invested."

"Well, if it was on the stock exchange, maybe it was lost."

"That's just it. Each investment shows a profit, but the investment company denies handling any funds. Then the loop starts all over. The question becomes, is it a misappropriation of funds if the money should have never been there or never existed?"

Interesting. Sacha sipped his coffee. "Okay, but what does that have to do with me?"

"In my digging, I found a name, a Maude Cheroncourt."

Son of a bitch!

"Didn't you represent a Cheroncourt not too long ago?" Kian continued.

Boy, did he. Harper Cheroncourt Fallon was the reason Sacha was sitting where he was. "Yeah, her great-grandson. He's doing thirty in a federal pen."

"Didn't the family go broke years ago?"

"That was the story. Maude's daughter married an Austrian aristocrat. Any money she had had come from her husband. But after his death, there were disputes with his family about the will, and Maude was awarded a small settlement, only a fraction of his total worth. What's left of that has been divided among her living relatives."

"Hm." Kian paused as if considering. "So, what am I missing here?"

"I couldn't tell you. Harper was charged with tax evasion and racketeering. He swore the only money he had was dividends from his vineyard in Napa Valley and his work as a documentarian. The DA found evidence of several offshore accounts, but by the time they moved to freeze them, all the money was gone. Couldn't locate a single penny, euro, peso, ruble, bitcoin, or whatever currency it was in. Just empty shell accounts."

"More ghost money. Did they find anything?"

"A whole lot of smut. Turned out Harper's documentaries were adult films with some questionable *adults*." He took another sip of coffee. "He swore everyone was of legal age, and no one has come forward—not that they can identify all the actors—to complain. But he shot his movies in locations with very loose age of consent laws. Plus, he may have dabbled in being the CEO of street pharmaceutical distribution. Of course, I didn't learn any of this until the bastard got convicted."

There was a knock on the office door, though the door was wide open. Sacha snapped his head up to see Mace in the doorway and waved him in.

"Hey, Kian, my cousin is here. Let me call you later."

"Sure, no problem. I need to go over my notes now. Thanks for the info."

"Any time, though I'm not sure it helped any."

"I'm not, either, but that's why it's called investigative journalism. Oh, and don't think I've forgotten about you getting your ass cherry popped."

Sasha's face burned with heat as he flushed every shade of red in the color wheel. "That didn't happen."

"We'll talk about it later."

Before Sacha could respond, Kian disconnected.

"This a bad time?" Mace asked, shoving his hands in his tailored pants pockets.

"Nope. I was hanging out in here until everyone else arrives. What can I do you for?"

"Do you happen to have a key to downstairs?"

"The archives?" Sacha shook his head. "I don't, but it all should be cataloged into the computer database. Let me log in and—"

"Don't bother. I already did, and it looks like records are missing. Besides, I don't know what I'm looking for."

"Huh?"

Mace helped himself to a cup of coffee and sat in a chair across from Sacha. "Have you ever had a case where the more you worked on it, the more it tap-danced on your fucking nerves?"

Nearly spitting out his coffee, Sacha choked down the beverage. "Wow, someone must have royally pissed you off."

"Is it too much to ask for detectives and prosecutors to do their damn jobs? I mean, sure, it's job security for us, but damn." His cool tone and relaxed demeanor were in stark contrast to his words. "And if I call that bitch assistant DA out and say she's got sand in her *cocotte* because I've decimated her in the courtroom every time I've gone against her, she's going to cry sexual harassment to the bar."

Dabbing his lips with a napkin, Sacha peered

through his lashes at his cousin. "That's a lot of pent-up hostility for a Monday morning."

"It's been building for a while. Plus, she interrupted my breakfast—caused my eggs and rice with that good Lord and Barrett sausage to go cold. I honestly wonder how she hasn't combusted into flames like a witch roped to a stake the instant she steps into sunlight."

"What has you so peeved?"

"Something isn't adding up." He leaned forward. "My client attended a party the night his parents were killed. Dozens of witnesses saw him at this party. He's even on the marina security footage boarding the boat." Mace counted each point he made on his fingers. "Yet no one sees him return. All the witnesses are missing. And a drug screen indicates positive results for Rohypnol. Instead of this raising a brow for the DA and police, they have a hard-on to pin the murders on my client. Trust and believe, if some of those detectives attempted to throw themselves on the ground, they'd miss—solid proof that evolution *can* move in reverse."

Scratching his chin, Sacha thought for a moment. "What's in the archives that you think will help?"

"That I don't know, but my client did state that the press had gotten a hold of confidential medical records, which are not only protected by HIPAA but also were sealed by courts due to him being a juvenile at the time. Even my client doesn't have a copy of those records, but he knows this firm handled the legal aspects. He doesn't remember doctors' names or hospitals, and I want names. Because if I find out it's a midlevel hospital employee or some coked-out physician leaking information, I'm going to sue them until their dick shrivels up like the underside nut sac of a naked mole rat."

Sacha snickered and crossed his legs. "Now, that's vivid... and specific."

"You know, I'm going to do us a solid and talk to Max about you helping me out on this. I could use you riding shotgun."

Vehemently, Sacha shook his head. "No, don't cause any trouble for yourself. You know what they say about no good deed going unpunished."

"Sach."

"I appreciate it, but it wasn't only my father. It was all the partners. Besides, I don't need anyone's permission to root around in the basement."

"Just a key."

"Correct." Sacha nodded. "People should begin rolling in the next couple hours."

Mace checked his watch and finished his coffee.

"Unfortunately, I can't wait around until then. I have a deposition in forty-five, and then I'm meeting Mother for brunch at some snooty place that's bound to serve scallops that taste like they've been shot from a wild boar's butt." He stood and rebuttoned his coat. "I swear, the elements of the universe have conspired to prevent me from having a decent meal experience today. I'll come back later."

"As I said, I don't mind."

"Okay, thanks. I doubt this is something that's going to be resolved quickly anyway. Something in the milk isn't white, and the math isn't mathing."

"It never is."

22

CORRIGAN

CORRIGAN'S DORM ROOM DOOR SWUNG OPEN without warning, striking the wall with a loud bang. Startled, Corrigan snapped his head toward Nguyen, who now graced the threshold with an ominous expression and a wadded ball of paper in his hand.

"Dude, what did you do?" Nguyen demanded.

"What are you talking about?"

"This." He tossed the paper he was holding on Corrigan's desk. "You gave an interview to Leo Warnock?"

Corrigan smoothed the wad to reveal it was the sports page of the latest issue of the *Minotaur Advocate*. He swallowed hard and gulped a deep, calming breath as he read the headline: **Ellery Top Runner for Captain**.

Shit, shit, shit! Like he needed to add another reason for his teammates to want to gouge out his eyes with a serrated spoon and impale his severed head on a spike.

"What were you thinking?" Nguyen began pacing as Corrigan quickly scanned the article. Throwing his hands up in the air, Corrigan's teammate continued, shaking his head. "This is so disrespectful to all the guys who have been on the team for years. We all work our asses off, but this?" Pointing at the paper, he threw his hands in the air again. "It chucks the rest of us away like rotting corpses in some serial killer's crawlspace."

Corrigan looked up from the newspaper. "I never said any of this stuff. I swear."

"Why would you even interview with him?"

"I didn't. I didn't even know he was a reporter. I only spoke with him for a few minutes at a frat party."

Nguyen's brows bunched. "He was trolling Gamma house?"

"No, the other one. I was—"

"Wait, you went to XDU, the most exclusive and sought-after fraternity on campus?" He squared his shoulders. "Ah, now it makes sense."

"What does?"

"Why you would have an invite. You did this to impress them?"

"No." Corrigan jumped to his feet. "We didn't talk about hockey. I mean, he asked who Coach favored—"

"And you said you."

"No, I told him no one, and that's the truth. Why would you think I'd do something like this?"

"Because everyone knows how much you hate Theriot."

"I don't *hate* him."

"Then why wouldn't you tell Warnock that Theriot's captain?"

"I don't know. I wasn't thinking, I guess." Shrugging, Corrigan stuffed his hands in his sweatpants pockets and swayed. "But is he really? I mean, do we know for sure he's going to remain captain? Or is it like Coach said and no one is secure?"

Nguyen frowned. "Look, I don't know how you did it back in New York, but this for sure isn't how it's done here. Not kosher. We have one another's back."

Seriously? The team has my back?

"For the last time, Bo, I didn't throw anyone

under the Zamboni." He snatched the newspaper from the desk and waved it in the air. "All of this is a fabrication. I mean…." Cursing, he raked his hand through his hair. The accusation in Nguyen's tone should have pissed him off, but Corrigan had to admit that the evidence looked incriminating. Plus, Nguyen really didn't know him—none of his team-mates did. There'd not been golden bonding moments. "Factually, everything is accurate—my stats, where I'm from, and all those things. But I never once said anything about me becoming captain."

Nguyen's expression softened. "Coach is going to be furious when he reads this."

Don't I know it?

STANDING IN THE LOCKER ROOM DOORWAY WITH nearly two dozen sets of eyes glaring at him, Corrigan reevaluated his life. His plan was, and always had been, to join a premier college hockey team. Perform impressive work while there. Win a Frozen Four—hopefully two. Get signed by a profes-sional team and go straight into the league as a starter. Gross enough money to be able to make a copious donation to the university like all affluent alumni and perhaps be honored with a building being named after him, or at least a wing. Of course, knowing his luck, he'd only get a bathroom, and maybe not even that—just a toilet: The Ellery Stall.

So when or where in this smashing plan of his had he inserted making friends? Because that shit had derailed before the train had left the station.

"Listen, guys—"

"You punk bitch," Theriot interrupted.

"Cool it, Theriot," Coach Massey ordered, a stern expression etched into the fine lines of his face. "That's no way to speak to royalty."

Oh damn. This is going to be bad.

"For twenty-three years, longer than most of you have been squirted out, I've been coaching, and it never fails that each year there is at least one prima donna who thinks he's All-American and knows how to direct a team better than I do. One who believes he's entitled to any position and doesn't have to *earn* his shift." The coach paced the center of the room, his stare downward at his shoes and hands clasped behind his back. "One who shakes his fist at God as being inferior. One player who is so omnipotent that he possesses the ability to glide on water and resurrect the dead. How blessed the rest of us menial and basement dwellers are to be graced with such eminence. Well...." He stopped pacing and looked up at his players. "I guess that means I have to prove that I'm the man for the job and earn my paycheck. Everyone on the ice in two minutes." He marched out of the room.

"Fuckwad!" Theriot mumbled, snatching his practice sweater from his stall.

"CORNER TO THE HALF WALL TWO VERSUS ONE," Coach Massey barked once everyone was on the ice. He wasted no time pitting Theriot and Kavanaugh against Corrigan.

On the first pass, Kavanaugh left Theriot uncovered, preventing Corrigan from gaining the puck without contact. Theriot, whose job in the drill was to pass to Corrigan, was slow to do so. And when Theriot did decide to pass, Corrigan had to overextend, leaving him off-balance and susceptible to being knocked off his feet—which happened—to reach the pass, only to get clobbered by Kavanaugh again. Any way it went, Corrigan found himself on his backside. And because of his poor performance, Corrigan had to perform the drill again with the next group and the next group and the next, all having the same results.

He got it. Basically, this was Coach Massey's way of allowing the entire team to have free hits on him. Bullying? Probably. But, at the same time, it was hockey—a contact sport. Hockey players had to be tough. They had to be willing to sacrifice their bodies to make plays. Most importantly, Corrigan had to endure if he expected to remain on the team.

Eyes on the prize, he reminded himself as he climbed to his feet from the ice. *Let them get it out of their system. Do not show weakness. Do not break.*

Eventually, the hockey gods intervened, and Coach Massey received a phone call he had to take, allowing the team to take a ten-minute rest break. Huffing, Corrigan made his way to an isolated end of the bench and chugged a sports drink. The cool liquid flowed over his parched tongue so quickly he didn't taste it as it slid down his throat.

"Do you need to borrow my pads?" Larousse asked, removing his helmet and leaning against the wall.

Corrigan responded with a tiny smile. "Wouldn't hurt."

"Well, if it's any consolation, you took that shit like a trooper."

"Thanks." Corrigan watched as two teammates skated past, eyeing him with all the compassion of a viper ready to strike. "Aren't you afraid someone will say something about you consorting with the enemy?"

A wicked expression crossed Larousse's face. "I wish a mofo would. Listen, I know Leo Warnock, and he has a knack for making a story where there isn't one. I suppose that's what he has to do to get anyone interested in reading that rag, but my guess is he wasn't trying to cause trouble. He argued a case for you, and it crawled between some people's butt cheeks."

"But not yours." Corrigan swiped his forearm against his forehead. "Why are you unbothered?"

"I'm a goalie. I can't be captain."

"Ah." Corrigan nodded with understanding. "But if you weren't?"

"Then we might be having a different conversation. Welcome to D1 hockey. It ain't all cotton candy and tata bouey. Fuck what you heard." Slapping Corrigan on the shoulder, he flashed a reassuring grin as he walked toward his other teammates.

"Hang in there. That which does not kill you lets you live to die a gruesome death another day."

"I don't think that's how that saying goes."

"Maybe not, but it doesn't make it any less true."

Survival. That was what Larousse had meant. Corrigan only had to survive.

But what if he wanted to *live*?

23

CORRIGAN

"GET YOUR SHOULDERS OVER YOUR KNEES, ELLERY," Coach Massey bellowed. "Knees over toes. This is basic edge work. What are you doing?"

If Corrigan had been asked that question two hours ago, he may have been able to answer. At present, his mind was mush and fogged with fatigue. He hiked his back leg higher and skated a backward C-cut on his outside edge left leg before turning and doing the same on his right. The neon orange cones strategically positioned on the ice distorted into clown faces mocking him, and the rink stretched endlessly in front of him like a deserted highway in a B-movie horror flick.

Of course it's endless. It's a circle. Circles are endless.

Well, no. Yes, circles are endless, but hockey rinks are rectangles—so not endless.

He sailed around another cone, leaning in more and feeling his blade bite into the ice. Fifty cones in fifty seconds, the coach had demanded. What was Corrigan on now? Twenty-five? Thirty? What was his time?

Go! he commanded himself. *Just go.* It didn't matter that everything was a blur and that sweat burned his eyes. He turned out his knee and toe and shifted his weight, slicing the ice. Left foot. Right foot. Left. Again and again. Cone after mocking cone.

Did they still think after two solid weeks of riding him hard he'd quit? They were delusional—or maybe he was. After all, he was the one seeing talking heads on this verglas polygon with an infinite number of sides. The sounds of voices, sticks striking against the floor, and metal on ice wavered in and out. His chest rose and fell with heavy but controlled breaths as he glided into the next maneuver, the sting digging into his thighs and glutes. His eyes focused on the obstacle course, making visible the invisible lines he needed to skate. He could do this. He *would* do this. He was living his vision and not his circumstances. Then a whistle blew. *Was that a whistle?*

He stopped, and holy shit, the pain! If he thought skating the drills was agonizing, it was nothing compared to the pain in his muscles when he stopped. He felt as if his lower half had been dipped in molten lava and sprinkled with cactus spines. *Mother of pearl.* He grimaced, clenching his jaws as he skated—wobbled—to the bench to join his teammates.

Suck it up. Don't let them see you hurting. Hold it in. He compressed his lips into a tight line. *Happy thoughts. Think of something happy.* Sacha's face immediately popped into his mind, and Corrigan's heart leaped to his throat.

"Per usual," Theriot sneered, "Corrigan's the last in."

Ordinarily, the statement would have bothered him, but at present, he was too winded and in pain for the insult to fully register. *Blah, blah, blah* was all he heard. Lips moved, but nothing made much sense, and finally, the coach dismissed them. The walk from the ice down the chute became a blur too.

Slouching on the bench in front of his locker, Corrigan fished his cell from his gym bag and smiled at the icon of having new text messages—well, at one in particular. The others—notification of uploads from his favorite YouTubers; messages from Hoyt Lemelle and Alton, two of the guys he'd met at the fraternity party; Panhellenic links for mandatory antihazing and sexual harassment videos—he couldn't care one way or the other. However, seeing Sacha's name, even without knowing the content, made his day.

Although they'd been texting daily since he'd left Sacha's home, he felt a distance—one of his own doing—creeping into their developing... relationship? Was that what they were calling it?

It wasn't fair to pressure Sacha to label himself, and, *technically*, Corrigan hadn't. But he'd walked away and left things as if their time together had been a weekend hookup. With a label, he would feel more... what? Valued? Secure? Assured? Guilt gobbled at his insides for feeling the way he did—to feel so emotionally drawn to Sacha, yet afraid to go all in. Becoming involved with someone sexually ambivalent—if that was the correct word—was tricky. Experiments went left all the time, and he had no interest in becoming a sacrificial guinea pig. Corrigan knew himself all too well. He didn't just fall for someone when he fell. No, he plunged without a safety net. And he felt himself falling harder, faster, and deeper for Sacha than he had for anyone in the past.

He leaned back against his cubby, disgusted. How hypocritical was he? Here he wanted Sacha to figure it all out, but what would Corrigan do if he did? Push him and their relationship into a closet so no one knew? Hide Sacha from his teammates and coaches? Lie about how much he meant to him? At least Sacha was being honest about having doubts about his sexuality. Corrigan knew but refused to admit it to anyone.

Then again, why should he be the only one to throw himself in a pit of fire? What would Sacha lose? He had the security of a prominent last name and generational wealth that could practically buy him anything he desired, including his pick of boy toys. His sexuality didn't jeopardize his future the way Corrigan's did his.

He scanned the locker room at his teammates in various stages of undress. The old, familiar questions cropped up in him again. Would they be uncomfortable knowing a gay man sat among them? Would they fear he was checking them out and awaiting an opportunity to pounce on them in the shower? Were they the kind of people who bought into the deleterious lavender panic stereotype that gay men lacked the restraint to curtail their sexual urges and held a main goal in life of *corrupting* straight men to the "dark side?"

He wouldn't create an opportunity to find out.

"What's up with you?" Theriot asked, planting his hands on his hips. "You about to hurl or something?"

"What's it to you?"

"Because as captain, it's my duty to know players on this team are healthy."

"Well, I'm fine, so you can move on."

Nguyen, undressing beside Corrigan, glanced at the phone in Corrigan's hand and smirked. "Looks like girl trouble to me."

Kavanaugh snorted from across the room. "Ellery with a girl? I doubt he's ever eaten pussy."

Nguyen shook his head but laughed. "Geez, Kav, you have zero tact. You must have been born in a barn."

Tossing his socks in his gym bag, Kavanaugh flashed a devious grin. "Hey, if it's good enough for the Divine, it works for me."

Larousse draped a towel around his neck. "Oh, I know you didn't just make that comparison. Can we leave religion out of this?"

"Yeah," Nguyen agreed, untying his pants. "We have enough issues. Is anyone else wondering how much longer Coach is going to keep trying to invent new ways to kill us?"

"Until," Theriot said, narrowing his eyes at Corrigan, "we look like contenders. Like we belong."

"If you have something to say, say it," Corrigan challenged.

"When I do, I will, but just know, affirmative action isn't going to earn you a spot on my line."

Corrigan leapt to his feet, jaws clenched and muscles coiled, and came eye to eye with the captain.

"Ah." Theriot scoffed smugly. "There it is. There's that bestiality. What are you going to do, Ellery? Hit me?"

Corrigan had a good mind to do just that; however, he reined in his temper after considering the ramifications of his actions and the conditions of his scholarship. He was already at the top of Coach Massey's shitlist. Adding to it would be unwise. But on the other hand, slugging Theriot would be so satisfying that Corrigan could practically taste it.

"I've taken dumps that have smelled better than you," Corrigan clapped back, glaring and not breaking eye contact. "You're not worth the toilet paper to wipe my ass."

Theriot parted his lips to speak but didn't. For a second, his eyes flickered with what Corrigan would have labeled in anyone else as hurt before he spun and walked away to the showers.

Nguyen tapped Corrigan on the shoulder. "Hey, a new zydeco band is playing at Lafourche tonight. A group of us is going to skip the dining hall and go. Care to pass a good time?"

Corrigan's face scrunched in confusion. "What?"

Nguyen chuckled. "Do you want to go, silly?"

"Oh. Um. Maybe. Sure. What's zydeco?"

Larousse gasped. "Saint Cecilia, pray for us, and Ellery especially!"

"You told me to leave religion out of it, and now look at you," Kavanaugh griped as he headed toward the showers.

"What can I say?" Larousse responded. "The boy needs prayers if he doesn't know what zydeco is."

Nguyen followed Larousse. "Cut him some slack. He's from New York."

"Yeah, and it's supposed to be a melting pot *and* populated with plenty of people of Haitian descent," Kavanaugh rebutted. "I'm not giving him a pass. I'm canceling his ass."

Nguyen glanced over his shoulder at Corrigan, hunched his shoulders, and smiled. "I tried."

24

SACHA

Frowning, Sacha waved off his approaching brother. "No," he grumbled, climbing the final two stairs and carrying a stack of journals as part of his glorified stock boy duties. "I've already had my mouth assaulted by a baking soda sandblaster this morning, and I don't need any more fuckshit." He marched down the corridor to the resource room.

Paxton followed. "I haven't said anything."

"But you will, and I won't like it."

"You don't know that."

"The hell I don't."

"Is that any way to talk to the person who got you in to see your first NC-17 movie and allowed you to have the last slice of Patti LaBelle's sweet potato pie at Thanksgiving?"

Sasha drew a face and dumped the books on a nearby table. "Yeah, after you dropped it on the floor."

"Don't be nitpicky. It's the gesture that counts."

Oh, do I have a gesture for you.

"If this is how you're going to behave, I recommend you never go to the dentist again and just allow all your teeth to rot out. You could rock a set of dentures."

Suppressing his urge to smile, Sacha crossed his arms. "Do you even think before you speak?"

"Well, there's always veneers, but you run the risk of making your teeth too big. I mean, you have lips the size of a guppy but a mouth the size of an anteater."

"Why are you still talking to me?"

"Because I need you to watch the kids this weekend."

"You have a nanny."

"And she has plans."

"I might have plans."

"Do you?"

Sacha shuffled uncomfortably. "No, but I could," he muttered.

"Oh?" Paxton's eyes gleamed with intrigue. "Are you seeing someone?"

Shit! He hadn't meant for the conversation to go here. "No. Yes. Maybe." *Fuck!*

"Well, I'm glad that's clear. Does this other person hold the same opinion?"

Hunching his shoulders, Sacha propped himself on the table. "Honestly, I don't know where his head is."

"So it's a *he.* How's that going?"

"I like him… a lot."

"But?"

Sacha shrugged and fiddled with a pencil left on the table. "He's young. Real young."

Paxton's brows bunched in concern. "How young? As in ten to twenty and a lifetime on a registry young?"

"Listen, I may be a touch flummoxed, but I'm not stupid. Or sick. He's legal… well, for some things."

Paxton's brows bunched more. "What?"

"He's twenty."

"Oh." He sighed with relief. "Twenty works… unless he doesn't. He trying to mooch off you?"

"No, nothing like that."

"Then what's the problem?"

"I remember when chatrooms were a thing in the nineties. This guy doesn't know a world where dial-up exists."

"So you're a geriatric millennial. It's not the end of the world. You'll just have to educate him on a few things, which could be fun." Paxton waggled his eyebrows.

"More like he's teaching me."

"Learning can be fun too. But I'm sensing something deeper is bothering you."

"We're at different stages in our lives. He's not going to want to get serious or settle down."

"Whoa. Wait a minute." Paxton held up his hand. "Did he tell you that, or are you assuming?"

"He's twenty."

"In other words, you're being an asshole. You should know better than to stereotype anyone."

Sacha winced at being called out on his bullshit.

"It's called communication, something necessary in every relationship no matter what age the participants are," Paxton continued. "Seems to me, you're creating your own fuckshit."

"Ugh! Stop reading me."

"If this is something you want, which it seems to be, then you're going to have to shimmy into your big boy drawers and work it out."

"You're right."

Paxton's beaming smile returned. "I know. I always am."

Sacha rolled his eyes dramatically.

"Now, will you babysit?"

"Fine. What time?"

"Seven." His smile widened. "So, how's the sex?"

"I didn't say we had sex."

"Yeah, but you did. I can tell because you've been too damn chipper these last couple weeks. I figured it's either because the Hounds have a chance of going to the Superbowl this year—and we both know that ain't happening—or you got laid."

"Sometimes, I really, really don't like you."

Sitting beside him on the table, Paxton patted his younger brother's knee. "This is a big step you're taking, and I want you to know you have my support. But I also want to know you're okay."

"I am."

"The last time we talked about something like this, you admitted that you'd never had a good experience. Has that changed?"

"Yeah. It's good. Granted, it's only happened twice, and there are things I haven't done."

"But?"

"No buts. I can see myself with him."

"Wow." Paxton smiled reassuringly. "You sincerely are smitten."

"It's more than that, Pax. I've fallen for him.

Hard." He shook at the words tumbling from his mouth. It was the first time admitting aloud what he'd been feeling for weeks. "But is it too much too fast? Is it just enthusiasm for a new lifestyle?"

"I can't answer that, but I can tell you that when I met Gretchen, I knew immediately."

"Seriously?"

"Yeah. I let her dangle out there a spell wondering, because you can't lay all your cards on the table the first night. But yeah, she had me from the giddy-up. I proposed on our third official date. Four months later, we were married, and look at us—still here. It doesn't always take the *Iliad* and the *Odyssey* and a Battle of Troy to figure out who you're meant to be with. And you don't need reasons to validate what you feel. It doesn't matter what anyone else thinks. It's what you feel that matters most. There are always going to be people who don't get it, who question the authenticity. People who complain that it happened all of a sudden. But guess what? It's not their relationship, and it's not their place to judge."

"But they will judge. I'm in a position of power… sort of. He's a Croneau Foundation scholarship recipient. At best, it's a conflict of interest."

"Why? Because if you're eliminating dating anyone who has any slim association with this firm in any way, you're back to dating your hand. Our health insurance is good, but do you want to meet your deductible on carpal tunnel surgery?"

Sacha's bottom lip jutted out. "Again, have I mentioned how I don't like you?"

"What else you got that's holding you back?"

Sacha parted his lips to relinquish. "Noth—"

"So, this is your payback to me," Maxwell Weymouth barked, standing in the doorway.

Both Sacha and Paxton hopped off the table as if snapping to attention.

"Father!" Sacha nearly swallowed his tongue. A pit formed in his stomach.

"Paxton, I'm going to need a word alone with your brother."

Distressed, Paxton stared at his brother, his eyes silently communicating that he would only leave at Sacha's request.

"It's okay," Sacha said, nodding slightly.

For a moment longer, Paxton remained motionless before begrudgingly exiting. Once his eldest son had departed, Maxwell one-handedly shoved the door shut.

"I knew," Maxwell stated slowly, his voice low, "that you were upset about the partners' decision to move you. I knew you held me responsible. But never did I imagine you would go to this length to hurt me or this firm."

"What I do in my personal life has nothing to do with—"

"You can't be so ignorant not to know that *everything* you do is a reflection of me and this firm. What do you think our friends will say once they learn of your deviant behavior? Think they'll continue to eat their crumpets and *mille-feuilles* and not be disgusted by the thought of you? Of course, they'll blame your mother and me for raising you around the wrong sort, for allowing you to befriend that Kian boy."

"Kian is one of the most moral and upstanding people I know."

"He's not our kind," Maxwell snapped. "Now he's put these debauched notions in your head."

"He didn't—"

"Shut up!" Maxwell warned, wagging his finger. "I just finished a call with Mace, who expressed his concern that the partners have been too harsh on you and I should bring the matter up for reconsideration. But after learning of your sickening behavior as of late, I'm not inclined to do any such thing until you stop engaging in this filth. Do you think your cousin would have put his good name on the line vouching for you if he knew what you are? It seems you're better here out of sight of everyone. Otherwise, you'll continue to disgrace this family."

"Is that what I am to you? A disgrace?"

"This is not how you were raised. Not only have you demonstrated unabridged incompetence, but you're now exhibiting flagrant doltishness. And if you ever want to be reinstated in this firm, you *will* end your foolish, vindictive licentiousness immediately."

Sacha attempted to keep his voice even, not from anger—which he was—but from the sadness that was stomping his soul. "It's illegal to hold my sexuality against me."

"Your sexuality?" Maxwell snorted. "You were transferred due to your failure and blatant inadequacy to perform. There's no mention of your *sexuality* in any records. None of the partners know— that is, unless you've told them. And I doubt informing them will improve your situation."

"You'd do this to me? Your son?"

"No son of mine would behave the way you have."

Don't cry. Don't cry. Sacha fought back tears swelling in his eyes.

Pivoting, Maxwell opened the door and left.

Shortly thereafter, Paxton reentered and rushed to his brother's side.

"Are you okay?"

Unable to speak, Sacha nodded.

"No you're not," Paxton replied, his voice laced with bitterness. He pulled his brother into a tight embrace.

25

CORRIGAN

After some thought, Corrigan had a change of heart and decided against going out with the team. Sure, it would have been an opportunity to bond, but why bother? Day in and day out, he spent his time with these people, and nothing changed. Besides, his body ached. The hot shower had done little to soothe his aching muscles, and he had a ton of reading to do for classes. And if he were going to spend the night out, he'd prefer to do it with Sacha, but that wasn't going to happen. For now, he was resolved to sit on the bench in the empty locker room, embrace the silence, collect his thoughts, and rest his muscles before making the long walk back to the dorm. However, a slamming door interrupted his plan. He looked up the same moment as Theriot rounded the corner lockers.

Well, hell in a handbasket.

Theriot startled. "What are you doing here?"

"Minding my own business and leaving yours alone."

Theriot grunted and then mumbled under his breath, "No need to be nasty."

"That's funny coming from you—a person who rarely has a civil word for me. Of course, why would you when you hardly think *my kind* is human? We're just a bunch of jungle monkeys, right?"

The color drained from Theriot's face. "You don't know me or what I think."

"Don't I? I think you've made your opinion clear from day one."

"No you don't. If you did, you'd know…." Shaking his head as if he'd had another thought, he shrugged. "Forget it," he mumbled, taking a step away.

Corrigan moved in front of Theriot, blocking his path, and crossed his arms. "I got time."

"I'm not that way, okay?"

Something in Theriot's tone made Corrigan want to believe him. Or maybe he wanted to believe him no matter what—that he wanted to find the good in everyone and not believe that in this age, people still treated other people as less than human. Perhaps he wanted the optimism of Anne Frank. However, this was Theriot, who'd never given him reason to believe anything different than the ugliness he'd displayed.

"Well, you're doing a damn good impersonation of it. Maybe you should test your skills in Hollywood."

"Maybe." He moved to step around Corrigan, but Corrigan moved with him, continuing to block his path.

"What, you're not so bold without an audience?"

Theriot sighed. "Just drop it." Again, he moved, and Corrigan blocked the way. "Look, it was never my idea."

Huh? Idea? "What wasn't?"

Closing his eyes, Theriot released a long breath before meeting Corrigan's gaze again. "None of it. I'm not supposed to tell you, but before you arrived, Coach called me into his office and told me to go in on you to toughen you up."

What the hell? Corrigan's mouth fell open. Would his coach seriously advocate something so depraved? Only one word came to mind. "Why?"

"Coach said we needed to do it before the other teams did, that they would say those kinds of things to goad you into drawing a game misconduct, and it would destroy you and this team. He said it would be your Achilles' heel and an easy target."

"And you willingly went along with it?"

Theriot shook his head vehemently. "No. I wanted no part of it, but Coach said it had to be me because as captain, the other guys would follow my lead." He dropped his gaze. "You don't know how sick it made me to spew such filth. He convinced me that it was for the best and that there was no other way."

Corrigan plopped down on the bench, his eyes glossed with disbelief and astonishment.

"I'm truly sorry if I've hurt you." Theriot sat beside him. "I just…." He stared at the ceiling as if searching for an answer. "It's hard saying no to Coach. I know that's no excuse, and I should have refused. But sitting in his office, listening to his rationale, it all made sense at the time. Tough love. Trial by fire. My father taught me to swim by tossing me in the Caney."

Silence emerged while Corrigan allowed Theriot's words to sink in. A swirl of emotions numbed him. Everything he thought he knew had been turned upside down once again. His coach had orchestrated the hell he'd been living. Was this a moment when the end justified the means if it was for a better good?

From his peripheral vision, he regarded Theriot, who looked as if he'd had his soul eradicated, and Corrigan's mood sank further. Why did he feel pity for the captain when moments ago he'd wanted to strangle him?

"You seriously didn't mean any of it?"

"Not a single word… well, except for you being slow. That part is true, but none of the other stuff. In all fairness, though, you have improved and are keeping up better now."

Corrigan nodded. He had improved, and for what it was worth, Theriot's taunting had become less distressing.

"So, can we start again?" Theriot's tone didn't exude the confidence of receiving a positive response. "I mean, we are stuck on the same team until I graduate."

"That's if Coach doesn't cut me."

"He won't. You're one of the best players we have."

Corrigan huffed, but his eyes widened at the unexpected compliment. "Tell that to Coach. I'm on the fourth line."

Theriot smiled knowingly. "No you're not."

"Yes I am. Where have you been living? I'm—"

"Do you genuinely think Coach would delegate Hansford and Kavanaugh to the fourth line?"

Hearing Theriot ask aloud drove in the ridiculousness of the notion, and Corrigan shrugged.

"Coach said it would make your line work harder if you thought you were fourth. He's grooming y'all to be a rotating first with my line. He thinks it'll give us more options."

"He sure keeps you in his confidence, doesn't he?"

"Only because he does a lot of his bidding through his captains. But it's like being a puppet sometimes."

Another silence ensued for several minutes before Theriot stood. "Look, I know it's a lot to ask, and I don't blame you if you say no, but I'd like for us to try to be, if not friends, at least cordial."

Corrigan nodded. "I can do that." And he could.

"C'mon. I'll give you a ride back," Theriot offered.

"Thanks." Corrigan gathered his belongings.

26

SACHA

"So you're just going to give up? End things?" Paxton asked.

"I don't see that I have much choice," Sacha replied, staring into the garden koi pond and swirling his bourbon in the glass. His mood had called for a drink stronger than beer. "Father has made his position exceedingly clear."

"And that's it? You sacrifice your happiness to indulge Father?" Paxton shook his head. "You can fight this, you know. Fight him. Legally—"

"It's not that."

"Then what is it? You said you care about this man."

"I do."

"Then what? You'd rather have a career than take

a chance with someone who's possibly your soul mate?"

"He *is* my soul mate." His own words stunned him, and he froze. When had he decided this? And even so, what possessed him to speak it aloud?

"Then why, Sacha? Why do this?" Paxton pressed.

"Corrigan is a Croneau Foundation scholarship recipient. Father could make life very difficult for him… find a way to strip him of his scholarship."

"Why would he do that?" Mace asked, entering the garden and removing his designer sunshades.

Sacha and Paxton grew quiet and turned at the unexpected arrival of their cousin, expressions of startle and discomfort on their faces.

"Sorry," Mace said, picking up on the tension. "Gretchen told me y'all were out here. Am I interrupting? Because I can leave."

"No, you're fine," Paxton replied, waving his cousin toward them. "I could use backup to reason with this knucklehead. How much did you overhear?"

"Only that Max will possibly interfere with the distribution of foundation funds." The fading sunlight glinted off his gray hair as he tilted his head. "My question is why."

Paxton turned toward his younger brother. "Do you want to tell him?"

Panic streaked through Sacha. He loved and respected his cousin the same as he did his siblings, and he held Mace's opinion in high regard. He appreciated Paxton leaving him the decision whether or not he wanted to come out to Mace. And Sacha did want to do that. He didn't like having secrets from his cousin, yet saying the words terrified him. He couldn't take any more rejection.

Mace picked up on the hesitation, and his eyes softened. "You don't have to tell me. Listen, I should go."

"No." Sacha grasped Mace's wrist as he turned to leave. "I want you here."

Nodding, Mace sat at the garden table and crossed his legs. "What's happening?"

"Father has disowned me."

"What in heaven's name for?" Only people who knew Mace well would have detected his outrage in what outwardly appeared as an unphased demeanor.

"I'm…." Sacha cleared his throat and collected his nerves. "I'm dating Corrigan Ellery."

Mace nodded slowly. "I see. And this Corrigan Ellery is a scholarship recipient?"

Sacha nodded.

"Well, I assume since the scholarship is awarded to college students that he's at least eighteen."

Sacha nodded again. "He is."

"Well, that makes you both legal adults. Scholarship recipients are decided by a board—which you're not a part of—based on the merit of application and recommendation. Did you know him before he was awarded the scholarship?"

"No."

"I see no impropriety. So, what's the problem?"

"He's a *he*," Sacha said.

Mace shrugged and waited for further explanation.

"I'm queer."

"Okay, I get that, but what does that have to do with the foundation?"

"Homophobia," Paxton interjected. "Father's threatening to block Sacha from ever returning to defense law in the practice if he continues dating Corrigan."

Mace's eyebrows pulled together. "That's preposterous. Besides, there's no such thing as homophobia. Phobia suggests fear. This is plain ignorance."

"I agree," Paxton said. "But Sacha here is going to end his relationship."

Mace focused on Sacha and completed Paxton's

thought. "Because you think if you don't, Max will eventually go after your boyfriend."

"I don't think it, Mace. I know that's what he'll do."

Mace shook his head. "He won't."

Sacha's eyes lifted. "What makes you so sure?"

"Because I represent Timothée Croneau, who is now the current president and CEO of the foundation. And for reasons that I can't explain due to lawyer-client confidentiality, I can say with the utmost confidence that my client would not be pleased to learn that he's overseeing a foundation with biased practices. While his mother may have held alliances with this firm, Timothée Croneau does not. He would have no problems taking his business elsewhere should such information *just so happen* to find its way into his inbox." Mace's lips curled upward slightly. "So, rest assured, he's no one Maxwell wants to offend." He leaned forward and patted Sacha's hand. "Don't let your father stand in your way—not on this."

"But he could still make trouble for him. I don't think Corrigan is out to his team, and you know how jocks can be."

"True." Mace nodded. "But again, I don't think

Max will want to go there. He'd be *honte* and would rather amputate a testicle than air family laundry."

"Unfortunately," Paxton said on a sigh, "we can't force the partners to let you back in."

Sacha set his glass on a table. "As long as Corrigan's safe, the rest doesn't matter. He's what's important."

Corrigan

As Theriot crossed the parking lot to Beauvais Hall, he looked to his right at Corrigan. "I'm glad we're getting a chance to start over. Honestly, I think it'll be better for the team if we're not at each other's throats constantly."

"I agree, but will Coach? He won't be happy that you're not following his orders."

"Maybe." Theriot hoisted his duffel bag higher on his shoulder. "But he's also always talking about oneness and the importance of being a team. As captain, it's my job to ensure we all come together."

"*As captain.* You say that a lot."

"A lot comes with it. It's not just a letter stitched

on a jersey or a chick magnet. Maybe one day it'll be your role."

Corrigan rubbed his hand on the back of his neck and winced. "About that newspaper article... I truly didn't—"

"I know."

"You do?"

Theriot nodded. "Anyone who takes that much shit at practice and doesn't beg for forgiveness is either a masochist or telling the truth. Besides, Larousse hit me up. He explained about Leo. Do you think you're the first player to get misquoted?"

"I wasn't quoted at all."

"It doesn't matter now. It's over. Time to move forward. Coach got his pound of flesh."

"And then some," Corrigan grunted.

Theriot chuckled. "You're a tough cookie, Ellery. Most would have broken weeks ago."

Cocking his head, Corrigan stared evenly at his teammate. "Is that the goal? To break people? Because I thought you said it was to toughen me up."

"It's both. Look, Ellery, this hockey program is bigger than both of us, bigger than Coach. Millions of dollars ride on us, and the powers that be are determined to squeeze out every miserable cent. That means casualties—good players pushed until they have nothing left to give. It means a billboard of shiny stars. They'll pamper us when we win and punish us when we don't."

"By billboard, you mean Coach's favorites?"

"I don't know if *favorite* is the appropriate word, but the ones who become the face of the team, yes. Players who motivate the boosters to dig deep in their pockets and the university to avoid cuts."

That resonated with Corrigan. "Yeah, makes sense. Sacha said as much."

"Sacha? Is that your boyfriend?"

Corrigan stopped in his tracks, his eyes wide as saucers. "What?"

"The guy with the Mercedes."

Corrigan's mouth hung open.

"Come now. Did you think I wouldn't know?"

"I never…. But how…?"

"How many times must I tell you? I'm captain. It's my job to know everything going on with this team. I'm my brothers' keeper."

"But you hadn't said anything, never used it against me."

"I also told you I'm not a complete dick. It's not my place. How you crumple your sheets is your business."

"Does Coach know?"

"Probably, but who knows? But listen, if any of the guys on the team ever try to give you shit about it, let me know. I'll take care of it."

Take care of it? Who is this guy?

Speechless, Corrigan nodded and willed his feet to start moving again. Stunned by the revelation, it hadn't crossed his mind to refute the allegation. Frankly, it was a relief that someone knew.

Only... was Sacha his boyfriend?

"The guys can talk all the shit they want to about me, but Sacha's off-limits. If anyone comes for him, I'll slam their ass to the asphalt like a skateboard."

"I doubt that'll happen," Theriot continued. "It's not like you're the only person on this team who has a boyfriend."

Wh-What? "Who?"

Theriot tilted his head and grinned. "I'm not telling."

27

SACHA

Sacha held his hand beneath the fried green tomato to catch any dripping remoulade and stared across the room at the taped box on the table. It wasn't much. He hadn't brought much when he'd transferred to the law center because he hadn't thought the move was permanent. The fact that he hadn't been assigned an office gave him hope of a short stay, and he'd temporarily stashed his belongings on a corner table in his father's office. When he'd moved in, he'd thought he hadn't brought enough. Now he was thankful he hadn't. It simplified moving out.

He would have been gone hours ago if Paxton hadn't bought him lunch as a bribe to stay until the end of the day. How was it possible that his entire life could be accumulated in one measly box? Sure, there would have been more boxes if he'd packed up his house, but how much of any of it would have significance to his impact on the world?

But *did* he impact the world? Did his life have meaning? Purpose? Or was he just a paper punch— one teeny circle cut from a flat, blank sheet with so many others? Insubstantial and unremarkable? Would his legacy be notable, or would he be forgotten the second his warm corpse hit the ground?

Contemplating life curtailed the enjoyment of his lunch, and he shook away the thought. He'd made a vow to step away with dignity and the type of elegant discretion his cousin frequently displayed. Few people recognized when Mace was flustered, and his impassive expression pissed them off. Not that Sacha was aiming to tick off his father— although that would definitely be a bonus—he simply didn't want to appear beaten by someone who obviously held him with little regard. Had his father ever loved him? He had to wonder, because it didn't seem feasible to him that anyone who truly cared for him could withdraw affection so easily.

Suddenly, an epiphany flittered in his mind, and Sacha stopped chewing. Perhaps he had suppressed acknowledging his sexuality because deep down he knew his father's convictions and had wanted to circumvent his rejection. And not only his father. His mother would be aboard too. She had supported every action Maxwell Weymouth had ever taken. He'd seen her quickly recant opinions—and not out of fear—once she realized her husband held an opposing stance. Perhaps Sacha had transposed this deep-seated fear of rejection onto his budding relationship with Corrigan. Maybe he snubbed the thought that Corrigan could care for him because his own father didn't.

Well, fuck! I have daddy issues. How fucking cliché?

A knock on the door snapped him from his thoughts, and he looked away from the box to his father's paralegal standing in the threshold.

"I'm sorry to interrupt your meal. Your father gave me a list of errands. I was about to go do them, but someone is here asking to see you. He doesn't have an appointment. What would you like for me to tell him?"

Sacha didn't feel like seeing anyone, but he also didn't want to inconvenience a student. Since classes had begun, he'd found that many students preferred to meet with him than his father—although, he couldn't argue that he blamed them. Many were confused by the syllabus and already overwhelmed by the readings. He could empathize, reflecting on his days of first-year law.

"You can send him in."

"Would you like for me to stay and answer the phones?"

"No, I can handle things. And you don't have to rush back. Take your time."

She smiled sweetly at him. Sacha knew his father didn't treat her well or pay her nearly enough for what he had her do. He returned her smile.

"Thank you."

"It's nothing." Grabbing a napkin, he wiped his hands and mouth, then closed his boxed meal.

"Hey," Corrigan greeted, stepping into the room and closing the door behind him.

Sacha's smile widened, and a warmth filled him. "Well, hello. I wasn't expecting to see you."

"I have a break between classes and thought I'd stop by. I was going to use asking for a fraternity letter of recommendation as an excuse. I've decided to pledge—not that I have much choice. They don't seem all that bad after all and may actually be fun. But the truth is I wanted to see you... since you're not responding to my texts."

Guilty. Sacha hung his head. Since his blowup

with his father, he'd been avoiding Corrigan. "Yeah, I'm sorry about that. Things have been a little crazy these last few days."

Corrigan tilted his head. "Are you sure that's all it is?"

"What do you mean?"

"Things got a little weird between us."

"Weird?" Sacha raised his brow.

"Tense. I guess I freaked out a little." He shifted his weight. "I had a plan to come here and play hockey. I never thought I'd meet someone like you and develop such strong feelings."

"You have feelings? For me?"

Corrigan shifted again and shoved his hands into his pockets. "Here's where I start to sound like a cheesy greeting card commercial. The thing is, I never believed a gay man would be accepted in hockey. I was struggling with that and resigned to keeping my personal life on the down-low. Then an amazing man who I thought was far out of my league enters my life and adds a completely new set of concerns. What if I take the risk to come out, and you aren't in it for the long haul? What if you're just... curious? Where does that leave me if you decide this isn't the lifestyle for you?"

"Cor—"

Corrigan raised his palm. "Wait. Let me finish. I realize now how selfish that was, and that's not what love is about."

Sacha blinked twice. "Love?" he croaked.

"I totally get it if you don't believe me. I know it's fast, and you may think I'm too young. But *I* know what I feel. And I want to move forward with you no matter the consequences. Any doubts or problems we encounter, we can work through them… together."

A moment of silence ensued.

"Say something," Corrigan urged, his voice cracking.

"Well…." Sacha moved toward Corrigan. "I like this commercial, but I'd prefer it to be a feature film. I don't know the right thing to say other than I love you too. Plain and simple. I want to be with you. Build a future with you. Be the creepy old man with the hot boyfriend."

"Stop insisting you're old. I got my first off-the-books paying job when I was twelve years old, working as a stock boy at a local grocer. I've been helping support my family ever since. By fourteen, I was navigating around New York City alone. Each night, I made sure my siblings were fed, bathed, and had homework done. And I was the person who got them to school in the morning. I've helped care for a disabled parent whose moods changed directions like the wind. I've lived a life many thirty-year-olds haven't. And while it might be nice and all to say I should enjoy my innocent youth, I can't go back and reclaim those days. Nor do I want to. I don't regret the choices I've made or even the ones that have been made for me. The years you've been on this Earth physically are pretty damn close to the years I've lived emotionally. Please don't look past me because of my age."

Grasping Corrigan's hands, Sacha shook his head. "I'm not discrediting your experience, but I don't want to hold you back or be the reason your dreams don't come true."

"If they don't, I'll go to Disney World. Besides, dreams are goals without a plan, and I have a plan." He squeezed Sacha's hands. "Look, I know realistically what my odds are to make it into the NHL. I know it's not peaches and cream with travel, practice, and all that jazz. In hockey, you start doing that stuff before you hit varsity if you're serious. Most times, it's the only way to make a varsity team. It's not like football where they wait until you graduate. If that dream doesn't come true for me, it's because it's the wrong dream. And there's nothing that says I can't have more than one." He stepped into Sacha's space. "I don't want to miss out on the dream of us."

Sacha trembled, and his heart pounded against his chest. If there was ever a moment he could feel his blood circulating through him, it was now. He stared at Corrigan knowingly. This man completed him.

Releasing his hands, Sacha trailed his long fingers along Corrigan's jaw and brushed his thumb across his bottom lip. His free hand wrapped around Corrigan's waist, pulled him in, and he tenderly pressed his lips against his younger counterpart. The contact caused Sacha to lose all sense of time and place.

"How dare you!" a voice growled, grounding back in reality.

Sacha peered over Corrigan's shoulder and into the incensed gaze of his father. How long had he been standing there? How had Sacha not heard the door open and close?

He stepped away from Corrigan and straightened his shoulders.

"Yes, I do dare, Father." Reaching across the table, he grabbed his suit jacket draped on the back of the chair. "I don't see a need for a written resignation, but you'll have mine first thing in the morning for your files. That should keep everything nice and neat. By the way, this is my boyfriend. I won't bother with a more formal introduction, as I'm sure you're uninterested and won't be civil."

"You're such a fool."

"I have been, but not as you would think."

"You're throwing away everything important."

"That's where you're wrong. I'm taking the most valuable things in this room—the man I love and my dignity—and I'm leaving." He glanced at Corrigan, whose dark eyes glinted, startled, alarmed, and bewildered simultaneously. "Let's go." Tugging Corrigan's hand, Sacha led him out the door. "I'll have Pax drop my things off to me."

"Sacha!"

"Good day to you, Father," Sacha replied.

Without looking over his shoulder, he exited.

28

CORRIGAN

"I didn't mean to cause problems for you," Corrigan said, waving his arms in the water and staring up at the stars that were beginning to pop out in the sky like scattered diamonds. In the city, he'd never had such an unadulterated view of the evening sky, and he marveled at the beauty before staring across at Sacha, who had his arms draped along the side of the hot tub, his head leaned back, eyes closed, and holding a glass of wine. He looked relaxed—more relaxed than Corrigan had expected.

When the two had parted earlier in the afternoon outside the law center, Corrigan had hesitated to leave. Sacha, despite his even tone, had looked absolutely wrecked yet wholly resolved. He'd explained to Corrigan the situation with his father and, in

Corrigan's opinion, had attempted to pass it off matter-of-factly, as if he wasn't affected. However, Corrigan saw through the facade. He'd wanted to skip his classes and spend the afternoon consoling him, but Sacha wouldn't allow it. Therefore, Corrigan had moved on to Plan B and hightailed it over to Sacha's place the second he was dismissed from hockey practice.

He'd arrived at Sacha's house as Paxton was exiting. "He's out back in the hot tub," Paxton had said, stepping aside for Corrigan to enter. "Fair warning, he's on his third glass of cabernet sauvignon. There's not much reasoning with him."

Corrigan hadn't come prepared for a hot tub rendezvous; therefore, Sacha had offered him a pair of trunks in the pool house, and again, Corrigan's mind was blown. Who kept a stash of new swimwear in varying sizes for guests in their pool house? Then again, if a person had a pool house that resembled a small cottage, it made perfect sense. Even with the copious selection, Corrigan had had difficulty finding a pair that accommodated his thighs and buttocks without too much strain—the quandaries of being a hockey player. After ten minutes of searching, Sacha suggested he go commando. Of course, that had also been Sacha's first suggestion, but Corrigan couldn't help feeling nervous and self-conscious being nude outside where the neighbors could possibly see. It ended up being the option he'd chosen.

"You didn't cause any problems that weren't already there," Sacha answered. "Scabs atop infections don't promote healing."

"But if it wasn't for me, your father—"

"Would still have an issue." Sacha opened his eyes. "His objection isn't with you. It's my entire life, and you happen to be in it. I want you in it." He took a sip of wine and smiled. "And I want you in me."

Corrigan sat up from his reclined position, his eyes wide and brows arched. "You what?"

"Since when did you go deaf?"

"Are you sure?"

"Why wouldn't I be sure?"

Corrigan shook his head. "It's a big decision."

"You don't think I'm a big boy capable of making adult decisions?"

"That's not what I mean." He moved closer to Sacha. "You've been drinking."

"I'm not drunk." He tipped his glass and took a sip. "Yet."

"You're new to this, and it's not a rite of passage

to queerdom. Some gay men never have anal. You've asked yourself, what if you don't like it?"

"What if I do?"

"Sacha—"

"Just because I struggle with a label doesn't mean I don't know what I want, and I'll never know if I don't try. And if I'm going to try, I want to do it with someone who I love and who loves me." He finished his wine and set the glass aside.

Nodding, Corrigan closed the space between them. "I do love you."

"Then I don't see the issue unless you don't want—"

Corrigan interrupted by cupping his hand around the back of Sacha's neck and drawing their mouths together with a kiss that was equally hard, rough, and desperate. There was no way he was going to allow Sacha to finish that sentence when it was not remotely close to being true. He wanted Sacha in a way he'd never wanted anyone. He pushed his tongue inside Sacha's mouth—sucking until they both released hungry growls—while Sacha's hands dug into the curve of Corrigan's lower back and splayed downward.

Pulling away slightly, Corrigan whispered on Sacha's lips, "I want this."

"Then I'll be right back."

Sacha

SACHA RETURNED MOMENTS LATER WITH A HANDFUL of condoms and packages of lubricant.

Corrigan chuckled. "Do you think we'll need all that?"

"If I have my way, we will." He placed the items on the shell of the tub, slipped out of his trunks, and slid into the water. "You don't think you're up to it?"

With hockey-quick reflexes, Corrigan snatched Sacha into an embrace and spun him to face away from him. "Overtime is my specialty." Positioning a foot between Sacha's, he pressed against him. His erection blazed against Sacha's inner thigh while his nipples raked tiny sparks of fire across his shoulder blades "I excel in one-on-one shootouts." He allowed his fingers to trail to Sacha's groin and brushed the short pubic hair. "You trimmed."

"You like?"

"Very much," he rasped, nuzzling his neck. "Lean forward."

Sacha complied, resting his arms and upper torso against the cedar decking that encased the hot tub. Corrigan's tone alone caused Sacha's entire body to flitter with uncontrollable anticipation. In the water's reflection, Sacha watched Corrigan retrieve the package of lubricant and squeeze a generous amount in his palms.

"Is that necessary in water?"

"Oddly, yes. You'd be surprised how drying water can be."

Sacha peered over his shoulder. "Sounds like you've done this a time or three."

"Don't be jealous, and no, I haven't. I just happen to be well versed in certain matters."

"And how did that come to be?"

"Oh, for Pete's sake!"

"I don't know Pete."

"A friend—platonic friend," he added quickly, "explained it to me. It's different in a big city, and he didn't want me to get hurt." Corrigan hesitated from rubbing his hands together. "Is that okay?"

"It's not *not* okay with me. At least one of us knows what to do. I just don't like the thought of you being with other men." He paused. "Or women."

"I've never had sex with a woman. I'm what some call a *gold star*." He pressed back against Sacha.

"Haven't you ever been curious?"

"Not really. I told you, I was young when I discovered my attraction to men. It's a heterosexual misnomer that a gay man needs to do a test run with a woman to determine if he's genuinely gay."

"I envy you."

Corrigan softened his voice and placed a series of gentle kisses on Sacha's shoulder. "Sacha, a label isn't everything. You've helped teach me that. Getting caught up on what we call ourselves can cause us to miss out on what's before us. I don't want to miss out on you." He slid his lubricated hands over the curve of Sacha's ass and kneaded his flesh in time with the movement of his mouth on Sacha's shoulder.

Whatever words Sacha intended to vocalize were preempted by the sensation of Corrigan's hands and hypnotizing tongue on his body. "Mm." *Yes.*

Corrigan's finger pressed against Sacha's opening but didn't push in. Instinctively, Sacha clenched.

"Relax," Corrigan whispered, nipping Sacha's earlobe. "I'll go slow. I won't hurt you."

Sacha exhaled, trusting Corrigan but doubting

there would be zero pain involved. "Kiss me while you do it."

Corrigan licked his way from Sacha's ear to his mouth. His kisses were softer but deeper, as if he meant to extract Sacha's soul. In truth, Sacha wasn't certain that wasn't what was happening as he felt himself lifting and floating. Nothing else seemed to matter or exist. However, a sharp pain bolted him back to reality, but only for a moment. Within seconds, the pain eased, and he felt the decadence of Corrigan's fingers rubbing the sensitive nerves inside his hole. Moments later, he felt his muscles relaxing, allowing Corrigan's fingers to glide in and out effortlessly. He moaned again, sounds that probably would have been embarrassing had he not been consumed with pleasure, until Corrigan withdrew to reach for a condom.

This is happening. His breath rushed into his lungs, heating his entire chest. "Don't just have sex with me. Make love to me," he murmured, bracing himself.

"I will." With his hips, Corrigan nudged Sacha's knees farther apart to gain a better position between them. Then, with one silky, slow glide, he entered him.

"Fuck!" Sacha uttered as his vision went black.

His head flexed forward, and he broke out in a gloss of sweat. He wasn't prepared. Corrigan's finger penetration was nothing close to his thickness, and Sacha's knees buckled. A thunderous delectation suffused him.

"You okay?"

Sacha wasn't certain if he answered with words, but he must have given some encouraging indication, because Corrigan continued until he'd filled him.

"Get at me," he purred, clutching the edge of the hot tub for balance. He didn't want Corrigan holding back, although, he had a feeling he might be asking to unleash a kraken that would ravish him into bits and pieces. The practical Sacha would have worried, but the lustful Sacha… not so much.

Nodding, Corrigan began moving with strong and slow thrusts that grew steady, his right hand stroking Sacha's shaft at the same tempo.

I'm going to implode. He pushed back to meet Corrigan's thrust.

"Damn, Sacha," Corrigan panted. "If you keep doing that—"

"Overruled!" Sacha cried, cutting Corrigan's sentence short. Corrigan had hit that magic spot that Sacha had no idea existed. "Again."

Corrigan rammed as deep as he could, and a guttural grunt of agony and delight tumbled from Sacha.

Sacha lost all sense of time and gravity as if he'd been sucked into a vortex. His mind spun, and a coiled tension in his abdomen tightened until it combusted into a million glorious shards of bliss and madness. Again, he wasn't prepared for the violent sweetness that overtook and shook him. Rolling waves of ecstasy gushed through him, and his pulsating cock splattered his release against the side of the tub.

This is what it's supposed to be. Finally, he understood the hoopla regarding sex.

He was still shuddering when Corrigan clutched him in a death grip and stilled. Sacha looked over his shoulder just as Corrigan growled and seemed disoriented with orgasmic rapture.

Beautiful.

For several minutes, neither moved nor spoke and enjoyed the connection of their limp and ravaged bodies. However, Corrigan finally withdrew, breaking their seal. Although Sacha logically knew his body needed a respite, he wanted Corrigan back in him.

"I'm going to assume from the circumstantial

evidence of moaning and groaning that you enjoyed yourself, counselor."

Turning, Sacha wrapped his arms around the neck of the younger man and smiled. "And you'd assume correctly. Seems you know how to handle a stick."

Corrigan winced at the pun. "Extremely corny."

"Do you have to go back to the dorm tonight?"

Corrigan nodded. "Not for a couple hours, though." He sighed. "College hockey life. It'll be like this for the next four years, you know."

"It's a curfew, not a prison sentence. We'll have plenty of time to see each other, just maybe not always as much as we want or when. Where would we be in this world if people gave up every time things got inconvenient?"

"Inconvenient? Don't you mean difficult?"

"Nope. See, that's the issue. People tend to be too egocentric and then write a narrative that life with others is too demanding."

"Relationships are a challenge."

"No they're not, but they are worth being challenged."

"You've lost me."

"I wanted to be an attorney. I studied, took tests. I didn't quit when I failed an exam."

Corrigan quirked an eyebrow and smirked. "*You failed an exam?*"

"Well, no, but that's not the point." He twirled his fingers on Corrigan's nape. "Being an attorney was important to me. Therefore, I did the things I had to do to make that happen, and sometimes that meant missing out on doing things I wanted to do with people equally as important to me or even doing things I didn't like to reach the end goal. Some people viewed that as me putting myself and what I wanted, my ambition, in front of the people in my life and what matters to them. But what would the flipside have been? What if I had done all those other things and flunked out? Would I have been happy? Would my misery have made others happy? Would I even have the capacity to make another happy?"

"I get what you're saying."

"No, I don't believe you do. What does it say about our relationship if we're the type of people who need to be underfoot twenty-four seven to remain connected? Psychopathic codependency? We'd fair better investing in cling wrap. Corrigan, when you love someone, you're there for them, and that doesn't always translate to a physical presence. It's emotional too. All couples face hardships, but they must make a decision to overcome them together. And it's best if they make this decision from the start instead of getting halfway in bumbling about with no plan to love each other every day even when the other doesn't deserve it. I fully comprehend that you're on a journey to be a professional hockey player, and I'm willing to make it with you."

"And I with you."

"Good. Now that that's settled, we should get out of this tub before we do some serious dermatological damage."

CORRIGAN

Corrigan snuggled beside Sacha, his legs slung across Sacha's thigh, on the handwoven double-quilted hammock hung between two massive dogwood trees in Sacha's backyard as the golden rays of the setting sun faded. With his head pressed against his companion's chest, Corrigan listened to the older man's heartbeat while his hand stroked down Sacha's side. He sighed, welcoming the breeze that brought with it the sweet scent of juniper.

"Tired?" Sacha asked.

"Hot. How do you deal with this heat? It's like Satan's sweatshop, only it's hot for no damn reason."

"It's the humidity. You'll get used to it."

"Doubtful." Corrigan gazed upward. "But I could get used to chilling in this hammock."

Sacha grunted and pointed at the trees. "You say that now, but stick around for the spring when these towers of kindling unleash their flower baby gravy. Your sinuses will loathe you."

"I guess that means we'll have to cuddle in your bed instead."

"Yep. What a hardship to spend hours upon hours together in my Alaskan king-size bed."

"I definitely could get with that." Closing his eyes, Corrigan smiled. As he began drifting off, a thought suddenly jarred him awake. "Could you get used to somewhere else? Like maybe a northern state?"

"Why would I?"

Corrigan shrugged as if he didn't have an answer but really did. "I don't know," he mumbled. "I was wondering if I got picked up by some team far away...."

"Ah!" Sacha drew it out as if a lightbulb suddenly illuminated above his head. "Then that's where we'll be. Or maybe we'd purchase a condo and live there during the season and keep this place as a vacation home."

"And your career?"

"I can set up practice anywhere." Sacha grinned and added, "Or retire and collect my Social Security."

Corrigan lightly punched him in the shoulder. "Stop that, Grandpa."

"You and I are a team."

Lifting himself to his elbows, Corrigan stared down at Sacha with a huge smile. "We are."

The best team ever, and the future is ours.

THANK YOU SO MUCH FOR READING *FUTURE GOALS*. IF your interest has been piqued and you want to discover more gorgeous hockey players, check out OUT OF THE PENALTY BOX. But why stop there? There are other players to get to know. Check out the entire LOCKER ROOM LOVE series.

ACKNOWLEDGMENTS

The process of writing and having published *Future Goals* has been a long one, and I have so many people to thank and shout-out for helping me along this journey. I must thank my mini who constantly reminded me I needed to be writing instead of watching YouTube and TikTok videos. (Yeah, that really happened.)

A huge thank-you to my alpha and beta readers, cover artist, critique partners, editors, proofers, and publishers for everything, and I do mean everything. I had questions, and y'all gave me the answers. Y'all even gave me answers to questions I didn't know I had, and I'm much appreciative.

Thank you to my family and friends for understanding all the times I bailed on events to research, write, or edit, and checking on me to ensure I'd maintained sanity during computer malfunctions. You each mean the world to me.

Last but certainly not least, I want to thank each

and every person who read, shared, tweeted, blogged, followed, reviewed, or help spread the word about *Future Goals*. It is for you that I write, and that this book is possible. Thank you so very much.

ABOUT THE AUTHOR

Genevive Chamblee is a southern darling and resides in the bayou country where sweet tea and SEC football reign supreme. She is known for being witty (or so she thinks), getting lost anywhere beyond her front yard (the back is pushing it as she's very geographically challenged), falling in love with shelter animals (and she adopts them), asking off-the-beaten-path questions that makes one go "hmm", and preparing home-cooked Creole meals that are as spicy as her writing. Genevive specializes in spinning steamy, romantic tales with humorous flair, diverse characters, and quirky views of love and human behavior. She also is not afraid to delve into darker romances as well.

As an author, I'm very much interested in knowing readers thoughts and feelings. One way that allows me to know is when readers leave reviews. I would appreciate you taking the time to leave a review on your favourite book site (e.g., Amazon or Goodreads). Good, bad, or indifferent, all feedback is welcomed as it helps me grow as a writer and produce the stories readers want to read.

If you would like to keep abreast of news and updates including all new releases, join my mailing list at HTTPS://GENEVIVECHAMBLEECONNECT.WORD PRESS.COM/NEWSLETTER/

I love to hear from you directly, too. Please feel free to email me at genevivechamblee@yahoo.com or check out my website Creole Bayou at WWW. GENEVIVECHAMBLEECONNECT.WORDPRESS.COM for updates.

ABOUT THE PUBLISHER

Hot Tree Publishing loves love. Publishing adult romantic fiction, HTPubs are all about diverse reads featuring heroes and heroines to swoon over. Since opening in 2015, HTPubs have published more than 300 titles across the wide and diverse range of romantic genres. If you're chasing a happily ever after in your favourite subgenre, HTPubs have you covered.

Interested in discovering more amazing reads brought to you by Hot Tree Publishing? Head over to the website for information:

WWW.HOTTREEPUBLISHING.COM

CPSIA information can be obtained
at www.ICGtesting.com
Printed in the USA
BVHW031211240123
656976BV00004B/47

9 781922 679420

LOVING A
VAMPIRE
IS
TOTAL
CHAOS

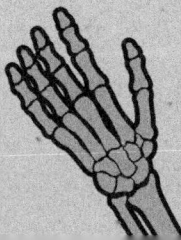

LOVING A VAMPIRE IS TOTAL CHAOS

AURA HAYES

DEDICATION

~~We would like to dedicate this book to~~
~~our families and~~

To me Zav because without me there would be no book.

TRIGGER WARNING

Loving a Vampire is Total Chaos features a sunshine vampire MMC who's a serial killer. There is on the page gore but we promise Zav only kills the worst of the worst! Other things you might want to watch out for are a parent with dementia, blood, and kidnapping.

The sound of grown men begging for mercy always brings a smile to my face.

Not sure what that says about me, but at three-hundred-years-old murder at least keeps life interesting.

"You sick fuck!" The repugnant, pot-bellied man yells up from the floor, clutching his now stump of a leg. Greasy hair is plastered to his face and spit flies in the air every time he shouts, nearly sullying my perfectly good shoes.

I frown down at the recent purchase that I've already become attached to. I take a step back to avoid any other potential incidents.

Shaking my head and laughing, I reply, "I've heard worse. And watch the shoes."

I don't want even a speck of his vile bodily fluids to land on them. Not because I'm worried about leaving behind any DNA or trace evidence, but because it's a game to see how clean I can stay.

Besides, I don't like blood unless I'm drinking it. Even then I'm a picky bitch.

Glancing around the room I take a moment to appreciate my handiwork. Puddles of blood and limbs are strung across the entire warehouse floor. Decapitated heads, broken teeth, and shredded intestines draped like tinsel. What originally started as a gang of forty men is now down to one and the scene it creates is a crimson masterpiece.

Grinning down at the sole survivor I start to slowly walk toward him, my steps echoing within the concrete box. The only other sound in the room is the pounding of rain outside and the labored breaths of my soon to be dead acquaintance.

He screams as I approach, eyes round with fear.

I do so love it when they scream. It's the terror in their eyes that really feeds me—knowing that these men who have done horrible things finally know a smidge of what their victims have felt.

"Why are you doing this?" he wails, doing his best to crawl backwards but the efforts are futile. All he's doing is speeding up the bleeding from his severed femoral artery, bringing him one step closer to joining his buddies in the afterlife.

"I think you know, Peter." I make a show of licking my fangs and shoving my hands in my pockets, continuing my slow stride.

It's a little too much fun taunting *powerful* men. I mentally scoff at the word.

They're all so pathetically human and easily breakable once I get ahold of them. I haven't had a good, solid fight in over a century.

"Please! I'm begging you." Snot pours out of his nose and his body odor sours the air making my own nose wrinkle. His pallor is ashen and not just from fear. His time is almost up, and he knows it. "I'll do whatever you want! Do you need money?

Weapons? Drugs? I swear I can make all of that happen. I have connections." He pleads with hands out, blood continuing to trail in front of him. His heartbeats slow. His eyes dulling from the loss.

"Hmm." I tap my pointer finger on my chin and pretend to consider his offer. "You think you could do that for me?" I taunt. "I am kind of low on cash."

He nods furiously. "Yes! Let me just call my guy and I'll get it squared away."

Amusing. Even with death imminent he's still trying to plead like there's something that can be done. I love seeing that small sliver of hope twinkle in their eyes before crushing it.

"You have"—I look at my bare wrist— "a minute left, Peter. Do be serious. You're wasting both our time."

"Turn me! Change me into ... into what you are."

That's why he's bargaining.

I do nothing to stop the amused chuckle that claws out of my throat.

I suppose my third century of life, or whatever one can call this, has made me a teensy-bit unhinged. But it's not like I can rely on the cops to actually do their job. I'm bored. I might as well help clean up the streets and wreak a little havoc of my own while I'm at it.

Grabbing his phone from the floor from when I had kicked it away earlier, I give it to him. Within the same breath I pull a rusted lead pipe from the severed hand of a previous victim and bring it down on his arm, making him cry out in pain and drop the phone.

It clatters across the concrete floor, screen shattering.

So fucking fragile.

Humans.

Their things.

All of it.

But not me.

"Shit!" Tears stream down Peter's face like raindrops on the windows outside as he sobs and cradles his arm. "What the hell? Please, please, please don't kill me. I've got a wife."

"Did you really think your measly offering would interest me?" I cock my head to the side, clucking my tongue. "I've been around for longer than you'd believe and have access to everything you offered and more."

I sigh, knowing our time is up.

"I thought you were going to make this more fun for me, Peter," I tsk, and wag my finger at him. "And using your wife as a means for sympathy? Do you think of her when you're allowing drugs onto the streets? Or when your kidnapping young girls and selling them? Or do you only think of her when it might save your sorry ass?" I look down at my perfectly manicured fingernails, inspecting them. "I bet you don't even love her, which is such a shame. Love really is the only thing that makes life worth living."

I'd loved once, but then she turned out to be off her rocker more than I am, so I skedaddled right on out of that relationship. I haven't been in a serious one since, but I've remained what you might call a romantic at ... well, I don't have a heart so I'm not sure where exactly. But it's there. Somewhere.

He pleads vehemently for his life, and I roll my eyes. It's always the "tough" ones that wimp out and sing like a bird. It ruins all the fun.

My ears perk up at the wail of sirens in the distance.

"Goodbye, Peter." His eyes go wide as he registers what I've said and a second later his head is rolling across the concrete floor. It thunks into another head with a wet smack and I chuckle when they roll together like bowling pins.

"Strike!"

The sirens grow closer, but I know with my speed I have

time to put a finishing touch on my artwork. Zipping around I carefully collect what I need and proceed to do what I do best.

After placing the heads exactly where I want them, I dip my fingers in a particularly viscous puddle of blood drawing my signature symbol. Standing up I wipe my hands off on a handkerchief I stole from one of the lackeys before throwing it behind my shoulder. Vampires don't have fingerprints, so they won't be able to track me.

That's another thing that makes this all the more fun—they're chasing a phantom, a ghost they'll never be able to catch.

I scurry up the scaffolding and head toward the window ready to make my escape.

Time to let the cops run around in circles like they always do. Idiots. They've been trying to catch me for years when really, they should be sending me flowers and a thank you note.

Bright red, white, and blue lights fill the warehouse. The sirens are so loud I wince.

I wonder what they'd think if they knew the serial killer masquerading in Chicago isn't even human. Their puny little minds wouldn't be able to handle that fact, I'm certain.

I smirk to myself and just as I'm about to take off into the night with the cover of lightning and thunder, I pause. I don't know what makes me do it, but I turn toward a police car that has squealed to a stop outside of the front door of the warehouse.

A flash of brown hair catches my eye, swinging around a woman's shoulders in a curtain of glossy darkness that resembles a raven's wing and my heart stops. I watch enraptured as she exits the car with toned legs encased in dark skintight jeans and black boots. I'm no stranger to attractive women, but it's like there's a magnetic pull leading me toward this one. I want to gather her hair back as it starts to stick to her face, slick from the pouring rain. Hardened eyes scan the scene. I can't pinpoint exactly what color her irises are. Vampirism isn't a cure for everything, and my shit eyesight carried over when I was changed. It's not entirely a bad thing since I can pull off a pair of glasses like nobody's business.

One thing I can see, there's something captivating about the way she carries herself. She's strong and yet I can sense a vulnerability within her. I wish I could pick up her scent but the storm and mix of blood inside of the warehouse make it difficult.

My reaction catches me off guard, I've never felt such a visceral response to a human. It's almost like ... *no, not possible.*

Settling myself into a dark corner of the scaffolding I lean back against the wall to observe and stretch my legs out instead of leaving like I planned. Tonight wasn't a total loss after all, not when I just found my latest obsession.

ost twenty-six-year-olds would be spending their weekend out with friends at the bar. Me? I'm currently standing in front of what looks to be a crude attempt at a smiley face made out of decapitated heads and body parts.

What the fuck?

I tilt my head in absolute bewilderment, trying to process what I'm seeing.

"Detective Brennan."

I snap my head up at the sound of my name, Captain Barnes pulling me out of my trance.

"Yes, Captain?" Shifting my weight and putting my hands on my hips I fully face him.

He scratches at his mustache. "I know this is your first case after getting promoted, but I have to say this isn't uncommon. I feel like you should know that."

Captain Barnes is a burly man with an imposing figure. His brown hair is shaved short to his scalp with dark eyes that convey a no-nonsense attitude that dares you to try to pull a fast one on him. It's no wonder he has the highest clearance rate with that scrutinizing gaze. I wouldn't want to be on the receiving end of his wrath.

I've known the man since I was a child. My father was a detective too, so Captain Barnes has practically watched me grow up.

"Sir," I reply in a deadpan tone. "You're telling me you come across bloody smiley faces made from body parts often?" I try to breathe through my mouth, because the scent of blood and bile is stifling.

What kind of predicament have I gotten myself into? Maybe I should've stuck with being a patrol officer.

The captain shakes his head. "Unfortunately, yes. We've had murders that all end in these crass, grotesquely childish depictions for years now."

I can swear I hear a disbelieving scoff of, "Childish?" but when I look around it's just Captain Barnes and me on this side of the warehouse.

He places a hand on my shoulder and squeezes. "I know you weren't fully briefed as we just promoted you, but you're one of the most promising in the force. Your recent work has already been outstanding and we need to get to the bottom of this." He runs a hand over his scalp. "I'll understand if this is a bit much. I've lost a few good officers that couldn't stomach this." He gestures at the mess of blood and limbs.

So much blood. I'm not normally one to be squeamish but even I'm having a hard time not gagging.

I try to calculate how many bodies we're looking at for there to be that much blood, but my brain can't seem to compute beyond *a lot.*

"Okay," I drag out the word, and look around the warehouse at the various corpses. "Thank you for your candidness, but I'll be fine." *I think.* "How many murders are we talking?"

Captain Barnes sighs and grabs a thick case file from a fellow detective who brings it over. Paging through, he counts out loud and lands on three identical crime scenes within the last month alone.

I gape. That's unheard of.

"Can I have that?" I offer my hand, and he nods.

The pictures contained within the manila folder are disgustingly vivid and I can't help my wince when I see human bodies manipulated in ways I didn't know were possible. Three offenses in a month is beyond excessive, especially considering each one has a minimum of ten dead. Killing *one* person in this kind of manner is exhausting on the human body let alone so many. It makes no sense. It doesn't seem possible.

"Always a gory mess and yet they have enough time to clean it up and leave a nice picture for us," he says clean with quotation fingers. "They also leave a signature in blood each time." Coming around to me he points at a bloody poorly drawn smiley face with—*is that fangs?*—found in each photo from the previous crime scenes. Walking over to our current massacre I delicately step over a dismembered torso to see the tell-tale 'signature' off to the side.

"What a bunch of psychos," I mutter under my breath. "It has to be a group."

There's no way one person is responsible for this.

Captain Barnes huffs a laugh. "It's like chasing a ghost. Never any DNA of any kind and anytime a shoe print has been left behind it's always been the same size shoe. One perp doesn't make sense and yet..." He trails off with a tired sigh. "Oh, and there's one more important detail." Barnes rubs the back of his neck and exhales. "The other common denominator

between all these murders is that they've been deaths of criminals or complete annihilations of organizations we've been
trying to take down for years."

I whip around to face him fully. "All of them?" I'm flabber-
gasted as to who would be capable of such a thing, let alone be
motivated to do it.

Like a real-life Dexter?

"Every single one." The captain looks just as confused as I
feel, and I know my work's cut out for me. He takes in the scene
and says, "I'll only say this to you, but I'm kind of relieved at
least someone is getting rid of the rapists, child predators, and
traffickers. We don't have enough manpower to take them all
down."

He walks away when his name is called by a squad member.

I sigh and brush soaking wet hair away from my face. I'm
glad one of us has faith. This crime scene is like nothing I've
ever seen or dealt with before. During training I saw all kinds of
crazy shit and I do love a good horror movie, but this might take
the cake.

Letting out a breath, the shift of a shadow above catches my
eye. I look up but find nothing.

"Probably a fucking rat," I mutter to myself. "I hate rats."

Throwing my apartment keys into the dish on the stand in my
entry I stand in silence. Crazy mass murderers who make art
with intestines and only target bad guys? Not on my bingo
card.

A furry head suddenly rubs itself along my calf and I look
down to find Midnight, my inherited cat. I refuse to claim him
as mine since I'm pretty sure he'd sell me for catnip if he could.

His pitch-black fur in the darkness makes him look like a mass of shadows with no visible form save for bright yellow eyes.

"I'm not petting you," I warn and walk away. He hisses at the insult. "That's what I thought. I know this game." Grabbing his wet food from a cabinet in the kitchen I start the process of feeding the crotchety cat. "You act all lovey-dovey and then go in for the kill."

Midnight struts over like the prissy prince he is and hops up on the counter to wait impatiently for his dinner. Tail curled perfectly around his fluffy paws he paints the perfect picture of innocence.

"I do feel bad you're getting this so late today, but better late than never, huh?" I rest my elbow on the counter as he delicately laps up the food when I set the can in front of him. I resist the urge to scratch behind his ear. He might be cute, but he's deadly. I have an automatic dry cat food feeder that goes off at scheduled times throughout the day, but Midnight needs his wet food or hell will be raised.

Looking at the cat I can't help but think about my father and his situation.

My parents were sickeningly in love until they weren't. It's supposed to be 'til death do us part, right? Apparently, my mother didn't believe that. My dad was diagnosed with early on set dementia when he was fifty and it rattled her. The symptoms started slowly with forgotten dates, items on the grocery list, and repeated questions of things that were just answered. Then it morphed into wandering, misplacing important things, and loss of recognition.

My mom panicked and couldn't deal with it, even though it's the responsibility of a loving partner to help their spouse through the best and worst of times. As soon as the doctor told us it was going to progress quickly, and he should be admitted into an assisted living community she ran for the hills.

I haven't talked to her in a long time. Although, she's tried to call me randomly over the years, for what I'm not sure. Out of guilt? To beg my forgiveness?

She didn't just abandon him when she left. I was only eighteen. I still needed my mom and she was just gone. It was a harder blow than my father's diagnosis. At least he didn't forget about me because he wanted to.

As his daughter it was hard to watch as the strong, proud man I once knew as my father slowly deteriorated into a shell of himself. A much loved and stellar detective himself when he was in his prime, I saw how much it hurt him to lose every part of himself.

I hope most people will never know the excruciating pain of walking into a room and having one of the most important people in their life not recognize them.

The first time it happened was a knife to my gut and after the visit I sobbed on my couch. I think that was the one rare occasion Midnight let me use him for comfort without scratching me.

Even though he was a little piece of shit, the cat was one of my last few ties to my father. He was his partner in crime for ten years. While he still had a sliver of lucid mind left, he asked me take care of him.

"I don't trust anyone with him besides you." He had said while giving Midnight an affectionate last pat on the head. I wanted to insist he keep him since pets can help dementia patients, but with tears in his eyes, he had said I needed him more, knowing I'd be alone.

"Ow!" I rub my ankle where Midnight has suddenly decided to take a bite out of my leg. Looking down he's glaring up at me with his beady eyes, tail whipping behind him. "I gave you your dinner and apologized for it being late."

He grumbles and I roll my eyes, heading back to my bedroom making sure to close the door so he can't follow. Exhaustion weighs heavily on me and sleep can't come soon enough. Not when I know the kind of work cut out for me tomorrow.

"**G**ood morning, Celine." A cheery voice calls out to me as I round my desk at the station the next day. Sitting down, I place my leather jacket over the back of the chair and grab the file placed in the center of my desk.

Ava, Captain Barnes's secretary, and my closest friend, smiles at me from outside his closed office door.

With wavy pastel pink hair and a white flowy shirt, she's the polar opposite to my ebony locks and black ensemble. I met her my first day on the job two years ago and we'd been fast friends, although her energy took some getting used to.

I suppose in our line of work you either compensated for the constant debauchery by being a bubbly optimist like her or a solemn realist like me. Some called me grumpy, but *I* wouldn't go that far. This was a tough profession to be in.

"Are you excited to take on the Mayhem Murderer case?" Her pen sways back and forth between her fingers like she has to find some way to let her energy out.

"Is that what they're calling these murderers?" I ask without looking up from my file but can see her animated hand gestures out of my peripheral. "You know we're not supposed to give them names." I arch a brow in her direction, trying not to smile.

"I know," she laughs, and folds her hands demurely on her desk. "But every murder is so..." She flings her perfectly manicured hand out searching for the right word. "...disgustingly gory and bloody with so many bodies. You have to admit that it's kind of fascinating that anyone can stomach committing crimes that involve so much gore."

"How do you know so much about the case?" I ask, since despite her position she shouldn't be privy to this much knowledge on it.

"One night over drinks Detective Kerr spilled his guts to me and some of the other staff in attendance. He went off about how he couldn't take it anymore, gave us all kinds of details he probably shouldn't have. I guess it was the case that finally broke that bastard. You'd know this if you went out with us more." She levels me with a firm look. "The team has a done a good job keeping it under wraps for the most part but with the media starting to get a hold of it, panic is going to set in with citizens." She taps her finger against a newspaper on her desk.

I remember Captain Barnes's mention of all the detectives that have dropped the case when we were on our way to the scene.

"Captain says he has total faith in me." Paging through the stack of papers, I mutter to myself, "No pressure."

I want to live up to his expectations. Captain Barnes has believed in me since day one. I think he feels like he has to make up for my dad's absence. I can't help but think he associates his legacy with my potential, which can be a bit much.

"I know you'll figure it out. You always do, and he wouldn't have promoted you without a reason." She turns back to her desktop and her long-manicured nails tippy-tap against her keyboard. I don't know how she stands having her nails that long. I keep mine filed as short as possible.

Standing, I walk over to the coffee machine in the break room even though I know it's the same terrible coffee they have every morning.

Man, I really need to convince upper management to upgrade to a Keurig or something. How anyone could do their best investigating on this lousy excuse for caffeine I'll never know.

Turning around at the sound of footsteps, I see Ava standing there with my leather jacket hanging off her fingertips and brows raised.

"Bean Hive?" She smiles as she mentions the name of our favorite local coffee shop.

"Bless you, my lord and savior." I grab my jacket and throw it on, following her toward the exit. "I don't think I could've done with this excuse for coffee today."

"I've got you, girl." Ava pats me on the back.

"It's on me though." I stop before she can open the door and give her a look. "You got it last time and it's my turn."

"Thanks, Sugar Daddy. I won't turn down free coffee." She steps in front of me and holds the door open.

The October air blows my dark tresses around my face. I unwind the elastic from around my wrist and secure my hair back in a ponytail. Bean Hive is a quick walk from the precinct and many of the staff make runs there for coffee throughout the day. I was going to suck it up with the station's coffee, but I can't turn down Ava's offer to get the good stuff.

Beside me, Ava sighs. "You have the longest, prettiest hair and you've always got it in a ponytail." She gives the end a tug.

I shrug, pulling my jacket closer around me when wind gusts around us. "It's so thick and always gets in my way."

Despite my statement, I can't bear the idea of cutting it short.

My dad always told me how much he loved my long hair. Even now, when he doesn't remember me, it's my hair he comments on.

Last time I saw him he said, *"My daughter is ten and she has the prettiest hair too. It's halfway down her back. I learned to braid just for her."*

We trek down the street to the shop.

Just before I reach for the door handle, I stop, causing Ava to run into my back. "What's wrong?" She glances back at the street when I turn and observe my surroundings.

In our line of work, you learn to be paranoid and the creepy crawly feeling spreading down my spine has me on edge. I look left and right and then behind us.

"Nothing," I mumble with a last sweep of the area. "It felt like someone was watching me."

Ava pauses, searching the street. "I don't see anyone staring."

"Must be my imagination," I say, but I can't get rid of the slippery feeling.

Stepping inside, the smell of freshly ground coffee hits me. I let out a happy hum and smile when the owner, Luna, makes eye contact with us, winking as she starts on our order. We find an open booth in the back corner shrouded by plants and wait for our lattes to arrive.

The shop is an eclectic mix of modern and rustic. The red brick walls have various plants hanging on them and the occasional hung photo frame in between with various art pieces of coffee beans that look like bees. A mix of booths, comfy chairs, and natural wood tables fill the room with hanging Edison bulbs illuminating the space.

"How's your dad doing?" The question pulls my attention away from our surroundings.

"The same." I trace a whorl in the wood of the table with my fingertip. "I can't help but hope one day he'll be magically cured but that's never going to happen. They take great care of him. I can't complain."

Sensing my lack of enthusiasm on the topic, Ava drops it and grabs a folded piece of paper from her purse, placing it on the table. "You know what you need? Some fun."

I eye the piece of a paper, finding it impossible to keep the disdain from my face.

"A club? Ava, I don't know how many times I have to tell you, but that's not my scene." I grab the flyer and try to straighten it out. It boasts the grand opening of a new night club downtown. "Can't we just paint pottery? Or go to a movie like we usually do? Our favorite actor is starring in one of the latest releases." I try to tempt her into a more introverted activity.

Ava is a social butterfly and flourishes in all kinds of settings, whereas I would much rather be at home, curled into the couch reading or at the small gym I like to box at. Boxing has always helped me clear my head and work out any frustrations.

"Oh, please." She rolls her eyes. "All you do is go home and talk to that damn cat."

I open my mouth to refute, and she gives me a stern look which makes me deflate.

"Celine." Grabbing my hands, she pleads, "You are an intelligent, gorgeous, single woman who deserves to have some excitement in her life. Let's go out, dance, drink, and have a good time! Maybe have a one-night stand?" She shimmies and I sigh seeing her scan the shop for any potential partners for me. "You, not me, of course. I have Spencer."

The other patrons are mostly elderly people and college students working on papers and projects. I swat at Ava when she catches the eye of a male student and winks at him, motioning toward me with an over emphasized head jerk in my direction. His eyes shift to me when she does, and he smiles softly, causing me to shield my face away from him.

I'm no virgin, but I fear my lady bits are covered in cobwebs at this point, and I have no interest in changing that any time soon.

Work and my dad come first.

It's not that I don't like the idea of finding a boyfriend, but you have to put in effort, whether that's by going out, or hopping on a dating app. And frankly, men are like plants, if you don't water them, they'll die, and I don't have a green thumb.

Luna walks over with our lattes saving me from more embarrassment. I tilt my head at her in a silent thank you, both for the coffee and the save. Ava glances over with disapproval like she knows what I just wormed my way out of.

"Any exciting cases on the rise ladies?" Luna asks with a twinkle in her eye. She's close to Ava and I's age, and has already managed to start her own business. Bean Hive is successful, too. The place often has a line out the door in the early morning hours. It's inspiring what she's done with this once dilapidated space.

I mime zipping my lips and Luna pouts, making Ava laugh into her coffee cup.

"Are you following the sex trafficking ring?" she asks it so blatantly I can't help but look around and make sure no other patrons have overheard.

"What?" I lower my voice. "Sex trafficking ring?" I hadn't

been briefed on one but that wasn't out of the ordinary. There are too many cases for me to know everything that goes on.

Leaning in, Luna whispers, "Word on the street is that the new night club, Vex, opening up is a front for them to nab women. Absolutely awful if it's true."

"Where did you get that information?" I balk at the accusation and Ava looks at me with wide eyes.

"I have my resources. Oh, just one minute, Z!" Luna calls to a waiting customer with red hair and glasses. He smiles in our direction, but I ignore it. I have more important things to do than to smile at a cute guy.

Turning to Ava with a smile I say, "You know what? I'm down for going out now."

Ava's body heaves with the weight of her sigh. "Why am I not surprised this is what gets you to go out? But hey"—she leans back, hands up— "if it gets you out, I'll take what I can get."

C eline Brennan.

My obsession and she doesn't even know it yet.

The one I'm killing a man for. Slowly, of course. I do so love it when they suffer.

"Why are you doing this?" The man in question squeaks at me from against the wall in the abandoned alleyway I dragged him into. His stomach is steadily dripping blood from the slices I made in his flesh, the dirty concrete beneath him drinks up the liquid within its cracks.

Can a plant survive being watered with blood? Might have to test that.

Sighing, I steel my patience. "I'm getting deja vu. Why do humans always ask the same questions?" Rolling my knife between my fingers I squat in front of him. "Fight back. Run away. Give me a show. Do *something*. You're all so fucking boring."

Humans think they want to live forever, but being immortal can be so fucking tiresome.

"What are you talking about?" A lone tear rolls down his cheek and I sneer before quickly stabbing the source of it, his left eyeball. He screams and lifts his hands up like I'm going for the next eye, but I don't. He needs to see for what's going to happen next.

I grab his hands and hear the rapid pounding of his heartbeat accelerating. A frightened rabbit in my trap, just how I like it.

"Are you a coffee or tea kind of guy?" Seeing the confusion in his good eye I continue, "I can't stand either. Never could."

When silence greets me, I squeeze his hands so the bones grind, causing him to yelp and stutter out, "C-Coffee."

I wonder what he'd think if he knew I was holding back. That I could shatter him without much thought.

"That was my guess!" I use his hands to applaud myself. "Actually, I don't like to cheat, but I have to be truthful and tell you I already knew the answer."

Sliding my hand into my back pocket I pull out a sleek black phone and open my photo album. Scrolling past various photos of the gorgeous creature that's haunted me since last night, I land on an incriminating one. The phone illuminates my new friend's bloodstained face when I turn it to him, and his eye widens when he sees the screen.

"You were watching me? What the hell? Who are you?" His sudden temper spike makes my nonexistent heart race.

"I think the real question here is, why were you talking to her?" I jab my finger at the dark-haired beauty the cretin is speaking to in the photo.

"She's just a random girl, man." I push down on his stomach wound, and he yelps, "I thought she was hot! We were flirting. I don't know! Her friend made it seem like she was looking for something. Seemed like it would be an easy hook-up." The man throws his head back clearly unable to handle the pain. Weakling.

He's so fucking boring. One day of watching Celine Brennan tells me this pathetic excuse of a man could never keep up with her.

Pushing my glasses up my nose from where they had slipped, I repeat, "You thought she was hot?"

Human men are a disgusting breed, never mind that I was once human too.

My patience wearing thin, I continue, "You want to know what I think?"

He slowly shakes his head and keels over, trying to fold into himself like it'll make a difference as I lean closer.

"I think..." His humerus bone snaps under my shoe. "...that I don't want a filthy creature like you..." His fingers crunch with ease in my hand. "...touching what belongs to me."

At this point the human is close to expiring both from the pain and the blood loss which means I have to wrap it up. Celine might not know she's mine, but she will soon enough, and I don't need human trash like this guy thinking they have a chance with a creature as ethereal as she is.

"A divine angel like her is a blessing to the eyes and you are nothing but lowly trash unworthy of looking upon her," I chuckle darkly, and soak in the fear emanating off the man. Even my laugh has him pissing himself. *Fucking pathetic.* "But me? I'm the monster under your bed, the shadows stalking your every move"—my breath fans across his face as I continue—"and a walking nightmare cleaning up the filth."

Making quick work of yanking his other eye out of its socket, I rip out his heart to silence the scream before it comes. There are days I relish in the sound, but today I want Celine back in my sights as soon as possible. It makes me twitchy not having her nearby. Like I've lost something vital, and I'll be the one bleeding out on the ground without it.

I cock my head to the side. This has never happened to me before. This *obsession* with a human. At the moment, I can't bring myself to ponder why that might be. I have an inkling but I'm afraid to hope in case I'm wrong. Instead, all I can focus on is locating her as quickly as possible. Once I see her, I'll be able to breathe again. Hypothetically, speaking of course.

I don't actually need oxygen to survive.

A blooming puddle of blood on the ground attracts my eye and I dip fingers into it to draw a smiley face with fangs that unfortunately look more like buckteeth, but I can't let someone else take credit for my work. I drop the body into a metal trash bin and dust my hands off. Extending my arms, I look myself over and smile when I find that I didn't get a single drop on me. Pleased, I head in the direction of Celine's apartment.

Following Celine home after the investigation last night was a no brainer. I had to know where she lived, my little raven wasn't going to fly away from me that easily.

I scale the chain link fence at the end of the path with ease and head out onto the sunny sidewalk as if nothing happened. A breeze ruffles my wavy red hair, and I tilt my head back with a happy sigh. I love this kind of weather and can smell the approaching rain on the wind. Hot and cold doesn't affect vampires like it does humans. Sometimes I miss the true feel of heat on my skin or the prickle of chills. Everything all feels the same to me.

Fingering the thin silver chain resting against my throat I give myself a chance to wonder what it would be like to inhale Celine's sweet scent up close. To run my nose along her collarbone and lick a path between her breasts before sinking my teeth into her delicate neck.

This fixation is all consuming. Not that I haven't stalked my prey before, but Celine isn't that. She's more and for the first time since becoming a vampire I feel the closest thing to fear. If she's what I think she is then she holds the power to weaken me.

Before I know it, I'm in front of Celine's apartment building.

I'm losing my mind—what's left of it anyway—over a human woman I don't even know. I'm not sure what's become of me, but I don't care to figure it out. For years, the only thing I've filled my existence with is killing those who are unworthy. At a certain point, even that can't fill the hollowness inside. But ever since last night, Celine has occupied a corner of my mind, and that space has become bigger and bigger to the point that I can't stop thinking about her. Obsession is quickly becoming too mild of a word for what I feel.

With a bounce in my step, I grab hold of the wrought iron door and I'm cognizant not to show how truly easy it is for me to open it. The man that walked in right before me struggled to wrench it open against the wind.

Deciding it'll be quicker with my speed to take the stairs and scent the hallway of each floor as I climb, I head for the stairwell. I make it to the twenty fourth floor in record time and stop dead in my tracks when her sugary blackberry scent hits me, making my mouth water and fangs ache. I'd gotten whiffs of it as I'd gone along like she took the stairs from time to time but this was thicker, heavier.

Following the scent trail down the hall like a kid in a candy store I stop at a door labeled 2431.

This is the one.

A wreath of fake red leaves and berries adorns the door along with a small welcome mat on the ground with a design of a black cat peeking out from the corner. It's a homey gesture that doesn't seem to line up with the hard-edged detective I've been following. But I like that there may be a softer side to her that few see.

Taking a step closer, I hold in the groan rumbling in my chest as I breathe deeply and ingest as much of her smell as I can.

It fills me up, fortifying me in a unique way—almost *feeding* me more than the blood that's essential to my existence.

With my forehead against the door, I can almost pretend she's on the other side about to let me in. She'd smile at me with her gorgeous mouth, brown eyes twinkling while leaning against the frame. I wouldn't be able to resist grabbing her around the waist and crushing her lips to mine. Her imaginary whimpers of pleasure shoot to my dick, and I can't keep in my groan this time.

"Can I help you?" A grating voice sounds to the right of me. I turn to find a man that looks to be in his twenties holding bags of groceries, a quizzical expression on his face.

It's embarrassing this human was able to sneak up on me.

Fake smile in place, I put my hands in my pockets non-threateningly, and reply, "Hey, yeah. I'm here to visit my cousin, Celine, she's kind of a ditz and gave me the wrong key." I hope the excuse covers for me as a groan of frustration and not lust that I was letting out a second ago.

He nods hesitantly, brown hair flopping in his eyes. "I've never seen you before and I don't remember her mentioning a cousin." Skepticism lines his features.

"Really? We're super close but I live in California, so I don't have the chance to visit too often." Holding out my hand he reluctantly shakes it, transferring his groceries to the other hand as best he can. He shivers at my touch, his eyes untrusting. "Trent." I'd be lying if I said I didn't squeeze his hand a little harder than I should've.

Despite what the stories might tell you, vampires don't stick out like a sore thumb. We're able to blend in without too much notice—it's part of what makes us such a threat to humans.

But no matter how human I look, I'm not, and some are far more aware that a predator lurks behind my eyes. He seems to be one of those people. I can tell from the way his shoulders curl slightly inward, and how his eyes dart around like he's taking stock of where he might escape to.

I don't plan to kill him, unless he says something stupid, so he has nothing to be worried about. Yet.

"Nice to meet you, Trent. I'm Cory."

The deadbolt unlocks loudly as he twists the key in and nudges his door open with his shoulder.

"Here let me help you." I rush over and hold the door open all the way, taking one of the bags from him. A plan formulates in my head. I don't care for eliminating humans who haven't done anything wrong, but sometimes it's necessary to get what I want. The man from the coffee shop definitely did something wrong when he touched my girl.

"Thanks, man." Cory shuffles in and I smirk as the door closes behind me with a soft click.

"Nice place you've got here." Gently placing the bag of groceries next to his on the kitchen island, I invite myself into his living room and glance around. I can tell he's put out by my barging in.

"Yeah, it's cool being in the heart of the city," Cory answers dismissively, head in the freezer.

He puts away his refrigerated items and I walk toward the balcony. Pushing open the sliding glass door I walk out, greeted by the sprawling city in front of me. I'm pleasantly surprised to find Celine has her own balcony right next to this one. Reaching out my arm I can easily touch the metal railing of hers. An adorable table and chair set decorates the space with string lights twisted around the railing. Eyeing her door, I see a piece of wood in the track preventing intruders from easily breaking the lock and entering.

My smart girl. Not that it would keep me out.

"Hey, uh not to be rude, but could you leave? I appreciate the help, but I have friends coming over." Cory motions a thumb over his shoulder toward the front door in a get the fuck out gesture.

I can smell the fear on him and the confusion too. He's not sure *why* he's scared of me, just that he is. He's certainly not the stupidest human I've encountered but he's an idiot if he thinks I believe him.

"Oh yeah, of course. Silly me." I hold my hands up and walk past. Halting in my steps when I pass him, I turn around. "Before I go I have one question, do you ever talk to Celine?"

"Sometimes." He rubs a hand through his hair. "I tried to ask her out but she's kind of frigid. Totally dismissed me without giving me a chance, but don't tell your cousin I said that."

"Hmm." If Celine dismissed this guy, it must've been for a good reason. I nod and roll my neck before fully turn back to Cory. A cold smile slowly curves my lips. "Then I definitely don't feel bad about doing this." A split second later, I swing my arm back to punch him square in the face for daring to say anything bad about her.

He falls back, entirely limp.

I kick his shoe.

Is he just passed out or—?

No heartbeat.

"Aw, fuck," I say out loud, annoyance drenching my words. Sometimes I forget to lessen my force. "Oh, well." I shrug. "This might be a new record of dead bodies in a twenty-four-hour period," I muse, staring down at Celine's former neighbor. "I didn't *mean* to kill you, at least not yet, but that doesn't matter, does it?" I chuckle to myself. "Like you can even answer me."

With a sigh, I plant my hands on my hips and look around the apartment.

"Now"—I muse, tapping my foot— "how am I going to get rid of you?"

It doesn't take me long to decide the side floor length window is my best bet. I can't throw him over the balcony as much as I'd love for Humpty Dumpty here to have a great fall. Celine saw enough gore at my hands last night. I don't need her looking out her balcony to a mess below. Best to toss the ilk out the other way.

It doesn't open and while it's made from glass that doesn't easily shatter it wasn't made to withstand a vampire. I knock out the glass and look down into the shadowed group of shrubbery and trees, perfect for hiding a body.

I heft Cory's body into my arms and carry him to the window. A quick check tells me nobody is around to see what I'm about to do.

"Look out below," I say with a laugh, tossing him into the void.

Seconds later the sound of impact meets my ears, and I swish the curtains closed. Pulling out my phone, I send a text to one of my contacts to dispose of the body and fix the glass. I can't have the cops sniffing around and alerting Celine to my shenanigans.

With a sigh I plop myself down onto the black leather couch and rest my head against the cushion. Staring at the ceiling my mind wanders to Celine who I'm now perfectly positioned next to.

As if summoning her, my sensitive hearing picks up on soft footsteps coming down the hall and the jingle of keys. Jolting to my feet I peek out of the peep hole in my door and spot her walking down the hallway with a determined look in her eye. She's holding her phone to her ear, and I can pick up on her friend's voice from earlier.

At least she was already in the building before I threw the body out the window.

"Ava. I already told you this is the perfect opportunity to snoop." She sticks her key in the keyhole of her door and quickly opens it, leaving my field of vision which is way too soon after not seeing her for hours. With a pout I move back over to the living room and continue to listen in on her conversation.

"Yes, our motives for going to the club might be slightly different but we can't turn a blind eye to something like this and you know it. I can't just let innocent people be taken and sold if that's what's happening."

Now my interest is piqued, and I find myself leaning forward hoping she'll give more information on what she's talking about.

"I'm going to see what I can find out online about the club owner. We'll get ready at your place if that's cool with you?" There's a rustling sound like she's taking off her jacket before she continues, "Okay. I'll see you later. Bye, Aves."

I whip out my phone and search for a club opening in Chicago, quickly finding a news article detailing the grand opening of Vex tomorrow night.

What trouble are you getting into, Celine?

5

"You have to wear the red mini dress. It shows off your calves." Ava sits with her hands splayed out behind her on her bed while I flounder under her gaze.

I roll my eyes. "I don't think anyone is going to be looking at my calves."

"You're right." She smirks triumphantly. "They'll actually be looking at your ass."

The club opening is tonight and she's dead set on dressing me, or should I say undressing me, in the least amount of clothes possible.

"Why can't I just wear this?" Waving my hands at my jeans, leather jacket and t-shirt she shakes her head and walks over, holding the red dress up to my body.

"Even though you're going into this with an ulterior motive it's a night club. Everyone's going to have their boobs and butts hanging out. You'll stick out like a sore thumb if you're not in a dress." Riffling through her closet she pulls out the same mini dress but in black. "How about we compromise on this one?"

I sigh holding my hand out for it, accepting defeat. At least it's black.

"Fine but I'm wearing my leather jacket on top of it." Ava claps and ushers me into her bathroom to change. I huff out a breath and a lacy push up bra is thrown over my head a second before the door is pulled shut.

"Ma'am! Watch where you throw! You almost took me out with that thing. It must have ten pounds of padding," I yell when my vision is obscured by the delicate fabric. Her answering chuckle is downright evil.

Standing in my plain black underwear, I tilt my head toward the ceiling and take a second to mentally prepare myself for the soul-suckingly tight dress. Grabbing it from the hanger, I roll it down my body and admire how good it makes my chest and hips look. I'm not particularly curvy or well-endowed in the breast region but the dress and push-up bra make it look like I have more than I do. I smooth down the stretchy material and pick off a piece of lint before shrugging on my leather jacket and pulling my hair out from under the collar. Ava might've succeeded in getting me into the dress, but I will be wearing my jacket. Some girls might be able to brave the chilly Chicago weather in skimpy outfits, but not me. I'll never choose beauty over function.

Turning to look at myself from all angles I'm pleasantly surprised. My hair is silky and pin straight from an earlier run through with my flat iron. With the odd amount of rain we've been getting lately, I don't trust the weather or my wild waves. The brown in my irises is accentuated by the mascara and fake lashes. Thankfully Ava carefully applied them on the corners only and not the full strip where it feels like caterpillars on my eyes. She learned from making that mistake when we went out a few months ago and I was blinking excessively. It had given her a good laugh though when she said it looked like I was fanning my cheeks with them. A warm shimmery pink shadow tints my lids, with a matte-black smoked out around the edges. I have to admit even though it's out of my comfort zone, all together it makes me feel hot, powerful even, like I can take on anything. With a finishing swipe of pink gloss on my lips I open the door for Ava's approval.

"Damn girl. You need to dress like that more often. Your boxing sessions have you in serious shape." Ava whistles and stands with her hands on her hips. "Oh, wait the finishing touch!" She grabs a pair of studded black ankle boots and sets them in front of me. I sit on her bed to pull them on while she steps into a pair of strappy heels. Her dress is a champagne color and showcases her toned body and mile long legs. She's adopted my high ponytail and strategic wisps of pale pink hair float around her face.

"How do we look?" Pulling me over to take a final glance in the full-length mirror against the wall, she loops an arm through mine and smiles. "Like a pair of seductresses," she answers herself.

"Spencer isn't going to be able to take his eyes off of you." I already know they'll be off in their own little world at the club when we step through the doors.

Ava always promises she won't abandon me, but she can't help herself. When her and her boyfriend Spencer are together, they tend to get lost in each other. A part of me is envious. I'd like to find someone like that—someone I love so much that the rest of the world pales in comparison to their company.

"Speaking of, he's here. Grab your purse and let's roll out." She spritzes herself with one last spray of perfume, making me cough when it beelines for my lungs. I wave the cloud of fragrance away and follow her out.

"I worry about you, Celine," she says in a soft-tone that belies her normal bubby exuberance.

"Why are you worried about me?" I ask, stepping onto the elevator.

She eyes me with a look that says *are you seriously asking me that right now?*

"Oh, please, you talk to a cat who you're in a constant love-hate relationship with and won't glance up long enough from your reports to see the attention you get from men." The elevator doors slide open, our heeled shoes clicking on the tiled floor. "I know you're not a partier, but you need to put yourself out there and meet people. Your life can't stop because you're taking care of everyone around you."

A slight breeze pulls some of my hair from beneath my jacket, tickling my nose. I quickly brush it behind my ear so it's out of my way. "If you promise to look around and listen when you can, then I'll promise to let loose a teensy bit." I pinch my fingers together with the slightest bit of space between them to emphasize my point.

"Deal. But hopefully it's more than a teensy bit." She wraps an arm around me and pulls me in for a side hug. "I think the only other time I've seen you loosey goosey is when we both got drunk over the news of Ren Evans." The day the leading man of our favorite romantic drama announced his departure was a sad day indeed.

"I still haven't recovered," I mumble wiping an invisible tear from my eye. Ava murmurs her agreement which is promptly ended by a squeal and her jumping into Spencer's arms who leans against his idling car.

Spencer is an attractive man, and I really like him for Ava. He balances out her chaotic energy with his even keeled aura.

He's an all-around gentleman holding doors open for her, bringing flowers by the office, and cooking dinner. As clingy as they are when they're together, they also know how to be autonomous and give each other space. Whenever I find my significant other, I hope he's like Spencer. I'm not sure I could handle someone who isn't self-sufficient and needs constant supervision.

"Your carriage, milady." With a sweep of his arm Spencer lets Ava into the passenger seat.

Tapping my booted foot on the ground I cross my arms in mock anger, "What am I, chopped liver?"

Spencer opens the back car door and winks at me.

"Of course not. Court jester? Maybe," he laughs at his own stupid joke.

I glare playfully at him and wiggle into the car best I can without flashing Ava's doorman and the general Chicago populus as they walk by.

"Remind me again who we're looking for?" Ava turns in her seat once we're on the road.

I pull up my notes on my phone. "From my research the club owner's name is Damien Black. He has two other night club locations, one in Los Angeles and another in Miami. Successful businessman and somehow not much to be found about him on the internet, he keeps to himself for the most part, doesn't have any kids, and doesn't have a partner."

Normally, I wouldn't discuss the details of a case fully with Ava and definitely not with Spencer present but since it's not a case—not yet, at least—I don't see the need to filter what I say.

"Hmm." Ava taps her chin thoughtfully. "How do we know he's supposedly involved with trafficking if there's so little information out there?"

"We don't. I'm just basing things off what Luna said." Locking my phone and looking out the window, I watch the city pass by in a stream of neon colors. I know it's bad to let my focus stray in this direction since it's not the case I should be working on. It's not even a case. But I can't help myself. Ever since Luna mentioned it, there's been something that keeps needling me about it. "There were also instances at his other club locations of women going missing. Somehow it was brushed under the rug and blamed on irresponsible behavior and unfortunate but realistic city nightlife." Spencer scoffs and I agree with his assessment. "He must have friends in high places to stay out of the drama."

"Do you have a picture of him?" Ava's phone dings right after she finishes talking and she laughs under her breath seeing I've already sent it to her. "Wow, that's not the crochety, greaseball I thought it might be. Kind of hot actually."

"Should I be worried?" Spencer tries to peer over and look at Ava's screen while simultaneously keeping his eyes on the road.

Kissing his cheek, she gazes lovingly into his eyes, "Of course not, Stud Muffin," she says sarcastically. Turning and holding a hand up in mock secrecy she loudly whispers, "That kind of money wouldn't be too bad, though."

Spencer lets out a snort and pulls up to the curb of the club. "I'm going to let you ladies out here and try to find parking. Wish me luck."

I once again finagle my way out and immediately pull the dress down as far as possible to cover my skin that's now pebbling under the crisp fall weather.

Why did I let Ava talk me into wearing this scrap of clothing?

The pink and blue neon club lights illuminate our faces as we take it in. A historic building that's been refurbished, it's truly a sight to behold. You'd never guess it was a club during the day with its white brick and imposing black doors. The party has already started and the bass of whatever EDM song is playing inside blares onto the city streets whenever the bouncer opens the door. Every few seconds the shine of disco balls streak across my vision through the stained-glass windows.

We shuffle through the crowd of people and wind our way around the building to the end of the line. Huddling closer for warmth, Ava and I thankfully make it to the door within a few minutes and present our IDs. With a silent nod from the bouncer and opening of the door we're inside.

It's an overwhelming scene for someone like me who much prefers the quiet solace of my apartment, and I think my eardrums might burst with how loudly the music reverberates around the room.

The refurbishment of the old building has been done in a tasteful way where it still showcases the original beauty of the architecture but brings modern flare at the same time. The white brick from the outside continues into the interior and reflects the light back easily around the room. Large archways looking down upon the floor can be found as you take the stairs up higher within the building. They don't seem to lead anywhere, just more alcoves for debauchery. Cages hang from the ceiling holding female dancers dressed in skimpy bustiers and panties.

A large circular bar is set in the middle of the room instead of back against the wall like I'd assume. Multiple bartenders take orders and deliver drinks to the flow of patrons who've stopped to drink after gyrating on the dance floor.

Private booths line one wall, shadows moving behind white curtains.

A blush heats my skin when I realize what's happening behind those curtains.

Running a hand through my hair I remind myself why I'm here and scan the room.

At first glance I don't see Damien, not that I expected to, but I do spot a large door which seems to lead to a back office or something else in the corner. Squinting my eyes, I can make out two burly security guards stationed in front of the door which further confirms my suspicions it's a room of importance.

"Spencer said he found a spot but it's a few blocks away so he'll be here when he can." Tucking her phone away Ava grabs my hand and pulls me toward the bar. "Remember what I said?" She gestures toward the menu, and I let out a breath turning to the bartender.

"Two shots of tequila, please." The blonde woman is already pouring our drinks before I even finish saying the words.

"Starting strong, are we?" Ava smirks, rubbing her hands together with excitement.

"Weren't you the one who said I needed to let loose? I'm going to need some liquid courage for that."

As soon as the shot is placed in front of me I down it and Ava stares at me mouth agape but pride in her eyes. "Hell yes, you go girl." Following suit, she slams the glass down and starts making her way toward the dancefloor. "Let's get out there and show them what we've got." She does a little shimmy to demonstrate her point.

"When you put it like that my immediate answer is no," I retort, but follow after her through the throng of sweaty bodies.

She giggles, grabbing my hand and dragging me to the middle of the crowd.

At first, I stand there like an awkward deer in headlights, looking every which way, trying to figure out what I should be doing. Ava must sense my nervousness because she bobs her head and starts to sway her hips giving me a reassuring nod. I follow her lead and try to lose myself in the music, closing my eyes and forgetting anything related to the world around me besides the song. After a few minutes I feel much better, maybe it's the tequila coursing through my system, but I start to enjoy myself.

"Come on," Ava says, mouth near my ear so I can hear her over the music. "Let's give them a show."

Giggling and putting our hands on each other's waists, Ava and I sway out of time with the music. I know she's trying to keep me in the moment, and I try to focus on the rhythm of the song. Just as I'm getting into a groove, the music transitions into a new dubstep track and I jump around with the crowd, throwing my hands in the air. I catch Ava smiling at me when I shimmy against her side, she lets out a loud whoop and claps with the beat. It's genuinely the most fun I've had in a while.

Spencer's dirty blonde hair appears above the crowd as he makes his way over to us. He's also brought another round of shots which I promptly throw back and thank him for. I try to tug Ava back to the middle to dance but she waves me off.

"Go on! Find yourself a hottie." Her brows waggle at me as she grabs Spencer's hand and leads him toward a table.

"Don't forget why we're here!" I shout over the noise, and she throws up a thumbs up in acknowledgment without turning around.

I blow hair out of my face and scooch back into the crowd but it's harder to get back into it. I probably look like a deranged puppet shuffling around trying to dance by myself while also scouting out the room. Just as I'm about to say screw it and walk off, a corded forearm snakes around my waist and pulls me back against a hard chest.

I squeak in surprise.

"Relax," a husky voice murmurs in my ear.

It's like time stops, the sweaty bodies gyrating around us slow down, and I swear my whole body shivers. Goosebumps rise on my arms at the sensuality in his tone and the strength with which his arm holds me against him allows me to feel how defined his abs are. Normally that command would have no effect on me, but something about his voice instantly soothes me.

I can't see the mystery man holding me past his black boots and dark jeans, but I desperately want to see more. His smoky vanilla and cypress scent envelops me, and I inhale deeply to savor it.

Coming back to myself I take stock of the situation and tense up. A stranger's holding me captive and I'm sniffing him like a weirdo.

I try to pull away, but he holds me tighter and breathes softly against my ear. Stroking my side in a soothing motion he lulls me into a sense of complacency. If I didn't know any better, I'd think I heard a small whine of displeasure coming from his throat when I tried to break away.

"Dance with me," he whispers seductively against the shell of my ear, and I melt against his warm body. "I promise I don't bite."

An amused chuckle rumbles through him at his own words.

Even though this is so out of character for me there's something about him that calms my nerves. Ava said to let loose, and I'm determined to prove I can. I have to sell my cover, right? Reaching an arm back around his neck I feel the brush of soft waves of hair. He tightens his grip once again when I make contact and lets out a sigh of relief when he realizes I'm not trying to leave.

I close my eyes as I lean my back against his front, rolling my hips into his. There's something exhilarating about not knowing what he looks like.

Swaying to the music my mystery man keeps his left arm around my waist and brings his other up to brush my hair to the side. He settles his face next to mine and gives an encouraging noise when I feel adventurous and start to grind back against his body. My heart rate picks up under his touch, and by the feeling of hardness against my ass he's just as affected by me as I am him.

"Such a good girl," he croons, and a soft moan escapes me at his words. I grip his arm with my free hand, needing something to hold onto, and allow myself to feel good for the first time in a long time.

Holding Celine in my arms and seeing her up close is better than I could've ever imagined.

It takes everything in me not to scrape my fangs along her neck and give in to my vampiric urges. Every cell in my body is screaming at me to claim what's mine in front of every idiot in this club.

Her fingers clutch my neck with a gentle touch and sift through my hair. I close my eyes hoping this isn't a dream and focus on her body against mine. Every time she rubs against my cock, I come closer to saying fuck it and dragging her away.

Patience.

I've spent enough centuries on this planet to have learned the art of patience, but I find with Celine Brennan it's non-existent. Lust, intrigue, and obsession are driving my brain.

And something else. Something purely primal and vampire.

Unwinding my arm from around her waist I reach up and grab strands of her hair to bring closer to my face. Her shampoo enhances her blackberry scent, and the dark tresses are soft to the touch like I knew they'd be. Watching her from afar I had to make educated guesses when it came to Celine. Now, I'm silently checking off each box on my mental checklist.

Intoxicating scent? Check.

Gorgeous doe eyes? Check.

Body that's molded perfectly for mine? Check.

The one thing I want now more than anything is to get to know her. Within those beautiful eyes is a sadness and isolation I have to untangle. Whoever put that hurt in her will pay dearly one day. It's an isolation I often find reflected in my own eyes, well that and boredom, but with her around I already know that will change.

My teeth nip her ear, allowing myself a small taste of forbidden fruit. Her small moans drive me crazy as we continue to grind against each other. I'm practically humping her like a dog, and I'd let her leash me any day.

I wonder if she's into bondage? The idea of tying her up or letting her do the same to me is intriguing.

Whether she is or isn't, I'm into what she's into. Whatever she wants I'll give her.

Except another man. I'd kill him before I'd let another man ever touch her.

"You are the most beautiful woman I've ever seen," I flirt, but mean every word. Being the one to bring a spark back to her soul will give me purpose.

Celine goes to turn toward me, but I grab her hips and hold her back tightly against my chest. A selfish part of me doesn't want her to see my face and break the bubble we're in. Not yet at least. Time isn't on our side because her pink-haired friend shouts her name through cupped hands from a booth. It hardly does much to amplify her voice amongst the lyrical chaos of the club but it's enough to catch Celine's attention.

I resist the urge to keep her from walking away, but I know I have to bide my time. As much as I'd like to bundle her up and never let her leave me, it will only scare her away. I need Celine as addicted to me as I am to her. With a last caress of my fingers to her face I let go and disappear on her next breath.

To the humans nothing has changed except a slight breeze left behind in my wake.

Watching her from a darkened archway up above, I cross my arms and lean against the structure. She turns in a circle, squinting, trying to find the stranger she was dancing with no doubt, but she won't be able to spot me. Ava calls her name again and she glances around one more time before setting off toward her.

My original plan wasn't to make contact with Celine tonight, but seeing the disgusting eyes of so many men on her left me enraged and with no other option. One piece of shit was quite literally on his way to dance with her when I intercepted. He was lucky all I did was break his wrist.

Celine sits down in the booth, and I watch as Ava animatedly tells her something she's overheard from the Vex staff. I chuckle to myself knowing I'm going to have my hands full with this one. She has a tendency to run toward danger and it's why it makes us even more of a perfect match.

Ava's mouth is moving but all I can think about is my mystery man who vanished into thin air. The way his hands felt on my body was unlike anything I've ever experienced. It felt natural for him to hold me. I wish I could've seen his face, because scanning the crowd does me no good when I don't know what he looks like.

"Hello?" Snapping brings me back to the present and I refocus to find Ava and Spencer staring at me with equally perplexed expressions. They've never seen me like this. "Have you been dickmatized?" She searches my eyes imploringly.

"Sorry, continue." I wave her on and give my head a small shake to clear my mind.

I don't think dickmatized is what I'd call it, but there's a definite hazy feeling that has me wondering if I imagined the whole thing.

She gives a knowing look but goes on. "I was fixing my makeup in the bathroom and overheard someone talking. There's a vent right above the mirrors that must connect somehow to an office or something. They weren't being very quiet, and it sounded like they were pissed off about a delivery gone wrong."

"Well, that doesn't seem particularly suspicious." Spencer frowns and leans back against the booth. He brushes his fingers lightly over Ava's bare shoulder. It's that small touch, that intimacy that has me momentarily wishing for what they have.

"Sure." Ava purses her lips at him, brow raised with sass. "Except he said a delivery of sangre."

"Sangria?" He scratches his head. "It's a club, Aves."

"No." She shakes her head, pastel pink curls flying. Sangre means blood in Spanish." Her eyes are wide, and she makes a duh expression at us.

"Are you sure you heard correctly, Aves? I know the whole situation is off but that seems like a stretch." He cringes when she glowers at him.

Even I'm struggling to fit the pieces together.

"I swear. Scout's honor." The disco lights reflect off her various gold bangles as she holds her hand up as if taking an oath.

Glancing between her and the suspicious door I make a decision. "I'll be back." The leather beneath me squeaks as I slide out of the booth and head to the bar.

"Screwdriver, please!" I yell above the music and place crumpled dollar bills on the tabletop. The bartender hands me my drink and I stumble away making a show of spilling some on the floor. Feeling my way along the wall I fake drunkenly walk toward the office. Lucky for me the bouncers just stepped away to escort a pair of actual drunks out of the club, so it's left unattended. Scanning the vicinity one last time I reach behind me and push down on the door handle which opens with ease.

My hair swings around my shoulders when I turn and start

to head into the space. Just as I'm about to get a visual a large hand closes on top of mine and yanks the door shut. My back is slammed against the wall and the burly guard from before glares at me.

"What the fuck do you think you're doing?" he spits out, dark eyes scanning me up and down.

Channeling my inner drunk sorority girl, I become boneless under his hold and try to look as dopey as possible. "Isn't this the bathroom?" I hold up my drink and spill a few drops on his black shoes. I throw in a giggle for good measure. "I really have to pee."

"You stupid, bitch. Just like all these other idiots." He flings me away from the door, forcing me to trip and shoos me with his hand. "Get out of here. If I see you again, you're getting kicked the fuck out. I only give one warning."

"But wait, where's the bathroom?" I continue my act as I find my footing.

"You'll figure it out. Go." The tone in his voice leaves no room for discussion. "You won't like what happens if you don't."

I throw in a whimper like I'm some poor, defenseless frightened little girl. "Fine. Fine."

I stumble away—not in theatrics this time—and grab ahold of a stranger's elbow to steady myself.

"Hey," the girl complains.

"Sorry. Almost fell."

Pushing my way through the crowd back to the table where Ava and Spencer sit, I plop down, setting aside my halfway empty drink.

"What were you thinking would happen?" Ava laughs as I wipe my hand of the sticky alcoholic beverage. "There's no way you were going to get back there."

"I know, but I wanted to check whether or not I could see anything under the door or overhear anything."

Spencer leans forward and lowers his voice. "Celine, be careful. If this is what you guys think it is, you could get hurt or worse."

His concern is genuine and sweet but not needed.

"I can't do anything. I don't have a warrant or probable cause."

If anyone has to follow the law, it's me. I just hate that people might get hurt while I'm forced to wait for something to happen that's big enough to force an investigation..

"How's the hangover?" Ava pats my shoulder as she passes by my desk toward the end of my shift the next day.

I hide in the shelter of my arms to drown out all light and sound. Every shuffle of paper and slam of the door grates on my eardrums. Despite the ibuprofen I've taken every few hours, and the water I've guzzled, I can't seem to knock the raging headache.

It's my own fault. I don't drink often so it doesn't take much for me to overdo it.

"Ugh." My muffled moan is pitiful. "I'm never drinking again." I hold up a finger, wagging it in her face. "And if you let me, I'm disowning you."

She grabs my finger and folds it down so it's no longer pointing at her. "You would never. You love me too much. Plus, all in the name of justice, huh?"

"Shut up," I retort, and the bitch laughs at me.

"You're such a lightweight. The fact your hangover is

lingering this long is crazy." She walks away to make a copy of the document in her hand.

"Thank you for stating the obvious." I lean back against my chair and slowly blink against the harsh light of the office. Whose idea was it to put these awful fluorescent lights in buildings?

I knew I shouldn't have ordered shots, they're always too much for me, but at least it did help play into me just being a stupid drunken girl act. I didn't miss the way the guard kept eyeing me for the rest of the night. It was unsettling to say the least.

Her boots tap on the floor as she walks back over and perches on my desk. "For someone who doesn't typically drink you were downing tequila like it was juice. I'm shocked you're able to function at all today." She extends her hands, admiring her sparkly pink polish that's nearly the same shade as her hair. "I fully expected you to take a sick day."

"Honestly, if Midnight didn't wake me up with his claws in my arm I would've slept through the alarm. Little shit is rabid until he gets fed." On multiple occasions I toyed with the idea of rehoming him, but I couldn't do that to my dad. He might not remember Midnight anymore, but I knew how he begged me when he was still lucid to take care of the grumpy feline. I was also partially scared the cat would somehow find his way back, slit my throat in my sleep, and go on his merry way if I ever rehomed him.

Ava clears her throat pulling me out of my thoughts. There's a glint in her eyes that makes me narrow mine in suspicion. "Ava," I draw out the last syllable of her name. "What are you scheming?"

"I'm setting you up on a blind date." She practically bounces where she sits, and I cross my arms, eyeing the clock on the wall behind her. Almost time for me to clock out.

"Oh really? When was I going to have a say in this?"

It's sweet Ava wants to see me happy, but it's also exhausting. Sure, I'd love to find someone I click with but that takes time and effort and a dedication that I just don't have right now.

"Spencer has a cousin that's a sweetheart. I think you'd really like him." She reaches out and grabs my hands. "Just give him a shot Celine. Please? For me? I wouldn't set you up with anyone I didn't vet myself."

This isn't the first time she's tried to set me up with someone. It's not that the dates have been bad in the past, but I still hold onto the romantic notion I'll meet someone naturally. But that would also require me to leave my place and put myself out there, which I don't.

"What's his name? What's he like?" I mutter after she shows no sign of backing down. Hopefully my questions will serve to appease her.

Grabbing her phone and rolling with the small glimmer of hope I've given her, she pulls up the profile picture of an admittedly attractive man. He has inky black hair and wears wire frame glasses that make him look nerdy but hot. I've always been a sucker for a man in glasses so that gives him bonus points. He's lean with ocean blue eyes. Bold letters highlight his name at the top of his profile. Asher Brooks.

"Isn't he a cutie?" Scrolling through his feed she shows me various photos of him competitively swimming, posing at the gym showcasing his abs, and cuddling with his Siberian husky. "Loves animals, hot body, and single? Please Celine this should be the easiest yes of your life."

"You dragged me to the club and now you're trying to set me up on a blind date?" Slowly spinning in my chair, I squint my eyes at her.

"So says Miss Having-Sex-On-The-Dance-Floor last night."

She leans over and gives me a playful shove. "We never did talk about your dance partner from last night."

I gaze wistfully out the window next to my desk and remember the dance from last night in my head. Our breaths mingling, warmth pressed against my back, and his muscled arm holding me like I'm something precious.

"A shame I didn't get to see his face." Suddenly realizing Ava was watching, I perk up. "Did you see him?"

Picking at her manicured nails, she says, "Our booth was pretty far back so I couldn't see much besides the top of your heads. It looked like he had darker colored hair, but the lights made it hard to see exactly what shade."

I slump back against the chair and wish I could've found out more about him. Obviously, it wasn't meant to be, and I'm a big believer in the natural order of the universe. My dad always said everything happens for a reason.

"Pity. Well, that just means you're a free agent and eligible to go on a date with Asher." Typing away on her phone she continues to talk like I've responded. "I'm going to give him your number."

Spinning back to my computer, I sigh, and she lets out a victorious hoorah before sashaying back over to her desk. Time for me to get out of here.

"Onto more important topics than my love life, since it's time for me to clock out, I'm headed back over to Vex." Turning off my desktop I gather my things and slide my aviators onto my head.

She narrows her eyes on me. "Celine."

I give her side eye at her tone. "I want to scope the place out while there's still some daylight left. See what kind of deliveries they might be getting. Plus, it's not too far out of my way."

She frowns, eyes darkening with a level of seriousness that's rare for her. "Please be careful. If Luna's right about what's happening, then it's not safe."

I nod and she grabs my sweater sleeve as I pass by. "Don't forget to answer Asher when he texts you." She winks and I flatten my mouth but nod.

Captain Barnes waves from his desk when I walk out of the building, and I head to our small parking lot. Being downtown means not much parking, but as employees we have first dibs. I manage to park in the same spot every morning with my early arrival.

Walking toward my red Nissan Altima, I click the unlock button on the fob. The smell of cypress greets me as I slide into the driver's seat courtesy of my air freshener. I stop in my tracks when it reminds me of the delicious smell of the stranger from the night before.

Let it go.

Blowing out a breath I hit the remote start and cruise onto the street and into Chicago traffic. Vex is about fifteen minutes away from the police department so I cycle through my Guns N Roses playlist and zone out.

I'm not sure what exactly I'm hoping to find running by Vex. Once I'm home I need to focus on the Mayhem Murderer case files but something in me says I have to stop here just in case.

I park a street over from the club and get out. I scan my surroundings and make sure there's nothing out of the norm. For some reason lately I've had the odd feeling of someone watching me but I've never able to spot the ghostly culprit. It could just be the case and my paranoia getting to me.

Closing the door, I cross the street while there's a break in cars and slink my way to a spot that gives me a decent glimpse down the narrow alleyway alongside the club.

Two hours pass, longer than I intended to watch and enough for my limbs to become stiff and my feet to hurt. I don't spot a single thing of notable suspicion. I suppose it's what I get for listening to Luna. Normally I wouldn't even entertain a civilian saying something like she did, but there's something about this whole thing that doesn't sit right with me.

Slowly backing away from the wall, I keep my head down and pull up my jacket collar, speed walking as silently as possible toward my car. The sun is just starting to set.

As I reach the street, I notice a black sports car parked near mine with the engine running. At first, I write it off but when I pull away, I notice it tailing me a few minutes later.

My heart thumps erratically at the uneasy feeling I have, and I drive a little faster.

I pull into the underground garage beneath my building, making sure the car didn't manage to get inside somehow.

The uneasy feeling follows me all the way up and doesn't go away. I make sure to keep my hand by my gun as I near my apartment.

I make one last scan of the hall when I turn and run face first into a hard wall.

A wall that grabs me.

drenaline spiking, I push against the hands holding me and whip my gun out, clicking off the safety. If I'm going down, I'm taking this stalking fuck with me.

"Whoa, Rambo!" A startled baritone voice has me instantly looking up and into a pair of vividly green eyes wide with shock.

I grip my gun tighter and train it on the stranger in front of me who then holds his hands up non-threateningly.

"Who the hell are you? Why are you following me?" I ask accusatorially, my breaths coming out in short pants.

"What? Following you?" His tone makes him sound oddly innocent. "I don't even know you," he says in an even tone. "I live on this floor. I take it we're..." He eyes my gun warily and cocks his head to the side. "Neighbors."

Giving the hallway another scan for anything that appears off, I look back into his eyes and see nothing malevolent.

You're paranoid, Celine.

These cases have me feeling a little edgy. Not that the club situation is an actual case, but it's weighing on me as such.

With a sigh I click the safety back on and pocket my gun. The man slowly lowers his hands and watches me cautiously. I swipe a hand down my face and center myself before untensing my shoulders and allowing myself to relax.

"Look, I'm sorry for pulling a gun on you. It's been a weird couple of days." I give a humorless chuckle and look back up at the stranger. I burst out laughing when I see a pizza box balanced precariously on his head. I'm not sure how I missed it. I blame it on the initial shock of thinking I was being attacked.

"Nice hat."

How he managed to get a pizza box on his head *and* balance it is beyond me.

Lush pink lips quirk to the side, and he releases me to grab the box.

While he's focused on that, I allow myself to fully examine the man in front of me. My heart races for an entirely different reason as I take him in.

His red hair curls over his forehead boyishly and tapers down the back of his neck. Rogue strands fall into his eyes, and I resist the urge to swipe them away. An adorable pair of glasses rest on his nose and act like a window into his oddly vivid green eyes. He's dressed in an outfit very similar to mine, a sweater and pants in all black. A thin silver chain peeks out from the collar of his sweater.

He doesn't appear outwardly dangerous. He's fit but lanky and maybe I'm being too confident, but I think I could take him in a hand-to-hand fight if it were necessary. The hours I put into boxing should be good for something. But there's a sharpness to him, something that makes me wary.

"Desperate times call for desperate measures. The pizza had

to be protected." He pats the top of the cardboard pulling me out of my trance.

I shake my head in disgust at myself for checking him out so thoroughly.

His small smile of pure masculine pleasure tells me he didn't miss it.

"Maybe you should watch where you're going and not grab random women. Then this wouldn't happen," I chide, even though it's probably my fault I wasn't paying enough attention.

"You ran into me," he muses, and I make a move to step around him toward my door. A hot shower, my bed, and a book are calling my name after this long day.

His arm shoots out and he grips my forearm. I look down at the muscular, veined hand clutching my wrist, dwarfed under his hold, before flicking my gaze back to his.

"Do you want to eat with me?" It comes out in a rush and a red curl manages to fall fully into his eye. He flicks it back with a shake of his head while his eyes remain trained on me. There's an almost predatory gleam to them, not in a gross way but in an intense way. Something internally tells me to still under his gaze, I'm not sure what it is but my guard shoots back up.

"Not really. I thought we established we don't know each other."

His eyes widen and he takes a step back once again letting go of me. "I apologize, where are my manners. I just moved in." He points to the door of the apartment beside mine and grins like it's that simple.

"What happened to Cory?" He's lived here the entire time I have and never made any comments about leaving. On multiple occasions he tried to flirt with me and failed. The douchey, frat boy energy wasn't my type, but we remained cordial and made small talk when we'd pass by each other. "I just saw him the other day and he didn't say anything about moving."

"Is that who lived here before?" he says in a way that makes me feel like he knows more than he's letting on. He shifts the pizza box to his other hand. "The leasing office called me with a very sudden opening since I was on a waitlist for this building. Said someone had an opportunity arise and they had to jump at the opportunity." For some reason this makes him smirk. When I squint my eyes suspiciously, he shrugs his shoulders.

I must be losing my mind because I come to an irrational decision. The words seem to tumble out of my mouth before I even know what I'm saying. It's almost like I'm being influenced by a feeling out of my control. For some reason I'm drawn to the stranger. I have my gun on me and people would notice if I went missing, so fuck it. "You know what, I've had a shitty day and pizza sounds great, so why not?" He pumps a fist in the air which makes me laugh. "Lead the way, Mister?" I drag out the last word, so he knows I'm searching to fill in the blank.

"I'm Zavier. But my friends call me Zav."

"Hi, Zavier." I purposely draw a line with the use of his full name. "I'm Celine." I offer up my hand and he engulfs it with his own. There's a spark of something when our skin touches, but it could just be my half-hungover and startled state imagining things.

Holding my hand for longer than necessary, he finally lets go. "Come on in." His keys jingle and I follow through the open door.

I've never been inside Cory's apartment when he lived here so I don't know what to expect. Seeing as we live in a generic rental building, I'd assumed the rooms were similar but his is much bigger than mine. The living room holds a large black couch and a humongous flat screen TV is mounted on the wall. There's not much decor besides some movie posters and sports memorabilia, particularly hockey based, placed around the room.

"Do you like hockey?" I ask.

"Not particularly." He sets the box on the counter.

Interesting.

"When did you move in?" My eyes continue to scan the space. I don't recall noticing any signs of anyone moving in, but I have been out of it lately. Sliding my hands in my back pockets. I graze the pocketknife I keep there just in case. My dad taught me growing up that there's no such thing as too paranoid.

"Yesterday," Zavier calls from the bedroom he disappeared into. "I planned to introduce myself then, but you didn't seem to be home. I went door to door distributing the lemon pound cake I made for all my new neighbors."

He made lemon pound cake?

I try to imagine the man before me with an apron tied around his waist baking in the kitchen that's off to the side. I hate to admit the visual of it is appealing.

There are a few boxes stacked by the kitchen bar just waiting to be unpacked.

"I was out with friends." Making myself comfortable I sit on a stool at the counter. "You actually made the lemon loaf? From scratch?" I need him to clarify so I can determine if my visual is correct or not.

He swaggers back in the room, and I have to make a conscious effort to keep my mouth shut when I see him pull his sweater off. His t-shirt rides up revealing smooth alabaster skin. Divots of muscle showcase his most likely frequent gym visits.

My core clenches.

Slow down. Let's not go there. Ava's right, you really do need to have sex, but sex with your neighbor is a big no-no. If it ends terribly you'll inevitably run into him from time to time.

"I'm full of surprises. Pizza?" Shiny white teeth reveal a

perfect smile as he walks toward the box. I nod and try to get my head out of the gutter.

"I hope pepperoni is okay." Grabbing paper plates out of a cabinet he divvies out two respective slices which I happily take. His large frame looks hilarious as he sits himself on the small stool beside me. Why he'd buy such tiny stools I'm not sure.

"Pepperoni is my favorite. Now if you said something like ham and pineapple then I'd have to kill you." I pick up the greasy piece and dive in. It's the best kind of pizza with fresh, stringy cheese and piping hot pepperoni. He laughs and the sound does something funny to my chest.

"Resorting to murder? I like it." The roguish grin he sports holds a mischievous gleam.

Companionable silence descends, and I find myself enjoying sitting here with Zavier, which is odd given my previous unease, but there's an aura around him that seems to silence my previous worries. "Where did you move from?" I find myself wanting to know whatever I can about this new neighbor.

He's already on his second piece and a bit of sauce clings to his lip. Sensing my stare his tongue flicks out to pull it into his mouth. "I'm kind of a nomad. Been here. Been there." Wiping grease off his fingers onto a napkin he stuffs his face with the last of his slice. "I find staying in one place rather boring. You?"

"I'm a Chicagoan, born and raised. I used to dream about traveling..." His head cocks to the side when I trail off and patiently waits for me to continue. "...But those dreams died when I took this job and assumed partial care of my dad. He has severe dementia, and my mom is...well, I don't actually know where she is. I have a fear of jetting off somewhere and something happening to him. Even though he's in good hands at the assisted living facility you can't help but fear the worst."

Swirling my paper plate on the counter I avoid eye contact. I'm not sure why I just unloaded all of that on him. I don't typically tell people about my dad, let alone someone who's practically a stranger. I find myself rubbing my lips, wishing there was some way to stuff my word vomit back inside.

A strong hand folds over mine, pulling my fingers away from my mouth and I look up. The sympathy is his gaze holds me hostage and I couldn't look away even if I wanted to.

"It sounds like you've done more than enough. You can't hold yourself back for the sake of others, Celine." A seriousness settles over our conversation and I'm in awe I'm opening up this way. Something about him invites me in and encourages me to say all the things that weigh heavily on my mind.

Clearing my throat, I gather our empty plates and crumpled up napkins. A stainless-steel trash can sits next to the fridge and I usher our garbage into it. Wiping my hands on my jeans I turn back to Zavier.

"Well, it was nice to meet you." I force a smile and slowly make my way toward the front door. My shoes remained on the whole visit, so it makes for an easy escape. "Thank you very much for the pizza and I guess I'll see you around?" Even though I say it, I secretly hope I don't see him too much. I fear my intrigue of Zavier could become dangerous to my productivity and I can't have an attachment like this distracting me.

Zavier walks toward me with the stealth of a jaguar and I gulp. The air feels too thick, and I back up into the entryway. He prowls closer and closer until I'm backed up against the door. He doesn't hold me against it but instead leaves a small breadth of space. I can break away if I want to, but I'm frozen in place.

"You definitely will." Soft lips brush the shell of my ear. "It was nice to finally meet you, Celine." His intensity is electric, and I fear if I don't leave something might happen.

"Goodnight," I squeak, extracting my body out from underneath him. As quickly as humanly possible I open the door and slip out not risking a glance behind me knowing he'll still be watching.

"You should've seen her. She was spectacular. I thought dancing with her had me dying all over again and going to heaven," I gush, remembering Celine's sweet body pressed against mine. "Although," I muse, tapping my lip. "If I'm being honest with myself, if there is a God, then I don't think I'd be let through the pearly gates. You know, for all the murdering and stuff ... and the indecent way I think about Celine."

Silence.

"You know what I mean?" I prompt, knocking my hand against his arm.

Silence.

"Are you listening?"

More silence.

"Hey!" I shout in annoyance. How can my one and only friend *not* want to hear about my love life? Rude.

"What!"

"You never fucking listen to me." I throw my hands up in exasperation.

"What are we talking about?" He turns his "good" ear in my direction, but frankly I don't see where it's any better than the other one.

"Celine, you old coot!" I shout at the old man sitting across from me at the table. "The love of my immortal life," I add under my breath.

My current chess partner is seventy percent deaf and almost completely blind. I met Tom sixty years ago. We hit it off when I would visit his family-owned bar. They ran into trouble with a gang who was bleeding them dry financially, and I took care of the problem.

We built a natural camaraderie after that, and I always made sure to stop and see him when I was in town. Thankfully, he didn't notice my ageless appearance due to his impairments. I have to admit it's nice having something constant and unchanged in a world that does nothing but that. Being a vampire is both a blessing and a curse with the passage of time. I've come to accept the deaths of my family and friends, but every once in a while, I find a soul I know I will mourn when their time comes.

Tom is definitely one of those rare gems. I've never gotten the chance to "grow old" with someone. Only him.

"Who are you calling an old coot, Zac?" He fiddles with his hearing aids. "We're the same age!" he yells at me from beneath his large mustache. I always tease him he looks like the prospector from *Toy Story* and beg him to dress up as the character for Halloween. I could be Bullseye. Giddy up.

"Take your turn. You know I'm going to whoop your ass just like I do every time." I push my glasses up my nose and fold my arms against my chest. I don't bother correcting him on my name anymore. He's insisted from day one that Zav is a dumb name and resorted to calling me Zac despite my annoyance.

Tom grumbles and leans up close to the board to move his queen, setting it in direct sights of my king.

"Check." I smirk victoriously.

"You're a fucking cheater." Tom knocks the pieces off the board, and I roll my eyes.

And he says *I'm* the dramatic one.

"And you're a sore loser." Kicking my feet up onto the table and crossing my ankles I survey the bar, our game now over. Tom's grandkids run it since he's too old and it's been converted into a restaurant as well. They seem like nice kids, but I avoid them to limit questions on my unchanged good looks.

Patrons murmur and piddle about the room like scavenging little bugs. A small human child runs by and nearly bumps into my shoulder. I recoil in disgust, wiping the invisible germs off my shirt. Children are one of my least favorite things with their whining, screaming, and messiness but it can usually be blamed on shitty parenting. My one exception for a crotch goblin is if Celine wants children. I'll give her as many as she desires. I look forward to practicing the baby making.

Wait.

Babies.

Celine.

I need to write that down.

Pulling my trusty notebook and pen out of my pocket I lick my finger and flip it open to a new page. Quickly scribbling, **Breed Celine**, under a new list titled *Goals in my long life with Celine.*

Besides, even though vampires *can* have children, it's rare which means if she wants them, we're going to be doing a whole lot of practicing. I rub my hands together in excited glee.

"You have that crazy look in your eye, Zac." Tom shakes a rook at me, and I snatch it out of his hand.

"I don't know what you're talking about and how would you know? You can't even see." I tease him but we both have a small smile on our faces.

Putting my notebook back in my pocket I set the chess board again, collecting runaway pieces from the floor. It had been a gift from me to Tom a few Christmases ago and was handcrafted by an artisan in France.

"That's what you'd like to think. My body may be failing me, but my mind is still fresh as a daisy. If you're not talking, I know you're scheming." He goes to stand up, arms shaking and hands gripping the tabletop tightly. I zip over to help him, and he immediately scoffs.

"Off me. My eyes and ears might be useless, but my legs work just fine." Shaking off my grip he walks away without another word. "Still don't know how you move so fast at our age," he gripes. "It's damn annoying."

"Bye, Tom," I shout as I stride out of the bar.

I can't help but shake my head at the grunt he responds with. One of these days my greeting will be replied to with silence, and I savor the small piece of humanity that remains in me at the sting of pain at how hard it'll be when he's gone.

Standing under the awning of the restaurant I watch as rain pounds onto the concrete. My cream-colored sweater darkens from the onslaught of droplets, pooling on the fabric when I stick an arm out. Sucking the water off my lip I head for my car parked around back. Lightly jogging over to the sleek black sports car, I tuck my large frame in and buckle up. Indestructible or not I am nothing if not an outstanding citizen.

I pull out my notebook before I drive away and scribble down;

Make sure Celine always wears a seatbelt. Safety is hot.

I already know the more time that passes the harder it'll be to rein myself in when it comes to my growing desire for her. The allure of a mate is impossible to resist long-term and I'm tired of denying to myself that she's not mine. I was scared at first to acknowledge it, to give truth to what I knew was staring me in the face, because I've been alone for so long and the small chance I was wrong held me back. It would've been devastating to think I'd finally found my mate after all these years only to realize I'm wrong.

But I'm not wrong.

Celine is mine.

I can't help but want to get to know her, though. Slowly. Properly. She's human and deserves to be courted. I want to do things *right* with her. The way she'd expect.

Except I'm me, and if I'm honest with myself I can never do things the 'normal' way.

I suppose it stems from living hundreds of years, but it's much more fun to do things out of the box. It keeps life interesting.

My wipers furiously swipe rain from the windshield as I bob and weave through traffic. The irregular weather pattern has me tilting my head in question. It's a known fact in the supernatural community that heavy and consistent rainfall is indicative of a large gathering of creatures in one area. We tend to keep to our own species and areas across the world. Bustling, populated cities are vampire territory, wooded seclusion is a werewolf haven, the sirens stick to the beaches, dragons in mountain ranges, and so on. The heavy rainfall could either mean multiple species crossing paths in a singular location or an influx of one. I'll have to keep my eyes and ears open for things going awry. Celine is my top priority, and I can't have trivial species drama interfering or putting her at risk.

One day in the near future I'll have to tell Celine what I am.

There's no way in hell I'm existing without her now that I have her. She might be human now, but I can change her one day. When she's ready.

And if she's never ready?

I shove that nagging thought away—the fear that's taken up residence in the space where my heart used to be. She'll turn. She has to. There's no way I'll survive my pathetic existence by finding my mate only to lose her to something as silly as aging.

But I know I have to be careful. Not only is she human, but a detective, and that means her skepticism is through the roof. I can tell after last night her walls are built high. I'd take a sledgehammer to them if I could, but I'll approach her with the care I know she needs.

I stop at a red light and run a hand through my unruly waves.

Rolling up to the parking garage of the apartment building I park in my spot. I know it's my spot because I've labeled it with a sign that says, "Zav's fucking spot so don't park here. Violators will be eaten." I included a smiley face with glasses and subtle fangs only I'd notice for a finishing touch.

I take the elevator up, inhaling Celine's scent that permeates the floor the second the elevator is open. I let it guide me to her door. Without looking around, and knowing by my vampire senses there's nobody else in the hallway, I let myself into Celine's apartment. Pocketing the universal key I stole from the front desk, I fall to my knees at the overwhelming scent of *her*.

It's both too much and not enough.

My mate.

I've heard how intense the scent of a mate can be, but I never grasped how it truly brings you to your knees. It's going to take a monumental effort to not give in to my baser needs and claim her before she's ready.

Somehow finding the strength to stand I slowly take in all the little details that make her apartment her. Fake candles with LED fires gently swaying to the invisible breeze are scattered throughout the space. Her tan-colored couch against the wall in the living room is covered in throw pillows and fuzzy blankets. It makes me irrationally angry these inanimate objects get to cover Celine's body and provide the warmth and comfort I'm desperate to give her. A singular framed photo of flowers hangs above the seating area, a modest TV across from the set-up. Books are piled up on the table. Slinking over I run my fingers across the fabrics splayed across the couch and bring them to my nose.

Delectable.

Mine.

My fangs drop of their own accord, and I run my tongue across them. I'm due for a blood bag soon at the rate Celine is affecting me. At my age I only need to feed every few weeks and only drink a certain caliber of bagged blood. I'd never stoop to indulging myself on the filthy liquid that runs through my kills' veins, that was equitable to sewer water. I shiver in displeasure just thinking about it and drop onto the couch with a dopey smile when a pillow falls right on my face, surrounding me with her unique scent that reminds me of blackberries.

A soft swat on my arm hanging off the couch gives me pause since I know it's not said pillow. Lowering the pillow, I squint one eye open. There's a mass of black shadow with two yellow eyes staring at me from beside the couch. A small tail swishes inquisitively behind the floofy black cat, and I turn on my side to better look at it. We stare at each other in a silent battle of dominance before the cat jumps up onto my stomach and starts kneading my chest.

"Who might you be?" I stroke the kitty's head, and it leans into my touch.

A metal jingle draws my attention, and I finger the small collar hanging around his neck.

"Midnight, huh?" I scratch under his chin which makes him purr like a motorboat. Smiling I place the cat around my neck like a scarf to continue my tour of Celine's apartment. "I would've thought Celine would've given you a more unique name than that. Like Bob. Or Hashbrown. Maybe Burnt Marsh-mallow." He seems to hum in pleasure at that name. "You like that one, do you?"

Knowing she's at work, I explore her space to see what she likes. The way she darted out of my apartment and back over told me how much she valued this place and sought it out when she was uncomfortable.

I stroll into her bedroom and slowly catalogue everything I see. A neatly organized closet with color-coded clothing, mostly black, draw my attention first. My footfalls are soundless as I walk over and place myself in the middle of the rack, sliding her clothing in half so I can stand comfortably. Midnight continues to purr, not bothered by my actions. Standing sentinel in the clothes for an indeterminate amount of time I spy a pile of clothes thrown off to the side on a chair. I know they're clean since the nefarious laundry detergent covers her natural scent.

I'll go ahead and fold them for her.

Midnight hops off my shoulders when I tilt my back toward the bed and settles himself on top of her pillow. Snatching up the pile of clothes I deposit them on the end of the bed and get to folding. A scrap of lacy black peeks out from under her bed and I grab it.

Celine's underwear.

Was this what she was wearing under her skimpy dress when we danced at the club? My nostrils flare as I inhale deeply and catch a vanilla undertone to her berry scent.

Did dancing with me turn her on? Her scent becomes more complex when she's aroused.

My lips curve at the thought that I affect her like she does me. I pocket the scrap of lace and continue to fold her shirts, pants, and socks. Once I'm done, I set the finished folded clothes on the end of her bed. My eyes take in her room as I spin on my heel and look for anything else I can do to help. Dust glints on the mirror in the bathroom light when I flip the switch, so I find the glass cleaner and some paper towels before I get to work wiping it free. This turns into using her cordless vacuum to sweep the place up, organizing her fridge and freezer contents, and making sure her pillows are arranged perfectly. Truth be told her apartment isn't a mess, but it looks much better now.

Hands on my hips I admire my hard work and notice the black cat eyeballing me from his perch on the couch now.

"What? You weren't going to do any cleaning?" The bombastic side eye continues, and I scoff at him.

"I know what'll win your heart." Foil crinkles as I locate a treat bag tucked into the back corner of the kitchen counter and shake it. An almost feral meow sounds followed by scampering paws on the hardwood floor.

"That's what I thought." Tiny claws prick my jeans as Midnight attempts to climb my leg in desperate need of the treats. Still not sure how I feel about the name. I wonder if Celine will let me rename him.

"Simple creatures, aren't we?" I toss a few of the tiny fish shaped treats on the ground and he runs after them. "Blind-sided by temptation." Celine pops in my head and I lean against the counter. "I know the feeling."

Celine doesn't have much on her fridge, just a couple magnets with info for local food places. A generic calendar she probably got free somewhere hangs on the side held up by a magnet that's also a photo. I trace her face in it and see the heartbreak that coincides with her fake smile. An older man sits next to her with a lost look in his eyes, the resemblance between the two uncanny.

A circled date on the calendar catches my attention and I lean closer to see on tomorrow's date she's written *Double date at Strike Lanes.*

Double date? Oh fuck no.

"Midnight, how could you let this happen!" If my hair could catch fire like the color it resembles, it surely would with the rage I feel in this moment. The cat, of course, ignores me curled up on the couch, not sharing the same disgust I do. He gives me a long look and then proceeds to lick his paws.

My girl on a date with another man? Unthinkable.

I need to take this situation into my own hands. My timetable for showing Celine how perfect we are together just moved up.

10

Collapsing onto the couch with a loud sigh, I rub my aching eyes. Midnight, who had been hiding behind a pillow, lets out a disgruntled harumph and disappears into my bedroom.

"Thanks for the warm welcome," I mutter, exasperated by the grumpy cat.

My original plan to head to the gym for a boxing session is dashed with the absolute exhaustion I feel.

A thick stack of manila folders sits next to me, and I rifle through them. Report after report of past Mayhem cases complete the stack. They're filled with gory photos and testimonies, not that anyone has actually seen the killer yet. I've spent countless hours going through them trying to glean any insight that might help us catch them but nothing has stood out.

The temptation to further stakeout Vex has been nagging at me. I have to let this club thing go, though. It's not the case I'm supposed to be working on. It's not even a case at all. Just a stupid hunch I can't seem to let go of because the feeling in my stomach won't allow me to.

I need to refocus and put my nose to the grindstone when it comes to the Mayhem cases.

First, though, I need to relax a little.

"I think it's time for a bath, a snack, and my book," I say to nobody in particular, because God knows my cat is ignoring me, and my voice echoes in the empty space.

The decor in my apartment is a slow and everchanging process. I wanted the area to be cozy and ambient with warm lighting but not sparse, with curated knickknacks that are cute but have a purpose. I hate when houses feel clinical and unlived in. I try to keep it as clean as possible especially with the constant cat hair piling up, but my job doesn't always allow for it.

With a groan, I heave my tired body up from the couch and snag a bag of gummy bears off the counter before heading for my room. I let my hair out of its usual ponytail as I do and sigh at the pressure relief. I massage the back of my neck before realizing something is off.

I pause in my tracks.

Where's the pile of clean laundry I left on the chair earlier?

I remember thinking to myself I should fold them before I left this morning, otherwise the job would be waiting for me now, but said clothes are folded perfectly and sit on the end of the bed just waiting to be put away.

My brow wrinkles as I wrack my brain for when I could've folded them.

Maybe after I had breakfast this morning?

No, it can't be that, because I got distracted when Ava called me.

"I must be losing my mind." Midnight gives an unhelpful

sigh; life is hard for a full-time freeloader like him. "I must have done it and just don't remember. Right?" I ask the slow blinking cat.

It's the only logical explanation. No one breaks into an apartment to fold clothes.

Swiping my current read from the side table, I head into the bathroom.

The metal knob squeaks when it turns, and I pour in some vanilla scented salts while it fills. A few tendrils of hair escape the high bun I throw it in after stripping off my clothes. Steam begins to fill the bathroom, and I settle into the water with a tray over top the tub with my book and snack once it's at the perfect height and temperature.

Despite the relaxing nature of the bubble bath, I can't help but think of the, no doubt, doomed double date tomorrow. My stomach begins to sour, and I soon find myself getting out of the bath. Freaking Ava and her need to get me into a relationship is ruining one of my favorite things. Drying off, I tug on my pajamas and climb into bed. I only read a few more pages of my book before my eyes are too heavy to continue and I drift off to sleep with the book still half open on my bed.

"You're a detective?" Asher's honey smooth voice fills the car as we drive away from my apartment to meet up with Ava and Spencer.

"I am. I recently got promoted." I try to sound enthused but fail miserably. I'm not in the mood to go on a date and it's showing, which isn't fair to Asher. He was conned into this as much as I was, I'm sure, but I should at least give the date a fair shot.

I feel the weight of Asher's eyes but can't find it in myself to look at him. Suddenly the dripping of rain on the window is the most fascinating thing I've ever seen.

"Look, I know Ava kind of forced this date on you, but you seem like a cool girl, and I'd love to give this an actual go." The genuine tone in his voice has me glancing over to see the sincerity shining in his brown eyes. I can't help but think about how dull they look in comparison to a certain pair of emerald eyes I've seen recently.

I deflate and my tough girl act crumbles. "You're right. I'm sorry." Wringing my hands uncomfortably in my lap I continue. "It's hard for me to say no to Ava when she sets me up on dates. I think I've gotten to the point where I shut down before the date even starts. I promise to be more engaged."

"Let's just have fun, okay? We'll bowl and chat and get to know each other. No pressure. At the end of the night if there's no chemistry, we go our separate ways with no hard feelings. Sound fair?" When he puts it that way how can I argue.

My high ponytail slips over my shoulder as I nod, and the relief is evident in his face.

"I've got mad bowling skills so prepare to be impressed." He breaks the awkward air with his declaration, and I huff out a laugh.

I arch a brow in challenge. "Oh yeah? My aim is spot on with my firearm training, so we'll see about that." Just then his playlist changes to a new song. "You're playing Motley Crüe, which I can fully appreciate."

We both smile and I relax for the first time since I got in the car.

We pull up to the bowling alley and I spy Spencer's white car idling next to an empty spot which Asher promptly fills.

"You're here!" Ava wraps her arms around me in a bone crushing hug when I step out of the car. Asher tries to sprint over and open the door for me but I'm not that type of girl. He does hand me an umbrella though to protect against the rain since I foolishly didn't bring my own. What the hell is with this weather lately?

"Of course I'm here. You forced me," I whisper in her ear, and she laughs.

"Well, someone has to. You're too much of a hermit. You know what they say, the best duos are made up of the grumpy friend and the sunshine one."

I let out a humorless laugh. "Watch who you're calling grumpy."

She gives me a playful shove, and we dissolve into giggles.

Out of my peripheral I see Asher and Spencer do the typical guy back slap greeting. Once they separate Ava skips over to her boyfriend. Linking arms with Spencer, she finger gun points at the front door and starts forward with a triumphant expression. I shake my head at her adorable dorkiness. Asher and I walk beside each other and stop just under the awning so I can shake off the umbrella. Water droplets spray everywhere as I dry it the best I can and wrap it up before we enter the building behind them. I already have a black cat and can't be bringing an open umbrella inside for even worse luck.

The bowling alley is a super cute spot outside of the city. The quirky 80's carpet with various shapes in neon colors fill me with a sense of nostalgia even though I've never been here before. A sign on the wall spouts cosmic bowling every Wednesday and I can see the blacklights hanging from the ceiling. It seems to be a family-owned business and employed by mostly teenagers.

"Let's grab our shoes." Asher takes charge and heads over to the counter.

I take a moment to appraise his form. I can't lie to myself, the man is insanely good looking. A football player in his past life he still has the stocky, muscled frame. A small slit out of his eyebrow due to a past injury gives him an edgy vibe but once he opens his mouth you can tell he's a sweetheart. He's wearing a red and black plaid flannel on top of a black shirt with light jeans which makes him resemble a lumberjack more than anything.

"What size shoes do you need?" A strangely familiar voice asks Asher, and I tilt my head in question.

Why do I know that voice?

Stepping around Ava and over to the counter my eyes widen in shock.

"Zavier?" The incredulity is obvious in my voice. "You work here?"

Low and behold my mysterious new neighbor stands behind the counter donning a blue striped Strike Lanes uniform. We never did discuss what he did for work, but I didn't peg him as this, not that there's anything wrong with it.

"The one and only." His thin silver chain catches the light when he leans over to grab Asher's shoes. "I pick up odd jobs around town to keep me busy. Shoe size?" He nods toward the rack behind him.

"Tens, ple—" I'm promptly cut off and shock floods my features when he's already handing me a pair of size ten shoes.

What the hell? How did he know?

I reluctantly accept the pair when he hands them to me. Our fingers brush and a familiar zap of energy passes between us. Our eyes meet and I'm held captive by the pure depth of emotion in his green eyes. In a blink it's gone, leaving me questioning if it was ever there and Ava and Spencer nudge their way to the counter.

"Eights, please." She eyes me with a questioning gaze, and I purposely ignore her, striding over to the lane Zavier assigned us where Asher already waits, typing all our names into the system.

By the time I reach him, he's taking off his shoes when I sit down and begin to untie my own sneakers. I love my trusty boots but decided it was easiest to go casual since we'd be swapping out our shoes for the ugly clown clompers.

"These always feel so clunky, don't they?" Asher's long legs stick out, heels clicking together like we're in The Wizard of Oz, reading my thoughts.

There truly is no place like home, and I'd love to be there right about now.

I hate that I'm like this, and even though Ava's meddling can be tiresome, I understand where she's coming from. I'm never going to meet someone if I don't get out. It's not like my knight in shining armor is just going to burst through my door and cuddle up on the couch with me and that be that.

Looping the shoelaces through and tying tightly I stick my own legs out. "They really do. Doesn't mean I won't kick your ass though." I give him a playful squeeze on his arm, trying to look like I'm more into this than I really am.

Asher laughs and stands, holding out one of his large hands for me to take. My hand slides across his roughened palm after a moment of hesitation and he pulls me up before awkwardly letting go. We walk over to the rack to pick out our respective balls. I'm sure there's a rhyme and reason to what ball you're supposed to pick but I just go with what feels right and doesn't seem like it'll rip my arm out of its socket when I throw. Asher on the other hand looks like he's taking it very seriously, even holding the ball up to his face to closely examine the surface. Happy with our selections we join the table again where Ava and Spencer have already picked out theirs.

"Celine, you're up first." Spencer points to the screen and I see my name at number one on the list.

Walking up to the lane I hold my red ball to my face and let out a breath in an effort to focus. Striding forward I wind back and let the ball go as my arm comes forward. It careens down the wood and knocks all ten pins down in one go. I let out a whoop and throw my hands up in the air.

"Damn girl!" Ava yells from her seat and I high five her when she passes by to take her turn. "You're going to wipe the floor with these fools."

Asher claps in disbelief. "Bringing the heat. I see how it is."

"Did I or did I not say I was going to kick your ass?" A triumphant grin graces my face, and I fling my hair to the side dramatically to bring home my point.

I can't help it that I have a competitive streak a mile long. I like to win. Who doesn't?

We all clap for Ava when she gets a spare. Spencer gives her a blush inducing kiss, and Asher heads over to the lane for his turn. He picks up his ball and wags a finger at me like he knows he's already got it in the bag.

Shaking my head and crossing my arms over my chest, I sense him before I hear him. An ominous yet comforting presence over my shoulder. It's odd how much he affects me when I barely know him.

Zavier.

"Where'd you learn to bowl like that?" His crimson head of hair appears in my peripheral as he stands next to my chair.

"Ava and I have gone a few times to another bowling alley." Glancing quickly at him I get my fill before watching Asher take his turn. He's who I should be paying attention to since we're on a date. I shouldn't be staring at my neighbor ... my very attractive neighbor.

Right as Asher winds up, Zavier lets out an obnoxious sneeze that has us all jumping in surprise, Asher included, whose ball goes right into the gutter. He turns and glares at

Zavier who suspiciously wipes non-existent snot from his nose and apologizes.

"I'm so sorry. That really came out of nowhere. The dust." He waves a hand nonchalantly in the air. "Should I turn on the bumpers?" Like the cat that ate the canary, he smirks to himself and walks back to the front counter to help customers without waiting for a response.

"What a weirdo," Asher mutters and sits down like a petulant child when his second attempt results in only three being knocked down.

"He just had to sneeze," I defend, even though that was the most obvious fake sneeze ever.

"Better luck next time." Spencer claps his back.

Time passes by quickly and we play until we have two frames left. I'm absolutely crushing it with a perfect game so far. Besides his initial miss due to Zavier's shenanigans, Asher is close behind with mostly strikes and a couple spares. Ava is third and poor Spencer falls in last place with his god-awful bowling skills. He blames sore muscles from working out and Ava placates him but rolls her eyes with mirth behind his back.

Asher seems like a super nice guy and I'm having fun but something's missing. I'm sure we'd get along as friends, but the chemistry is lackluster. Throughout the night, I continue to feel Zavier's eyes on me and have to make a conscious effort to hold back the shiver my body wants to let out. I don't risk looking back since I don't know what I'd be tempted to do.

Asher pulls me from my thoughts when he motions toward the restrooms, and I nod. He walks away and Ava slides over to my side of the chairs, taking his recently vacated one.

"How's it going with you lovebirds?" Her shoulder knocks into mine.

"Ava. I just met the man."

"It seems like you're getting along though!" she defends

herself. "Whenever I've run into Asher at Spencer's family functions he's been so sweet. Plus, if you end up getting married and
I'm married to Spencer we'll be like distant sister wives. Kind of.
Really keep it in the family," Ava laughs as she tries to make
sense of her own joke.

I take a sip of the pop I bought halfway through the game
and try not to laugh at her confused face. A weird, distant
growling noise tickles my ear but looking around I don't see
anything out of the ordinary. Must be the lane machinery.

Setting my cup down I finally respond. "He's super easy to
get along with but I don't know if the spark is there, you know?"
She nods in silence and doesn't push the issue any further, but
there's no mistaking the flash of sadness in her eyes.

I wish she understood that I'm *okay*. Sure, I'd love to find a
man I enjoy spending time with but I'm content on my own. It's
going to take someone special for me to want to be around
them like how Ava is with Spencer.

I almost groan at how good it feels to stretch when I stand
and reach my arms up. Taking in the room I see the bowling
alley is almost completely cleared out since the facility closes
soon. A few stragglers remain finishing their games like us, but
it's gotten much quieter. I risk a glance toward the counter but
am slightly disappointed to see Zavier isn't there. Sitting back
down on the hard blue chair I settle in to wait for Asher when
it's like I manifest the man I was hoping to see.

A long, elegant finger taps my shoulder, and I turn to see
Zavier with a hand extended and a piece of paper with a
message written on it. Confusion must show on my features,
but I accept the scrap of paper any way.

"Saw your friend doing the boot scoot and he asked me to
deliver this message. I won't charge a delivery fee." Tipping his
head toward the note with subtle amusement in his eyes I
quickly read it.

In scrawling handwriting it says;

So sorry for the abrupt departure but I have a family emergency I have to attend to. I had a great time tonight! -Asher

"He left?" Ava asks incredulously, peeking over my shoulder to read.

"Looks that way." Zavier shrugs his broad shoulders and walks away.

"Well, that's shitty. I guess a family emergency is something you can't mess around with but he picked you up," she sighs, and I swear she's more upset than me if the dejected tilt of her shoulders is anything to go by. "Let's just leave, we were almost done anyways. Spence and I can drop you off at your apartment."

We start to gather our things and put our less clownish shoes back on. Slinging my purse over my shoulder we head toward the front door and drop our bowling shoes on the counter. Just as we're about to make it out we're stopped by a familiar figure.

"I'd be happy to take Celine home. I'm clocked out and we're actually going to the same place." Zavier's back in regular attire and holds car keys in his hand. I'm mesmerized when he swings them around with ease before catching them out of the air.

"Wait, you two know each other?" Spencer points between us and I see Ava perk up at the statement. She clocked something was going on from the start at the counter.

Zavier's pressing gaze forces me to answer when he doesn't. "We live close to each other actually. He just moved in." I wince knowing Ava's going to have a field day with the information.

"Are you now?" Her blond brows raise. "What a small world." Eyes darting back and forth between the two of us I avoid eye contact but don't miss her grin.

"Do you feel comfortable going home with him?" I don't

miss the wrinkle in Zavier's brow when Spencer asks. "Neighbors or not, that doesn't mean you know him well."

I swear I see a flash of something like appreciation in Zavier's eyes at Spencer's concern for my safety.

By how dejected Ava seems to be feeling at another of my failed dates, I don't know if I can sit in a car with her right now. I'd also hate to make them go out of their way to drop me off at home.

"Thanks for the concern, Spencer, but I'll be fine. Zavier's harmless." Shifting over to stand by the man in question, I look up at him. Craning my neck slightly to take in his full form, I find he's already watching me. "Plus, I am an officer and between that and my boxing sessions, my self-defense skills aren't lacking." Zavier smiles at my comment. "So there will be no funny business."

Ava clears her throat and breaks the spell. "Okay, well, I'll see you tomorrow, Celine. Text me when you make it home." I nod in understanding, and she gives Zavier a scolding look. "Take care of her."

"You never have to worry about that," he responds with a slight growl in his tone.

They continue their stare down until she must see something that sets herself at ease. Spencer wraps an arm around her shoulders and pulls her outside with a last small wave.

Zavier holds the door open for me and winks. "Shall we?"

11

Celine touched me.
Celine.
Touched.

Me.

"Zavier? Hello?" Her delicate hand waves in front of my face and cars honk behind us. I startle and step on the gas. Catching me off guard is no easy task and yet Celine does it effortlessly.

My brain short circuited when she brushed an eyelash off my cheek a second ago. It's the first time our bare skin has touched, and I want to cement the memory so five-hundred years from now I still know how it feels.

"Are you okay?" she presses. "I shouldn't have touched you without your permission," she apologizes.

"No, no, it's not that." I swallow down my desperation to say *yes, please, touch me some more. Touch me everywhere. Touch me any time you want.* "Just lost in my thoughts," I finish with instead.

"Thanks for driving me home. I would've hated to make Ava and Spencer go the opposite way of their apartment just for me."

My steering wheel squeaks in alarm when I squeeze too hard in an attempt to calm myself down. Her words are going in one ear and out the other as I focus on deep breathing just like the yoga instructor in the class I popped into a few months ago told me to do.

My teeth grind together, and I bite down to cover my fangs that have popped out involuntarily.

No. *No.*

Now is not an appropriate time for a fangboner!

I can't seem to control them around her and that's going to quickly become an issue because I fully plan on spending more time with her.

"Mhm." The garbled response is uncivilized at best, but it's all I can do.

Celine leans forward to look at me when she finally realizes something's wrong. I try to lean away and let the collar of my coat hide my face.

Go away! I will the pesky canines to retract, but so far they're not going anywhere.

"Are you okay?" Her sweet voice holds so much concern, and I jerk when she lays her palm on my thigh.

I'm already dealing with a fangboner. The last thing I need is an actual one too.

"Just started to feel a little weird." I mumble around my fangs, willing them to recede.

Stupid fuckers never listen.

"Do I need to drive? Do you want to stop?" The concern in her voice amplifies and I curse myself for worrying her.

Wait. She's worried about me?

If I could blush, I most certainly would be. My sweet girl is worried about me, when all that's wrong is me wanting to take her to pound town and mark her as mine.

"No, I'm fine." I try to reassure her. "We're close to the apartment."

She makes a noncommittal noise, and I know she doesn't believe me but keeps quiet otherwise.

The remainder of the drive is spent in silence, and I hate it. I haven't had much one-on-one time with her, and I want to ask her so many questions. What's her favorite color? What makes her laugh? What makes her heart race? How can I make her smile? I look forward to finding the answers out to everything and more when the time is right.

Rolling into the parking garage, I pull up to the nearest elevator and stop the car.

"I'm going to drop you here."

Confusion wrinkles her brow when she turns to me. "Is your spot far away or something?"

"Yeah," I choke out, and will her to head upstairs.

As much as it pains me to leave her, my episode has caused me to burn through the remaining donor blood in my system. Any that remains has rushed straight to my dick and I need to visit my supplier stat, or I won't be able to hold myself back.

I'd never hurt Celine but a vampire in bloodlust, even a more mature one like me, is bad news. Mix in the fact Celine is my mate and I'll be trying to claim her before she's ready for it, which I refuse to do. Mates are a temptation like no other and it's rumored their blood is a rush of adrenaline.

"I'd rather you get out here, so I know you're safe in the elevator. I ... have an errand I need to run," I add when she hasn't made any progress on getting out of my car.

"An errand? This late?"

"I need to pick up something from a friend."

"Oh, okay." She looks a bit disappointed. *Does she want to spend more time together?* Annoyingly for me, it doesn't matter if she does, I need blood. Tightening her purse strap on her shoulder she opens the car door and steps out. "Thank you again." She dips her head in and slides out, heading for the elevator.

I don't dare pull away until I know she's safely inside. Blowing out a breath, a wheeze of pain escapes and I dig out my phone. Speed dialing my contact she picks up in one ring.

"What do you need?" Her voice is young sounding. A stark contrast to her age.

"Five pints. Stat."

"Rough night, huh?" The teasing lilt in her voice is not appreciated.

"Shut up. I'll be there as soon as I can. Just have it ready."

My wheels squeal on the road and splash rain everywhere as I drive like a bat out of hell.

"You're so fucked." A chuckle and the line goes dead.

An aggressive clang of metal on wood sounds as I throw open the front door to my supplier's business. The bells tied to the top nearly fall off in my rush to get blood.

"Slow your roll, Speedy." The blond-haired woman scolds me and places a cooler in front of my face on the countertop.

Without any acknowledgement I tear open the lid and rip into a bag of O negative. A moan slips out as I feel the rush of liquid into my system. I'm sure I look like an absolute savage but the burning in my throat was almost too much to bear up to this point. I haven't been this close to falling into bloodlust since I was first turned.

"Celine's really got your panties in a twist, doesn't she?"

Luna arches one perfectly manicured brow and taps her fingers on the table while I start on my second bag.

I give her a scowl while I continue to drink and only when I'm finished with my third bag do I finally feel like myself again. Sighing, I sit down on the barstool of the coffee shop bar and level her with a no nonsense look.

"How'd you know?"

"I could see you perched on the roof of the building across the street like a ginger gargoyle the other day watching her. You're not slick. You killed one of my patrons." She raises a brow at me, but I don't apologize. "I've known you for twenty years, Zav, you don't stick around unless something catches your eye, and I think that something is a five-foot seven-inch-tall brunette. Spill." Her smile is teasing, but curious.

"You're too nosey for your own good, Luna." My empty blood bag lands next to her, narrowly missing her face when I launch it her way.

She wipes a fleck that's landed on her wrist. "How else do you expect me to live out my eternal life? Gossip is what makes the world go round." Wavy hair cascades over her shoulder as she grabs all the emptied blood bags and tosses them in the incinerator she keeps in the closet.

Luna and I met in the early 2000's in New York City. A one-night stand gone wrong solidified her fate as a forever twenty-four-year-old. The bastard was a one pump chump who turned her and ran—the guy nearly drained her by accident and felt bad about it so he turned her.

I'd be lying if I said we didn't mess around in the beginning, both lonely and needing companionship, but we quickly found we were better as friends. She was someone I made sure to stop and say hello to if I was in town.

Plus, she keeps a blood stock for vamps in the area. A coffee shop by day and blood bar by night, it was the perfect cover.

Humans would never be able to fathom what walked among them right under their noses.

"She's my mate." I drop the bomb figuring I should get it out of the way.

It's probably wrong of me that she's the first person I tell, but I'm pretty sure Celine would run screaming from me if I told her. Or worse, laugh.

A clunk echoes throughout the room when she drops her phone on the ground. Her mouth is a perfectly round "O" shape that would be comical if the shocked expression on her face wasn't as annoying as it was.

Here come the twenty questions.

"Are you fucking kidding me?" The shrill squeak she lets loose makes me cringe. She gives me a punch in the shoulder.

"Why would I joke about that?" Already exasperated by the conversation I start to sip on my fourth blood bag thankful my fangs have fully retracted now. I've already run through my head how ludicrous the situation is, not that I'd trade Celine for anything.

"Zavier Lockwood." Her face holds the biggest smile I've ever seen. "You have a mate. And it's Celine." Her face morphs back to shock. "A human. That's rare!" A slight breeze tousles the hair falling over my glasses when she rushes over in a blur. Plopping down on the barstool in front of me, I lean back when she encroaches into my space. "Tell me everything. How did you find out? Does she know? Of course, she doesn't know, that means you'd have told her what you are. When are you going to tell her you're a vampire? You'll have to since she's a human! Will you turn her? How will she rea—"

"Luna. For the love of God shut up." Already fed up with her questioning I cover her mouth with my palm and pull it away once she stays quiet. Her teeth nip at my hand like a little fledgling and a hiss comes out. I bop her on the nose. "You brat. I'll tell you if you promise to keep your lips zipped."

She mimes zipping her lips and I smirk.

"I was leaving one of my ... art scenes," I say for lack of a better idea of what to call it. "When something tugged me toward her." Luna rolls her eyes at the mention of my "art". I know she hates when I talk about it, but I continue. "She took my breath away. It felt like I got hit by a truck. When I finally caught her scent, the world was ripped right out from under me. It's like my life starts and ends with her now and I can't let her go. The fact she's a human and I'm a vampire doesn't matter. I know it's rare, and definitely odd she's human, but it doesn't change anything."

Mates aren't all that rare for those of us who are of the supernatural variety—vampire, fae, shifter—but having one that's human is. It's uncommon enough that I've only ever met one pairing in my three-hundred years. It was a wolf shifter and her human mate.

My eyes flutter shut under my glasses at the memory of how she looked that first night on the scene. Celine was a stunning and intelligent creature and all *mine*.

"You've got it bad," Luna laughs and pats my hand. "I'm happy for you. Truly. Celine is one of the nicest humans I've ever met, and I know she'll be good for you. But shit. A human."

"I won't be good for her?" I balk, pure offense sharpening my words.

Spinning around from me on her stool, and walking away she volleys back, "She needs to keep her wits about her around you. You'll corrupt her, Zavier."

"That's what I'm counting on," I chuckle, but stop when I remember a crucial detail. "Wait. You were the one that encouraged Celine to go to Vex's grand-opening weren't you?" I cross my muscled arms over my chest and glare.

"Yeah. I've heard whisperings that something is going on there. She's a damn good cop and I pointed her in the direction of a case." Shrugging her shoulders she continues to put away clean dishes.

"It was a club! One where she wore essentially nothing and looked like a walking snack." Raking a hand through my hair, I fight back my anger and remember the men and women who stared at her with covetous eyes. I stepped in to stake my claim as quickly as I could, but the damage had been done. "Do you know how horrible it was to watch her basically dance naked in front of everyone?"

Pursing her lips, she rebuttals, "She deserved some fun and you're not her parent. Let the girl live. Plus, like I said, she was investigating a case. And how was I supposed to know she's your mate? She doesn't smell of you yet."

"What exactly did you have her investigating?"

"I think it's a drug front that's dabbling in trafficking. It's been hard for even me to get the straight of it."

"Luna! You sent Celine there knowing that?" I explode, standing straight up.

The anger I feel is all consuming and if this is a peek into what I have to look forward to I don't know if I can handle it. If I'm a possessive bastard on a good day, I'll be downright murderous on a bad one. Celine is *mine* and she'll come to no harm under my watch.

"Chill." A dirty dish rag hits my face. "She was obviously fine and can take care of herself."

Grabbing the soiled cloth before it stains my shirt I lob it back at her. We push each other's buttons, but I need moments like this to rein myself in and she knows it, too.

"You're going to be the death of me." A sigh leaves my body, and I deflate.

"You're already dead."

Silence fills the space as I stare at her for a few beats before I turn on my heel and walk toward the door. "I'm leaving." The door jingles as I open it. "And you're an idiot."

Luna's melodic laughter follows me, and I stop, remembering my reason for initially coming in. My feet pound on the wooden floor as I sprint over to her backup cooler and steal a few extra bags of blood.

"You greedy little pig," she calls out. "I'm adding that to your tab."

I stick out my tongue and dart out into the night.

12

"How's he doing today, Sharon?"

The woman slowly ambles next to me as we make our way down the hall of the assisted living home. Pictures of smiling couples and families line the walls, aiming to incite happiness but instead fill me with dread with their hollow smiles.

Today's the day.

Marked on my calendar every third Wednesday of the month.

It's my day to come see my dad.

Will he remember me? Will he be docile? How long can I stay this time?

Guilt gnaws on my stomach that I can only manage to come once a month. Not because I don't have the time, but because it's so painful for me I just can't make myself do it more than once every four weeks. The facility isn't exactly close—nearly two hours from Chicago with traffic so that serves as a deterrent as well.

"You caught him on a good day, sweetie." She rubs my shoulder in reassurance, and I instantly relax, letting out a sigh of relief.

"I know you deal with it every day, but it never gets easier, does it?" My forced smile hurts my cheeks and I zero in on the familiar door at the end of the hall as we inch nearer.

"Unfortunately, not. Being a nurse and helping patients is one thing but having to see family and friends visit someone who's a shell of their former self is heartbreaking. The good days are some of the happiest, but the bad days stick with you. I don't regret working in this profession, but you need to have tough skin."

Glancing at the older woman's face, wrinkles from years of laughter and hard times line her skin. Sharon has helped my dad ever since he was first admitted to Avery Corr Living. A stoutly woman with a bob of brown hair, sunspots around her face and kind brown eyes, her optimism and support have always been appreciated. When you're in a place like this it's hard not to expect the worst every time you walk in but having staff like her truly keeps hope in peoples' hearts.

I hesitate to ask my next question since I know the answer, but I have to. "Has my mom stopped by?"

With a sad shake of her head Sharon confirms my suspicions.

Mom never stops by. I hate that even now I hold a tiny flicker of hope that someday the guilt will be too much and she'll visit.

"Sometimes all I can do is hate her." Our steps slow as the door draws ever closer, but I halt my steps. This conversation isn't one to be had in front of my father. "The way she abandoned him ... who could do that to their spouse?"

Sharon stays quiet and simply listens. She's amazing at that.

"But then there are times I hate myself because I understand in a way. It's tough. Look at me, I can only manage one visit a month." I give a humorless laugh. Toeing the light green carpet with my boot, I gaze at nothing. "But at the end of the day, my dad can't help his situation and being here for him is what's right."

"You're a wonderful daughter. I hope you know that. When he's coherent he always mentions you." She tucks a strand of flyaway hair from my ponytail behind my ear and smiles at me with a motherly grin. It's more than my mother has done in the past fifteen years. "Let's go see him."

I nod and reach for the long silver handle when we walk up to the gray door. Soft music can be heard when I open it, and I turn the corner to find my dad sitting in his favorite chair. He turns at the noise and for a second I hold my breath.

"Celine!" A huge grin splits his mouth, and I nearly collapse on the spot. His good days are rare, and I didn't know how badly I needed one until he says my name.

"Hi, Daddy." My voice is barely a whisper, and I can't hold myself back any longer. Rushing toward him I give the biggest hug I can muster. His arms come around me, now frailer than ever before, but the strength and love in them can't be mistaken.

"What's going on? Something wrong at school?"

My shoulders tense at his question because this is one of the worst parts. He remembers things but not always correctly. Yes, he remembers me, but his memory right now is from a past self when I was still in high school. It's best to meet him where he's at so I go along with it.

"No, nothing like that. Classes are great just happy to see you." I mask the pain in my voice with false cheeriness.

"Hopefully Mrs. Masters isn't giving you too much trouble?" His bristly eyebrows draw together, and I laugh.

"She's just mad I get an A on every assignment and call her out on her bullshit grading."

Untangling our arms I sit on the couch beside his armchair and wave to Sharon as she sees herself out.

"Language, young lady." My dad always was a stickler for proper etiquette.

I lean forward and rest my elbows on my knees, chin in hand and simply observe this man that's half of me. He turns his attention back to the television that's playing over on the entertainment stand, content with the silence. If I ask too many questions, it can set him off and I want to enjoy his good mood for as long as possible.

The wear of his illness is evident. Wrinkles bring his eyebrows lower into his once shining brown eyes that are so much like mine. His dark hair has lightened significantly from stress and is unkempt around his face. He dons a simple baseball tee and grey sweatpants, a blanket covering part of his lap.

My physical features reflect his, instead of my mother who had blonde hair and blue eyes. I'm grateful once he's at peace and no longer on this Earth I'll be able to look at myself in the mirror and see a reminder of him.

We continue to sit in mostly silence for the next hour and I soak in my time with him.

He's slowly becoming less verbal and struggles for words much more now than before. I try to help when I can, but I can tell it frustrates him. We share simple commentary on the game, and he asks a few questions related to school. I don't correct him and follow along.

In my relaxed state I jolt when he suddenly stands up and shouts. Frantically running around the room he slams open cabinets, throws open doors, looks under cushions and I follow behind the whole time.

"What's wrong?!" My heart races and I inch toward the front door help button.

"I can't find him. Where is he?"

"Where's who, Dad? What are you talking about?" I put my hands up when he approaches, and a glint enters his eye.

"You. You took him. You did this." He grips my arms painfully and I let out a squeak. There's no recognition in his eyes now. "He's not here!"

Slamming my palm on the buzzer I shout for Sharon and try to keep calm. Even though he's my dad, I'm not his daughter in this moment.

"My friend. You stole him." He's hysterical now repeating himself and my heart breaks.

"I still don't know what you're talking about. Dad, please!" I plead and hold onto his arms as he falls to the ground in dismay.

"Midnight," he wails and I suck in a breath.

He's done this before and it's why I pushed for him to keep the cat, since the facility allows it, but he was insistent I take him. He must have a memory of giving him away, but it's warped, and he thinks I stole him.

Footsteps pound outside the door and it's flung open when Sharon and two male nurses enter the room. They quickly take action consoling my dad, helping him to his bedroom. Sharon gives me a pitying look and I wipe a tear that has escaped from my eye.

"I think it's best I leave." My voice sounds hollow to my own ears and Sharon nods. "Thanks, Sharon. For everything."

With a last pat to my back, she walks with me to my car and closes the door behind me when I get behind the wheel. No more words are exchanged but there doesn't need to be.

The drive home is excruciating. There's no way in hell I can listen to music or an audiobook and pretend what happened didn't. That means I'm left with my thoughts as I stare blankly and go through the motions of driving home.

Was the light I just passed green?

I don't even know, but the fact my car hasn't been smashed by someone else's probably means I'm fine.

My thoughts continue in an endless cycle of nonsense and I'm honestly not sure how I make it to my building. Besides making a stop on floor five for someone to go up to fifteen I'm left blessedly alone in the elevator. The ding of the cabin lets me know I've finally made it to mine.

I step off and walk like an emotionless zombie down to my door. Standing in front of it I freeze and then suddenly the dam breaks. It's like standing in front of my apartment far away from what just happened gives me an excuse to let go. The sound I let out must sound like a dying animal, but I can't hold it in any longer. I made it so close to safety just to lose it now.

My coat catches on the textured wall as I back up and slide down it, collapsing in a heap on the ground. My keys fall from my hands, sliding out of my reach. Tears stream down my face in a constant flow and I curl up into a ball, tucking my head into my knees. I can't muster the energy to pick myself back up and get inside so I just sit there and let the emotions carry me away.

I cry for my dad who's been dealt a fate he didn't ask for. I cry for myself who's lost both of her parents. I cry for the uncertain future that seems to hold nothing but isolation and agony.

I'm distantly aware of the creaking of a door opening and the thud as it shuts. Clothing rustles and a warm presence to my right has me peeking out from under my arm. I find Zavier crouched, watching me with a melancholy look on his face. He's wearing a black sweater that looks so soft I want to cuddle into it and his silver chain lies around his neck. When he tilts his head, his silky red hair moves and covers his glasses adorably. He watches me watch him and slowly opens his arms.

The silent show of comfort somehow has more tears flooding out of my eyes and I dive into his arms. They wrap around me so tight I feel my own heartbeat echo between us.

"Shh, Celine. I've got you, pretty girl." He holds my neck with one hand and undoes my high ponytail with the other to allow my hair to cascade down my back. The pressure relief feels wonderful, and he gently strokes my tresses. I swear I feel him press a kiss to my head but it's so soft it could be my imagination.

His words only make me cry harder and I'm embarrassed by the way I melt into him, but it feels so good. He's practically a stranger and yet the comfort I feel around him is undeniable. The invisible pull between us is magnetic and I can't figure out how he's always there when I seem to need him.

"I've got you. You're safe," he continues to murmur in a soothing tone. His voice vibrates against my chest, and I settle further into his lap, fully surrendering myself to the warmth. "Whoever hurt you, just tell me and I'll kill them."

"It was my dad," I say, voice hoarse. "I told you about him. He has dementia. Today was ... a bad day."

We stay like that for God knows how long and I selfishly linger for longer than I should. When his arms randomly tighten, I feel like he needs this as much as I do. My face is tucked into his neck and his vanilla and cypress scent fills my lungs.

My hiccups finally quiet down and I know I can't stay any longer in the safety of his arms. I have to pull on my big girl pants and bring myself back to reality.

Slowly pulling away, I'm stopped short when Zavier pulls my forehead back to his and keeps me there. My eyes widen in surprise but his are closed tightly like he's trying to savor the moment. His thumb comes up to wipe my cheek with a gentleness that has my eyes blurring again. I blink and the moment's over and he's pulling me to my feet. I awkwardly avoid eye contact, slightly embarrassed by my actions and not wanting to talk about what just happened.

Zavier must sense how I feel because at my mumbled thanks he simply strokes the side of my head one more time. He picks my stuff up and slips my key into my door for me. I back away with one last small smile of appreciation and head into my apartment but not without one last glance at him where he stands with a sad smile.

13

Resting the back of my head against the door as it closes, I rub my eyes and groan. What a shit show of a day. I'm glad I got to see my dad, but it was a rough one. It was going so well initially that I let down my guard and was rewarded with a slap in the face.

"Meow." A black floof yells at me from the floor sitting like a perfect angel. I know better, but still risk it and reach down to hold him close. Midnight allows it like he knows what's happened and I need comfort, animals are smart like that.

I pet his soft head and run my finger down his little nose. In a rare show of affection his pink tongue flicks out to lick my pointer.

"See, we can be friends." Rocking him like a baby in my arms we have a moment that's promptly ruined by a knocking at the door. Midnight yowls and scratches my arm in the process of sprinting away.

"Ow, you little shit!" Assessing the damage and finding no

blood drawn I open the door, expecting it to be Zavier although I don't know for what.

"Ava?" Her face appears and she pulls me in for a hug.

"Aw, my girl. Look at your poor face." Wiping under my eye she pulls her hand away to show black streaks. "I hoped it would be a good day, but I guess not."

"Oh my God, I must look like a clown." Rushing to my bathroom, and leaving her to let herself in, I stare at my appearance and let out a squeak. "Jesus, I look awful."

Mascara is smeared everywhere, and my eyes are puffy and red rimmed. My face is blotchy from my outburst, and I make quick work wiping off as much gunk as I can with a washcloth. I turn my head from side to side and don't see any other makeup but it's not great. I just have to accept my sorry state for now.

"Get out here and let me comfort you," Ava calls from the living room. "I didn't drive across town for nothing."

"What're you doing here, Aves?" I question, plopping down next to her when I meander my way back in with a forced smile.

"I knew today was that day of the month, so I wanted to stop by and check in. And I'm not talking about your period." She supports her head with her hand and leans her elbow against the back of the couch. Warmth shines in her eyes and I'm instantly surrounded by her healing aura.

"Thanks. I'm all right." I fold my arms across my abdomen and lay back against the couch.

"Oh, I know you're all right, you hussy." Ava swats my shoulder, and I scoff.

"What are you talking about?"

"I ran into Zavier in the hall. He literally lives right next to you! Not just in the same building but next door." She draws out his name when she says it and I know I'm in trouble. "Did you sleep with him last night?" Her voice goes up a few octaves and I jump up to defend myself.

"What? No!" Frantically waving my hands I try to put her suspicions to rest. "Yes, he lives next to me, which is a crazy coincidence, but nothing happened. He got me home safe like a perfect gentleman."

I don't mention the weirdness when he dropped me off, or him comforting me during my meltdown, knowing that'll add fuel to her gossip bonfire. I pray Zavier didn't mention it during whatever conversation they had.

Ava gives a disappointed noise and slinks back down on the couch.

"I wouldn't have judged you if you did. He's a hot piece of man and from the little I've seen he genuinely seems into you. If you don't feel a spark with Asher, why don't you go on a date with Zav?"

"Zav?" I question incredulously.

Since when were they besties and on nickname basis?

A loud thud followed by several bangs next door has us both jumping out of our seats and running to the door.

"The fuck? Was that his apartment?" she asks as I'm already knocking on his door to make sure he's okay.

The man in question appears within a few seconds. One emerald eyeball shines back at us through the small crack he's opened of the door.

"Zavier? Are you okay?" I try to see more of him through the tiny sliver to make sure.

"Uh. Yeah, why?"

Ava and I share a confused glance and look back at him.

"We heard some pretty loud thuds coming from your direction. Did something happen?"

Zavier sighs and fully opens the door to show blood trickling down the side of his face.

"What the hell happened?" I jump into action, shoving him aside and racing toward the kitchen.

Ripping off a piece of paper towel I run it under water and wring it out before blotting his forehead when he sits in front of me. I grip his chin gently and push his glasses up onto his head to properly wipe the stream of blood away.

What starts as frantic concern on my part turns into intense heat as our eyes lock. There's an emotion reflected in his eyes I can't place, but it makes butterflies awaken in my belly. With his glasses out of place I can fully appreciate the sharp angle of his cheekbones, the curve of his jaw, and the perfect symmetry of his face. My eyes dart back and forth between his and I step further into his body. His arms firmly wrap around the backs of my thighs, and I let loose a sigh I didn't know I was holding.

The bubble is broken when Ava gasps and I abruptly step back clearing my throat.

"So." Ava purses her lips. "That thing I was talking about?"

She gives me a knowing look and I threaten to throw the bloodied paper towel at her. Bloodborne pathogens be damned. Tapping her foot, she sets her sights on Zavier who pushes his glasses back in place. God, he's fucking hot.

She came over here to comfort me and now she's pushing me into yet another date. I know she means well, and I *do* like Zavier, but I wish she didn't feel like she has to worry so much about my love life or lack thereof.

"Celine wants you to take her on a date."

"What?" Zavier and I shout simultaneously, a grin quickly spreading across his face.

"Ava," I hiss vehemently.

"I'd love to," Zavier responds cheerily, linking his arm with mine.

I turn to him in shock and quickly regret it when I tweak my neck with the force of my whiplash. A small whimper leaks out and my eyes widen once again when Zavier gently cups the back of my neck. He twists my head to the side and traces the curve of my décolletage, momentarily zeroing in on my pulse and rubbing it with his thumb.

I swear I see a dulling of the vibrant green of his eyes when he zones out but in a flash it's gone. The concern reflected in them is crazy considering he's the one who was bleeding a second ago.

"Are you okay?"

The care in his voice makes me want to curl into him and never let go. Between our moment of comfort in the hall, Ava stopping by, and him caring for me now, I've felt more care than I have in a long time, and I don't know how to handle it.

"Cel?" Ava comes into my field of vision, and I straighten, slowly removing Zavier's hand from my neck. He frowns but doesn't comment. I notice him clench his hand and cradle it in his other reverently like the one that touched me is something to be treasured.

"Totally fine." I stretch my neck from side to side to gently work out the kink and direct attention away from me. "What about you? You're the one with the cut on your head. What happened?" Zavier's cheeks stain red when I focus my gaze back on him.

He mumbles something unintelligible, and his embarrassment is palpable.

"What?" Tucking my hair behind my ear I lean closer to him feigning deafness. "I didn't catch that."

"I fell off a chair and nailed my forehead on the ground."

Zavier says it so quietly I can't help but laugh. Ava tries to hold in her snort but fails miserably when it comes out around the hand she holds to her mouth. Envisioning this elegant force of a man, eating shit falling off a chair is hilarious.

I peer around the kitchen island and see the chair in question tipped over onto the floor as well as one of the posters that had been hung on the wall. The frame is shattered and it's shocking he's not cut worse than he is.

"Who would've thought you'd be a clumsy one." I chuckle under my breath and head over to the living room to help right the fallen pieces. "Do you have a broom?"

"You don't have to do that." Zavier jogs over with the cleaning tool and starts to sweep it up himself.

Ava passes me a plastic bag she found, and I carefully place the larger pieces of glass in the bag. When I'm done, I pass it to Zavier to finish up. Our fingers brush and I feel the familiar tingle I only experience around him.

"Well, we're glad you're okay, Zav." Ava nods her head at him, and we start to head toward his front door.

An amused chuckle makes me stop and turn back around. "What?"

He stands and places his large hands on his hips. A smirk tilts his gorgeous lips up and my brows furrow.

"I just think it's funny you've known me longer than Ava has and yet *you* never call me Zav. It's always Zavier this, Zavier that."

A scoff leaves my mouth as I place my own hands on my hips to mimic his stance.

"You just moved in! I'm sorry if I don't think we're in the territory of nicknames."

He levels me with a stare of challenge, and I know I'm in trouble.

"I think you're afraid, baby."

The sputter that leaves my mouth is immediate. "Baby? Afraid of what? Who do you think you are?"

This little bastard.

Ava stands off to the side watching our showdown with interest. If she could have a bucket of popcorn for the performance, I'm sure she would.

"Getting close to anybody." Zavier struts over like a peacock with his feathers out. "For the short period of time I've known you, I've read you like a book, and you don't like to let people in."

I would love nothing more than to smack the stupid smile right off his gorgeous face right now.

"Oh, please. Zavier whatever-your-last-name-is-know-it-all." I inwardly cringe at myself and the shitty comeback, but I'm too riled up to care. "You don't know me." Poking his chest with a finger I emphasize my point.

He grabs my finger so quickly I can barely react and nips at it. I try to pull away, but he refuses to let go. "Lockwood. Zavier Lockwood. L-O-C-K-W-O-O-D. Why aren't you writing this down? It's going to be your last name one day, too." His grin is downright wicked.

I sputter incoherently.

His pink tongue slips out to lick me like a popsicle and I try to suppress the shiver that wants to wrack my body. In one swift pull from him we're toe to toe, and my heaving chest brushes his hard pecs.

I should be grossed out, angry even, but I'm not.

I'm ... intrigued.

And maybe even a little turned on.

"And I want to know even more about you, Celine Won't-Face-The-Truth-Brennan."

Our height difference doesn't help with me trying to be intimidating so I rip my finger out of his grip and pull a stool over to stand on top of it because I'm petty like that.

"Ha."

Zavier shakes his head and grabs my hips, pulling me off the stool with ease. His flexing arms let me down but not without letting our fronts rub against each other as he slowly lowers me. The hardness in his crotch is undeniable and I fight the growing blush on my cheeks both from anger and lust.

"I'm leaving."

I turn and purposely hit him in the face with my hair. The groan he lets out proves to have had the opposite effect than intended. I don't know what to do with him. Grabbing Ava's hand in mine, I yank her out into the hallway and fumble for the keys in my pocket, trying to get away as soon as possible.

"Where are my damn keys?" I pat down my clothing but can't find them. A jingling noise has me turning to Mr. Frustrating himself. Zavier has one sassy hand on a hip and the other holding my missing keys nonchalantly.

"You dropped these," he drawls, only serving to piss me off even more.

"Give me those." I storm over and snag them from his hand then run out of his apartment like my ass is on fire. Ava continues to watch like we're providing endless entertainment.

"Oh, and Celine?"

"What?" I shout louder than I mean to and glance around the hallway hoping my neighbors aren't out.

"See you on Saturday for our date."

He pushes his door shut and locks it before I can verbally attack him. Smart man.

"You asshole," I whisper shout, and hear his chuckle on the other side of the door.

Even with my annoyance I can't help but smile at Ava, who smiles right back at me.

"Want to explain what that was?" she asks, pointing over her shoulder toward Zavier's apartment. "It's like you forgot I was standing there. I've never seen you get so wrapped up in someone."

"I couldn't if I wanted to, because I have no freaking idea."

My coffee table is a mess of scattered magazines, pictures, and pamphlets. I'm scrolling through my phone on the couch and have my laptop set up as well, all in an effort to come up with the best date idea possible. Our date is in two days, and I can't fuck it up. It has to be perfect.

I could kiss Ava for convincing Celine to go out with me. Much like myself, Celine can't ignore the magnetism between us. One day it's going to turn into an inferno neither one of us can deny.

My notepad of ideas sits next to me based on my research so far and I glance over it.

Zavier's Date Ideas for Whooing His Mate:
~~Bowling~~ - Asher's bitch ass ruined this one

Karaoke - Show off my golden pipes
Navy Pier, Ferris Wheel - Basic and done before
Skip everything and go straight to fucking her
senseless - My favorite

Number four is by far my pick but nothing realistically is jumping out at me. It has to be special. I chew on my pencil in thought and tap it on my fang. Suddenly a brilliant idea strikes me.

Snagging my coat, and throwing it on, I grab my car keys and head out the door but not before I pause at Celine's door and inhale her scent.

Ever since I moved in, I've spent as much time as I can listening and watching her go about her daily routine. She sings in the shower, talks to Midnight even though he doesn't seem to be the biggest fan of her, and loves to read with oddly specific ambience music playing in the background. Who knew cozy and calming rainy bookstore in Chicago lo-fi music was a thing?

After a short drive, I park my car in front of my first stop. The rain is coming down hard and I open my umbrella, prepared this time. Overcast weather has still been common lately and I can't ruin my perfectly waved hair. Tossing it out of my eyes I look down at a large puddle that shimmers in front of me. Red, orange, and blue city lights reflect in it capturing the bustle of the city. My chest tightens when my eyes play a trick, and I see a blurry Celine standing next to me. Quickly turning I see a brunette passing by in a rush. Not Celine. I knew it wasn't her by the smell but still my shoulders droop and I trudge sullenly into the restaurant.

Scanning the room, I spy my unsuspecting victim where he always sits in the back corner of the bar. I make my way over, steps silent. His eyes are closed, and a plan concocts itself in my head. Creeping over stealthily, I avoid running into customers and tables before I lean down behind the man and yell in his ear.

"Boo!"

Nothing.

"Hey!"

Nothing.

"Are you kidding me, Old Man?"

The fun officially sucked out of my plan, I plop down on the chair unceremoniously in front of him. He decides to open his eyes right then, and I swear his hearing and vision are perfect, he just likes fucking with me.

"Oh, Zac, it's you. When did you get here?"

Wrinkled and time worn hands rub the sleep out of his soulful blue eyes. From young man to now he's always been a kind human but that doesn't mean he doesn't drive me batty.

Ha. Vampire jokes.

"You're the worst," I mumble, but fold my arms in front of me and get right to business. "I need date ideas."

"Date ideas? What do you take me for? I haven't gone on a date in fifty years." Mirth dances across his face. "You haven't either, you crusty old fart. Who's the lucky lady?"

"The one I've been telling you about, Celine, and please, if anyone's crusty it's you." My chair tips back as I lounge.

"You finally ballsed up and asked her out, huh?" A raspy chuckle comes from him ending in a deep cough. Time, the ever-silent killer, has caught up to Tom and I cringe internally at every cough and sputter that comes out of his body, not ready for our friendship to end.

"Something like that." I clear my throat leaving out the detail of Ava forcing the date on Celine. "I'm glad you find my situation so funny, but seriously, I'm desperate." My knees thud on the ground as I grab his hands and plead in front of him dramatically. "Please, Tom."

"Okay, okay," he grumbles and throws my hand off his leg. I settle in my seat once again.

"Back when my Betsy Jo was still alive, we loved to go to Navy Pier and ride the Ferris wheel." A nostalgic look smooths out his wrinkles, and his eyes zone out, lost in a memory. "We'd bribe the attendant to let us ride multiple times without getting off and kissed whenever we reached the top. She always scolded me for doing it, but I knew she secretly loved it." He winks at me and a sigh leaves his lips. "The view is fantastic at night and there are plenty of establishments to get dinner at so that's my vote."

I rub my chin in thought. I already came up with the Navy Pier idea but crossed it off due to my fear that it might be too cliche. Something with a beautiful view is a great idea, though.

At my silence, he continues, "Something else we did was grab dinner and then catch a movie afterwards. If Celine's a detective like you said maybe she'd like the new thriller flick." Tilting his head in thought he laughs to himself. "Or there's a showing of that 2000's vampire romance. If you're into that stuff."

"What's wrong with vampires?" I gasp.

"Immortal beings that either sparkle or burn in the sun? Pfft."

"Well, both are untrue ... so..." He can't hear me over his laughter, not that I want him to, but I still feel the need to defend myself. Fucker.

"Just don't overthink the date thing, Zac. Women aren't as hard to please as you'd think. Just show that you put a lot of thought and care into it."

"How did you know Betsy Jo was the one?" Curiosity gets

the better of me. I've never flat out asked him before in fear of bringing up old wounds.

Tom flashes the biggest grin, and I can't help but smile back at the adoration in his eyes. There's also a sheen of sorrow and loneliness that I know stems from the loss of his person. Having his kids and grandkids around helps soothe the ache but he still misses his love.

If Celine was ever taken from me...

No. I can't think that way.

I suppress a growl that threatens to rise up in my throat and lick my fangs that have descended in anger. The napkin on the table in front of me shifts slightly at the breath I blow out to calm myself. My canines thankfully retract.

This whole mates thing is hard. I've had three-hundred years to learn how to control myself, but finding my mate has thrown all that out the window.

"It was love at first sight. Well, maybe not for her, but it was for me."

Out of my peripheral I spy a few patrons listening in. Tom has a way of drawing people in even though he can come off as brash at first.

"People think it's crazy, but I swear time stopped when she walked in the room."

His eyes go distant and I just know he's reliving a memory.

Shaking himself free, he says, "All right, that's enough of that, scram everyone. I can only be mushy for so long." He waves his hands in the air as if swatting the crowd away. They disperse and it's left just us once again.

"Next time we're having a rematch so I can beat your ass in chess." He smiles at me, and I lightly pat his back, glad he's not letting our last conversation ruin his mood.

"You got it, Tom."

"What?"

"Bye Tom!"

"Uh huh." He makes a shooing motion with his hand. "Now get out and go plan your date."

Back to our usual banter, I tip my invisible hat to him and rush out the door an excited but nervous mess.

15

aptain Barnes ambles over to my desk and taps it with the folded papers he holds. "Witness here for you, Brennan."

"For me?" I wrack my brain for what it could possibly be for. Running my fingers through the long strands of my ponytail, I give him an imploring stare.

"Well, Detective Waters would be doing intake but she's out until tomorrow afternoon on vacation so you're up." He crinkles the papers, shoving them into his pocket. "Once she's back she'll take over."

I collect a notebook and pen, standing from my desk. "No problem."

He nods and walks away with a whistle.

Approaching my destination, I spy Captain leaning against the interrogation room door. His thick legs are crossed, and he holds a cup of coffee and a donut, not doing much for our stereotype.

"You okay to take this? Not too busy with the murder case?"

Straightening my posture and righting my jacket I give him a confident smile. "I've got it, no problem."

"Good luck." Captain gives me a small smile and disappears around the corner.

Turning, I push open the door to reveal a stunning woman seated at the metal table. She looks up at me with teary brown eyes framed with thick lashes. Luscious black hair flows in a silky curtain down her back. Her makeup is flawless save for the black streaks of mascara running down her cheeks, not that it dulls her beauty. Dressed in a maroon sweater and dark jeans she could say she just got off the runway and I'd believe her. An intense energy emanates from her. It's slightly intimidating and pressurized which is odd since her body language is so demure.

"Hi, my name's Detective Brennan." I ease into the room offering my hand. "What's yours?"

She sniffles and takes mine in her respective dainty hand. "Genevieve."

"I brought you some water if you'd like it." I extend the glass, and she wraps elegant fingers around it to take it.

"Thank you."

"Genevieve, I want to help you however I can. Do you feel comfortable telling me what brought you in, or do you need a minute?" Gently sitting in the chair across from her, I slowly place my notebook and pen on the table, ready whenever she is, but not wanting to pressure her.

"No, I'm okay to proceed." She blows her nose in a tissue and takes a deep breath before launching into her story. "My best friend Katie and I are like this." She holds her entwined fingers up for emphasis. "We text constantly to keep each other updated on our day, no matter how stupid the update may be." Genevieve gives a watery smile. "The other night we were out clubbing, and I decided to head home first. I told her we should share a cab, but she lives in the opposite direction, so she insisted on taking her own." She sniffles and stares at the table in front of her, lost in a memory. "I got home fine and waited for an update from her saying the same and I just ... never got it." Tears continue to stream down her cheeks. "I've called her so many times I can't even tell you and tried to get into her apartment but nothing. Poof. I'm worried something happened to her. This isn't like her."

Genevieve is now a blubbering mess, and I set my stationary on the table. Walking over, I squat down in front of the crying woman and pat her knee.

"Hey, it's okay." I soothe her the best I can. "We can take a break for as long as you need."

Tearfully, she looks down at me apologetically. "I'm sorry. I'm not typically this much of a mess but I can't shake the feeling I'll never see her again." Suddenly, she grips my hands. "You're going to get her back, right?"

I grip her hands back just as tightly. "I'll send in my report and start investigating. Detective Waters will take over once she's back tomorrow so you'll be hearing from her not me." I hope my sincerity can be heard and the relief in her eyes tell me it is.

"May I ask you what the name of the club was you were at?"

She lifts her tear-stained face to me. "Vex."

My heart jolts in my chest, and I try to school my features so as not to give any emotion away. There's no concrete evidence Vex has anything to do with her friend's disappearance, but the fact I've had a bad feeling, tied with what Luna said, the whole thing is shady.

"Just a few more things and then I can get started on opening an investigation."

Sitting back down in my seat I cross my jean clad legs and begin writing.

Blowing out a frustrated breath I look back down at my notebook.

Wrinkles litter the lined paper from shoving it into my pocket and my list is completely crossed off except for one scribble. I've visited every surrounding business on Vex's street save for the one I now stand in front of.

None of the establishments knew anything about the situation, and one, ran by a crotchety old woman, refused to answer my questions. I left quickly afraid she'd take a bite out of my arm with her crazy ass dentures. Every time I spoke, she inched closer to me and bit at the air like a piranha. I'm not sure if she was just messing with me or truly off her rocker.

"So fucking weird," I mumble, my breath swirling in the cold air. At least it isn't raining for once. "Let's get this done." One last place to visit.

The Throwing Wheel is an adorable pottery shop with all kinds of ceramics displayed in the front window. Mugs, vases, decorative pieces, and more, line shelves showing off both the owners' and customers' pieces. Fake pumpkins and leaves are dispersed throughout the art, and I file the location in the back of my mind for a future girl's day with Ava. I'm shit at pottery, but so is she, so it would make for a great laugh. Last time we did it, I dropped my mug in a bucket of glaze and her piece got stuck to mine in the kiln rendering them useless.

I push open the door and step inside. The smell of clay and earth hit my nostrils and soft jazz plays over a speaker. Shelves of pottery continue throughout the entire room and the buzz of pottery wheels fills the space. It's a quaint but quirky store full of character.

A class is in session, and I hear the teacher instructing the attendees on how to throw a clay cylinder.

Quietly walking toward the middle of the room, I try not to disturb anyone. They all seem to be doing a great job molding and forming their shapes by cupping the clay and cleaning their wheel surface with a sponge as they go. The class is men and women of all ages, some couples, some friends, and others on their own. An older woman smiles up at me as I walk past. Pieces of grey hair escape her bun, and I can tell by her skill and technique she's done this hundreds of times.

"Okay, class, now that we've got the cylinder down, we're going to move on to shaping a mug and adding a handle." A man's voice rings out and I freeze where I'm at, not daring to look up.

Wait a damn second.

Sure enough when I glance up I spot none other than Zavier.

My neighbor Zavier.

Fucking Zavier who seems to pop up everywhere.

My eyes narrow when he looks my way, not seeming surprised in the least to see me, like I am him. His long sleeve shirt is covered with a green apron that's tied at the waist and his hands are caked with dried clay. A perfectly thrown cylinder rests in front of him and I'm blown away when the owner, an old man who looks to be in his sixties, walks over to Zavier and pats him on the back.

That's it.

I speed walk over to my victim and give him the death stare. Fisting his apron in my hand, I drag him away from the students and over to the kiln in the back corner of the room. He grins the entire way like he enjoys me yanking him along like a dog on a leash.

"What are you doing here?" I hiss the accusation.

His smile widens, flashing perfect white teeth. "I work here."

"Since when?"

Zavier popping up *everywhere* is nothing short of suspicious.

He pouts his bottom lip, thinking. Picking at a piece of lint on his shirt, he answers, "Today."

I throw my hands in the air. "The other day you were at the fucking bowling alley."

He shrugs, unbothered. Reaching between us, he picks up a strand of my hair and twirls it between his fingers. I should bat him away, but for some strange reason I don't.

"I work a lot of odd jobs," he finally answers. "Pays the bills."

"You..." I sigh, planting my hands on my hips. "There's something strange about you."

His smile somehow gets even bigger than it was before. "Oh, darling, I'm so glad you noticed."

Darling?

"Anyway"—he removes the apron in one lithe motion and hangs it on a rack beside us—"since we're both here, how about dinner? Hmm? Get the date started early?"

I narrow my eyes.

"No. Ava might've coerced me into a date with you, but it's not supposed to happen until tomorrow."

"Oh, come on," he cajoles, undeterred. Cool fingers skim my arm, sending shivers down my spine. Not bad shivers—not the ones I get when I know something strange is up. This feels good. Too good. "It's dinner time. You need to eat."

I stare at him, trying and failing to come up with a decent enough excuse. My shoulders sag in defeat. "Fine. But only because I'm hungry."

"Excellent. Shall we?" He leads me toward the exit with a

hand on my waist. For a moment I allow it to happen, enjoying the warmth of his arm and strength of his side against mine.

How did we go from me dragging him across the room to this? It's like he puts me under some sort of fog every time I see him. It only lifts when I'm no longer in his vicinity.

When we step outside the shop, I finally come out of my fuzziness and pull out of his grasp.

"Wait. I'm not ready!" I shout in exasperation. "I still need to do my job! I have to ask the owner if he saw anything that could help my case. It's the last stop and then I'll go home and get ready, okay?" Knowing Zavier won't take no for an answer I plead with my eyes. "Well, I have to stop back by the precinct first and pass off my notes to the detective that's taking over the case." His smirk grows and I resist the urge to stomp my foot. "Besides, aren't you working?"

Zavier crosses his arms and watches me in silence, brow lifted in silent accusation.

"I promise."

"I don't believe you." He sounds like a toddler fighting with his mother which I most certainly am not.

"Zav, are you fucking kidding me?" I think I've cursed more in the last five minutes than I have in the last month. This is what he does to me. The smug bastard with his perfect face, adorable glasses, and kissable lips.

I find myself wondering what it would be like to kiss him which is a worrying stray of my thoughts.

Silence continues to greet me, and I look back up into Zavier's emerald eyes to see excitement bursting in them. For a second, I'm worried he saw right through my inner monologue, but then he smiles the creepiest clown grin I've ever seen and bobs his head from side to side while doing a little shimmy dance.

"What's happening?" My arms shoot out in self-defense as I lean away from the clearly unhinged man in front of me.

"You." He squeaks out and puts his hands up in front of his mouth to rest on his chin like a little kid.

"Me? I'm failing to see the point." Tapping my booted foot on the ground I watch him continue to flail in confusion.

"You. Called. Me. Zav." A girly sounding *teehee* comes out of his mouth and I roll my eyes.

"I'm going inside now. Goodbye ... Zav." I throw the last part in as I enter the building, and the door shuts behind me, but not before I hear the second squeal, he lets out causing me to shake my head in amusement.

Where did he come from? It's like this man dropped from the sky from some alien planet.

Plastering on a smile, I introduce myself to the owner and ask my questions, all while steadfastly ignoring the man that comes back inside and resumes his class like nothing happened.

"You look stunning. You're such a catch anyone would be lucky to have you. Me? Oh, please you flatter me."

Batting a hand at the mirror I chuckle and turn away.

My reflection doesn't respond, but Midnight watches from his cat bed with one eye open and one closed. A paw outstretched making air biscuits, the end of his tail lightly sways while he sprawls like he's king of the castle.

"I have to practice, Mr. Meow Meow. You don't get it." Midnight harumphs before closing both eyes. I run my fingers through my hair, the nervous tremble impossible to ignore. "You've obviously never been nervous to go on a date with your dream girl."

At this point I'll have to comb my hair again with how many times I've run my fingers through it. Being a three-hundred-year-old vampire doesn't mean I'm invincible from human emotions and I can say for a fact I haven't been this nervous in a long time. I've dreamed about spending time like this with

Celine since the day I spotted her in the warehouse, and now that it's here I'm floundering.

I don't like feeling like this ... so out of sorts like I don't know what to do or how to act in my own body.

"This has to be perfect. By the end of the night, I am kissing this woman and convincing her we're meant to be together."

Sure, a first date is probably too soon for that, but we're mates. How can anything be too soon when you have an eternity together? I'm steadfast in my need for Celine to turn, but I still have to go at her pace.

"Meow."

"Exactly, my friend. You and I know she and I are meant to be together, but she has to admit it to herself." Bending down and stroking Midnight's fur I smile. "Thank you for the vote of confidence. This is precisely what I need."

"Meow."

"I'll see you soon, bud."

With the silence and swiftness of my kind, I slip into my apartment when I hear the elevator and Celine's scent becomes stronger. Did I sneak into her apartment to get a pep talk from my hype kitty? Absolutely. Midnight is my best friend. I just can't let Tom find out or his feelings will be hurt.

Our earlier run in today has had my non-existent heart racing and my fangs refusing to retract as per usual. The fang-boners are getting out of control. It's a miracle I get away without her noticing my lisp that happens when they're in the way.

Honestly, I'm not sure how much longer I can stay away from Celine. Well ... I already don't do that great of a job at it, but my inner beast is clawing at its cage every time I walk away from her without staking my claim.

It goes against every animalistic cell in my body to not mark her slender neck with my bite for all to see. It's part of being mates—the animalistic need to claim one another.

Although, in our case, I'm the only one with those urges it seems. As a human she's certainly drawn to me, but she doesn't appear to have the same need to claim me.

I've always been told that during the time of claiming— before the bond completely snaps into place—that it's possible to lose all rational thinking. But it's not something I ever gave much thought to before. After all this time alone, I didn't think a day would ever come where I'd meet my mate.

Stepping out onto my balcony my nostrils flare as her perfumed berry scent floats from her patio door. The sounds of her getting ready meet my ears—the opening and closing of a drawer, the smooth glide of a brush through her hair. If I didn't know it would freak her out, I'd come in right now from the back and watch her get ready.

I head back inside and busy myself straightening up around my apartment and call my contact to make sure everything is in place for the date since I had to move the timeline up.

"T-minus five minutes until pick up." Rubbing my hands together in anticipation I sit on the couch and bounce in place.

Figuring I should have a snack just to be on the safe side, I snag a small glass of blood from the leftover supply I got from Luna. While I sip, I think about the possibility of turning Celine one day. How she might look as I drained her of nearly all of her blood and gave her mine to replace it—solidifying our bond and forever changing her into a vampire.

I'm so lost in my thoughts that when I finally look at the clock it's two minutes past the time I'm supposed to get her.

Shit.

I'm out the door in a flash, fist raised to knock on her door. The knock sounds impossibly loud to my ears as the fresh blood fills my veins.

The door swings open revealing the most ethereal being I've ever seen in my life.

I think my brain short circuits at the amount of skin on display with the dress she wears. It's not the same as the one she wore to the club when we danced, but similar in style. Black and lacy it hits her mid-thigh and is topped with a black leather jacket. The sweetheart neckline showcases her gorgeous tits.

Her hair is pulled up in its signature high ponytail, which I love since it gives me direct access to her scent that is strongest at the pulse point in her neck.

As I continue my perusal up her body, I let out a whistle of appreciation that makes her cheeks stain with the prettiest blush. Her brown eyes flutter when they finally make contact with mine and I can see the desire reflected in hers while she gives my body a once over. I made sure to wear a black sweater and pants that would match her outfit, she didn't need to tell me what she was wearing for me to know.

The dark clothing serves to make my hair and eyes stand out. A silver watch glints on my wrist in the light, and I spare a quick glance at it. I don't want to look away from Celine for any longer than I have to, before offering her my arm.

"Your knight in shining armor is here."

She accepts it with a smirk.

"Knight in shining armor," she says in a playful, mocking tone. "I'm no damsel in distress."

"No, you aren't," I concede. "But that doesn't mean I can't sweep you off your feet." My brows waggle and she lightly swats me with her free hand.

"Let's go, Casanova."

Celine locks her door behind her, but not before I wink at Midnight who sits on the counter and watches us go. "See you later," I mouth at him. He swishes his tail in response, and I swear his eyes are all too knowing in that moment for a simple cat. Huh.

"Where are we going?" she asks as we step onto the elevator, and I'm surprised it's taken her this long to ask and that it wasn't the first thing out of her mouth when she opened the door.

I smirk at her. "If I told you, it wouldn't be much of a surprise."

She grumbles but accepts my answer as we make our way out and I walk her to my car. I backed it in earlier, blocking the sign I painted. I know Celine isn't an idiot. If she sees it she'll begin to connect the dots on exactly who I am and I'm not ready for her to know that part of me.

I hold the car door open and her eyes rove over me for the fourth time—yes, I'm counting—as she slides into the passenger seat. I cross in front of the car and slip into the driver's side. The engine purrs to life. I wet my lips with my tongue. She tracks the movement, and I smell the faint irresistible scent of her arousal. Metal crunches slightly under my grip but thankfully Celine doesn't notice.

Oh fuck. Pressure in my gums. God help me. These insufferable fangs. Incoming boner of both kinds.

As much as Celine pretends to be unflappable the mating bond is an inevitable bitch. That's not to say mates can't reject the bond, because they can, but it makes it hard if there's a natural attraction present like we have.

I take a moment to center myself before I pull out.

Pull out.

Pull-out method.

Get your head out of the gutter, Zav!

Sitting in a confined space with my mate while she's aroused is going to test my limits and it's just the start of our date.

Dead puppies. Tom in his underwear. Pineapples.

My breath whooshes out of me, and when I finally feel composed enough and confident my fangs won't come out, I head toward the parking exit.

The drive isn't too far, and we make small talk on the way to our stop. If I had the capability of sweating, I would be, but I try to keep my expression as smooth as possible.

"Willis Tower?" Celine questions as soon as she sees the sign.

There's incredulity in her voice and I'm sure it's because the tower isn't anything special when she's lived in Chicago all her life. Sure, it's an amazing sight but doesn't hold the sparkle like it does for tourists.

Grabbing her hand and kissing the back of it, her eyes snap to mine. "Trust me." She melts a little under the gesture and I head out to open her car door.

"Thank you," she mutters when I tuck her under my arm. There's stiffness for a second before she lets herself settle into my warmth. Her tiny body fits perfectly, dwarfed by mine, and the urge to protect her from everything bad in the world rides me hard. I can tell she's been dealt a shitty hand in life and can handle herself but that doesn't mean I can't try my best to keep her away from it in the future.

Remnant puddles litter the streets and the last thing I want is Celine falling as we make our way to the front door of the tower. It also serves as the perfect way to slow my steps and hold her as long as possible. Strands of her hair blow in my face and I soak in the sensation before she pulls it away in apology.

"Did you get everything squared away for your case you were investigating?" I question.

"For now. I passed off my findings to the detective who's going to continue investigating since it's not my main case but..." she trails off.

"You're too deep in it now?" I muse.

"How could you tell?" Celine chuckles. "There's just something nagging at me about it all. I'll tell Detective Waters to keep me in the loop on what happens."

She smooths out the windblown ends of her ponytail to sit on her shoulder and picks a few fly aways that have stuck to her lip gloss. The shimmery pink color accentuates the natural pigment of her lips, and I'd love to have it smeared all over both her mouth and mine.

She gives a slight shiver, and I use it as an excuse to tug her closer. "Come on, small fry. I can't have you freezing out here before our date really begins."

"Small fry? What are these nicknames?" She shakes her head, lips curling in amusement.

I drag her toward the front door and tamper down my excitement. I can't wait to show her my surprise. Even with the date timetable moved up, I easily pulled off what will soon be the date of the century. It's amazing the things you can pull off with an unlimited budget. Sure, if Celine knew how much this had cost me she might go into cardiac arrest which would be unfortunate, but my girl deserves the best.

The wind is picking up and I smell rain in the air, a storm coming in no doubt.

As we enter the building it greets us with an open, modern, and slightly industrial looking lobby. There are lots of benches to sit at and large windows throughout the space to highlight different floors. I don't let us linger too long and we take the escalator down to filter through the expedited entry lane. I already handled everything with my contact's help and rented out the tower so it would only be us. I see her wide-eyed expression as we walk through without anyone intercepting us, but Celine continues to blindly follow me as I lead her.

"Have you been here before?" She breaks the silence with a question.

When I turn to look at her my glasses slip lower on my face. I make a move to adjust them when her delicate hand comes out of nowhere and pushes them up for me. To say I'm shocked would be an understatement and she giggles before walking ahead and observing the exhibit we're now walking through.

"Uh no, actually." My sheepish admission has her back-tracking to me in surprise.

"Never?"

I shake my head. "I don't get out much."

She narrows her gaze on me, head cocked to the side. "Zav, be for real. You have like twenty odd jobs."

I laugh. "Those are jobs. Usually, I'm just at home by myself."

You know, if I'm not out killing people who deserve it.

Her eyes scan the train exhibit as we continue to walk through the long hallway. Simulated windows showcase different Chicago scenes as we stroll, and the lights reflect off her skin like little fireflies. Our hands are so close right now they could touch, and I strain my pinky to brush hers before stopping myself from grabbing her hand. Celine's lips tilt like she knows what's happening but doesn't comment. Good. I want her to know what she does to me.

"Are you a true Chicagoan if you haven't come here once?" A light touch has me glancing down to see her pinky wrapped around mine.

Ahh. Oh fuck. She's touching me again.

"Skydeck is this way," she says with a little hop, using my pinky to tug me along.

Her smile undoes me. If I wasn't a sucker for her before, I am now. In my long life I'd seen all kinds of "beautiful" things.

Beautiful places, beautiful people, beautiful acts but never something so beautiful as Celine.

As the elevator goes up and we get closer to my surprise I begin to grow nervous all over again.

Turning to face the opposite direction, I hope to filter out some of her delicious scent while waiting for the elevator to climb. Of course it doesn't work, and I let out a tense breath. Finding a sense of composure, I allow myself to face forward again.

I must've been so focused on myself that when I turn, I jolt at Celine being right next to me.

God how long was I standing in silence.

Her brow is slightly wrinkled at my behavior, and I give a small smile in an effort to ward her off.

The door chimes as it opens to our floor, and I let her walk ahead of me for our first date—her *last* first date if I have anything to say about it.

17

oly fuck.

Stepping out into the space of the deck I'm in awe at what I see. The main lights are shut off and the area is lit solely by the illumination from buildings outside and the hundreds of candles littered throughout the room. Rose petals are dispersed strategically through the flames. Soft music hums in the background. There's a classic checkered picnic blanket and basket in the middle of the room and I can't help but laugh. It's such a simple touch on an over-the-top date of him renting out the whole place.

"Zavier, what the hell? How can you afford this?"

Who knew this goofball could be so romantic?

He must take my comment the wrong way because a frown starts to work itself onto his sweet face. He clears his throat. "I have family money. I work odd jobs to keep myself busy."

I look around, still taking it all in. I've never had someone care enough about me to go to this much trouble. "I can't believe you did all this. *How* did you do this? It's extraordinary."

He puffs out his chest under my praise. "Nothing is too much when it comes to you."

"Thank you." I hope my genuine appreciation translates. "Zav." I throw it in at the end because I know he wants to hear it. The blush that stains his cheeks lets me know it has the intended effect.

"Have a seat." Zavier waves toward the picnic set up and I kneel down. He settles across from me and pulls out different containers of prepared food.

As he goes about his task, I take a moment to appreciate the man across from me and slowly take him in. Crimson red hair gleams in the candlelight and the flickering flames dance in the lenses of his glasses. His black sweater perfectly frames his lean torso and his thin silver chain rests on his neck, begging me to grab it.

Long, lean fingers carefully set our plates up and I gulp at the veins standing in sharp contrast along the backs of his hands and forearms. There's something sensual and downright sinful about them that has me tightening my thighs together. Once he has the food arranged, he scrutinizes the placement to make sure he's satisfied and the way his gaze narrows is adorable.

"Zav?" His attention immediately hones in on me when I pull out the nickname once more "It's perfect. Don't stress yourself out about the plates."

"It needs one last finishing touch and then it'll be perfect." Digging into the basket once more he pulls out a bottle of champagne. "Some bubbly?"

Turning my head to the side I can't help but look away from the blinding cuteness he radiates. His determination to please me is adorable, so I play along.

"Yes, please."

Zavier pulls out two glass flutes and fills them with champagne. He's careful not to let the froth overflow and fills it as close to the top as possible.

"Trying to get me drunk?" I accept the drink as he carefully passes it over. "Planning to disarm me and have your wicked way?"

"Oh, Celine. I don't need champagne to do that."

I'm scared he might be right. I've never been drawn to anyone the way I am him. Despite his dramatic personality I'm drawn to him. I *like* him even if he drives me mildly crazy.

A clinking sound rings out when he taps his glass against mine and with a wink he sips the sparkling drink. I take a deep breath when a small trail of liquid dribbles out of his mouth and down his chin.

"Cheers," I murmur and down more champagne than I should in one go.

My stomach rumbles and I grab my fork to dive into dinner. The plate in front of me is stacked with all kinds of delicious smelling food. A creamy pasta dish with broccoli, red pepper, and sausage fills one corner. Cubed fruit and roasted potatoes with some kind of seasoning on them fill up the rest. Along with the champagne, Zav's also poured us both glasses of ice water somehow without me even noticing.

"Did you cook all this yourself?" I'm amazed at the burst of flavor I'm met with when I eat my first forkful of pasta. "Mm." The moan that comes out is instant and I melt right where I sit.

Zavier stares and his throat slowly works as his eyes lock in on my lips. It's then I realize how obscene of a sound I let out and down more champagne. I'm a mess.

"I did." He takes pity on me and answers. "I've had a lot of time to refine my cooking skills."

"Tell me about yourself," I prompt. "I feel like I don't know much except you work odd jobs around Chicago, live next to me, and apparently have enough family money to afford to rent out this place." I arch a brow.

"Nothing too special to tell. I already told you I've been around and never really stay in one place. I've traveled a lot and as for this"—he gestures to the space around us— "you're worth spoiling." His long legs stretch out as he makes himself at home. "Lately, though, I must admit I'm finding a reason to stick around." His eyes warm as he takes me in and heat rushes to my cheeks.

"Smooth." His gaze bores into mine and I clear my throat, looking away to break the tension. "What's your middle name?" I throw out a random question since he doesn't seem keen on the other one.

"Don't have one. What's yours?"

Zav fires it out so quickly it takes me a second to process.

"Everyone has a middle name."

"Hi! My name is Zavier. I'm the exception." He grabs my hand and shakes it which I toss away with a scoff in mock outrage.

"It's just odd." The blanket underneath us is soft against my legs as I stretch mine out too. "Mine is Rose."

He grins. "Beautiful, just like your first name. Did you know Celine means heavenly in French? It aligns perfectly with my theory that you're an angel. Heavenly flower is even more appropriate if you ask me."

Zav's statement makes me choke on the champagne I start to sip but he simply grins like a kid with his hand in the cookie jar. He loves that he always manages to catch me off guard.

"You are quite the flirt. Does this work with all the girls?" Clearing my throat and setting the offending champagne down I rest my hands in my lap. A loose thread on my dress is suddenly very appealing. I've never been the jealous type, but suddenly just the thought of Zavier with other women has me feeling like I want to stake claim to him.

"Wouldn't know. I haven't dated in a long time. My last girlfriend was even crazier than me if you can believe it," he says it so matter of fact it makes me tilt my head in question. A good-looking man like him must draw in quite the crowd on a daily basis. How could he not indulge?

"Rapid fire." Zav claps his hands. "Favorite color?"

"I wasn't asking questions fast enough for you?" I cross my arms over my chest and may or may not push my cleavage up a little more than necessary to accentuate the little bit of boobs I have.

His eyes flick down for longer than a quick glance. Zav takes his arms and does the exact same thing a moment later making me snort.

"Green." This isn't exactly true but the vibrance of his eyes in that moment eclipses my old favorite color of purple.

"Red." He points at himself like it's not clear whose favorite color he's stating. "Least favorite food?" Finger poised back at me.

"Get that thing out of here." I grab the offending appendage and trap it beneath my hand on the blanket. "Pickles if you must know. Good thing you didn't pack them for dinner." After a second passes I point my finger at him, and he smiles. "Do as I say and not as I do." His smile widens.

"Pickles. Favorite season?"

"Fall. You?"

"Fall."

Now I have a sneaking suspicion he's not playing the game correctly anymore, so I test my theory. "Favorite book? Mine's *Fifty Shades of Grey*."

"Same."

"Zavier!"

"Celine." His white teeth are showing in a full faced smirk now.

"You're just repeating whatever my answer is."

"How do you know? You said you don't know me, and I happen to love getting kinky in the bedroom." Yanking his pointer finger out from under my hand he goes back to eating his dinner.

Antics done, we continue to devour the delicious dinner. At one point I have to restrain myself from wiping sauce off his face when it smears on his cheek. I swear he's like a little kid when he eats, the food goes everywhere but his mouth. After packing our empty plates back in the basket, I hit Zav with another request.

"Tell me a truth."

Rubbing my hands on my suddenly chilled arms under my jacket I pull my knees up to my chest. I rest my head on them and watch as he eyes me suspiciously.

"A truth? I thought we were already doing that." He scoots slightly closer to me on the blanket as if I won't know. The man seems to have a pressing need to be touching me.

"Firstly, you were simply saying whatever I was saying. Secondly, I know you're a jokester and like to keep things light, but I want an actual truth from you." Rain pounds harder on the surrounding glass and I watch it slide down the panes. "It could be serious, maybe even a little painful." My eyes meet his as he watches me discerningly. "It's a safe space here but I want something real if we're going to know each other."

He seems to be running through answers in his head as he looks toward the ceiling. I give him the time he needs to formulate whatever he wants to tell me. I'm not sure what made me ask this of him but for all his jokes I can see pain hidden beneath them. I know firsthand how hard holding onto those kinds of emotions can be and when you can lighten the load by sharing them with someone else it helps just a little bit.

"My parents died, and I didn't get to say goodbye." Zav adjusts his seated position to where our sides rest against each other in a search for silent comfort. I press myself a little harder against him in encouragement. "We were estranged at the time, and I knew they didn't have long due to an illness. It was absolutely heartbreaking letting them leave this Earth knowing I'd never see them again and yet not doing anything about it either."

Our pinkies touch beneath the blanket, and I wrap mine around his just like I did not too long ago. His chest stutters at my touch and his head turns toward mine waiting for my reaction to his admission.

"Why didn't you go to them?" He must've had a reason especially if he's this broken up about it.

"I couldn't." Zav tightens his hold on my finger, his Adam's apple bobs as he swallows down a wave of emotions. "Circumstances out of my control prevented it from happening." His head drops and I've never seen the lively man look so sad before.

I want to press further on what those circumstances were, but I feel his guard rising the more he talks about it.

"If I could go back, I'd spend as much time as possible with them as I could before the sickness took hold. I suppose even that was out of my control." He loses himself in the memory before he shakes it off and gives me a sad smile. "Well, this date is going downhill real fast. Sorry for being a downer."

"Not a downer." I shake my head. "Thank you for your truth, Zav. I guess it's my turn now?"

"Celine, you don't ha—" He goes to stop me, but I insist.

"No, no it's only fair if you shared a truth that I do too."

Zavier closes his mouth and sits silently waiting for me to continue.

"Sometimes I think I'm doomed to live an endless cycle of people pleasing. Ava pointed out to me recently that's what I am—a people pleaser—and she's right. My mom abandoning my dad and I, then him leaving me in his own way has done more damage on my psyche than I like to acknowledge. I know it's not his fault, but sometimes it still feels that way." I give a mirthless laugh. "Part of why I find it hard to say no to Ava is for that reason. The few people I have in my life and care about, I struggle to go against them because I worry they'll leave me. Stupid, I know."

"Don't say that." Zav growls after my confession. "It's not stupid and you're valid in everything you're feeling." He speaks like he has his own experience with the pain.

"That's not the only thing, though." I bite my lip trying to hold the words inside, but I fail. "I'm not sure how I feel about my job. I'm slowly coming to the realization it's yet another piece of my dad I've been trying to hold onto. Being a detective was his thing, and he was so good at it." I picture Captain Barnes's face, full of expectation. "It's a high stress job and the burden of his legacy feels so lofty."

"What would you do otherwise?" Zav asks quietly.

"I'm not sure. I love the gym I box at, so maybe something with teaching other women self-defense?" I murmur and stroke the fabric of my skirt until it lays straight on my leg. "It's been a long time since I've thought about what *I* want."

Long fingers gently lift my chin, and I let my gaze wander over his masculine features before settling on his eyes.

Our faces slowly creep closer to one another's before a startingly loud thunderclap sounds and I jump. The building almost feels like it quakes, but I know that can't be true. It's more likely me that's trembling at Zav's proximity.

I can deny my feelings, my attraction, all I want but the truth is I'm drawn to this man in a way I've never been to another person.

"Should we go see if we can spot some lightning?" I clear my throat and stand up, the somber mood disappearing like a popped balloon.

Zavier's footsteps echo lightly as he follows me. We step out onto the Ledge deck and peek over at the view below. An unbelievably beautiful sight greets us, and the pouring rain adds to the ambience of the whole scene. A grid of thousands of lights in various colors, mostly yellows and oranges, stretch as far as the eye can see. Having the view surround us completely including under our feet is breathtaking. Even though it's a touristy thing, seeing it now with nobody else in the room is pretty magical.

"What do you think?" I ask Zav without taking my eyes off the view in front of me.

"Beautiful."

"Isn't the view spectacular?" I gush and trace a falling raindrop on the glass with my finger.

"Magnificent." I feel his stare on me as he says it and fight off the blush wanting to stain my cheeks.

"Let's sit down. I want to watch for a while."

We situate ourselves after Zavier runs over to grab the blanket and sets it down, so the glass won't be as cold to us. I rest my head against his shoulder, and he stiffens for a second in shock before wrapping an arm around my back. Somehow, he's beginning to lower my defenses in a way no one has before.

Cars zip by beneath us like little ants.

I'm not sure how much time passes, but Zav suddenly breaks the silence. "Thanks for agreeing to come on this date. I know I can come across as a lot sometimes, but I really do like you." He strokes my shoulder with a featherlight touch. "I wasn't sure you'd say yes, and then Ava pushed you into doing it so, yeah, thanks for coming." He sounds so small when he says it, but it warms my heart.

I pick my head up from his shoulder and smile. "Of course. I had a wonderful evening with you."

Determination fills his emerald eyes, our faces inch closer once more. He gives me time to pull away if I want to, but I don't. I want this. I want *him*.

"Wait."

Zav pulls back immediately when I say it, but I'm not protesting for the reason he thinks.

Properly facing him I gently rest my hands on his lean chest. The muscles tighten under my hold beneath his black sweater, and I clutch him tighter. I slowly push his glasses up onto his head where they sit out of the way. While I love them on him, I want complete access to his gorgeous face. Fingering a lock of red hair that has fallen into his eyes I brush it away. We both lean forward and the anticipatory breaths we release mingle in the air.

Zavier grabs my wrist when I move it up his shoulder and cups the back of my neck with his other hand. It's strong and warm but not suffocating. A pause is given as if he's allowing me one last chance to stop this, but I break down that barrier by closing the last bit of distance between us.

My lips are on his.

It starts as a soft, sweet peck and we pull back after it happens, staring into each other's eyes, as we revel in the moment. Then, like a raging inferno our lips slam back together and I'm holding onto his shoulders, fully seated in his lap. We consume each other, weeks of sexual tension building to this. The floodgates have finally been opened.

Zav yanks the hair tie out of my ponytail, the length cascading around my shoulders, and he fists it, controlling the direction of the kiss.

Our cores grind against each other and a moan slips out of me. Zav's answering moan tells me he's as affected by this as I am.

His tongue swipes across my lips asking for entrance and I part mine letting him in. Our tongues tangle and he continues to clutch me like a life preserver. A small prick against my lip has me questioning the contact but with another quick swipe of his tongue I'm consumed by pleasure. My fingers run through his silky crimson strands, and I pull on the silver chain around his neck just enough for a bite of pain to leave him whimpering under me, asking for more.

I love that sound.

A man who whimpers and moans for his woman is such a turn on. While I love to be dominated, sometimes I also love to do the dominating. My sexual history isn't extensive by any means but enough for me to know a few of my kinks.

Coming up for air we rest our foreheads against each other.

Zav whispers my name like a prayer and tucks his face into my neck. He peppers kisses along the column of my throat, and I hug his broad back reveling in the feeling of being worshipped.

Teeth scrape along my skin and when he starts to suck, I know a hickey is going to be left behind. His heavy breaths bring goosebumps to my flesh when he pulls back slightly to admire his work.

"Shit, Zav." I can't help but call out his name when he flips us and lays me down flat on my back. The hard floor smooshes me against the full length of his body and I clench my thighs together. His thick cock presses against my thigh and I moan his name when he licks over his work.

"I had to mark you." One last kiss to my neck before pulling back. "Look at you splayed out beneath me." Checking the silver watch on his wrist he smirks. "Just in time for dessert."

God help me.

18

'm hard as a fucking rock.

I'm talking dick absolutely weeping, steel rod in my pants, borderline moaning mess. The whole nine yards.

All it took was Celine's body laid out in front of me and now I'm having a hard time keeping my vampire instincts under lock. My stupid fangboner already popped with the initial excitement of our kiss. It got worse when I accidentally nipped her lip and got a taste of her blood. The honey flavor was the sweetest thing I've tasted in all my life. It's taken me years of practice to control my thirst, but Celine's blood calls to me like no other.

I turned the almost bite into a hickey both to soothe myself with a mark of some sort and to hide my mouth until I could get my fangs to recede.

"As much as I'd love to have you for my dessert"—I stand and offer my hand which she grabs with a frown— "I have actual dessert for us."

Her hair tickles my face when I lean in and whisper in her ear, "When I officially make you mine, it'll be on a lush bed and not on hard glass. You deserve more." Her eyes soften at my explanation, and I place a soft kiss on her brow letting my lips linger. "Come on, I made crème brûlée."

"Is there anything you can't do?"

"I'm shit at patience." The irony isn't lost on me what with how long I've been alive.

Her eyes sparkle with humor. "I could've told you that."

When I place the blanket down once more, carefully avoiding any fire hazards, I sit and she settles beside me, close enough that both our legs are touching.

Celine's dead set on torturing me by being this close.

"We could have this for dessert instead?" I hold up the bag of gummy bears I stashed away.

Celine gasps and makes grabby hands.

"How'd you know I like gummy bears?" She wastes no time digging into them. "Never mind, with you I don't even want to know."

I chuckle and go about my task while she eats her dessert appetizer.

I grab a ramekin out of the basket where it sits on ice packs. A small butane torch is tucked away, and she reaches for it which makes her scent even stronger than before.

Fangboner incoming.

"Celine." A growl sounds in my throat. "Unless you want me to cover your neck in my marks and spank your ass raw, you'll sit still." The gasp she lets out is telling, and I know if we were at the point where I could slip my fingers into her panties I'd find her fucking soaked for me.

I need to be on my best behavior. I don't want to take Celine to bed until I tell her we're mates and what I am. It feels wrong to take that step with her without her knowing the full extent of our connection. I might be a lot of things; killer, stalker, psychopath—but I won't take advantage of my mate like that.

I torch the sugar covered top of the dessert. Once it's caramelized to perfection we dig in and the gummy bears are forgotten. Celine taps on the top a couple times before giving it a firm crack to splinter it so there's a bit in each bite of cream.

Small noises of appreciation come from her, and I soak it all in. How I'm sitting here with my mate, my human mate no less, I'll never understand. I'd long given up on meeting my other half and figured I was unworthy with the blood I had on my hands. Killing vermin who deserved it aside, I had innocent blood staining my soul as well. Fledglings struggle with their hunger and mine was hard to keep in check for a while.

"This is delicious. Whenever I've tried to make crème brûlée in the past I either scramble the egg or end up warming the cream underneath too much and ruin the sugar." Her pink tongue flicks out to get the remnants of the dessert off her spoon. "You'll have to teach me your secrets."

Celine lets out a startled cry when I gently bite down on her earlobe. "You just want me for my crème brûlée." The temptation to break skin is dangerous but I can't seem to keep my fangs off her. The need to claim her is nearly all-consuming, but I won't do it. Not yet.

She swats at me and rolls her eyes. "Yes, you've found me out. Once I get the technique down, I'll toss you to the curb because you'll be of no more use to me."

Rain still pounds on the glass and a particularly aggressive strike of lightning illuminates her blushing cheeks.

"On the contrary, I think you'll find me very useful. In more ways than one." The last part I whisper and she shivers.

Her cheek brushes mine as she turns to me and just when I think her lips will be on mine once more the shrill cry of her phone ringing ruins the moment. Her eyebrows furrow when she sees the name on the screen and quickly answers.

"Captain Barnes?" After a few seconds she jumps up to stand. Her bootsteps echo on the floor as she paces nervously. "What? Just mine? Fuck."

A vampire's hearing is stronger than that of a human, so it's not hard to listen in on the conversation. I don't want to invade her privacy, but I have to know what has her so stressed. I need to know if I can fix it.

"From what we can tell nothing's been stolen but you might want to get here as soon as possible."

"Oh my gosh, Midnight!" Celine turns to look at me, eyes wide with fear. "Is he okay?" Tears well in her eyes and I rush over to grab her hand in silent support. She squeezes mine but lets go much too quickly for my liking.

"Yes, he's fine, don't worry." Just then a telltale meow echoes through the phone line and Celine visibly deflates like all she needed was the meow of confirmation. Her valuables could've been taken, but of course with her soft heart she's more concerned about the cat.

"I'll be there as soon as I can. Thanks, Captain." With an abrupt sign off they both hang up and she pockets her phone.

"What's going on? Everything okay?" I play dumb.

"Apparently some psycho broke into my apartment." Celine starts to gather up her things. "I'm sorry to cut our date short, but I really need to get back to survey the damage and talk to the officers." Her eyes dart around the room realizing how much is left on the floor. "Shit, I should help you clean this up." The genuine upset in her tone while she debates between staying to help me and getting back to her broken in apartment makes me smile internally.

"Don't worry about it. I have someone that can handle it for me. Right now, I want to drive you back and make sure everything's all right." Her watery half-smile in response guts me and we rush to the elevator to make our way back home.

"Captain!"

The police captain is standing outside her door, but no other apartment on the floor seems to have been broken into like hers has. Interesting. Multiple squad cars were parked outside of the complex and a few officers still mill about her space, taking pictures for evidence.

"Ah, Celine." His eyes shine with pity as he watches her take in the pillaged space. "One of your neighbors got home and saw the door broken in and the place a mess so they called the police. We've surveyed the building and surrounding area, but the culprit seems to have gotten away. From the surveillance cameras we believe it to be a male, but his features were obscured so we need to investigate further."

"Do you have a picture?" She crosses her arms and tries to stay strong like always when I know she wants to break. There's a subtle tremor in her lips that betrays her emotions despite her stoic appearance.

"Here." Another detective walks over and holds up a monitor with a grainy picture of a figure.

The person's tall and bulky build points to them being male. An all-black outfit with a hoodie covering their face doesn't help narrow down our search but I'm already formulating a plan to track down this asshole. Nobody fucks with my girl and gets away with it.

I sniff the air as discreetly as possible, but with so many officers having already disturbed the scene it's going to make it impossible to single out one specific scent.

Fuck.

"Shit." Celine scrubs a hand down her face and her eyes brighten slightly when Midnight creeps out from around the couch. "Come here, boy." She grabs him and holds him close to her chest, stroking his black fur for comfort. I reach over and scratch behind his ears which makes his yellow eyes narrow in pleasure.

"I need to look around and see if they took anything." She starts her search and I watch helplessly from the sidelines.

"Can I help?" I trail behind her like a helpless child. I don't like her shutting down.

"That's okay. I want to do this by myself," she sighs, and looks at me over her shoulder. "I'm so sorry I ruined our date, but thank you for everything. You don't need to stay here while this happens."

She's kicking me out? Fuck that.

"You didn't ruin anything, Celine. You didn't ask for your apartment to get broken in. I want to be here." We hold eye contact before finally she nods and silently continues to look around.

"Who are you?" The police captain must finally notice a stranger standing in the room.

"Zavier. Her neighbor," I answer like that's all he needs to know. "Who are you?" I already know but I'm a petty bitch, so I ask anyway.

"Chip Barnes. The captain of this force."

"All right, Captain Chip nice to meet you." I shake his hand when he holds it out.

"Captain Barnes," he corrects me.

"That's what I said." I stuff my hands in my pockets and start to walk back toward Celine's bedroom. "Captain Tortilla Chip." A snort sounds behind me and a grin pulls on my lips.

I can't seem to help myself. The man seems nice enough, but it's a laughable name.

The apartment looks like a tornado was taken to it. Furniture lies upturned on the ground, clothes that once sat folded in drawers are strewn across the floor, and even the fridge has been raided and torn apart. Her bedroom seems to have the worst damage, and I cringe at the shattered picture frames and TV screen on the floor.

My anger continues to rise when I see a pair of her panties half-hanging out of the drawer. She must feel so violated. My jaw ticks and I clench my fist in an effort to withhold my need to punch something.

"Captain?" Celine's crystalline voice rings out from her bathroom area.

"Coming."

He heads over to her, and I coincidentally find a small mess that needs cleaned up outside her bathroom. Slyly, I peek to see what they're looking at.

"What do you make of this?" She points while still holding the cat, floofy tail swinging in the air.

Blood splatter litters her vanity counter and they both inspect it.

"There aren't any other blood trails that I can see in the apartment, and I don't know where he would've done it either. Sure, there's shattered glass in the room but again, no other blood."

Interesting. I discreetly inhale to scent the blood and keep the memory of it locked down for future investigation. It is odd there's no other sign of injury with how much was wrecked save for this one spot.

"I'll have the boys take a sample for the lab. Very odd indeed." The captain rubs his bald head and walks back out to the living room.

I speed over to the closet and hide behind the door before he can catch me eavesdropping. Once he's out of the room I walk over to Celine.

"We'll get to the bottom of this, I swear." Inching closer I slowly wrap an arm around her shoulders, and she leans into me. Midnight must be anti-hug sandwich because he yowls and hops out of her arms. Without the cat between us it allows me to fully hug my mate. Her hair tickles my nose, and I nuzzle into it.

Celine sighs and tears soak into my shirt.

"You don't have to be strong all the time." She silently sobs harder. "I'll be strong for both of us right now. Let it out." I back us into her bathroom and sit us down on top of the toilet lid under the guise of privacy. Officers and detectives still mill about but they keep a wide berth between us understanding the situation.

It seems like a lot of cops for a break-in, but my guess is they realized it was Celine's address and more of the force came out than necessary. It's nice to know her team has her back.

After a few minutes of letting herself feel all the emotions she sniffles, and I dry her remaining tears with a tissue.

"Celine?" Captain Potato Chip calls out from around the corner, and I can see him rubbing his neck awkwardly while interrupting our moment.

"Yeah, Captain?" She gives a last swipe to her face, and I see the moment where she puts her mask back on.

"We're going to head out. The investigation will continue, and we'll look at cameras of the surrounding area to try and nail this guy. I don't know why he targeted you specifically, but it seems you're the only apartment that was broken into. Anyone come to mind that could've done this?" He holds a pen at the ready above his notepad.

"Uh, I don't know. You know how it is with this line of work,

there are a lot of people that could have it out for me I suppose."
Her brow wrinkles and I want to smooth the delicate skin out.
"Nobody specific comes to mind but you never know." She
shrugs and the captain takes a few notes.

"All right, Detective. I'm sorry this happened, and we'll do
our best to catch the culprit. For now, do you have somewhere
else you can stay?" He shifts his weight to one booted foot and
tucks his notepad into the breast pocket of his vest. "The lock
on the door is busted and even if it wasn't I don't feel
comfortable with you staying here after everything that's
happened."

A flash of surprise crosses Celine's face like she hadn't even
considered the fact she couldn't stay here right now. It goes to
show how flustered she is.

"Yeah, I can call A—" She starts but I promptly interrupt
her.

"Me. She'll stay with me." I flash my perfectly white teeth
and the shocked expression on both of their faces is comical.

"You?" They ask in tandem.

"Me." I smirk.

"Don't you live right next door? Does that make much sense
when the apartment one door down got broken into?" The
captain scowls.

"First off, I resent the fact you think I can't protect her."
Celine rolls her eyes at my comment, but I continue. "Second,
it's kind of perfect, isn't it? I doubt they think she'll stay this
close to the scene of the crime and if they come back, we can
catch them red handed. Third, how dare you? I'm perfectly
capable of watching out for Celine." His comment hits a nerve,
and I can't help but defend myself.

"Celine." Captain Corn Chip gives an exasperated sigh her
way. "It's up to you. No matter what you decide we can post
officers on watch just in case."

LOVING A VAMPIRE IS TOTAL CHAOS   153

Celine rolls her lip between her teeth and by the determined set of her eyes I know she's going to agree with me.

"It's fine. I'll stay with Zavier."

"I swear I'll keep you safe, Celine. The captain here will get to the bottom of this I know it." I nuzzle into her, and she stands there stiff as a board, which I don't like. She was loosening up to me on our date, but this break-in has shut her down.

"Right." He eyes us warily. "Take the next few days off, Brennan."

"Captain—" Celine starts to argue but closes her mouth when he holds up a hand.

"Having someone break into their home would shake anyone. You haven't had time to process, and I want you to take time off. Okay?" He pleads with her, and I give her a reassuring stroke down her back. "Nobody will think less of you, and we have everything handled."

Celine nods reluctantly, and I dance a little on the inside at the thought of extra alone time with her.

The squad slowly makes their way out of her apartment and close the door best they can with the busted lock. They leave caution tape for us to put up once we're done escorting Midnight and some of Celine's things over to my apartment. It doesn't take more than two trips.

"Got everything?" I snag Midnight and flip him over in my arms like a baby. She watches expectantly like the cat will shred my skin for attempting such a thing, but he purrs contentedly.

We're best buds.

"Yup." She gives one last cursory glance around her living room and shuts the door. Taping up the frame she covers it in record time and trudges over to my apartment. The sad slump of her shoulders hurts me to watch.

Midnight hops out of my arms as soon as we enter the

living room, and he makes himself comfortable on the couch. I hope Celine can settle in just as easily as him.

"I'll take the couch." She announces suddenly and I have to resist the urge to hold my hand to my chest like a Victorian child with the plague.

"I think the fuck not," I refute.

"Excuse me?" A small laugh comes out of her and she crosses her arms, ready to argue. Little does she know I'm a stubborn vampire and would never let my mate sleep on anything less than a comfy bed I personally vetted.

"I'm not making you sleep on the couch, Celine. You're my guest."

Quicker than she can track I grab the blanket and pillow she just sat on the couch cushions and deposit them on my bed. Vampires don't need much sleep, so I hardly ever use the king size mattress. The crisp black comforter is ready for her to dive under. Fluffing the pillows I stand back and admire my work.

"I'm not sleeping with you. Just because we went on a date doesn't mean we're cuddling."

"Aw, but I'll be the little spoon." My lip juts out and she slugs my shoulder. "I'm just kidding. I'll take the couch." Snagging a pillow and fleece blanket off a chair in the corner of the room, I set them up on the couch.

"I feel bad kicking you out of your bed." She stands awkwardly in the doorway of the bedroom with her blanket hanging loosely from her fingertips.

Even amidst the chaos of getting here in a rush, rain slicking back her hair, makeup running down her face, and red eyes from unshed tears, she's still the most beautiful creature I've ever laid my eyes on.

"Zavier." Snapping pulls me out of my daydream. Celine taps her foot in rapid succession on the hardwood floor and lets out a huff. "Did you hear me?"

"You want to get married and have my babies? Great plan. Love that plan."

Her cheeks burn red, and she chucks a pillow at my head.

"Shut up. You know what? I don't care that I'm stealing your bed." Hair flows around her shoulders as she abruptly turns and closes the door behind her.

A snort comes out at her thinking a flimsy piece of wood would keep her safe from me.

"Meow." The disgruntled sound behind me shows Midnight making himself at home on my makeshift bed. The bakery has opened, and he is working overtime to produce biscuits.

"Make yourself at home, my friend. Neither you nor your owner will be leaving." It sounds ominous but I'd be damned again if I let her slip through my fingers.

19

Sweat rolls down my temple as I jab the heavy bag in front of me.

The room is quiet besides the occasional grunt from fellow boxers.

I've come to Vitality for as long as I can remember. Run by a retired female MMA fighter, it's a female only gym tucked downtown. It's a safe and supportive environment I love coming to.

Boxing has always been an outlet whenever I have too much on my mind. Usually after I visit my dad it's one of the first stops I make. When I'm stuck on a case it also allows me to clear my head. There's something about boxing that makes everything else in my life fade away.

Right now, I'm overflowing with frustration, confusion, and horror at what happened last night. Someone broke into my apartment, my safe space, and ransacked the place. Violated doesn't even begin to cover how I feel. My chest is tight, my stomach coiled from the defilement.

With one last punch that leaves the bag swinging, I squat down to catch my breath.

"You okay, Celine?" Olivia, a regular I see often, asks.

I peer up and find her standing in front of me with a concerned look. I must seem possessed over here, absolutely pounding this bag like if I beat it hard enough whoever did this will feel it too.

"I'm all right." I blow out a breath and attempt to wave her off.

"Are you sure? You've been going to town on that bag." She gives a small smile, and I accept the hand she holds out to pull myself up.

"Lot going on in here." I tap the side of my head and cringe at the amount of sweat I feel in my hair. A shower before I go is a must.

"Maybe class will help. We have a new instructor today and he's *hot*. If you're not too tired that is." She claps and flits over to other girls that have started to filter in, not bothering to wait for my response.

There are rotating instructors and classes they teach within the gym. I try to hit them when I can, and today's is focused on shadow boxing.

Jogging over to the back wall, I grab a quick sip from my water bottle and text Ava back. She'd heard about the break-in this morning and immediately texted to make sure I was okay. After reassuring her she didn't need to take off work to be with me I said she could come over for a girl's night in. Zav didn't mind and even encouraged it.

I zip my phone back in my bag and stretch my arms over my head for some relief before class. I hadn't planned on joining but I still have some frustration I need to vent.

Footsteps echo in the room and girls start to murmur about something that's gotten their attention.

The steps continue until I hear them stop just behind me. A heady, masculine scent fills my nostrils and now I can't catch my breath for a different reason.

"Boo." A familiar tenor sounds next to my ear.

I close my eyes, taking a deep breath.

I should've known him letting me leave the apartment alone was too good to be true. He resisted when I first brought it up, wary of the intruder stalking me, but then it was like a light bulb went off in his head and he agreed.

Now I see why.

"Fancy seeing you here." I face a certain red-headed fiend. The girls are tittering near the classroom door, watching us.

"Did I mention boxing is one of my secret hobbies?" Zavier quirks a brow and I narrow my eyes.

"Everything seems to be a secret hobby with you."

"What can I say"—Zav nips at my earlobe before I can stop him— "I'm a man of many talents."

We walk together over to the classroom, and there's no mistaking the gossip that's circulating.

"Does she know him?"

"Is he her boyfriend?"

"I didn't think she dated!"

"Let's circle up everyone!" Zav claps his hands, and it doesn't take much for him to become the center of attention. I can't say I blame him. He is annoyingly gorgeous.

From there we run through various exercises during all of which Zav doesn't stray far from me. When I hold back during our sparring session, he tells me to let it all out. Poor guy gets hammered by my fists but it's exactly the cathartic release I need. I suppose I shouldn't feel too bad since he grins the entire time.

When class is over, Zav refuses to let me walk back to the apartment.

"There's nothing wrong with my legs," I protest.

His lips purse. "Get in the car, Celine."

I don't know what it is about his tone that has me listening. I slide the seatbelt across my body as he gets in the driver's side. "Since you're insisting on driving can I put in an order for Mexican food and pick it up before we go back?"

He hands me his phone and I take it, despite the fact I'm perfectly capable of using mine.

"What's your passcode?" I ask when the phone prompts me.

"Zero, three, One, Three."

I put in the numbers and search for the Mexican restaurant's information. I stop before hitting the call button, my finger hovering above the screen.

"That's weird. Your passcode is my birthday."

He glances over at me, sliding his glasses up his nose. "Huh. Funny coincidence."

I shake off the weirdness and call to place the order. Since it's going to be twenty or so minutes before it's ready, I have Zav drop me by Luna's shop since it's on the way and get some of her treats for later.

Once we have the food, we head straight back home and Zav pulls up to the elevator to let me off with the stuff before he goes to park, so we don't have to carry it all the way over here.

While I wait for him to return, a text comes from Ava.

Ava: Be there in 10!

I'm excited to see her and have some much-needed girl time, but I'm not sure I'm ready for the nebula that is going to be her and Zav together.

"Stop touching it!" Ava slaps Zav's hand as he reaches for his face mask once again.

We're sprawled on the couch looking like we just stepped out of Phantom of the Opera with our white face masks. Zav insisted on participating in girl's night and now is facing the consequences of his actions.

"It's been five minutes," he whines. "You're telling me I need to wait longer to be pretty?"

"Beauty is pain and patience." Ava folds her hands across her chest and settles back into the couch cushions. "Plus, you know you're a pretty princess already, so shut up."

"Aw, am I?" He bats his lashes at her, flashing her a winning smile.

They've been going back and forth since she arrived. It started with him sneaking a bite of her enchilada and her hangry self retaliating by making him do masks with us. Truth be told I think he enjoys it.

"Should we throw a movie on before I head home?" Ava asks.

"You know it." I grin.

Between my boxing session and having Ava here, it's been a welcome distraction, and I already feel much better about everything than I did when I woke up this morning. Ava has made it a point not to bring up the break-in which I appreciate. For now, I'm happy to stay ignorant and enjoy this time with my people.

The movie starts—an early 2000's rom-com—and Zav hops up to stick some popcorn in the microwave. When it's all popped he settles between us with a giant bowl for us all to share from.

"I think I like girl's night," he muses.

Ava pats his arm. "Oh, sweetie. This is only the tip of the iceberg of what girl's night can be."

He gives her a dopey grin. "I can't wait for the next one."

"That is not edible. It's still hard!" I protest, spitting out the pasta.

I might not have to eat human food for sustenance, but if I'm going to then it ought to taste good.

"It's called al dente." She pouts her perfect pink lips. "It's supposed to have some form. If we cook it like you want it'll be a mushy, wet mess. Trust the process." Celine grabs the pot of boiling pasta and strains it through the colander sitting in the sink.

After a grocery run this afternoon, due to the lack of products in my fridge and pantry, we swung by Luna's so Celine could get some coffee and I could sneak some blood bags.

When we got back, Celine made quick work of putting everything away. I grinned the entire time, because whether she realizes it or not she feels at home with me.

After she decided she wanted pasta, we began cooking together side by side. It's an oddly intimate activity, which I hadn't expected. Celine brushing against me to grab a utensil, me reaching over her to grab a hard-to-reach plate, and small smiles she sends my way every now and then.

She's letting her guard down little by little.

Midnight observes from his perch on top of the fridge like he's Gordon Ramsey. Every little bit, he'll interject like we've gone about the process wrong. Cat thinks he's a human, I swear.

"This is how my dad always did it. I promise it'll work out in the end." Steam billows out of the metal bowl and disperses in the air. "Do you have the egg mixture ready?"

I crack my last egg as she says to stir to combine with parmesan and parsley. The counter looks like a warzone since I'm not particularly good at keeping things tidy.

"Got it right here."

She grabs it from me and pours it over the pasta now in the skillet resting on the stove with cooked bacon. Her arm works furiously stirring it around until it's all evenly coated and the egg is cooked within the heat of the bacon grease and fresh pasta.

"Can you hand me the heavy cream? It's time to add that, too."

Her tongue sticks out adorably in concentration. I'm not sure she's even aware she's doing it.

I grab the cream and pass it over. She pours it into the mixture and gets back to stirring. I'd take over and help but I'm enjoying watching her way too much for that.

"This smells delicious." I sneak behind Celine and wrap my arms around her middle. Her dark berry scent is delectable, and I can't help but nuzzle her neck. The beating pulse of her heart accelerates, tempting me to do something I know she's not ready for. "My little chef."

"Don't say that before you've tried it." Her back settles into my chest. "You might think it's terrible."

"Never," I scoff.

I kiss Celine's cheek before letting go and grabbing the now finished peas from the microwave. Out of my peripheral I see her rub the spot my lips left with a small smile.

Cute.

"Do you want these added in too?" I pull a spoon out of a drawer.

"Bring them over to the island and we can add however much we want to our bowls." Celine shuts off the stove top and sets the finished pasta skillet on the waiting potholder.

Our placemats sit ready with plates and silverware. We each dish up a portion of the carbonara and dig in.

Creamy sauce sticks to the noodles and I spear a large portion on my fork. Shoving the enormous bite into my mouth, I'm shocked at the taste. It's delicious and the wait was well worth it, not that I'm complaining about spending time with Celine.

Celine's pink tongue darts around her pasta and the moan she lets out is downright sinful. I feel my cock tightening in my pants. I close my eyes, counting to ten in an effort to calm myself.

We don't talk much as dinner goes on, the delicious food consuming our focus. I do find out a few more of her favorite things by asking silly questions simply because I can't help myself. I fill my plate with thirds while Celine finishes off seconds. By the time we're done we're both nursing a food baby and reluctant to clean up our mess. I haven't eaten that much human food in one go in a long time.

"My dad always said a good cook cleans as he cooks but we have not heeded that advice, have we?" Celine laughs and pats her flat stomach as we both face the mess.

LOVING A VAMPIRE IS TOTAL CHAOS   165

I eye her hand on her stomach, thinking about what she might look one day round with my child.

"First to clean their dishes wins," I blurt out to derail my thoughts and rush to the sink.

"Wha—" Celine sputters, but wastes no time in bumping me out of the way.

I could easily win the challenge put forth, but I find I don't want to. Seeing the competitive gleam in her eye is a welcome sight after everything. She's tried to hide it well, but I've seen the disquiet within her brown eyes. She's more shaken up over the break-in than she wants to admit.

"Done!" she shouts triumphantly. "What do I win?"

Truth to be told I hadn't thought that far ahead and follow my gut.

I plant a kiss on her nose and enjoy the shock that floods her features.

"That's it?" Celine breathes, the air in the room suddenly getting sucked out.

"I've wanted to do it since you poured the noodles into the pot," I admit.

"Oh." She rocks back on her heels before seeming to come to a decision. "Kind of a lousy prize. I think you can do better."

I'm shocked at my little vixen's boldness, but I don't have to be told twice.

Advancing toward her with the grace of a panther, I lift her by her curvy hips onto the counter. Wedging her legs open I lean toward her so we're chest to chest. Both breathing heavy, we simply exist together in this moment in time.

Celine traces a line around both of my brows, and I push an errant strand of hair behind her ear. She leans an arm across my shoulder and pulls me closer with her other.

"I might've thought about it too," she whispers as our noses touch.

"Yeah?" I moan at the sensation of her body pressing into mine.

Celine tugs my hair, and my fingers splay on the counter, digging into the granite hard enough to leave behind a dent. I quickly raise my hands, hoping I didn't do enough damage for her to notice. I lean into her, inhaling the scent at her neck. I could easily lay her out here and make a meal out of her.

As our lips brush, a timer goes off on the stove and we jump apart.

"Fuck," Celine breathes. "Forgot to turn that off."

I back away in disappointment, but not before making sure she feels every hard inch of me as she slides off the counter.

Celine excuses herself to change as I turn off the timer.

I hear her milling about in my bedroom and the shower cut on a second later.

The visual of her naked and wet in a shower is doing nothing for my raging hard-on.

"Midnight," I grind out. "Your mother is going to be the death of me. Not the literal death, since I can't die easily, but at least the death of my dick."

"Meow."

I sigh, "Thanks, bud."

Celine finishes her shower and pads out into the living space with bare feet and dressed in a pair of tiny blue cotton shorts and a matching tank.

Fucking temptress.

She knows what she's doing to me.

"I'm going to shower," I mumble, passing her by.

My cock practically cries in protest at leaving her behind. But it's not time. Not yet.

After my shower I find her curled up on the couch under a fleece blanket. Midnight blinks over at me from his cat bed where he kneads the fabric in the corner.

I settle beside her on the couch, grabbing her ankle and carefully pulling her legs to settle in my lap. She gives me a lazy, tired smile in return and adjusts the blanket so it's over both of us.

There's a movie on, something gory and hilarious that instantly sucks me in.

About an hour later, movement out of the corner of my eye has me looking at Celine. Dark lashes brush the tops of her cheeks where she's starting to doze. I watch her struggle to keep her eyes open and slowly slide further to the side of the couch before I give in and gently pick her up. Walking slowly to not jostle her, I lay her prone form on the mattress. I pull back the comforter and place her on top of the sheets. She doesn't say anything, just mumbles sleepily when I shut off the lamp and tuck her in.

I take a second to sit on the edge of the bed and watch her surrender to sleep. Her long dark hair is free of its typical confines and splayed across my pillow. The sweet sound of her breaths fills the space, and her chest rises and falls steadily. The stiff peaks of her nipples poke against the thin fabric of her tank top. The soft swells of her breasts tease me each time she inhales.

I stroke her cheek as gently as possible without waking her up. She smiles softly in her sleep at my touch and it feels like some sort of victory. Even unconscious, she knows she's safe with me. I would never hurt her, nor would I let anyone else harm her.

Anger surges, because someone *did* hurt her. Maybe not physically, but they invaded her personal space, ransacked her entire apartment, and made her feel incredibly violated.

Soft mumbles and a furrow in her brow encourage me to leave the bedroom. My rage is starting to become palpable and the last thing I want to do is wake her. I need to go kill something. Or someone.

Certain she'll be safe in my apartment after I secretly had state of the art security installed while she slept last night, I give Midnight a pat where he sleeps curled up and make my way out of the building and downstairs.

My phone dings and I glance at the screen. A slow smile spreads over my face.

Perfect fucking timing.

Death's Assistant: I have a target for you.

nder the cover of night and falling rain, I run through the streets, so fast that all anyone who's looking would see is a strange blur. I could take my car, but I crave the cold bite of the elements on my skin right now. It serves to keep me centered and remember my ultimate goal— ridding the streets of the worst kind of scum.

I reach my destination in the form of a luxury hotel downtown. What seems to be an exclusive, high-class establishment that's invite only to humans is actually a central meeting place for supernaturals in Chicago. It is indeed a hotel, but it's also used for more than that. Conferences, social gatherings, secret meetings, and sexual debauchery all go on within these halls.

A group of powerful supernaturals own the building and keep it running smoothly. I've used it many times when I've been in the area over the years for meeting purposes and it's the perfect place to do so now.

Flashing my membership card to the doorman he nods and

holds it open for me. I swiftly zip to our agreed upon room and spot my contact leaning against the window.

"Whatcha' got for me?" I ask.

A man of few words, the vampire simply holds out a folder for me and I grab it from him. He crosses his thick arms over his chest and continues to survey the city while I review the information. His hair is cropped close to his scalp, his eyes a bright shade of blue.

"Good one this time." I whistle gleefully. It's a sick fuck I was stalking for months that got spooked and even though I was careful to always cover my tracks, he got paranoid that he was being watched. "Pleasure doing business as always." I pat his shoulder and receive a growl for it.

Not wasting time, I exit the hotel in record time. I don't stop until I'm slipping into the entrance of an abandoned, dilapidated building on the outskirts of the city. It's positioned perfectly to hide a piece of shit like Frank Denvers.

He's somehow given the police the slip while wreaking havoc in various cities. Abuse and murder are just a few of his offenses and I'm putting a stop to it right now.

My boots are silent as I slink along the edge of the building and spot a small fire burning in a stove in the middle of the room. Frank himself is sat in front of it on an old holey couch, without a care in the world. I can't help but snort at the fact that he's even hooked up a TV. I guess he doesn't want to miss his favorite reality shows while he's hiding out.

Blood steadily drips from a body he has strung up in one corner of the room. I wrinkle my nose at the stench of body odor and sweat from Frank as well as the decaying corpse.

The taste and scent of blood changes drastically as a body decomposes. It becomes downright rancid, like spoiled milk to a human.

I was hoping my contact gave me the information fast

enough that I'd be able to take Frank out before he added another kill to his list, but unfortunately, I'm too late. I can at least guarantee this will be his last ever kill.

Ashes twist and float through the room with the scent of sulfur. The rain helps cover it where any typical human wouldn't be able to smell it. Frank thinks he's safe here. He thinks he can come back to Chicago and go about his typical bullshit. Instead, he'll be paying with his life.

Getting back to one of my favorite pastimes feels good since it's been put on the sidelines with Celine occupying my time lately.

Not one for delaying my entrance, I stroll into the space and openly greet Frank.

"What's up, Shithead?" I lean against a pole feet away from him and cross my ankles.

Showtime.

"Who the fuck are you?" He startles and jumps up from his seated position one the couch. Despite the fire, his breath puffs in front of him and nasty yellow teeth flash at me when he opens his mouth.

"I could be cliche and say your worst nightmare, but it's kind of the truth." My footsteps echo when I slowly approach. The idiot doesn't have anyone here with him, so it'll make for an easy kill. Kind of disappointing though, I wouldn't say no to a mass murder. "You've been a very bad boy, Frank." I see the exact moment my aura hits him, and he quivers. His body knows he should run but his mind is stubborn like most humans, and he stays rooted where he is.

Frank rips a glock out of his pocket, and trains it on my chest, but I continue my advance. "I'll shoot!" Shaky fingers unlock the safety on the gun, but I simply smile.

"Frank, Frank, Frank." A piece of trash crunches under my shoe much like Frank will very soon. "I had hoped you'd make this more fun for me. What do you say? Let's make a game out of it." A brilliant idea pops into my head. "Hide and seek. If you can manage to outsmart me, I'll let you go."

I won't, but humans do love the illusion of winning.

"What are you talking about? How about I shoot you right now and be done with it." Spit flies while he yells. He grips the gun tighter and holds it up to my forehead when I stand right in front of him.

Am I risking him shooting me? Of course, but I'm faster than he could ever imagine and would be out of the way before the bullet even left the chamber. And even if he did manage to shoot me, it might hurt like a bitch but I won't die.

"You want to know what's going on? Fine, I'll give you a hint." I roll my neck and I'm rewarded with a satisfying crack. "Laura. Chloe. Eleanor." Muddy brown eyes, nothing like Celine's, widen in fear as he catches my drift. "All broken and bloody by your hand. There are others I can name too. Shall I continue?"

"You don't know anything about anyone." Tremors flood his body, and the gun violently shakes in his grip. I clutch it and twist his wrist behind his back in one fell swoop. His yelp of pain fuels my fire.

"Pieces of shit like you can't hide from me. You're my only source of entertainment in a long life full of annoyance." Minus Celine, of course, who I now have at my side … sort of. "I know everything. Now be a good boy for once." Sidling up to his ear I whisper the last part, "Run."

Frank doesn't need to be told twice, so perhaps he's not as dumb as he looks. He turns and attempts to run, but he's not paying attention and trips and falls. With a look of terror that fills me with glee he looks back and makes sure I'm staying put before getting up and stumbling out of the room. There's absolutely no way he'll escape me or win our game but why tell him that? It would take all the fun out of it and hope is the one thing that can keep a person going.

Heavy breathing and clumsy footfalls fill my ears, and I pull out my phone to play Sudoku while I give him a few minutes to do whatever he thinks he's going to do. The fire has started to die out without its creator here to tend to it and I decide I'll give him until the flames have extinguished before the chase ensues.

Fuck, I thought there was a nine in that row.

The digital sudoku board flashes red when I attempt to place the wrong number in the wrong spot. Just then, a rat skitters across the ground to grab a piece of moldy food scrap not far from where I stand. Disgusting, just like filthy humans like Frank.

In record time I solve my puzzle and skip over to the dying fire as the app plays a celebration song for me. I "accidentally" blow out a huge breath to put out the rest of the fire because I'm getting impatient.

"Oops." Shrugging my broad shoulders, I feel my muscles shift to a predatory stance and close my eyes.

Frank has made it farther than I thought he would, I'll give him that, but his heart races like a frightened bird no more than a few blocks away. He's stationed himself in the dumpster of a fast-food restaurant behind the place probably in the hopes it'll muffle his breathing, and I won't smell his horrid body odor. A valiant effort but still a failure.

Wind streamlines my sleek body as I launch myself toward the miserable excuse for a being and adrenaline races through me.

I'm not sure when I decided to start hunting these pieces of scum but at the end of the day, I'm helping the human population by getting rid of them, aren't I? It also gives me something to do. Some people might say murder is murder and it's wrong but you can't please them all.

I rest on my haunches on the roof of the building across the street from where Frank hides.

Unfortunately, he didn't provide as much entertainment as I would've hoped but I plan to make him suffer for every dirty deed he's committed and for what he did to all those women.

"Time's up," I call even though he can't hear me.

I launch myself from the top of the building when he pokes his head out of the dumpster. Before he can retreat, he spots me. The smell of urine quickly soaks his pants.

I smile at him and then I get to work.

22

Rain pelts my body and slides down my face. I'm beyond soaked at this point but it's a welcome shower from nature with the amount of blood that coats me. At this rate, there won't be a trace on me by the time I make it home.

Frank sung like a canary, like I knew he would, and freely admitted to his wrongdoings by the time I was done with him. Dragging him back to the abandoned building he'd been hiding in was the appetizer to his main course of torture.

Skin shredded and bleeding profusely from the scrapes, he wimped out early on, but I made sure to catch his confession on tape.

I wasn't necessarily in the bad guy killing game for the police but there were certain situations like Frank where he flew under their radar, so I lent a helping hand. I could only handle their idiocy for so long. The case of the missing and abused girls would be wrapped up in a pretty bow with the confession from Frank. Hopefully those girls' families could finally rest easy knowing the killer is gone.

I hope the cops won't take too long and still find my masterpiece while it's fresh. I left a blood drawn heart this time instead of a smiley face. Just for Celine. Even when I'm killing, I'm only thinking of her.

Rain continues to pour as I head back to the apartment. One quick glance at the cameras via my phone show Celine sound asleep right where I left her. She's shifted in her sleep and hugs my pillow like she's sought me out in her unconscious state.

I whistle as I skip down the street having made it back to the building. Water flies as I splash in a particularly large puddle, dispersing the last of the blood remaining on my shoes.

Sudden movement out of the corner of my eye distracts me from my warpath to the front door of the apartment building. A hulking form emerges from the shadows and moves toward the door, but I can sense something is off.

It stops and erratically sniffs the air before turning abruptly in my direction. I have less than a second to process exactly what I'm looking at before it launches at me with lethal intent.

A fucking feral vampire.

I can tell by the pungent smell. Essentially a mindless zombie, this beast must've been turned hours ago by someone.

Whether it was purposeful or not, he hasn't fed enough to complete the transition and is mad with bloodlust. Left to simmer in it too long he'll never be able to come back since the grace period isn't very long.

Ugh. This is going to get messy, and I just got clean.

A vicious snarl rips from the throat of the imposing creature, and I go into defense mode, fangs dropping down. Talon like nails rip at the fabric of my shirt and tear through like butter. The long nails take me by surprise, like whoever this once was, has been held for a long time before being turned.

Ferals are animalistic in their half-turned state, and it gives them an edge. I grit my teeth at the sting when he grips my arm, nails biting into my skin. Venom pumps through my system but only a small amount since the feral doesn't know what he's doing. Young vamps have particularly potent venom due to imbalanced systems, and it hurts like a bitch. I bite my lip to stifle the pain, blood coating my tongue from the force. He chomps at the air, and I swerve out of the way, so he doesn't snag my neck. Like a piranha on steroids, he attempts to bite any part of me he can and manages to get my pec.

"Fuck!" Finally gaining purchase, I rip him off, but he tears a chunk out of my skin. "Asshole! I like this shirt." The feral vampire growls in response, and launches himself back at me. "I would rather nobody but my mate leave love bites on my chest."

We're lucky there aren't any humans passing by, but I don't want to take a chance of anyone seeing and getting caught in the crosshairs. This fucker will have to die.

I grip his shirt and toss him down the side of the building where I know there's a blind spot from the street cameras. It's like moving a mountain to get him where I want him and I'm already panting with exertion.

It's odd he attacked me the way he did. Feral vamps are hard to control both by themselves and others, especially once they're past the point of saving, but they don't tend to go for aged vampires like he did just now. A small part of them recognizes they'll lose the battle against us while they still hold a semblance of consciousness. Something about me set off his hunting instincts.

Having had enough of me he grabs at my back and shreds through my shirt causing it to flap in the wind and rain. So much for salvaging that.

I grab his arm and try to flip him over me and onto the

ground which works, until he pulls me down with him. Normally, I'd be in a better position to resist but I'm at a disadvantage thanks to Celine. She has me burning through my supply like crazy. My libido and need to claim her are riding me hard and living together has only made it worse. I should've stocked up again tonight but didn't realize getting attacked was in the cards.

He attempts to bite my leg but with a swift kick to his face I dart away from him. His jaw dislocates but it doesn't deter him and the crazed look in his eye only gets worse. Scanning the area around us I spot a "No Thru Alley" sign planted in the ground and make a quick decision. Dumb enough to not understand he doesn't make any move to stop me when I rip it out of the ground and smash him over the head with it.

How does one kill a feral vampire? Stereotypes don't hold true. Sunlight, garlic, fire, and holy water are all out but it sure would make it a hell of a lot easier if they weren't. The only sure way to execute a feral is a stab to the heart.

In our first hundred years of undead life our heart still exists within our bodies. It pumps blood just like any human heart but at a much slower rate. The older we get the more our hearts will disintegrate until finally they wither away into dust making it a sign of our maturity.

A vampire like myself is much harder to kill because of it.

Vampy attempts to get back up, apparently not one to give in. I toss the sign in the air and grip it closer to the bottom portion. My boot plants onto his chest to keep him down and I straddle his broad chest for better aim. Slamming the base of the sign through his chest it cleanly slices through the vital organ, pinning him to the concrete. An awful screech leaves his mouth, and he flails in a last-minute attempt to save himself. Eyes bulge out of their sockets as his life is extinguished right in front of me.

Just as I move to get up thinking I'm home free, the slick fuck gets a second wind and slashes me deep in the stomach. Intense pain radiates through my entire being, his venom partially paralyzing me from the new dose and the slow burn of the initial cut. Lifeless eyes stare up at the sky as his body falls to the ground with a resounding thud. Knowing I can't leave him here looking like this I do the best I can to toss him in the dumpster beside us. It's slow going with my wound and exhaustion but I manage to toss him over the edge.

For a second his arm doesn't want to go in until I nudge it and close the lid to hide his mangled body. Not a perfect disposal but it'll have to do.

"Bye bye!" I wave at the dumpster.

I need to get upstairs. At this rate I'll waste away on the pavement. My emergency blood bag is in my closet and it's vital I get it as soon as possible. The venom is screwing with my natural healing. Vampires have some of the fastest healing in the supernatural community but I'm not healing like I should.

Come on, Zavier. Pull yourself together. You've been through worse.

Somehow managing to make it into the building and onto the elevator I slam my palm against the floor 24 button. I pant loudly as I struggle to stay with it. My vision blurs, and my legs don't want to support my weight. My stomach feels like it's gone through a meat grinder, and I try to press my arms against it best I can. Blood flows steadily and I know the amount I'm losing is enough to warrant more than the one blood bag I have on reserve.

Fuck.

The elevator dings to signal I'm in the homestretch and when the doors open, I almost pitch forward onto the ground. I keep hold of my waist with one arm and plant my other against the wall to drag myself down the hallway. Celine's scent faintly fills the long corridor, and I use it to fuel my slowly dying ember of motivation. Dark spots take over my sight and I gasp when the pain becomes unbearable.

This fucker got me good.

I've been hurt many times over the last three hundred years, a few times where I wasn't sure I'd make it through, but this is skirting death a little too closely for me. Lesson learned; always make sure I'm full.

So. Close.

The door is within reach, but I'm fading fast. As I reach for the door handle my body finally gives in and I collapse, falling into the door face first. It's such a hard fall my nose crunches under impact against the sturdy wood. The resounding thud of my body sliding down is deafening and I hear a distant startled yelp from the other side.

Celine.

She shuffles out of bed, and I hear her muttering in question, not understanding what the culprit of the loud noise is. My vision is almost fully gone now and the pitter patter of her feet against the hardwood making her way to the door is an echo in my ears.

Celine.

My mate.

This can't be the end.

She doesn't know how big of a dick I have yet.

I'm going to die and she doesn't even know.

This is the worst.

23

jolt out of a deep sleep with a yelp of terror as a loud crash invades my dreams.

Midnight, who sleeps beside me at the edge of the mattress, gives an answering yowl. My heart races from the unexpected awakening and immediately I scan the room for intruders.

To be safe I grab my gun from the holder on the side table and quietly slide out of bed. Shoving my arms in my sweatshirt I cover my braless form and slip my phone into my pocket in case I need to make a call for backup. Gun trained in front of me, I start my patrol of the bedroom, bathroom, and closet.

Nothing jumps out at me, but I don't let my guard down. Has the man that broke into my apartment come back to finish the job?

Wait.

Zavier.

He's the first line of defense sleeping out on the couch and if there truly was an aggressor he'd be attacked first. Is that what the loud bang was? Shit.

Stealthily, I walk toward the door leading to the main living space and take a deep breath to center myself. The man has done so much for me I need to help him if he's being murdered out there. God, I hope that's not what's happening.

Yanking on the door I hold the gun in front of me. No sounds emit from anywhere but that doesn't mean anything. They could be hiding and waiting to make their next move. I shut the door behind me, so Midnight isn't stuck in any cross-fire and crouch behind a fake plant in the corner. Nothing occurs with my appearance, so I stand slowly and walk around the living room, checking behind the curtains and couch.

A low groan comes from the front area of the space, and I hold my gun back up in preparation of an attack. Nobody pops out and the kitchen seems to be clear. Another small thud against the front door followed by a mutter calls me that way.

I peek through the peep hole but don't see anyone standing there. From what I can tell there's nobody on either side of the door.

"Celine." It's spoken so softly I almost don't catch it. "Celine." In a voice sounding suspiciously like Zav's, I glance down, not having thought of the floor right in front of the door, and see him sprawled out like a broken doll.

"Zavier!" His name rips out of me, a cross between a gasp and a scream.

As carefully as I can, I open the door since he's leaning partially against it. Despite my best efforts, his head flops fully onto the ground with a sound that has me cringing. Hopefully he didn't get a concussion on top of whatever else has happened to him.

His breath leaves him in heavy pants, and he barely moves when I squat down next to him.

"What happened?" I squeak getting a better look at the mess that is the man in front of me.

"Blood," he murmurs. "I need blood."

Blindly he grabs at the air trying to find me and I grasp his waiting palm. It doesn't seem like he can move much in his current state, so I do my best to hoist under his armpits and drag him into the apartment. The crimson trail he leaves on the floor will be interesting to get out of the hall carpet and flooring.

His small moans of pain hurt my heart, but there's not much I can do.

"You need what?" I couldn't have heard him right. He's in a half delusional state.

"Blood." This time his answer is a small, strained breath.

Awful skid sounds ring out as I continue to drag him further into the apartment. His chest seems to be giving him the most pain, so I gently flip him over to survey the damage.

"Zavier. Oh my God." I cover my mouth with both hands at the sight before me. Skin lays torn and disfigured across his lower abdomen. Bits of his shirt that remain stick to the cuts and barely hang onto his lean frame.

Blood steadily pumps out of the slices, and I can't figure out what could've done this. They look like claw marks, but the size and shape make it seem like it was a large animal. How he made it all the way up here I have no idea. I hover my hand above the gaping wound not quite knowing what to do to help.

"I need to call 911. We need an ambulance and a hospital." Gulping in air while my thoughts run frantically through what I need to do, I'm halted when Zav weakly grabs my wrist.

"No." Green eyes reflect back at me in pain. "No ambulance and no police."

"What the fuck do you mean?" I'm frantic at this point as blood pools around his prone form. "You're dying! You need medical attention." With shaky fingers I grab my phone from where it rests in my sweatshirt pocket and attempt to dial. As I'm about to type in "9" Zav swats the device out of my hand, and it goes sliding across the floor hitting the wall on the far side of the room.

"What is wrong with you? I'm trying to help!" I attempt to get up again, but he somehow keeps me rooted in place.

His gasps for air are sounding more and more dire. "I ... told ... you..." Another wheeze and a groan of pain. "...blood ... I need ... blood." Fingers unwind from around my wrist to grasp his chest. "There's an emergency blood bag in my closet." He points in the direction of the bedroom. "It's...in a safe...password is... 235463." Blood sprays across my front when he coughs.

This is all too fucking weird.

Scrambling for the bedroom closet I nearly trip over my own feet. Midnight almost gets mowed over when I rip open the door since he's laying right in front of it. He must be just as confused with what's going on as I am.

"Blood bag. Safe. Blood bag. Safe." I chant to myself shoving clothes aside trying to locate what I seek. "Bingo!"

A square safe hides underneath a pile of clothes in the back corner and I shove them aside to access the keypad. Beeps confirm my password is correct when I type it in and reveal a stereotypical hospital blood bag sitting inside. A cool draft of air hits me and the bag is cold to the touch when I snag it. Plastic mushes under my fingers as the liquid inside sloshes around. Trying not to think about how weird this is, I rush back out to the living room and over to Zav where he lies on the floor.

If it's possible he looks even worse than a minute ago. His skin is pallid in color, eyes mostly closed, and pain contorts his handsome features. Resting my fingers against his neck I feel for a pulse and panic when it's very faint.

"Zavier!" I grip both of his shoulders and shake him lightly. He moans which I take as a good sign, he's not dead yet.

"I'm ... here ... pretty girl." His arm trembles from the exertion of trying to hold it up. He extends his hand to me and makes a grabby motion. "Blood?"

"Right here." I use both hands to place it into his, helping him hold it when he almost drops the bag. "I ... you need more than just a transfusion and Zav I'm not a nurse, I'm a cop. I don't know how to give you a transfusion in the first place. How do you even have blood on hand?"

He shakes his head. "Just give me ... the ... blood. That's all I ... need."

His lips are nearly white in color and fear roots me to the spot.

"You ... what?"

Green eyes meet mine and there's fear there. Strangely, enough, though I don't think it's to do with the injury. "I ... need ... to ... drink."

I look at the blood bag clasped between both our hands. Surely, he can't mean?

He nods like he reads my thoughts.

Fuck.

"Do I need to take the top off for you?"

How the fuck am I being so calm about this? It has to be a dream, right? A really strange nightmare?

In silence, he nods again, and I quickly execute the task of pulling the plug off.

Zavier tries to sit up to not spill it on himself, but struggles to lift his head off the ground. Shifting behind him to help support his weight I jostle him as little as possible, but he still winces. Then, I watch in fascination and horror as he drinks the blood. Greedy slurps of the viscous red liquid have dribbles sliding down his face and onto his neck. Even through my confusion I stroke his hair back and try to hold him up the best I can.

What the fuck?

Before my very eyes Zav's wound starts to slowly knit closed. I blink as if that'll make it untrue but between blinks it looks better.

That's not possible.

In record time, Zav downs the whole bag and slumps back against my legs. For a second I panic that the blood did him in, but his face is lined with sleep, and I watch his chest rise and fall. I run my finger over one of the angry, puckered scars of the previously bloody cuts and feel nothing but smooth skin. The wound isn't fully healed, but it's way more than any human being should ever have healed in the amount of time he has.

Midnight perches in the doorway of the bedroom observing the whole scene with a swish of his tail.

I glance back down at the unconscious man in my lap and reach behind me to snag a blanket off the couch.

With his weight and the blood all around us I don't want to do more damage to the room, myself, or Zavier. Situating it around him, I ease out from under his frame and stand. Blowing out a breath I stand there for a second in disbelief.

"What the fuck?" My eyes bounce between Zavier and the empty bag on the ground next to him. "A man almost died in front of me *and* downed blood like it was Kool-Aid."

Ambling over to the bathroom, I wash Zav's blood off my hands. Risking a glance in the mirror I see a nightmare reflecting back at me. Hair tussled both from sleep and panic. Eyes full of dismay and tinged with exhaustion widen at my appearance. I look like shit, but Zav is so much worse off than me.

Is he really going to be okay?

The sensible part of my brain says there's no way any of that just happened and yet he's out there lying on the floor passed out. I need to go to bed and wake up in the morning. Maybe it really is all a dream and when I wake up, we'll both laugh at my crazy imagination.

24

The sound that comes out of me is equivalent to a dying animal getting run over by a car. I certainly feel that way as well.

"Fuck me," I wheeze, as pain radiates from the top of my head down to my toes.

The last thing I remember is making it to the front door of the apartment and Celine dragging my sorry ass inside. Even though she tried to be careful, every pull against my arm felt like razor sharp needles. That feral vamp really did a number on me.

Thank God I had my emergency blood bag, but I can tell it hasn't done enough for my body's natural healing to kick in. It may have sealed some of my gnarlier wounds, but venom still courses through my blood keeping me from a full recovery. I need more blood, but I feel like complete shit and thinking about moving already has me sweating.

I look around the room and I'm shocked to see a small lump

on the couch. The black comforter from my bed covers said lump. A dainty hand peeks out from underneath, dangling off the side of the couch. I can't help the smile that finds its way onto my face at her sleeping out here with me. I must've scared the hell out of her, and while drinking blood in front of her was the least of my worries from last night, I know I'll have to explain myself.

With Celine being my mate, I knew at some point I would have to tell her what I am. This might not have been the timeline I planned to do that on but it's the reality. I'm not sure how she'll take it since she's pretty strait-laced, but I feel like at the same time she's far more perceptive than people realize. Of course, she's a detective and it's her job to be, but I'm not what people would call normal, and I think she recognizes that.

Holding in my groan as much as possible so as not to wake her, I shuffle along the floor using my forearm to hold my torso up and slowly scoot along to the couch. The distance is only a few feet, but it feels like it's a mile away in my current condition. I have to stop multiple times before I finally drop myself not so gracefully next to her on the floor and reach up with a trembling hand to grasp hers.

Her hand feels so small in mine, and I revel in the feeling of her soft skin against my palm. Right then a particularly immobilizing jolt of pain shoots through my chest and I yelp unable to keep it in. Celine startles and rustles around beneath her blanket cocoon. Her hand stays in mine, and I grip her hand to help myself through the episode.

"Zavier?" Alarm fills her eyes when she glances down at me in my sorry state. "Oh my God, it was real!"

I probably look like a ragdoll gone through a meat grinder.

"Howdy." I wave my other hand in the air weakly and promptly regret the action. "Shit."

She jumps out from under the covers and squats down next

to me. Her cold hand feels heavenly on my forehead as she flits around me like a mother hen. If I knew coming close to death would get her to feel me up, I would've done it sooner.

"You still look rough. I thought last night was a bad dream." Her eyes zero in on the empty blood bag over on the kitchen floor and I see the moment everything floods back to her. "You..." She gapes at me, mouth open ready to catch flies.

"Listen"—not wanting to waste any more time I plead with her— "you need to go see Luna and get more blood for me."

"Blood? Luna?" Celine's face turns pale as color leaves her.

Time is of the essence, and I don't have the time to fully explain myself to her. I need more blood as soon as possible to finish healing and then I can explain everything better.

"Celine, please." Another shiver wracks my body as the venom slowly eats away at my insides. "I know I have a lot to explain to you, and I promise I will, but right now I need blood. My body isn't healing like it should and the bag last night wasn't enough."

"Zavier ... what is going on?" she asks incredulously. "You're drinking blood like it's normal and asking me to go get more? Not to mention you showed up last night looking like you had one foot in the grave." Her voice is getting higher and higher, and I continue to hold onto her hand even when she goes to rip it out of my hold. "No one should've survived those wounds."

"I know. I know." I wince when I hold my arm up since it tugs on the wound in my abdomen. "I promise you, you'll get your answers, but please go to Luna and ask for more blood. Tell her I sent you and be as conspicuous as possible."

"Luna? Like Luna *Luna* from the Bean Hive? *That* Luna?" At my nod she pales. "She's in on whatever the fuck this is, too? Is it some kind of weird blood drinking cult?" I give her a look and she sighs in defeat. "Fine. I'll go talk to her."

Despite her obvious frustration she helps me onto the couch.

"God that fucking hurts!" I whine.

Celine pokes at my wounds and after wrapping me up mummy style on the couch she nods in satisfaction.

"Okay," she mumbles to herself and after dressing quickly picks up her keys. "You stay here, and I'll be back." Seemingly in a haze she goes to leave. "You owe me an explanation, though, Zavier." She points at me with what I assume she thinks is a menacing expression. "You're not wiggling out of this."

"I'm not going anywhere, Shnookems." My joke doesn't land, and she walks out without another word.

A soft meow from behind my head on the arm of the couch and a tickle of fur against my forehead is a welcome presence. Midnight paws at a strand of my hair.

"Hey, buddy." He purrs in response. "Let's hope I didn't just scare your mother away."

25

"Luna!"

I burst into Bean Hive with none of the grace and stealth Zavier asked me to. The woman in question halts what she's doing behind the bar when I yell her name. She must sense my panic because she apologizes to the customer she's helping, handing off the mug she's holding to another employee, and rushes over.

Luna's blonde hair waves behind her and I'm hit with a cloud of her delicate perfume when she stops in front of me.

"Celine, what's wrong?" Her eyebrows furrow and I glance around noticing all the patrons staring at me after my outburst. "Is it something with work?"

"Actually, I'm off but my vacation time just took a turn for the worst. Come here," I hiss, and grab her arm, dragging her into the supply closet behind the bar.

"What's going on? You're scaring me." She crosses her arms over her chest and peers imploringly into my eyes.

"I'm scaring you?" Her comment strikes me as funny after everything that just happened. "A man just bled out, almost to death might I add, on the floor in front of me and now has me here to request blood. *To drink*." The last two words leave in a barely audible gust of air.

Luna's eyes grow big as saucers at my words. "Zavier? Is he okay?"

"How'd you know?"

"Oh, girl, he is down *bad* for you. Who else could it be?" She's already rummaging around in a fridge hidden behind a shelf full of different syrups and coffee cups. "What trouble did he get himself into? If he sent you here, it must've been bad. Gosh, he better pull through or we'll have to deal with him haunting us, I'm sure."

I sputter at how casual she's acting. "How are you okay with this? I'm certainly not!" My level of hysteria is slowly rising. "Are you in kahoots? In some weird ass cult where you drink blood? Zavier wouldn't give me any answers."

Luna stops what she's doing to give me a pitying glance. "If Zav hasn't told you yet, then it's not my story to tell." She casually holds multiple blood bags and closes the fridge, setting them in a small portable cooler. "Here. You need to get back to him with these as soon as possible. If he's injured, he's going to need these and the sooner the better."

Shooing me out of the closet and toward the front door she gives me one last sad smile. "Just hear him out, Celine. I know it all sounds fake and downright insane, but it's real. He genuinely likes you so don't do anything rash. There's so much about the world that none of us really know and now you're getting to see a side of that very few humans ever have the curtain pulled back on."

I give her a hesitant nod and high tail it back to the apartment. I have a multitude of questions for her, it's in my nature, but there's something tugging at me telling me I have to go.

"I'm here!" The front door slams against the wall as I throw the keys down and rush inside. "Zavier, you better not be dead! I haven't gotten to interrogate you Detective Brennan style yet!" A low, weak wheeze sounds from the living room, and I let out a breath I didn't realize I was holding.

"I haven't gotten to go down on you yet, how could I pass away?" he questions, and I marvel at his ability to be flirty even in the state he's in now.

Unzipping the cooler and yanking out two of the blood bags I jog over to his prone form on the couch.

"Here." Thrusting it in his face when I rip the cap off, he grabs it and slurps down the crimson liquid.

"That hits the spot." He licks his lips. "AB negative is my favorite. Luna must be feeling bad for me." Zavier chuckles and swallows another mouthful of the bag to finish it off. "I'm gonna owe her big time."

Wordlessly he motions for the other bag and does the same thing. Each suck brings color back to his pale skin and it's like his once gaunt face is full of life and warmth again. He drinks the other two bags I have in the cooler before finally thudding back against the couch with a relieved sigh. Long fingers push the blanket aside to reveal perfectly smooth skin where there once were nasty wounds. Not even a scar is left behind.

"How is that possible?" I murmur and back away, thumping clumsily to the floor in disbelief. In my rush to help Zavier and get him more blood, my adrenaline has kept me going until now. I didn't give myself time to question what was going on, but now that immediate danger is out of the way I'm back to a state of what in the fuckery is this. Zavier must realize the predicament he's in because his eyes dart to mine and we stare at each other in silence, neither knowing what to say next.

"Might as well rip the bandage off." He runs a hand through his red hair much like the color of the blood he was just downing. "I'm a vampire."

I wait for him to say more but he doesn't. No punchline to the joke, no ha I got you, Celine. He says *nothing* else and sits there waiting for me to reply to his ridiculous statement.

"A vampire," I reply in a deadpan voice. He nods. "I vant to suck your blood ... kind of vampire?"

Zav rolls his eyes at that one.

"That's a harmful stereotype, how dare you bring that up?" He crosses his arms, sporting a mock pout on his lips, but I don't budge in my serious stare. Zav deflates, and I swear there's a twinge of worry in his emerald eyes. "Yes, a vampire. I know it sounds crazy but it's true. There's no easy way to explain it so there. That's the truth."

"You're right. It does sound crazy. You know what else is crazy? Luna acting like giving away blood is completely normal and you showing up on death's door but recovering in an insanely quick amount of time after drinking blood. None of it makes sense."

I mean, I guess it *does* make sense if I choose to believe him.

Feeling antsy, I get up and start to pace around the living room. There's no way I can stay still with the turbulent emotions inside of me. As a detective you need to have solid facts to build your case and put criminals behind bars. Simple opinion and educated hypothesis won't get you anywhere.

I just need to think about this logically even though it's completely illogical.

Through my internal debate Zavier sits still as a statue but his eyes follow me as I pace back and forth. I try to ignore his heavy gaze, but I feel the weight of it, it's impossible not to.

Midnight decides to make himself known and gives a short hiss at me when I almost mow him over before prancing over and jumping up next to Zavier on the couch.

That in itself is one piece of evidence to consider, as much as Midnight hates me, because he's a grump, he loves Zav. Animals are intuitive and if Zavier is the predator he claims to be, I don't think Midnight would be so chummy with him.

Another piece to consider, the state he was in and the healing that took place after he had blood is undeniable. I don't think I can blame it on being tired or half asleep when he's right in front of me perfectly fine. His blood spilled from last night still covers the floor and has started to dry around the edges.

Something else to consider is how strange Zavier is.

The man has always carried an ethereal grace to him. There's just something about his aura you can't put your finger on, but you know it's more than what's "normal". He walks with a stealth and confidence you'll never find on most human beings.

"Prove it." Even with the thoughts running through my mind I still can't wrap my head around it.

He arches an almost mocking brow. "The sort of dying and coming back to life with blood thing wasn't enough for you?"

Zavier gives a half snort but gives Midnight one last stroke before standing. He slowly approaches me where I'm positioned over by the TV stand and I back up right into it, pinned between him and the furniture. I should be screaming, maybe shaking in terror, but instead I find my body subtly lurching toward his. His large palm cradles my cheek, and I lean into him before coming to my senses and pulling away. A flash of hurt fills his face, but I look away and try not to feel guilty.

"Please, don't be afraid of me. Don't pull away." His baritone voice cracks, breaking my heart. "I can't stand it." Thankfully he doesn't make another move to touch me and backs up slightly.

A soft clicking sound fills the space and I glance back at Zavier with a gasp. He looks exactly the same minus the deadly sharp fangs that now poke out from underneath his lip. The deadly curve and shining pearlescent finish to them give a lethal edge to this already gorgeous man.

Drawn like a moth to a flame, I can't stop myself from softly running my pointer finger along their edge. Zavier suddenly grabs my finger and pulls it away.

"I'd be very careful if I were you." His voice is barely a whisper full of restrained desire. "My fangs are very sharp and I'm not feeling particularly in control right now."

"Are you going to hurt me?" It's a question anyone in my place would ask. Cornered by a wild animal who barely seems to be holding themselves back.

"No." Zavier breathes out. "Never. Never you." With the utmost gentle touch, he slowly folds his arms around me and deflates in relief when I don't automatically pull away. I should. This whole situation is fucked and there's still part of my brain that can't fathom the man in front of me being a creature from mythology that most definitely shouldn't be real. "I'd rather die than hurt you." He passes his long fingers through my messy strands.

I look up at him, unable to keep the question from leaving my tongue. "If you were so desperate for blood ... why didn't you ... drink mine?"

A small part of me can't help but be curious what it would be like. Would it hurt? Would it feel good?

Zavier lets out a strangled sound and I stiffen. He immediately loosens his grip on me. Soft lips against my ear cause shivers to ripple through my body. The magnetic pull between us is particularly strong in this moment and it's like I couldn't move if I wanted to.

"I couldn't. Especially right then, if I drank from you, it wouldn't end any other way than with my cock inside your pussy." His filthy words send a flush of heat through my chest. "Like I said before, you deserve more than that. I also refuse to take you to bed and fully claim what's mine until you've accepted what I am and you're okay with it. I know right now you aren't." With that, he backs away and sits back down on the couch, one lean leg crossed over the other. "You must have other questions so hit me with them."

Wanting to keep some distance between us with the tension in the air I choose to grab one of the stools from the bar and drag it over to sit across from him.

"All right, let's talk." I wrack my brain for which question I want to ask first. "So, do you deposit your paychecks at the blood bank?"

can't stop the boisterous laugh that bursts out of my chest.
Celine continues to astound me. Here I am a living,
breathing vampire and her first question is a vampire joke.

"You think you're so funny."

A small smile tugs at her mouth which turns into her biting
her lip. I want to tug it out from her teeth to prevent her from
hurting herself. I wasn't lying earlier when I told her I'd never
hurt her. Vampires physically can't hurt their mates. The worst
we can do is lose ourselves to the pull of the mating bond and
let our baser instincts to claim take over.

"You're a vampire." Celine reiterates like she still can't quite
believe it. I don't blame her. The world likes to tell you what is
and isn't true and when that philosophy is challenged it's hard
to accept. "You drink blood. But I've seen you eat food."

I understand what she's getting at. "Vampires can eat
normal food. Obviously, we prefer blood and that's what
sustains us, but some vamps, depending on their age, still like

to eat human food. Whether they still like the taste or it's a nostalgia thing, it happens." I shrug, personally falling into both categories.

"Hmm." She's so cute when she's thinking. Her brow furrows and her mouth twists to the side in contemplation. "When were you turned?"

"Oof. Going straight for the age, huh?" I try not to show it, but a large part of me is afraid once she gets her answers, she'll be turned off by me. Vampires feel the pull of the mate bond much more strongly than humans and I don't want to run her off. Besides, I want her to choose me for more than just the bond. "You sure you want to hear about the old fart you went on a date with?" I try and cover my concern with humor hoping she won't pick up on it.

"The fact you're a vampire is the biggest shock. I don't think your age will be more shocking than that," she reasons, and crosses and uncrosses her legs for the fifth time in the last few minutes.

"I'm three-hundred years old. I was born in 1725 and turned when I was twenty-six." Even with her earlier statement of reassurance I still see her brows creep up her forehead.

I am indeed crusty, but hey, at least I'm the sexiest crusty vampire she'll ever meet.

"Okay." Celine takes it better than I thought she would and keeps on trucking with her questions. "How did it happen? Is it the whole other vampire bit you, drained you to the point of death, and then fed you their blood sort of thing?"

I smirk at her hypothesis. "You read too much fiction." The plush pillow behind me pushes against my back as I settle in to tell her. "The shows and movies have always gotten paranormal creatures wrong. Vampires didn't start by supernatural means."

"Wait, what do you mean?" Celine's voice goes up an octave and she rubs her palms nervously on her thighs.

"The start of us actually came from scientific experiments. It's not like in fiction where some witch cursed our ancient ancestors and it led to vampires or some other nonsense." Midnight's fur is soft against my hand as I stroke him for comfort. "Back in the 1700's the world was rampant with illness and disease it had no cure for, at least none that were guaranteed cures. Smallpox, dysentery, cholera, I could go on and on. Countries around the world decided to start putting the dead and dying to good use and began to experiment on them. How could we come up with a medicine to strengthen humankind, so they were stronger and didn't fall ill to these silent killers?" My hair falls in my eyes as I shake my head in disgust.

"Were you one of the people they tested on?" Celine asks quietly.

I hesitate before answering. "Yes. But not in the way you think." Guilt wracks my body as I remember one of the darkest periods of my life. "I offered myself up for it."

"What? Why would you willingly offer yourself up for testing?"

"I had no choice." Midnight curls up next to me with his tummy in the air and I grab his little paw in a handshake. "My family was in a bad way, and I caught wind they paid for healthy candidates to test on. Thought I could help the family out by doing the tests and coming back but..." I trail off and stare into the corner.

"That didn't happen, did it?" Celine slowly stands and walks toward me when I shake my head sadly. Since Midnight is sprawled by my side she perches on the arm of the couch and rests a hand softly against my arm.

"As I'm sure you can imagine the testing resulted in ... this."

I let out a humorless laugh and gesture to myself. "We were indeed stronger beings, but we were also mutants and changed in a way that was unnatural. Both in awe and disturbed by the results they tried to see how far they could push us with experiments. How tough was our skin, how much pain we could endure, what kind of conditions we could live in before our bodies gave out. All in the name of furthering the human race."

Memories of needles, poking, prodding, and dark cells flash through my mind, and I cringe. My happy go lucky personality helps me cover up my pain and trauma but it's seeping through right now.

Fuck.

I try so hard to keep it locked away.

Pain.

Suffering.

Darkness.

My breathing quickens and I squeeze my eyes shut, trying to pull myself out of the prison in my mind. Whips, chains, musty air, and blood. So much blood.

A gentle hand grabs me around my neck and pulls me to a soft chest. Celine's scent fills my nose, and I lean into her. Breathing deeply, I whimper and feel myself slowly grounding in reality. Silent tears track down my cheeks and she wipes them away with the pads of her fingers. The steady rhythm of her heart and the comforting touch of her hand on my shoulder calms me down.

"You're okay. I've got you." Her hands are warm and comforting on my cheeks.

Twisting toward her, I hold her to me like the most precious thing in the world.

Because she is.

"Man, hydrogen peroxide really does wonders getting blood out of hardwood floors and carpet, doesn't it?" Celine muses as she finishes wiping up the kitchen floor.

I made quite the mess.

After my embarrassing episode on the couch, we decided to finally clean up the absolute carnage I inflicted on the apartment and doorway. I had told Celine I'd take care of it, but she refused to let me do it alone.

"I could tell you all kinds of ways to get blood out of things." I flash a fang at her from where I scrub, and she stills for a second before trying to pretend like it didn't happen.

Too soon.

"Sorry, I didn't mean to do that. It's just an involuntary reaction. I promise I'm not scared of you, Zav." She winces in apology. "Even though I probably should be," she adds under her breath with a nearly questioning tone. "I'm still processing everything you told me. I know you'd never hurt me." Celine sets a hand reassuringly over mine and then gets back to scrubbing.

I can't blame her for needing time. I'm overzealous and want to jump headfirst into things with her. No other human has even known my true nature and for once I don't feel lonely. She still doesn't know we're mates, but I think for now it's safer to keep that information to myself. I don't want to overwhelm her more than she already is.

A chirp comes from Celine's pocket, and she pulls out her phone to check the notification. Whatever she sees must excite her, because she jumps up and rushes to the bedroom.

"Celine?" I call after her now phantom form. "Are you okay?"

She hops back into the room, pulling a boot onto one foot and nearly falling over into the wall. I rush over to steady her. Her hair is back in its standard ponytail, and she grabs her black jacket from where it rests on one of the barstools.

"Yes! It's fantastic actually." I follow behind her as she practically skips to the front door. "Ava just texted me and said there's been another murder. My main case has been a little stale lately, but the serial killer left us another body." The gleam behind her eyes is that of a predator with a scent of their prey. I should know, since I've seen it reflected in mine many times.

"That's sounds promising." Flashing my smile sans fangs at her she nods, and opens the door. I follow her out and she stops abruptly when she realizes I'm right behind her.

"What are you doing?" She peers at me over her shoulder. A neighbor a few doors down walks past and nods in greeting. I notice him staring at Celine's chest a little too long and bristle.

Welp, another one to add to my list.

"It's take your man to work day. I've dubbed thee so." My arms flare out and I bow exaggeratedly.

"You are not coming to a crime scene with me." Celine tries to push me back in the apartment but I'm not budging. "And my man? Man-child maybe." She tops the comment off with a roll of her eyes. I make a mental note to spank her ass for that later.

"Pfft. Hurry up and close the door or you'll let Midnight out." Minty fresh breath teases my face when I hover right in front of her. "And yes, *your* man-child. Now onward!"

Slyly wrapping an arm around her shoulder and pulling the door closed with my other, I propel us forward. I can't wait to see her in action up close. Stalking from roofs and trees just isn't doing it for me anymore. I crave more. I need more of her. Plus, Frank was a big bad they've been trying to catch, and I know she'll be impressed.

"Obviously, you're not budging on this, so you need to listen to my ground rules before we get there." Celine presses the elevator button and turns to lecture me while we wait for it. "Number one, you stay in the car." She inches closer to me. "Number two, you stay in the car." Toe to toe now. "Finally, number three, can you guess?"

"Hmm." I tap my chin in mock thought. "Stay in the car?" She smiles widely when I answer appropriately.

"Exactly. Shall we?" The elevator dings and we walk in. I purposely stand as close to her as possible even though there's nobody else with us. Her short breaths bring a smile to my face when I realize she's still affected by me even after the vampire revelation.

"Most people would be terrified to be stuck in an elevator with me." Goosebumps flare along her neck where I whisper by her ear.

"Good thing I'm not stuck in here with you," the smart-ass replies.

Slamming a hand against the emergency stop button I cage her into the corner of the elevator. One arm frames her head against the doors and the other stays on top of the button stopping any escape she might hope to make. It's silent except for both of our stilted breathing.

"You were saying?" I murmur.

My nose drags through her hair, and I let loose a small growl of pleasure. Time to test the theory I've been wondering about. I give into my baser, animalistic urge and let my fangs click down.

If I didn't let them, they would've barged in anyway. Fangboner, hello.

With the utmost care I scrape a fang along her delicate throat like I've dreamed of doing since the day I saw her. I make sure not to draw blood, as much as I'd love to. If she protests, I'm ready to back off immediately.

A moan climbs out of her throat, and I feel the vibration against my canines. Her back is a solid weight against my chest, and I bring my left hand down to collar her throat on the opposite side of my mouth. She melts under the contact, and I gently tighten my grip.

"Mm."

Fuck she's so sexy.

"Very interesting." I feather a finger along her jawline. "Looks like I was right."

She recognizes my power over her and yet isn't afraid of me. In fact, it turns her on.

My words break the sexually charged spell, and she turns, pushing against my chest. She might as well be a small child trying to push a large boulder up a hill. I don't move in the slightest. Thankfully I had closed my mouth over my fangs, or she would've ended up a bloody mess when she pivoted.

"What the hell, Zav!" Celine shuffles away as far as she can from me and runs her hands over her hair adjusting her jacket along the way. She shakes her hands out like she wants to rid herself of the arousal she's currently perfuming the elevator with. "Start the freaking thing again."

Her glare is meant to be intimidating but just makes my erection that much harder. I simply smirk in response and hit the button. It starts back up and we take the rest of our ride down in silence.

27

Police lights flash, casting shadows on the surrounding buildings.

A forensic photographer's camera flashes, blending in with the reds and blues. The bloody scene is just as much of a massacre as every other time this serial killer has struck.

A stray flash of heat rolls through my body as I approach Captain Barnes. Flustered from the elevator earlier and needing distance from whatever that was, I drove as fast as humanly possible on the way here. Thankfully, Zavier took pity on me and didn't say anything else about it in the car. Feeling his dominating aura in such an enclosed space afterwards, though, was torture.

Holding the caution tape above my head and ducking under, I cast one last glance back at my car. True to his word, Zav sits in the passenger seat like a seemingly perfect angel. His tall form looks hilariously normal folded into the vehicle and at the same time too ethereal for this world.

Zav must feel my eyes on him because he tilts his head in my direction and smirks. He waves mockingly and I shoot him my best no-nonsense glare to which he only grins more. Shiny white teeth sit in a perfect row, no fangs to be found. I roll my eyes and try to forget he's on the scene with me when he definitely shouldn't be.

"You okay, Brennan? You're not supposed to be here. Time off, remember?" He arches a scolding brow in my direction. "Do you feel up to being here?"

His concern is sincere. Shoving my hands in my pockets, I kick a rock that sits right in front of my boot. "I'm good as I can be. That's not to say it's not shocking but I've been distracted for the most part. But I heard there was another crime from the Mayhem Murderer so I wanted to be here to see it first-hand." I'm sure he knows Ava blabbed to me, who else would have, but I don't want to explicitly throw her under the bus.

If I'm honest with myself, it's been kind of nice not working and the small voice in the back of my head that says I should think about a career change is getting louder and louder. It makes me feel guilty thinking that way, and I shake my head at the thought for now. It's not something I have time to dwell on at the moment.

Captain Barnes glances at my car and back to me before he nods. It's impossible for him not to notice Zavier, but he doesn't comment on the giant six-foot-plus man squished into my tiny car.

"I wish I had a better update for you, but we're still trying to locate the bastard who broke in. We spotted him on a CCTV downtown at one of the clubs, but we haven't gotten a name yet." A folded-up photo crinkles in his hand when he pulls it out of his back pocket. Sure enough, the same hooded figure can be seen in the darkness of night slipping into the back door of none other than Vex.

My lips part in surprised horror.

This has to have something to do with my suspicions surrounding the club. Nothing else makes sense.

Mistaking my silence for fear, Captain Barnes rests a reassuring hand on my shoulder. "Don't worry, Celine. I promise we'll find him."

I nod and clear my throat. "I appreciate it, sir. Now"—I turn to head toward the crime scene— "what's going on here?"

Captain sighs and his hand falls back down to his side knowing I'm not one for emotion. "Frank Denvers. Charged with abuse, murder, and other things I don't care to reiterate. He's been on the loose for the last two years and somehow stayed under the radar, but it seems like he's met his match with Mayhem."

My eyes widen at the captain's use of the nickname since we usually try not to use such language when talking about perpetrators.

Strolling around the perimeter of the body, I take in the scene before me. Just like all the other murders, the body has been mutilated and broken apart into a mass of limbs and stringy tissue. It's disgustingly gory and formed in a hauntingly macabre picture as is the signature of the killer. Instead of the smiley face it's been in the past it's a heart.

I bend down, inspecting it.

Captain crouches beside me, his eyes boring into the side of my face. "Why do you think it's different now? After all this time what changed?"

Standing, I plant my hands on my hips. I open my mouth to respond but stop when I feel a drop of rain hit my cheek. Another drop and another follow soon after before a torrential downpour berates us.

"Stay here! I'll grab an umbrella!"

The captain jogs away as a team of crime scene officials hurry over with a pop-up tent to keep the body out of the rain until we can move it since the abandoned building's roof is littered with massive holes.

These crimes are gruesome—to say the least—and now that I know vampires are real, I can't help but wonder if the Mayhem Murderer is one or another type of supernatural. It couldn't be Zav, I don't think. He's too goofy to go around slaughtering people like this.

"Celine, here you go." Captain Barnes huffs, now out of breath, and holds his own umbrella in one hand and an unused one in the other for me to take.

I give him a grateful smile as I open the umbrella to cover myself from the relentless downpour. "Thanks."

I eye the scene before me, and Captain does the same.

"I think he might have an accomplice. Or at the very least a new muse," I say softly. Rubbing a finger over my lip I scan over eyeballs plucked out of the man's face and placed strategically to make a smiley within the limbs. "Something's certainly changed."

"What?" Captain asks, fuzzy brows knitting together.

"You asked why it's different now." I gesture to the crime scene and squat down. "The killer's M.O. is the same, but the signature is slightly different. Whoever they are, they're trying to make a statement." I glance over my shoulder again, back to where I know my car is parked. I can't see Zav from this distance but somehow I can still feel his eyes on me.

It's hard not to shiver with how cold the rain has me in my soaked clothes, so I stand and shift from leg to leg to try and warm myself up.

"This killer? A statement?" A fellow detective asks with a scoff. "Every crime scene is a fucking statement piece." He waves a hand in the general direction of the body although calling it a body is generous considering nothing is attached to anything at this point.

"I just mean serial killers like to use the same signature and posing to communicate something. Obviously, this is different and there's some kind of reason behind it."

Captain Barnes lets out a deep breath. "You're on to something, Brennan. For it to change after all these murders there must've been something to cause this."

The other detective huffs a laugh and mutters, "Maybe he got a girlfriend," before walking off.

My frown deepens.

Dots are connecting right in front of me, ones I very much want to ignore.

The squad wraps up their on-site investigation and cop cars pull away as a few of us are left. Thankfully the rain lets up and allows us to put our umbrellas away.

It's frustrating this case seems to go on and on without any path forward in sight. Even though I was recently assigned to it, I did my research, and it dates back years ago. Always executed in a gory positioning and somehow the killer manages to avoid cameras at every turn. Nobody is that good unless they have a lot of experience both with murder and getting away with it— or unless they're not human.

Captain Barnes claps me on the shoulder. "Take the rest of the day. There's not much we're going to be able to do on this murder until evidence is processed."

"But—" I protest.

He shakes his head. "Crime scenes like this take a strong mental toll. Believe me, I know, and you're still dealing with the break-in. I'm just looking out for you, Celine."

I nod. "If you're sure."

"Positive."

I trudge back to the car, shivering from my wet clothes.

"You need to put on dry clothes," Zav says as soon as I open the car door. "I can't have you catching a cold. I brought a fresh set for you. It's in the back."

My eyes dart from him to the backseat. Sure enough a set of my clothes rests on the bench.

When did he snag those and how did he know it was going to rain?

"Or we can head back to the apartment, and I can change there. Not in the back of my car. I'm not about to flash any pedestrians with my ass or boobs," I gripe.

"I, personally, would welcome any flashing you'd like to do to me." He gives me a smile that has my tummy doing somersaults. "But no, we aren't going back quite yet. There's somewhere we need to stop and it's on this side of town. If we went back, it would be out of the way." I can tell he's trying to appease my more rational side. It doesn't make sense to waste precious gas. Not in this economy. He pulls his thin chain out from under his sweater collar. "We're already in a secluded section of the street, Celine. Nobody is going to see you." The gleam in his eye tells me someone might and that someone is in this car.

With a sigh, and ignoring the raging storm of feelings attacking my stomach, I close the car door before opening the back and sliding in.

"Turn around," I scold when he turns in his seat to watch me change. Like a kid that got caught in the cookie jar he slowly turns back around.

My face is probably a brilliant shade of red. I've never been the super confident type, and I can't help it if my insecurities are raging their ugly head wondering what if he catches a peak and doesn't like what he sees.

Silly, I know. Zav's proved endlessly that he's obsessed with me, but I've learned over the years that insecurities are rarely rooted in logic.

Letting out a huff, I slip down as far as I can in the back. There's a folded up blanket next to my clothes and I throw that over myself as I work off my pants. It's no easy feat with how suctioned they are to my skin, and I probably look like a demented worm, but I manage. My underwear pulls off with the pants and the fact I'm sprawled out here completely bare from the waist down with Zav in the front I can't help the spike of lust that shoots through me.

Fuck! What if he can smell my arousal?

A clicking noise draws my attention and I pull down the blanket, being sure to cover my front, to meet Zav's eyes in the rearview mirror. My gaze drops to his mouth where fangs have popped out. He runs his tongue along one of them and I gasp.

"Fangboner." The word lisps around his teeth.

That should not be as sexy as it is.

Looking away from him, I duck beneath the blanket again and reach for the underwear hiding under the shirt on top of the pile. My jaw drops when I come away with a sexy lace pair of panties I had hidden in the back of my drawer since I refused to touch them. Ava had gotten them for me as a gift.

Not wanting to waste any more time in my remaining wet clothes I make quick work of divulging myself of the wet shirt and bra. Trying to finagle the clasp is a struggle, but I finally hook it and get the new shirt on.

Fully dressed in fresh clothes, I rip the blanket off my head and blow out a breath. I push open the door to dangle my legs out and yank on socks and my boots.

Feeling much warmer, I get back in the front seat and try to work my fingers through my wet, knotted hair the best I can.

"Ready to go, my little wet kitten?" Zavier asks from where he watches next to me.

"Strike that nickname off your list." I fiddle with the vent so warm air blasts me in the face.

"Would you prefer sweet cheeks? Or honey bun? Or pudding pop?" He purses his lips in thought. "Oh, I know, pookie."

"Shut up," I groan. "I beg of you. No pet names." He grins maniacally. "Where are we headed?"

Zavier taps his phone a few times and pulls navigation up on the car's screen. With a mysterious smirk he simply nods toward it and mime's zipping his lips.

I put the car in drive and leave the crime scene behind.

28

"Seriously, Zavier, where are we?" Celine muses as we walk up the steps to our destination.

"My sex dungeon." I drop my voice a few octaves to answer, and she scoffs while playfully shoving me. "If I told you the truth that would take the fun out of it."

I rest my hands on her shoulders and squeeze. We parked not far from the front door since rain has decided to start up again

"Honey, I'm home!" I shout as we walk into the building.

"Not you again," a grumpy voice responds from around the corner. Celine shoots me a confused look, but I smile reassuringly. I see her taking in her surroundings with the curiosity of a detective's gaze.

I knew nobody would be in the restaurant today because once a month they close for restocking and deep cleaning. It was the perfect time to introduce Celine to Tom.

"Oh, hush, you know you look forward to my visits," I

refute. "I brought a friend this time, too." Gently pushing Celine along with a hand on her lower back we wander to the back of the restaurant.

Tom sits in his usual spot surrounded by napkins and silverware. He's slowly folding and rolling them up so they're ready to go for patrons. A few of his family members mill about but give us space to chat.

"I thought I was your only friend," Tom mumbles making me laugh.

"This is my special friend I've been telling you about." Celine and I settle in at the same table as Tom and he puts his supplies down when I gesture to her. "This is Celine."

"Who?" Tom shouts. "Francine?"

"Celine!" I reply. "Like Celine Dion. Why is your hearing so selective when it comes to us chatting? I swear you only hear what you want to." My sweater stretches across my chest when I cross my arms.

A quick glance at Celine tells me she finds our bickering amusing.

"Like I was trying to say"—I give an exasperated sigh and gesture toward the old man—"Celine, this is my friend Tom who I've known for a long time." Looking at Tom I gesture toward Celine. "Tom, this is Celine, my friend who I want to be my girlfriend, but she won't admit it, so I just say friend." She shoots me a look as per usual, but I pretend not to see it.

"So nice to meet you, Tom." Celine extends a hand and he shakes it in a gnarled, wrinkle ridden one in response.

"Wow, very soft skin. What's your secret at our age?" Tom asks and I snicker.

Celine glances at me in confusion and I lean over to whisper in her ear. "His hearing and eyesight are shit. We met way back in the day and he doesn't know what I really am. He's assuming we're all about the same age." I wink when I pull back and she nods.

"Lots of lotion?" she replies hesitantly, and it comes out as a question.

"Make yourselves useful and help me out with these." Tom gestures toward his task he paused when we sat down, and we get to work rolling silverware.

"So, Miss Francine, how did you meet Zac here?" Tom asks.

"He's my neighbor."

"Your what?" Tom asks again.

"We're neighbors, old fart!" I enunciate. Celine swats at me when I call him the name, but I don't dish what he can't take or return to me tenfold.

"You're going to get rid of the remaining hearing I do have, bastard." Tom's chuckle is in complete contrast to his gruff statement. We bust each other's balls but it's just our love language. "Now what did she say?"

"Celine said we met because we're neighbors," I inform him, crisply folding the napkin I'm working on. "We had a chance run in in the hallway and the rest is history. Now she can't get enough of me. What can I say, I'm a stud." Puffing out my chest I risk at glance at Celine to see her sporting a wry grin.

"Sure, let's say that," she giggles softly, and I'm a goner.

I must look like a lovesick fool because the next thing I know I pull my gaze away from her and see Tom watching me. A fondness fills his squinty, time worn blue eyes, and they dart back and forth between her and I. He nods to himself and continues about his business.

"Tom met his late wife because she was the daughter of the mob boss that had been threatening their family restaurant. The sly dog made a pass at her, and I guess she responded well seeing as they got married and had kids," I tell Celine.

"Really? That's so romantic," she sighs dreamily, and looks at Tom for more information.

His tired eyes melt with love that still remains strong. "Betsy Jo was the love of my life. We both knew it and even though our situation wasn't ideal we didn't waste any time in being with each other." His thick gray eyebrows knit as he loses himself in memory. "Life is too short to not spend every minute letting your person know you love them. It doesn't have to be some grand gesture every time. It could be leaving flowers on the table, sending a quick message, or cleaning up after each other without saying a word." He brushes some lint off his pants. "You never know when your last I love you is, so sprinkle them around like confetti." He reaches over and pats Celine, then me, on the arm.

"Wow, Tom, that's actually pretty insightful. Who knew you had it in you?" I try to lighten the mood when I can tell he starts missing his wife. "But thanks for the great advice."

"Sometimes I spread wisdom." Tom goes to stand, and I wince when more bones crack than I can count. "This old man needs a rest. Finish this up for me, would you? Lovely to meet you, Francine." He shuffles along until one of his grandkids rushes over and helps him up to the stairs to the attached apartment.

"Celine," I mouth to her, but she simply shakes her head at me.

Both of us do as we're told and finish up what Tom started with the silverware. I notice Celine being more contemplative after what he said. I can't help but wonder if she's applying it to us and our situation.

I haven't told her we're mates yet, but should probably do it sooner rather than later.

I want to get started on our forever.

29

The shuffle of papers, low murmurs, and footsteps echoing through the precinct are music to my ears. It feels so nice to be back at work. I've never been the type to sit back and mope at home but the break-in rattled me more than I would like to admit.

Zavier wasn't happy about it when I told him I was headed back to work this morning. The mopey pout he sported, and koala hug he latched onto me with were pitiful. At least he has Midnight to keep him company, plus he's a grown ass adult ... vampire ... man thing, so he'll be fine.

I still haven't fully wrapped my head around the fact Zavier is a vampire. You hear about vampires in myth and lore and think it's exactly that.

A story.

Not real.

But what I saw can't be explained any other way than supernatural.

As humans we're taught something and forced to believe it to be true. Hell, we spend years of our lives in school being fed facts to remember. To come to the realization anything could be a lie, and our history books could be so off base is a wild thought.

My phone buzzes in my pocket and I pull it out with a smile I can't seem to stop.

"Yes?" I cross my arm under the elbow of my other that holds the phone to my ear. Silence greets me. "Hellloooo?"

"I miss you," a sappy voice croons from the other end.

"Zavier." I pinch my brow. "I just left." I can't help but chuckle at his demeanor.

"My non-existent heart hurts when you're not here. Just come back home. Who needs work?" Zav pleads. My heart jolts at his use of the word home like it's our shared space.

"I think you'll live. Aren't you used to it with hundreds of years under your belt?" I mosey over to my desk from the window I've been standing by. "It'll make it that much sweeter when I get back to the apartment."

"I've never had the patience for edging. But I'd love to do it to you."

Just like that I'm hitting the end button, but not before a zap of desire hits me.

My phone buzzes again, but I ignore it this time.

Needy vampire.

I have to work and Zavier is just going to have to deal.

I plop down in my chair, and scoot in to be closer to my computer screen. Jiggling the mouse to wake it up I type in my password and do my initial read through of my email. A message from Detective Waters pops up reminding me I need her to brief me on the movement of the Vex case. I scan the email, my eyes latching onto the words *new evidence.*

"Hey, Ava!" My hair swishes as I quickly turn to call to my friend but she's nowhere to be found.

Now that I think about it, I haven't seen her yet this morning which is odd.

Walking over to the captain's office I knock on the door-frame so as not to barge in. Captain Barnes looks up from the paperwork he's filling out.

"Did Ava come in yet?" I question.

"Yes." Captain gives a quick nod and gets back to his work. I don't envy the huge stack on his desk and take it as a sign to leave. I doubt he'd know exactly where she is anyway.

I check her usual spots; the lounge, the front window she likes to look out of, and her desk once more to see if she returned while I was looking elsewhere. I'm passing by the bathrooms when I hear an almost inaudible sniffle come from the women's restroom. Backing up slowly, I stop and lean in waiting to hear it again. A louder sob comes out but is quickly stifled like whoever it is doesn't want others to hear.

Walking as quietly as I can, I nudge open the door and look around the corner. A rose gold head of hair hangs down, shoulders drooping, and a stash of used tissues sit on the counter next to her. I debate for a moment on whether I should interrupt or not, I've never been that good at comforting people, but this is Ava. I'm her best friend and need to make sure she's okay.

For her to hide away like this and cry it must be something big.

"Ava?" I walk toward her as if approaching a frightened bunny.

Her head jerks up and the red splotches on her face give-away the fact that she's been in here for a while. I can tell she's embarrassed when she tries to push the pile of tissues into the trash can and primp her hair like nothing's out of the ordinary.

"Are you okay?" Stopping right in front of her, I wait for her to respond not wanting to push too hard. Her mouth opens and closes a few times like she's attempting to reach for the right words.

"No," she squeaks out and dives for me.

Her delicate arms wrap tightly around my back and the smell of her floral shampoo tickles my nose. I respond in kind and hold her back as tightly as possible. Whatever's got her so upset is hurting my own heart.

"What's going on?" I pat her back soothingly. Her sniffles start up again and I wait once again for her to feel comfortable enough to talk.

"It's Spencer," Ava cries, and holds me even tighter if possible. Her anaconda grip borders on painful.

"What did he do?" I bite out. "Did he hurt you?" Spencer didn't seem the type, but if she's this distraught anything is possible.

If this asshole did something to her, I'll rip him a new one.

"No! He'd never do that." She snags one of her tissues from between us and wipes her nose. "A job opportunity came up in California. He wants to take it."

"Are you leaving me?" Now it's my turn to hold her tighter.

I'm hit with a wave of sadness when I think about not seeing Ava in my day to day. Sure, our personalities couldn't be more opposite but those made for the best friendships. I considered her a bright spot in my life that kept me afloat. Whenever I needed cheering up Ava was there. Now, I have Zav too, as weird as it is to admit.

"No, I ... I think I'm leaving *him*," Ava sighs, and tears stream down her cheeks once more. "When he first brought it up, I was so excited but the more I think about it the more it doesn't feel right for me and where I want my life to go. I love him, but it just feels like a fork in the road situation. A decision that can change my trajectory."

I rub her arms up and down and peel her off my chest. Gently arranging her hair so it isn't a tumbleweed around her face, I hold the sides of her cheeks so we're looking eye to eye.

"You need to do what's best for you. Think on it, don't make any rash decisions, and take a deep breath." I breathe with her, sucking in a huge breath through my nose and blowing it out. She does the same and I can tell she's starting to calm down. "Have you talked about your reservations with Spencer?"

Ava fully pulls away from me and holds her arms to her chest. "No. I need to. He can tell something's up because I've been distant. I need to have the conversation, but I'm scared. I don't want to hold him back when he clearly wants to take the job, but I don't want to leave Chicago. This is my home." She rubs her eyes and laughs at the makeup that comes off on her fingers. "It's hard to envision finding someone else when I've been with him for so long, but my gut is telling me California isn't where I should be. It's like a magnetic pull keeping me here." She finally turns to the mirror and jumps back. "Geez Louise I look like a killer clown."

Both of us laughing, I help her wipe away evidence of her cry session.

"It's your gut saying you'd be lost without me." I wink at her, and she smiles. "Come on girly, let's get back to work and forget about boys for a little while."

"Whoa, whoa, whoa." Ava halts in her tracks when I try to nudge her out the door. She gives a sly smile. "Speaking of boys. We need to talk about yours."

"Or we could not?" I reason and once again try to open the door. Ava slams a hand on it next to my head very much reminding me of Zavier cornering me in the elevator.

"Stop right there and put your hands up." Ava mock points finger guns at me and I hold my hands up for some reason like I'm in trouble. "I told you my news, now you tell me yours. That boy is down so bad, I could see it in his eyes the other night." Her eyes widen comically when she comes to a realization. "You never told me about your date after everything that went on!"

"Oops." I guess between the break-in and Zav being around when we were hanging out there wasn't a chance.

"You only gave me bare bones of what happened, and I need all the deets!" Suddenly full of energy, and color filling her cheeks back up, Ava continues to pepper me with questions. "Please, Celine." She reaches for my hand. "I need the distraction." She pouts her bottom lip.

"We might've kissed?" I mumble.

"Celine! How can we be best friends and you didn't tell me you kissed. Did you sleep with him? I would've jumped his fine ass so fast, I don't blame you if you did. You need to get laid. It's been too long." She grabs lipstick out of her pocket and applies it in the mirror with quick precision.

"No!" I cry out a tad defensively. "All we did was kiss and just the once. We haven't done anything since then."

Ava locks her arm with mine after one last pout in the mirror and we leave the bathroom.

"You're stronger than me. Spencer and I had sex on the first date."

I laugh and Ava seems lighter than before.

"Shall we continue this conversation over lunch?" Ava asks as she sits down at her desk outside Captain Barnes's office.

"It's a date." I head back to get some work done before the grill session that I know is coming.

30

pick up the laminated menu set down in front of me and scan for my usual favorites. We decided to try out a new local spot that serves burgers, flatbread, wings, and other bar food.

Sometimes a burger with all the fix-ins is in order to pick a girl up and be productive.

"I think I'm going to go for the Caesar salad with salmon," Ava muses while tapping her chin.

"I should've known," I laugh.

Ava and I are both creatures of habit.

I swirl my straw in the glass of water sitting to my right.

"At least I got this." Ava holds up her fancy sparkling lemonade. "You got water, you plain Jane." She sticks her tongue out like the mature adult woman she is.

I crumple up my straw wrapper and throw it at her face. It falls pitifully short and doesn't make it anywhere near its mark.

"Hello ladies! I'll be your server today!" A cheerful voice I know all too well pipes up.

Ava's light blue eyes dart back and forth from the server to me, and her grin gets so wide I think it'll split her face in half.

"Do I even want to look?" I shield my gaze from the side where the new presence stands and look at Ava who nods vigorously. Shutting my eyes, I rub the heel of my palms against my eyeballs for the oncoming headache I'm sure to get.

Ugh.

Sure enough, when I turn my head and peel open my tightly closed lids, a crimson-headed Adonis stands there, apron and all.

Zavier tilts his head at me like a dog begging its owner for attention.

Where did I find this one? In an abandoned alley?

Well, kind of.

"I don't want to know how you knew we were here or how you got this job on such short notice. You couldn't go the day without me, huh?" I laugh but it is endearing in a twisted, unhinged way.

He leans over and rubs his cheek against the top of my head.

"Of course I couldn't. I missed my pumpkin too much."

"All right, get off me." I shove Zav off, and he rocks back and forth on his feet. Now that I know he's a vampire, I realize he *lets* me do this. He's strong enough to not go anywhere if he doesn't want to. "What happened to our original waiter?"

Zav certainly wasn't the one to take our drink order and ask if we wanted any appetizers.

Zavier smiles mischievously, and I make a point to ignore it and not let my mind wander to what could've happened.

Ava and I rattle off our orders which Zavier writes down and takes to the kitchen.

"Speak of the devil." She smirks at me while sipping on her lemonade. "How's it going living together?"

"He's attentive that's for sure. I thought he was going to have an aneurysm when I told him I was going into work today." I run a hand through my hair tucking flyaways behind my ear. "Midnight, the little shit, seems to love him for some reason so he's living his best life. I wish there was movement on the intruder in my apartment, so I have a timeline for moving back in but so far nothing. I don't want to be a burden to Zavier, you know? I basically took over his space and he refuses to let me sleep on the couch so I take his bed. It's not fair to him."

What I don't tell Ava is I sleep better than I ever have in his bed. His scent which I thought would fade, only seems to stick to the sheets and lull me to sleep each night.

As much as I try to hold myself back from the goofy vampire, he continues to wiggle under my skin and into my heart. I'm not sure how much longer I'll be able to hold back from pursuing a full-on relationship with him.

I keep that tidbit of information to myself. Zav would probably throw a parade in his own honor if he found out I'm thinking about asking him to make things serious.

"I doubt he's bothered by you living with him," she laughs. "He's a walking boner for you. From everything I've seen he's going to be heartbroken when you leave." I spy Zav watching from the corner, but he quickly disappears when he's caught. "It's an interesting situation, but maybe you moving in is the universe telling you to follow your heart and not your head." Ava gives me a pointed look and sucks down the last of her drink. "Get yourself laid and see if your natural chemistry bleeds into sexual chemistry and decide if you want to take it further. Nothing wrong with walking away if it goes south."

"Yeah, maybe." She has a point but there's still part of me

reluctant to take the plunge. He's also an immortal being and I'm a human. How the hell would that work?

I take a sip of my water, and a different waiter appears with our plates of food. Ava's salad does look delicious, but my burger has me salivating.

I reach for my water for another sip and frown when I find it empty. I must've downed it without realizing in my discomfort answering Ava's questions. Before I can dwell too long on my dry throat, another full cup of water is placed in front of me and a lemonade in front of Ava.

I slowly run my gaze up the apron covered chest, corded throat, and strong jaw in front of me. Zavier smiles and walks away without a word.

"See? He knew what you needed before you did." Ava digs into her salad and draws her new lemonade closer.

"Pfft. It's his job to stay on top of that. I'm sure he'd do it for anyone," I reason with her, but know it's more than that. I just don't want to say it out loud.

I stifle the moan that wants to come out when I bite into my burger and flavors burst on my tongue. The meat is perfectly cooked to my liking and not too greasy. All of the toppings flow together seamlessly, and the fries are delicious too.

"This was a great idea." I point a fry at Ava, and she nods in agreement.

We finish our meal in relative silence, both enjoying our food. A certain someone is mysteriously gone but I still feel his eyes on me. I don't think I could miss the heat of their gaze if I tried.

Ava's phone rings as we're winding down and she holds the screen up to her face with a sigh. She hesitates answering, but rolls her neck and scoots out of the booth. Flashing the screen to me I see Spencer's name and understand. I nod at her, and she walks away to chat with him.

While she's gone, I take the chance to clean up our table a bit. Stacking our plates and wiping up crumbs I neatly place them on the corner. Customer service jobs in any capacity can be tough, and I try to help the workers as much as possible when I can.

I'm shocked when Ava slides back into the booth minutes after her phone rang.

"That was a short conversation," I marvel, and look up, only to find someone who is very much not Ava sitting in front of me. Unless Ava grew a few feet, dyed her hair red, and sported a set of fangs.

"I can't leave a lovely lady like yourself unattended." Zavier picks up my water and strategically places his lips on my lip gloss prints on the edge of the glass. His green eyes bore into mine and I fight the shiver that comes over me.

This man.

"Are you trying to move out of my apartment already?" he remarks, and I internally sigh. Of course he overheard that. "I know what you're thinking, and I promise I try to tune out your conversations to give you privacy, but I'm a vampire and we hear extremely well. Ava's loud so it was hard to miss."

Free of his apron I see Zavier's full outfit of a black tee under a gray flannel. The contrast really brings out the color of his hair and eyes.

"I just feel bad I'm all up in your space, and don't want to intrude that's all."

Zav's eyebrows wrinkle at my statement and he reaches across the table to grab my hands which I'm wringing in front of me.

"Celine. I promise you are not a burden in the slightest. I've been alone for hundreds of years and now I have you." His eyes soften and I melt a little. "I love waking up to you in my apartment. I love hearing your soft snores through the door. I love learning what I do that makes you roll your eyes. I love seeing how wild your hair looks when you walk out of the bedroom in the morning." That one earns a flick on the hand from me and a chuckle from him. "Please don't think you're a burden. You're a light in my life." A small stroke on the top of my hand. "Well, Midnight comes first and then you." He winks and I purse my lips.

Zav pulls the check out from under the table and sets it in front of me. When I open it, it says it's already been paid for.

"On the house." He disappears in the next breath before I can look up.

Freaking stalker vampire.

31

Ava came back not long after Zavier pulled his disappearing act, so did the waiter he "relieved of his job". She seemed somber and her eyes were ringed red, but she smiled and waved me off when I asked if she was okay. Her and Spencer finally talked about her feelings on the matter and were going back and forth on what to do. They love each other but Spencer sees his life in California with his promotion, and Ava sees hers here. While I think Spencer is a great guy, I fully support my best friend and any decision she makes on the matter.

Heading to Detective Waters office, the one who's been handling the case where the girl went missing after being at Vex, I raise my fist and rap my knuckles on the door frame.

She looks up at me with a soft smile.

Pin straight blonde hair falls around a heart shaped face. Fairly new on the team, Detective Stephanie Waters has so far shown that she's a kind and caring person. I can tell there's something off about her today, though.

"Hey, Brennan." She waves me inside, and I have a seat in the vacant chair in front of her desk.

"Was there confirmation of disappearance?" I reach for the file folder she extends. "Thanks for keeping me in the loop on this one."

"Of course." Her vanilla lotion scents the air. "Yes, unfortunately we found her." She sighs and I know what that means. "She wasn't alive when we did."

Flipping through the crime scene photos I take it all in. A body fully intact, unlike my serial killer, but with cuts and bruises all over her body. Her legs, arms, chest, neck, no spot was left untouched, and I cringe at what the girl had to do endure.

"Poor thing. What did they do to her?" Squinting I see grass around the body. "Where did you find her? It wasn't near Vex?"

Detective Waters leans back in her chair and spins slightly. "Oddly enough we found her because of an anonymous call very early in the morning. She was found in Millenium Park. Thank goodness we got to her before the general public to keep down on the panic." She shakes her head in disbelief and I'm sure my face reflects a similar expression. "Nothing tied her explicitly back to Vex like her friend said. We double checked the businesses surrounding the club after you did and talked to Vex employees themselves. Nobody saw anything, but a bouncer did say they saw her with her friend out front, not that that's much to go off of."

"Anything on the cameras to prove a kidnapping?" I ask glancing up at her.

"Nothing. It doesn't make any sense." She takes the folder from me, and we sit in stumped silence. "The lab is still running some tests, but nothing is adding up. Hopefully it gives us some kind of lead, because the captain is pushing for us to close the case now that we've found the body."

Something fishy is going on with this case. It bothers me more than anything when bad people get away with what they've done, and I refuse to let it happen here. Even with my other case I might have to do some more investigating myself.

"Did you tell Genevieve yet?" I ask the question I'm dreading the answer to.

"Not yet and I'm really not looking forward to it."

Detective Waters loses a little of the spark in her eyes that afternoon.

I slump onto the couch with a pathetic moan. Midnight lets out a disgruntled meow as he jumps off the couch from where he was sitting. I didn't touch him, but God forbid we sit within five feet of each other.

"That bad, huh?" Zavier asks from the kitchen where he's working on dinner for us. "What happened since I saw you at lunch?"

My answer is a muffled groan, and I hear his soft footsteps as he pads over to me. I shove my face further into the cushion and grip the blanket underneath me to my chest. A strong hand lightly strokes my head, and a weight pushes down on the cushion by my waist.

"Come on, sweetheart." He pulls me up from my pitiful state and pulls me into a side hug. His hand directs my head to rest on his shoulder. "Tell Daddy Zav what's going on."

Faster than the speed of light I pull back and glare at him. "Never say those words to me again."

"Sweetheart?" He plays dumb. "Well, okay. I didn't mind that nickname, but I guess I'll keep trying. What about, toots?"

"Zavier Lockwood," I scold and he straightens to attention at the edge in my tone and use of his full name. "You know what I meant. Don't play dumb."

Smirking in response, he pulls me fully into his lap where I'm straddling his trim waist. I can feel the ridges of his muscles as I settle myself in. My nose rests in the crook of his neck where his smell is the strongest and I blow out a deep breath, relaxing into him. I don't know what it says about me that all my inhibitions go away when I'm around this man. Vampire or not he's a safe space, and I'd be dumb not to admit it. Arms wind around my back and he lets out his own sigh of contentment.

"What's going on?" He tries again and I finally relent.

"Just typical frustrating detective stuff. That case the other detective took over ... a body was found."

"I'm so sorry, baby."

Zav holds me while I ride out the wave of emotions that come with death. I'm no stranger to it in this line of work, but it doesn't make it any easier. Did I know the woman? No. That didn't make her life any less important.

"Between not finding any concrete evidence for our serial killer and now this, it feels like I'm running in circles. What kind of detective am I if I can't solve any cases?" I mutter.

Zavier doesn't say anything else and simply holds me. We sit in silence with only the sounds of our breathing, the ticking of the clock, and the occasional pop from the oven where dinner cooks.

I become aware of my breasts pressed against his lean chest. My nipples are pebbled and hard under my shirt. His nose skirts along the column of my neck, mouth dangerously close to my artery. I know I should be scared. An apex predator holds me within his grasp and I'm a sitting duck with no chance of getting away, yet I don't find myself wanting to.

We haven't talked much about what him being a vampire means for our relationship, but I think I want to soon. He's still the same Zav I've known since the beginning.

My hands, with a mind of their own, wind themselves in his wavy crimson hair. Zav's breath hitches when I massage his scalp and place a light kiss on his own neck. Knowing I affect him as much as he affects me makes me feel powerful.

The pure masculine strength with which he holds himself is so hot. I need to feel good, taken care of, after this shitty day. I'm not used to coming home to someone who will hold me.

Pulling back, my eyes meet his hidden behind glasses. Heat simmers behind those endless irises and our noses brush in a butterfly kiss.

We simply sit and breathe in each other before making any other movements. His hands feather down my sides and inch underneath my shirt at my hips. Skin against skin, his fingertips burn a red-hot trail as they find their way under my bra. Soft lips press against every inch of my face.

My cheek. My forehead. My chin. My nose.

"Kiss me already," I growl, all patience leaving me.

"So demanding," Zav murmurs against my cheek.

He drives me crazier by kissing around the outline of my lips, so close to where I want him and then he stops. Sick of the games I take matters into my own hands and hold his head in place before smashing our mouths together. Our teeth clash and tongues tangle in a burning inferno of tension. We haven't kissed since our date, and it feels like coming home as weird as it is to say.

"Careful of the fangs," he whispers, voice slightly lisped talking around his enlarged incisors.

Smiling against his lips, I respond, "I'm no stranger to a little blood."

Diving back in I moan and his chest rumbles in satisfaction.

My shirt quickly finds itself on the ground and I urgently push his up and off his head needing to feel more of his skin against mine. His cock is hard underneath my ass, and I'd love nothing more than to take it out of the confines of his jeans. He teases his fingers down my body and under the waistband of my pants.

"Zav," I gasp when one of his long fingers finds itself along the seam of my panties.

"What does my girl want?" Another teasing stroke. "Tell me. I'm yours."

He breathes deeply against my neck and a need I didn't know could be this strong fills me.

"Bite me," I murmur.

Zav stills and I whimper pushing myself against him, needing more friction.

"You don't know what you're asking for." His voice is raspy, and I can tell he's slowly losing control. Just how I want him.

"It won't change me into a vampire will it?" I question.

"Well no but ..." He trails off with obvious desire in his eyes fixed on my neck.

"I trust you." I pull his head snugly against my pulsing throat and encourage him to do what we both so badly want. "Bite me, Zavier."

32

'm hanging on by a thread. My control is a flickering flame that will go out any second now, throwing me into darkness. I would never hurt Celine, but I'm afraid of what my instincts will make me do with my mate squirming and pleading beneath me.

"Wait." As much as it pains me to stop, my dick screaming at me, I have to tell her the truth before taking this plunge. I haven't wanted to overwhelm her, finding out I'm a vampire is enough to send any sane human screaming, so I've wanted to be cautious approaching this topic.

"Hmm?" Celine's confused gaze is cute.

Lust is written across her features, and I can't help brushing a stray hair out of her face.

"I haven't been completely honest with you," I stall.

"You're not a vampire you actually shift into a hamster?" she replies dryly.

Faster than she can track, I bend her over my knee and give

her ass a slap. She cries out but by the smell of her arousal I can tell it's just fueled the fire.

Good to know.

"No, you sassy thing. I am indeed a very sexy, very humble vampire." I stroke her butt over the spot I slapped. "It's something other than that," I say slowly.

Don't be a pussy, Zavier. Tell her.

I help her up until she's facing me. I need to gauge her feelings on this.

I blow out a breath and adjust my glasses where they've slipped down my nose.

Spit it out, I command myself. *Just say it.*

The words tumble out of me in a blur. "You're my mate. We're mates."

Silence.

"What did you say?" she asks, nose scrunching in confusion. "You said that so fast I didn't catch a single word."

I lower my head. "Mates—vampires have mates, and you're mine."

"Mates?" she repeats back to me.

This time she adjusts herself so she's sitting next to me on the couch, and I already miss her warmth. Looking in her eyes I attempt to decipher what she's feeling but my girl is a difficult one to read. I'm sure her detective training gives her a stellar poker face, but I want to see her true face so bad right now.

"Mates," I confirm.

"Huh." She continues to stare into my eyes, and I've never felt more vulnerable than under her gaze in this moment. I start to squirm, terrified of her reaction. What if she doesn't want to be mated to me? "Okay. What does that mean?"

"Uh, well." I fumble for an explanation at the casual tone in which she asks. "Every vampire has a mate somewhere but not everybody finds them. The world is large and especially vampires find it hard to stay in one place for too long. It's a rare thing, honestly, and even rarer for a vampire to have a human mate." I rub the back of my neck nervously. "Our souls call to each other. It's one of the purest loves you can have."

A heartbreaking expression crosses Celine's face, and I want to hold her in my arms and crumple at the same time.

Will she reject me? For her to accept I'm a vampire but not want to be my mate would be crushing.

"So, we're fated to be together?" She sinks back into the couch behind her, gazing off into nothing. "*Forced* into liking one another? Was any of this even real?" Her eyes begin to water and fuck I hate it.

"What? No!" My hair flops around as I shake my head vehemently.

I see where her thoughts are headed. Celine thinks the mate bond is the only reason I want to be with her. That a cosmic attraction is why I'm drawn to her and want to pursue a relationship. Despite her grunt of initial protest, I grab Celine and deposit her back in my lap. Easing us down so I'm flat on my back, and she's perfectly on top of me, I cradle her face and hold her gaze. The unshed tears break my heart, and I kiss away the wrinkle in her brow.

"Listen to me, Celine Brennan. We may be fated mates but no magnetic pull dictates who or what I do. Yes, it may initially bring us together in a way it wouldn't for others, but we still have free will. If I wasn't insanely attracted to you both mentally and physically, I wouldn't be here. You are the most stunning, intelligent, kind creature I've ever crossed paths with, and I worship the ground you walk on." Her cheeks stain a pretty pink at my praise so I continue. "Pretty girl, you're my everything. We haven't known each other long considering the length of my life thus far, but up until now its paled in comparison to being with you. The mate bond doesn't force us into doing anything. Okay?" I reiterate my point, and she nods. "Get it through that gorgeous skull of yours that I'm here for you because I want to be here. You can't get rid of me." Trying to break the serious moment because I don't do well with them, I proceed to kiss every inch of her head and face until she giggles. "And it goes both ways, just so you know. You might be more attracted to me than usual because of the bond … and my insanely good looks." I can't help but smirk. "But it doesn't force you to like me."

She rests her head against my chest when I'm done, and I slide my palm up and down her back. Her smooth skin feels heavenly.

"I freaked out for a second there thinking it was all out of our control. For the first time in a long time, I have something for me that makes me happy. Someone wants to take care of me instead of the other way around and the thought of it being based on a forced bond hurt to think about." Her small hands tighten against my pecs.

I grab them and press a kiss to each of her delicate fingers.

"Nah. You just have this vampire trying to get in your pants because he wants to." I nuzzle my nose against hers. "Also, just have to say, I will bite you. One day. That's a given. I've heard a mate's flavor of blood is quite the aphrodisiac." I lick her neck, and she giggles again. "Imagine both my teeth and my cock holding you captive." She hums at the promise in my words. "It'll be worth the wait."

Her chest rises in quick succession at the visual I'm giving her.

"I didn't want your first bite to be based on a half-truth. Plus, if I bite you as your mate, it'll begin to solidify our bond and I'm not about to force you into anything without all the vampy facts on the table. See? I'm quite the gentleman."

Rubbing her arms up and down I relish in the feeling of her body on top of mine. "I want you to be sure of your decision."

Sure of me, I don't say.

Just then the oven beeps signaling dinner's ready and I sigh. Our sexually charged moment has passed as much as I'd love to continue it. Fumbling around for our shirts I grab them off the floor and help pull hers on. Her hair is a beautifully, chaotic mess around her head once it pokes through.

"Go get dinner before it burns." She nods toward the kitchen.

I flatten her tangled strands and place one last kiss to her forehead before I walk away to do just as she said.

I'll always do whatever this woman tells me to do. She's the only being on this earth that can do so.

"Oh, I have a gift for you!" I remember the thing I snagged from my contact while she was at work.

"For me?" Celine gracefully unfolds herself from the couch and walks over.

The natural sultry swing of her hips distracts me, and I stare dumbfounded before coming back to myself and willing my fangs to recede from the little bit where they poke out of my gums. The twist of her lips tells me she caught me watching.

Good. I want her to know on a daily basis how much she affects me.

I reach over and open one of the cabinets to pull out a small gift bag I stashed there.

"Close your eyes." I tease and plant a kiss on each of her eyelids when she does. Depositing the bag in her palm I step back. "Open."

Celine peeps open one eye like I might've handed her a bomb. She moves aside the tissue paper. Pulling out a smooth leather holder she unlatches the snap and slides out her gift.

"A knife?"

Turning it this way and that she observes the silver metal crafted to perfection.

"Whoa. That's freaking sharp." Celine marvels at it.

Delicately poking the edge, I teeter between wanting to rip her finger away from it, so she doesn't come to harm and hoping she nicks herself, so I'll be able to smell her delicious blood.

"What's this for?" she asks.

I tug her closer to me by her belt loops and she puts the knife away before resting her hands against my pecs. She fiddles with the silver chain resting on my chest, and I press my forehead to hers.

"With everything going on lately I want you to be as prepared as possible. I know you're perfectly capable of taking care of yourself, but I can't see you hurt." The subtle caramel highlights in her hair shine in the remaining sunlight streaking through the window. "It would destroy me."

"I'll be careful. Thank you for the gift." Celine plants a small kiss on my cheek. "It's a beautiful knife."

"The hilt was hand carved," I explain. "I chose the butterflies because you're beautiful, but deadly, and I thought your knife should match."

She laughs softly. "Thank you, again."

We stand there like that for a while as I bask in the contact and simply breathe her in.

She probably doesn't realize it, but there will never come a time when I tire of her. She is the single, most important thing, in my immortal life.

33

"You want to go back to the club? The one where a woman was supposedly kidnapped and killed?" Ava waves her ceramic mug at me with a deadpan stare. "You who doesn't even enjoy clubbing?"

It's the weekend and I invited her over to the apartment to hang out. Things with Spencer haven't been going well since she's not positive what she wants to do. Spencer hasn't committed to the new job yet either, but I can tell they've both made up their minds and just don't want to say it.

"I'm not going there to have a good time." I wrap my fingers around my own mug. "I'm going to check things out." I give a small shrug. "I'm still fighting a nagging feeling something's up with that place." I implore her with my eyes to indulge me. I need her help. The more eyes the better.

"If you're doing that, I'm coming this time!" Zavier shouts from the bedroom.

I roll my eyes, and Ava hides a chuckle behind her sip of

coffee. He refused to leave the apartment when Ava came over, but he compromised by staying in his bedroom with the door shut for "privacy." Load of shit if you ask me now that I know vampires have strong hearing, but Ava's none the wiser so that's what really matters.

"If you're coming"—I call back, raising my voice even though it's unnecessary— "then that means you need to help me. That means eyes open and ears listening."

"Not a problem, dear," he sing-songs through the door.

"I'm always down for some sleuthing." Her frame droops a little and her rose gold hair shields her face from my view. "It's over with Spencer and me."

I shake my head, jolted by the sudden change in topic. "What?" I blurt, reaching over to place my hand over hers.

Ava sniffles and smiles through watery eyes. "It was a mutual decision. Heartbreaking but mature all the same. I'll always love him, and I wish nothing but the best for him but we both wanted different things and couldn't get past it. I didn't want to hold him back, but I also didn't want to leave my life behind, you know?"

"Aw, I'm so sorry, Aves."

Her sweet perfume hits me when I pull her in for a hug. I'm not a huge hugger but she is, and I know she needs it right now.

"I should've put a shot of vodka in our coffee," I throw out, and I'm rewarded with a laugh. "Not too late for it." Inching toward the refrigerator I pull out the bottle and she nods.

I startle when Ava suddenly shouts. "Zavier get your fine ass out here!"

He appears before us in a tumble of crimson hair. Rocking a black hoodie and somehow making it sexy as hell he holds Midnight stretched across his shoulders. The cat looks perfectly content, yet when he makes eye contact with me, he hisses. Still no progress there for me.

"You rang for me and my emotional support pussy?" He strokes Midnight's tail like an evil villain waiting expectantly in their chair.

"You, me, Celine, the club. Be there or be square."

She holds up a finger as she names each thing and ends with a palm in the air. Zav slaps it with no questions asked.

These two together are trouble.

"All right let's go. Nobody misbehave please, this is a perfectly legal observation, and it'll stay that way."

I glance pointedly at Zavier, and he holds his hands up in surrender before answering.

He pouts and adjusts his glasses where they've slid down his nose. "Now when have I ever misbehaved?"

Music pulses through the large space and I'm hit with déjà vu sitting in a booth with Ava in Vex. This time is different, though, because we have a particular redhead with us who glances around and takes everything in with sparkling inquisitive eyes.

"I can't believe we're back here." I try to ignore the heat of Zavier's palm where it rests on my thigh under the table. The man insists on being glued to my side at all times.

"Believe it," Ava responds mid crunch. "Funny enough, we're here for the same reason as the first, which is not in fact to have fun, but to scout out the scene." She gives me a pointed look which I stick my tongue out at.

I laugh sheepishly. "Sorry."

Ava wags a finger at me. "Don't apologize. We both know you're not one bit sorry."

"Speaking of, we're not going to find out anything just sitting here." Zavier nudges me out of the booth and hops out with a flourish. "Will you do me the honor of a dance?" He holds out a hand like we're at a regal ball and not a nightclub and tops it off with a wink. "We can check things out inconspicuously that way."

He offers me his hand, and I slide mine onto it. Pointing at Ava before Zav can pull me away, I say, "Why don't you hang out at the bar and see if you can glean anything from the bartenders?"

She picks up her drink and slides out of the booth. "You got it, boss."

Zav weaves us through the throng of bodies to not quite the edge of the dancefloor and pulls me in tight. I gasp at the feel of being pressed so firmly against him. My eyes flick up to his. I know I'm here for investigative purposes and can't afford to get distracted, but I can't help it the way lust shoots through me.

I've always wished a man would look at me the way he does.

He might not have told me he loves me, but there's no mistaking the emotion reflected in his eyes behind his glasses.

Brushing my ponytail off my neck he blows lightly on the delicate skin raising goosebumps in his wake. I close my eyes and take a deep breath. He turns me around and my back fits effortlessly to his front as our bodies move to the music.

Realization trickles through me and I gasp, flipping back around to face him. "You fucker!" I yell over the music. Spinning around to face him, he simply grins in response, knowing exactly what I'm going to say. "It was you!"

"What was me?" He plays dumb like he loves to do.

"My sexy stranger from the club that night."

How long has he been lurking around? How could I have been so blind?

"You think I'm sexy?" His long eyelashes bat at me.

"I know you like to stalk me, but exactly how long have you

been watching?" I inquire, poking his chest as his hands drift down my body, settling low on my waist.

"I can't hear you over the music!" Zavier points to his ears.

"You liar! Of course you can hear me!" I purse my lips at him, and he grabs my hand, twirling my body into his and holding me tightly.

I'll let it go. For now.

"You're thinking too much. Just feel the music with me. And *look around*," he reminds me. "Don't forget why we're here."

I hate that I got so distracted by him that I forgot the whole reason I had asked to come here in the first place.

I spot Ava at the bar, where she chats with the bartender. When her gaze flits my way, I see the hurt in her eyes. I wish I could wave a magic wand and make this whole situation with Spencer better for her, but I just have to hope the saying of time healing all wounds applies here too.

"Move me more this way," I tell Zav, trying to nod as discreetly as possible to the door that I believe leads to something of interest. The guard by the door pays us little attention, his gaze skipping over us as he scans the crowd.

He does as I say, but it does no good. No one is coming or going, and the door remains firmly shut.

"I think tonight was a waste of time," I admit, feeling a bit beaten down by that fact.

It's driving me insane that I can't get answers when it comes to this place.

"I hope you don't think I'm a waste of time," Zav laughs softly.

He swipes a hand through his hair and my knees go a little weak at the action. I want this man, and I want him bad.

"Never." I press a kiss to his cheek before we claim a table.

"Anything?" Ava asks as she joins us, sliding a much-needed glass of water in front of me.

"No," I admit, biting my lip. "No one went in or left." I angle my head toward the door that remains guarded.

Ava frowns. "Maybe there's nothing funny going on here after all?" she suggests with a lifted brow.

I feel the weight of Zav's gaze. "You still think there's something going on here?"

"I do," I admit. "It just ... it's a feeling."

I push away from the table. "All right, guys, I'm going to the restroom so don't do anything too crazy while I'm gone." I point a finger in warning at each of them. Ava and Zav are not to be trusted left to their own devices.

Slipping out of the booth, I make a beeline for the restroom because I do genuinely have to pee. Narrowly avoiding a puddle of vomit in the hall I blessedly find one open stall.

Quickly doing my business, I hover in the stall for a second, waiting for the girls at the mirrors to vacate the premises.

Thankfully they don't take too long, so I wash my hands in record time. Spinning on my heel, I'm just about to head back to the table when I hear something from above that makes me stop. Voices come from the vent on the ceiling right above my sink.

I remember Ava mentioning that the first time we were here and try to drown out everything else except for the voices. One in particular has me standing in shock. A voice that sounds oddly familiar.

It sounds like ... but it can't be.

It's difficult to listen since it's not crystal clear through the vent. I tuck my hair behind my ear like that'll help and close my eyes.

"Are you fucking kidding me?" The female sounds pissed. "It's like I have to do everything myself."

"I'm sorry." A panicky male responds.

"How are you this incompetent?"

He mumbles something in response, and I can't quite make it out, but the yelling definitely helps with understanding her.

"Enough! You're going to give me a headache which is saying something." Her tone brooks no argument. "Get your shit together. You won't like what happens if you don't."

I stand around a little longer after that, but don't hear anything else.

What the fuck was that?

Something odd is most definitely going on with this club and I'm not just crazy.

That conversation proves it, because I swear the female voice I just heard was Genevieve's.

34

All color has leeched from my skin and my wide eyes reflect back at me in the mirror. I have to compose myself before going back out there. Even though part of the reason for coming was to observe the club for any weirdness, I don't want to bring Ava any further into this. She's not naïve to the situation, but she's also not a cop and I won't risk my best friend getting hurt.

Come on Celine. Compartmentalize. You're great at that.

Trying to center yourself in a hectic bathroom with a constant flow of drunk women isn't the easiest thing to do but I tune them out. Adjusting my ponytail and reapplying my lip gloss, I give myself another once over. Much better. Someone nearby sprays an excessive amount of floral perfume, and I duck out of the door before it can suffocate me.

I make sure to slow my steps once I'm back in view of our table and tell myself to act normal when I sit back down.

Ava gives me a once over and I force a smile back. She seems to buy it, thank God.

"I'm grabbing one more drink. You in?" Ava asks us as she scooches out.

"Rum and coke for me, please," I manage to squeak out hoping it sounds normal.

Zav says the same for him, so I pull a twenty out of my pocket and hand it to her. She grabs it and shimmies while tucking it in her bra before wandering off to grab our drinks.

Glancing at Zavier, I find his eyes zeroed in on me and I look away. He's oddly serious and it's freaking me out since I'm so used to his usual comical manner. His burning stare drills into the side of my head and I shift on the seat.

Fuck, he's too good at reading me.

In an effort to distract him, I smooth a hand down his thigh. He jolts as soon as soon as I make contact, and a mischievous thought crosses my mind. We're sitting in the back corner of the booth where shadows cover any debauchery. My hand brushes dangerously close to his crotch and I know I'm playing with fire when he grabs my wrist in a tight grip.

He doesn't pull it away though, instead he holds it prisoner resting against his hardening cock. A streak of boldness has me squeezing him and I balk at the girth I feel against my hand. He's huge. His hold doesn't allow me much room, but I stroke him as much as I can within his confines. A whimper so low I almost miss it comes out of his throat.

That's hot.

Up until this point I've avoided eye contact, partially because I'm worried if I do, I'll lose my nerve. This has become less about distracting him and more about me simply wanting to touch him.

It's like a magnet drawing my eyes to his face and I'm rewarded with the sexiest expression I've ever seen—head thrown back against the booth with his tumbling red waves falling over his forehead, mouth slightly parted, with his eyes closed.

"What are you going to do with me?" he growls, voice low and husky.

Zavier looks like he's experiencing exquisite torture and it's at my hand. I give another squeeze, and he blows out a breath that morphs into a growl.

"Celine." Teeth clenched, I can see his fangboner, as he's dubbed it. "Harder," he begs.

Ignoring his plea, I cross my legs and stare out into the crowd with a bored expression trying to look normal and not like I'm giving my booth buddy a hand job. There's plenty of other depravity happening in the club so it's not like we're the worst offenders.

But I'd rather not have Ava call me out for this, and she's glancing over from the bar. I nod and she looks back at the bartender who's working on the rum and cokes.

"What do you think?" I purr. "Can I push you over the edge before she gets back?"

He whimpers again. "You are in so much trouble." He sounds breathless but doesn't make a move to stop me. Instead, he uses my hand and rubs up and down in conjunction with his at a rapid pace. By the pants coming out of him and the tensing of his abs I can tell he's getting close to release.

Teasing him, I stop. He lifts his hand off mine in question with a tortured moan at being left high and dry, but it's about to get even better for him because I unzip his fly to reach in and pull his dick free.

I can't see him but by the feel and girth he's larger than I've ever handled before.

Here I am holding his cock in my hand, in public, and I

haven't done anything except kiss the man a few times. Power radiates through me as I edge him near his release.

I could get used to this feeling—knowing that my touch alone brings this vampire to his knees.

My core clenches at the velvety hardness of him in my hand. It's a pleasant sensation against my skin and I rub my thumb gently around the head. Zavier squirms under my ministrations and grips my hand, encouraging me to rub his cock harder.

The little sounds he makes has me biting my lip.

If someone took notice to us, they'd know exactly what we're doing. The motion of our arms can't be mistaken for anything else. With a quick glance back at Ava, I see her grabbing the last drink from the bartender and know our time is almost up.

"Ava is about to come back to the table," I whisper, starting to get a little frantic.

"If you think getting caught by Ava is a motivator for me to hurry up, you're sorely mistaken." He turns his head to the side to burrow his nose in my hair and hide his pained expression. "But I know it makes you panic, so I'll be a good boy and come," he whispers against my ear, and I squeeze my thighs for more friction. My clit is throbbing with need at this point.

Both our hands work him, squeezing and rubbing up and down, twisting when we near the head. It's like the rapid beat of my heart is timed up to the ticking clock of Ava's footsteps as she grows closer.

With one last twist, Zavier lets out a long breathy moan and hot cum spurts out onto both of our hands. He tucks himself away and I look into his eyes, nervous that maybe it wasn't good enough for him.

He leans over and presses a kiss to the side of my forehead.

"I know what you're thinking and that was ridiculously sexy." He takes our drink napkins off and wipes my hand off underneath the table. "Don't think what you were just thinking. Anything you want to do to me is always welcome." I think he's done when he leans back over. "You are in for it later, though. Just because you've won the battle, doesn't mean you've won the war. I never lose." Flashing fangs at me he excuses himself to go to the bathroom just as Ava sets down our three glasses.

"Where's he going? I just brought the drinks." She watches his retreating form.

"Diarrhea," I blurt out, immediately regretting my answer. "Dinner didn't sit right with him."

My throat works overtime when I take a huge gulp of my drink. The burn makes me wince but not more than the lousy excuse I gave. I don't typically crack under pressure, yet when it comes to this I fold like a deck of cards.

"Huh." Ava slides in across from me and I grip my fresh napkin tightly. I need to run back to the bathroom myself to properly wash my hands, but I know Ava will clock that something is up if I go back to the bathroom so soon.

Ava pulls something out of her purse and slides it across the table with a cough. She looks off into the distance and sips her own drink. My cheeks heat when I see what it is.

Hand sanitizer.

35

Pouring myself a cup of coffee, I settle on the barstool with a sliced orange. The combo doesn't make much sense, but in my slightly hungover state it sounds like exactly what I need.

I stifle a yawn and set my coffee aside while I eat most of the orange, leaving behind two slices.

Picking up my mug, I inhale the French vanilla scent.

Perfection.

I haven't had a chance to take a sip yet when warmth envelops me from behind, arms wrapping around my torso to hold me hostage. A chin settles on top of my head a second later, a soft humming sound emanating from the man child behind me.

"Zav," I groan. "You almost made me spill my coffee."

"Shh," he hushes. "I'm getting my morning cuddle time in."

Ugh. It's so hard to be annoyed with him when he's so sweet. I relax into his hold and close my eyes. His lips brush the top of my head in a hint of a kiss before he finally lets me go and pulls out the stool beside me.

He snags my last two slices of uneaten orange and flashes me a fang-tipped smile.

My stomach rolls deliciously. I'm not sure what it says about me that I'm attracted to his fangs. I don't dare tell him, because something tells me he would take too much pleasure in that fact.

My phone rings, interrupting our slow and quiet morning.

Captain Barnes's name flashes on the screen so I quickly answer. "Hello?"

"Hey, Celine. I know you're not due in until later, but I thought you might want to head to the precinct soon. We finally caught the intruder on CCTV downtown and he's being brought in now for questioning."

"Yes," I cry, hopping off the stool and knocking the mug over in the process. Zav quickly rights the cup and grabs a rag to mop up the mess. "I'll be there as soon as I can."

"All right. Don't rush too much though. Now that we've got him he's not going anywhere anytime soon."

"Thanks, Captain."

I hang up the phone and I don't bother to fill Zav in because I know he heard the whole thing.

"I'm going to change and head in."

He nods. "I'll drive you."

"You don't—"

"I'll drive you," he insists.

I throw up my hands in a cease fire. "All right."

It doesn't take me long to change and then I swear Zav drives a hundred miles an hour to get there. I'm not prone to motion sickness, but my stomach doesn't feel great as I walk into the building.

"Brennan! Should I cuff you for speeding?" Captain eyes me

as I walk in. "There's no way you didn't break laws to get here this fast."

"Ooh, kinky. Celine arrest me." Zav sticks his wrists out and I push them down with a hiss.

"Don't listen to him." I swat at him to get behind me.

Captain arches a curious brow. "He seems to be popping up at a lot of crime scenes lately even though he isn't on the force. Why is he here now?"

"I'm her personal security detail," Zav pipes up from behind me. "Don't like it? Take it up with my lawyer."

I swat at the annoying vampire behind me wishing I could duct tape his mouth.

"So, you caught him?" I attempt to change the subject.

"Yup. Like I said we spotted him on CCTV downtown by that coffee shop you love. His prints match the ones we took from your apartment." The captain halts in front of the interrogation room with a hand on the silver handle. "We haven't questioned him yet in the hopes you could come in and be here to help do it yourself. I know you're worried the break-in was personal and hope that if you meet him, it will help assuage your concerns on that front. Ready?" He waits for me to respond.

"Let's do it." Besides my small exhale of breath, you'd never know that I'm nervous.

I feel Zav go to follow me into the room and I turn around and plant a hand on his chest.

"Celine," he whines.

"I let you come, but you need to stay out here. If you happen to hear anything I can't help that, but you won't be in the room."

I can tell he doesn't appreciate being sidelined but he also recognizes that this is something I need to do on my own.

Entering the interrogation room, I pull out a chair and sit.

The man sitting across from me is unassuming.

He appears to be in his mid-twenties, if that. Sandy blond hair, blue eyes, and a basic hoodie and jeans outfit. I'd never pick him out as a criminal. I suppose there's no right appearance for a criminal, though. The quiet ones are honestly the ones you have to look out for, and he seems to fit that bill. He fidgets nervously as we sit there in silence, and I stare him down.

Captain Barnes sits next to me to moderate. I'm sure it's in case I slip and allow feelings to flood in. I've gotten very good at tucking those pesky things away though and refuse to let them out now. I drum my fingers on the metal table and the culprit's eyes dart down to follow the motion.

Definitely a little twitchy.

"What's your name?" I start off easy.

"Derek … Fallows," he stammers out.

"Do you know why you're in here, Derek?"

"No. I really don't," Derek replies. "One minute I'm heading out for a late-night cup of coffee and the next thing I know I'm sacked by the police. I'd honestly love an explanation myself." He begins to get defensive but his genuine confusion, in turn, confuses me.

Furrowing my brow, I glance at the captain but he's still writing.

"Playing dumb isn't going to get you anywhere. In fact, it could get you into more trouble, Derek." I enunciate his name and lean forward to look in his eyes he tries to keep downcast.

"She's telling the truth, son. Answer Detective Brennan, please," Captain finally speaks up in his authoritative tone.

"I'm telling you the truth!" he shouts, the side of his fist slamming against the table. "I have zero idea why I'm here and what you're talking about. Are you sure you've got the right guy? I've never committed a crime in my life!" Derek shoots to his feet and I do the same. I see Captain Barnes's hand slide down his thigh for his taser just in case things get hostile.

"Hey. Okay, calm down." It's best to deescalate the situation and somehow this guy seems to believe he's innocent, so I choose to play along. "You didn't break into an apartment a few weeks ago?" I don't want to give him all the details in case he decides to tell the truth.

Derek slowly sits back down in his chair, but I stay standing.

"What? No!" Once again, I'm baffled by the conviction in his statement. This doesn't appear to be some guy just trying to fuck with us. He seems truly distraught over the whole thing.

A subtle knock on the door catches my attention and I remember Zavier in the hallway who must be listening to everything.

"One moment please." Avoiding the Captain's knowing look, I peek my head out of the interrogation room. Sure enough, Zavier is standing there looking like he's going to explode if he doesn't tell me something.

I slip out and shut the door softly, so as not to be overheard.

"He's telling the truth," Zavier looks perplexed.

"What? How do you know?" Him confirming what I suspect leaves me very confused.

"His heartbeat. When humans lie their heart races and has this little jump that is a telltale sign. He's nervous and his heart is racing but I can tell the difference at this point in my life. He doesn't know anything." Zavier scratches his head and pushes his glasses up his nose.

"That doesn't make any sense, though."

"It doesn't make sense to me either, but even though it's him he either doesn't remember or..." Zavier trails off and a spark lights in his eyes. "...he's been compelled to forget." He stares at me with horror on his face.

"Compelled?" He's speaking another language now and I play with the ends of my ponytail for comfort.

"Vampires of a certain age can compel humans very easily into doing what they want. They become a mindless puppet for them to play with." Zavier stares at the ground but I can tell he's working through things in his head.

"You think he did break into my apartment, but he was compelled to do it and forget? How come we couldn't find him for forever?" I muse.

"It could've been part of the trance he was put in. They didn't want him to be found until a certain point in time or he somehow broke the compulsion. Wait a minute." Zavier pulls a small notebook and pen out from his pocket and dramatically draws a line under what looks to be a pre-existing list and writes a new one. "The constant rain, the break-in with this, and the fucking feral vampire outside of our apartment." He taps at the new list and sticks his tongue out in an adorable thoughtful way while he pieces together a puzzle I'm not aware of. "Vampires and maybe even other supernaturals are gathering in Chicago for some reason."

I blink at him. "Say again?"

"There's something supernatural at play here. I don't understand why or how yet, but this has vampire shit written all over it," he concludes and shuts his notebook but not before scribbling something on a small piece he rips off and sticks in his pocket.

"Why would vampires be targeting me?"

"I don't know." Zavier pulls me in for a short but comforting hug. I allow myself to snuggle into his warmth for just a second. "I'm going to get to the bottom of it though. You might want to get back in there. I don't think it'll get you anywhere, though." He nods toward the interrogation room and with a last pat to my butt opens the door for me.

I send a stink eye his way, but somehow, he's disappeared. I don't want to know what Zavier loose in the police station looks like, but it probably ends with him in a jail cell. Hopefully he can behave himself for however long I'm still occupied.

"Everything okay, Detective?" Captain Barnes asks when I sit back down.

The culprit seems to have settled down some, but still looks wildly confused at being here.

"All good," I reassure the captain. "Back to you, my friend," I address Derek. "You truly have no recollection of breaking into the apartment? Or hiding out from the police?" I already know what his answer will be but want to ask a final time, because I find the whole situation hard to believe.

"I swear on all that I love." He holds a hand up like he's taking an oath. "Captain Barnes showed me the footage on the CCTV, and it looks like my build and that's my DNA. I know it's irrefutable, but I don't have any memory of doing this. I swear." Derek works his jaw and sits back with a defeated sigh.

"I believe you," I reply.

"You do?" Both Captain Barnes and Derek say at the same time.

"Detective, don't make any rash conclusions. We have the proof it's him. I can schedule a polygraph test, and we can hold him in a cell here."

Captain looks like he's having a hard time understanding and I get it.

"Trust me on this one." I pat his shoulder. There's no way to make him understand. It's not like I can tell him about vampires and their freaky mind magic. I can sympathize with Derek and a supernatural flipping his life upside down.

"I don't understand it but fine." Turning to Derek he sighs. "You're still going to be fined, and it seems based on Detective

Brennan's decision your lawyer can negotiate a deal that potentially doesn't include prison time."

"We'll get your paperwork processed and have you out of here in a few, Derek." I nod at him and the relief on his face is immediate. You would've thought I'd given him a key to the city.

"Brennan." Captain tries one more time and I simply smile at him. "You're not going to pursue this? He broke into your apartment."

He enunciates the last few words like I'm crazy and I kind of am. I feel bad for the guy, though. He most likely had his mind invaded without his permission.

"Nope. I know you probably want to wring my neck right now but trust me." With a shake of his head, he follows me out and heads down the hall to his office. He gives me one last bewildered glance and shuts his door behind him.

"Well, that's the clearest what the fuck is wrong with you expression I've ever seen," Zavier whistles out from behind me.

"Really?" I spin on my booted heel to look at him. "With how long you've lived and your personality I find that hard to believe."

"True." He gives me a wolfish grin and slings an arm over my shoulder. His nose buries itself in my hair and his chest rises with the deep breath he takes of my scent. "God, you smell delectable," he murmurs, and I push him away before he gets me hot and bothered at my place of work.

After that, we have Derek fill out some paperwork for his release. He's in our system, but I don't feel right punishing him, so he walks out of the building a free man. Zavier sits none too patiently with a bouncing knee in a chair in the corner. I can tell he's antsy to get home and figure out what all is going on since we discovered it has supernatural ties.

"Ready?" I tap his shoulder, and he rises so quickly I almost pull a muscle in my neck from looking up at him.

"I thought you'd never ask." Just then Zavier goes ramrod straight and his eyes go big as saucers. *"Shit,"* he curses and reaches for my hand, lifting me into his arms in a blink.

Zav runs out of the building with me in his arms before I can question him, and we go down the block and around the corner into an alley.

Sitting slumped against an alleyway wall is none other than Derek's freshly murdered corpse.

36

sift a spoon listlessly through my bowl of Cheerios and tuck a stray hair behind my ear. It's a mess of curls this morning since I let it air dry, which I usually try not to do. Yesterday was a long one. Finding Derek's body in the alleyway threw us for a loop and had me headed right back to the station.

Zavier discreetly checked the body out before I told the captain and found something unusual. No blood or bite marks just a clear snap of the neck resulting in instant death. He couldn't smell anyone on Derek, but I knew he attributed it to the supernatural. Too many odd things lined up now and I could tell it bothered him how many things were starting to center around me.

He was insistent on sleeping in the room with me last night and I welcomed the comfort. Even if he latched onto me and didn't let go. At least his temperature seemed to run cooler than that of a human, otherwise I would've been sweating in his hold.

"Celine." Zav taps me on the head with one of Midnight's fluffy paws. The cat hisses before cuddling right up to Zav's neck like the two-timing hussy he is. "Are you okay? I think your Cheerios have turned into a cereal smoothie at this point."

Looking down I see he's right. Lost in my thoughts the cereal has gone soggy and mushed together.

Gross. This is why I prefer to eat it dry.

With a sigh I dump the mess down the drain and run water. It swirls away and I look back at Zav. He's giving me puppy dog eyes not knowing what's running through my head or how to help me. I still can't believe this gorgeous, thoughtful vampire is my mate.

Mate. That's strange in itself.

"I want to move back into my apartment." I finally say after roving over his handsome features. As soon as I say it, I want to take it back because they contort into horror.

"What?" He sets Midnight down, so I know he's serious.

In a flash, he's over by my side. The breeze rustles my hair, and he grips my shoulders to steady me when I sway from his sudden appearance.

"Derek is dead, so I don't have to worry about him returning. I've been living with you for weeks and I want to be back in my own space again. I can't keep taking up your space, mate or not." I try to reason but he's having none of it.

I don't want to be in your way. I don't want you to get sick of me, I don't say out loud. It's old insecurities stemming from the way my mom left, and I know Zav would never abandon me like she did, but sometimes logic doesn't override feelings.

"Yes, he's dead but we know there's someone bigger at play that's still very much alive. You're not safe!" His green eyes spark with fear. "You can't get hurt. On my life I swear I can't go on if you're hurt and I could've done something about it. Celine, please," he pleads and it's the hardest thing to watch him in such distress. "If you want to go back to your place then I'm going with you."

"Zavier." I wrap my arms around him and try to keep from crumbling under the guilt I feel at causing him distress. "It's going to be okay. Nothing's going to happen. You'll be right next door if anything goes awry, and I trust you to take care of me *if* that's the case." He's borderline shaking underneath me and I continue my ministrations until he calms down. "I just need to be in my own room. It'll make me feel better to be around my own things."

His brows knit. "Do you … not feel safe … with *me*?" he mumbles, voice cracking on the last word and breaking my heart all over again.

"No!" I take a breath, softening my tone. "I mean no, that's not it at all." I fumble over my words to explain myself. "You're not…" I bite my lip. "I know you'd never hurt me, and I do feel safe with you, it's just been a lot lately. I know I'd feel better in my own space."

It truly has nothing to do with not feeling safe with Zavier and I'd be lying if I didn't say I was tempted to continue to live together in our little bubble. It's been … nice. Nicer than I expected, that's for sure. He can be a bit much at times, but shockingly I think I love that about him.

He thought I didn't notice, but one night when I woke up needing to pee, I saw his sleeping form next to me in the bed. Long lashes fluttered lightly against his cheeks while he dreamed about something.

Since I no longer resided next to him his hand tried to find me and resulted in him grabbing my pillow and burying his face in it. A sweet smile pulled at his lips then and I felt myself falling for him that much more. Sneaking in every night but being gone by morning was his routine and I thought it was cute, but didn't call him out on it.

I needed to have something for myself again with the chaos my life had wrought recently. Having Zavier next door should be safe enough, at least for the next few weeks while I take time for myself to decompress. I still don't have enough evidence to be any step closer to finding the murderer wreaking havoc in Chicago and I hope being back in my apartment will allow me to think clearer and settle my mind when it comes to the case.

"Come on, you can help me get my stuff together." I stroke my finger over his eyebrows, and he lets out a disgruntled sound but heaves his body up to follow my lead.

Over the next hour we clean the apartment and get my things together. Truth be told, I hadn't brought much over to Zavier's, just the essentials. With our arms full we head over to my apartment and unlock it. The door was fixed right after the break-in, but I haven't stepped back inside until the moment. Everything is returned to its rightful place, and I can't help but eye the man at my side, knowing he has to be the one responsible.

He gives me a smile. "I couldn't leave it a mess for you."

Unshed tears burn my eyes. "Thank you." I lean up on my tiptoes to press a kiss to his cheek.

"I'm going to put this down," he says, nodding to the box in his hands.

Zavier plops the box filled with miscellaneous clothes and toiletries on my bed. Stopping, he zeroes in on something at the bottom of the box. Gasping he pulls out a pair lacy black underwear I found him hoarding in his dresser.

"You stole these!" He holds the lacy panties to his chest like they're something precious.

"That's what I should be saying to you, mister." He pockets them once again but I roll my eyes and let it go.

We walk over to Zav's one more time and I do a quick scan. It's not like it's hard to pop back over if I forgot something but I want to make sure I did as well as I could grabbing stuff. The last thing is Midnight who's currently pouting in the corner of the couch like he knows what's going on.

"Hey there, grumpy kitty." I slowly approach with a hand outstretched to show I come in peace. "We gotta go back home. Will you be nice for once and let me grab you?" So far so good, I reach out to grab him and he takes a swipe at me. "You little shit."

"It's because he knows you both belong with me." Zavier stands behind me, leaning against the wall looking like he just walked out of a GQ shoot. Ankles crossed he examines his nails and sunlight streaming in glints off the thin silver chain around his neck. His hair is perfectly in place and his glasses rest on his nose adorably. I'm probably a sweaty mess from cleaning and packing, yet he looks like he just stepped off a runway.

"Let the record show," he begins, smirk growing on his lips since I can't seem to stop checking him out. "I'm against this. I think we need to stick together."

He waits for me to give him an invitation, but I don't. I've spent so much time with him lately and I just ... I need a breather to sort through my thoughts—to see how I feel when he's not right beside me.

"Grab the cat, please." I gesture toward the black void that wants nothing more than to suck me into endless darkness.

"I think we need a schedule." He doesn't make any move to grab Midnight.

"Schedule?" I question with a hand on my hip.

"Childcare schedule. You get him one day and then I get him the next." He finally makes eye contact with me and shrugs. "Or better yet, you both stay here and that way we all get what we want." A flash of white teeth showcases his smirk of defiance.

"Fine. You can have him today since he's in a shit mood," I relent, not wanting to argue with Zavier.

I stroll past him and back over to my apartment. His footsteps echo behind me and once we're standing in my kitchen there's a stretch of silence.

Shifting from foot to foot I flatten my lips together. Not sure what to say, I glance at him, and he looks to be in the same position. Two socially awkward beings, one immortal and one not.

"This isn't … I'm not trying to make things difficult," I tell him.

"I want to take care you," Zavier's honey smooth voice replies. His white sneakers appear in my line of sight as he steps chest to chest with me. Looking up, he grabs my chin between his fingers and pulls me closer. "Listen here, mate, if I had my way your ass would be over my shoulder, and I'd lock you in my bedroom until I convinced your mind and body exactly who you belong to." He leans up to my ear and whispers. "I'd wring so much pleasure out of you you'd be boneless, and orgasm drunk for days. Maybe I'd sneak a bite in here or there but not until you were writhing beneath me and screaming my name would I claim you."

Holy. Shit.

"You can run and hide from me—from this, from us, all you want but you're going to think about me when you touch yourself tonight." He kisses my cheek and backs away out of my apartment. I wouldn't have known he was even here if he didn't leave behind his scent behind.

I lean against the counter for stability and close my eyes trying to slow my heartrate.

I swear I hear a deep chuckle through the wall.

37

toss and turn, trying to get comfortable but my body refuses.

With a sigh, I shove the covers off and sit up in bed.

Sleep is futile.

I can't stop thinking about Zav. He's invaded every crevice of my mind.

Why do I keep resisting him so hard when he's clearly what I want? Sometimes I wish I was different, not so closed off, but it's not that easy for me to open up and let other people in—to share myself and my body with another person, but god do I want to do that with Zav.

My feet seem to take me to my front door of their own accord. I'm not sure what my plan is, but I guess I'll figure it out.

Opening the door, a figure falls inside and a black blob runs past me into the room.

A scream tears out of me, and I slap my hand quickly over my mouth when I realize it's Zavier and Midnight.

"What the hell are you doing?" I hiss, bending to grab his arm and drag him inside my apartment. It's giving me flashbacks to when he showed up at his own door bleeding out, but a quick scan shows he's unharmed.

He lies back flat on my floor as I shut the door and blinks up at me, eyes almost owlish behind his glasses.

"Hi."

Hands on my hips, I level him with a glare. "Explain yourself."

He flashes a smile, incisors the tiniest bit elongated. My treacherous body responds, and I squeeze my thighs together.

"Just keeping you safe, darling. Why were *you* sneaking out?"

I cross my arms over my chest, and it pushes my breasts up in the tank I went to bed in. My nipples pebble against the fabric and he takes it in, licking his lips.

"I wasn't sneaking."

I'm stalling, I know, but I don't care.

"Are you not going to offer me a hand?" he jokes, still sprawled in my entry.

"No."

He hops up in one lithe movement that reminds me that this man is very much not human. That fact should probably deter my attraction, but strangely I think it only heightens it.

"I'm going to ask you again, Celine." He stalks toward me with lethal grace. "Why were you leaving?" He keeps moving forward until I'm backed against the door. He lowers his head, lips grazing my cheek on their way to my ear. "You really don't have to answer. I can *scent* it on you. Your arousal. Have you finally decided to put me out of my misery?"

My breath stutters out of me. "I ... I don't know."

"You don't know?" His words are a growl against my skin. "I think you do. I might not be able to read minds, but I'm not stupid, Celine." His fingers graze my jaw. "Be honest. If you lie to me, I won't hesitate to throw you over my knee and spank you."

I whimper at the warning. "I was ... I was coming to get you. I didn't have any plan after that."

He smirks. "Lucky for you, I do have a plan."

I gasp but the sound is quickly swallowed up by his mouth. His left hand slides from my cheek to the back of my neck, guiding my head to the side as he claims me.

Every kiss we have is electric but this ... this is all consuming.

Zav worships my mouth, kissing me like if he doesn't, he'll suffocate.

My body practically melts beneath his touch and when my legs begin to give out, he lifts me effortlessly, encouraging me to wrap my legs around his waist. I moan into his mouth at the feel of his hard length pressing against my core. The cotton shorts I have on provide little barrier against his sweatpants.

"Zav," I gasp his name as his lips move down my neck. He sprinkles kisses over the tops of my breasts.

He pulls back to look me in the eyes. "Do you want this, Celine?" he asks, voice raspy from a mixture of desire and the hint of fangs poking out. "Do you want me?"

For a moment, fear threatens to choke me. Deep down I know that if I cross this line with Zav there's no going back, but I'm not sure if I *want* to go back. What am I so scared of? Is loving someone really so terrible? I can't let my mom abandoning my dad rule my entire life. I'm not her and Zav's not him. I need to live my life for me and a future where I'm happy.

I stroke my finger down his cheek and his eyes soften at my touch.

This is what I want.

He's what I want.

I know Zav, and yes won't be a good enough answer, so instead I say, "I want you."

The look of relief on his face makes my entire body shake. I'm surprised he assumed I'd say no. I might be insane for falling for a vampire, but he makes it obvious at every turn that he cares about me more than any human man ever has. With that, I know if I said no he would set me down and walk away even if it killed him. Blue balls of the century.

"Celine," he croons my name and the way he says it is better than any outlandish pet name he could possibly come up with. "Did you touch yourself in the shower?" he asks softly, peppering kisses along my jawline.

"No," I lie.

"Liar," he immediately calls me out. "I could hear you." His lips trail down my neck and I gasp when his fangs graze against the spot where my pulse beats steadily. "Smell you." He inhales that spot of my neck, and I shiver. "And now, I'm going to taste you."

A squeal rips out of me because one second he has me against the door and the next I'm lying on my mattress staring up at him. He grins down, fangs on proud display.

"If you only knew how many fangboners I've sprouted because of you."

"How many?" I taunt.

He hooks his thumbs in the back of his shirt, and it takes a concerted effort on my part not to openly gawk at his chiseled body. Every inch of him is rippled with lean muscle. His skin smooth and pale. I haven't wanted to admit it to myself, but Zavier isn't just *hot*, he's otherworldly.

My pussy clenches in anticipation.

He smirks at the fact that I'm actively checking him out as he lets the shirt drift to my floor.

I might have to steal that one like he loves to do with my clothes.

"I'm so fucking hungry, baby. You have no idea." He drops to his knees at the end of the bed. "Been dreaming of this pussy for so long."

I whimper as his fingers curl into the cotton of my shorts.

When they're gone, a groan rumbles in his throat when he finds me bare. I feel like I should be embarrassed with the way he stares at me, studying my pussy like he's going to need to pass an anatomy test by the time he's done ravishing me.

"So pink. So fucking wet. Just for me." The words are a lisp around his fangs.

For a moment, fear holds me hostage. What if one of those needle like incisors stabs me down there?

But like he can read my worries, he spreads my thighs wide open with a firm hand on each leg, and he says, "Don't worry, pretty girl, I'll be careful."

I cry out, my back bowing off the bed at the first lick of his tongue against my pussy.

He licks and sucks, lapping at my center like I'm his own personal feast.

My heart thumps in my ears, the beat out of control with no real pattern. Between my legs, Zav moans. This man is *moaning* just from the taste of me. Talk about a fucking turn on.

His hips grind against the bed as he goes down on me. That's how desperate he is for friction. It's the hottest thing I've ever had the pleasure of witnessing.

His tongue swirls around my clit and then he sucks on it, sending a riot of fireworks up my spine to explode behind my lids.

"Oh, god. Oh, god. Oh, god," I chant, my fingers seeking and searching for purchase and finally finding it in Zav's silky soft hair. It's his turn to whimper as I yank.

When I come down from my high, I find him watching me from between my thighs, his eyes wide with awe and something like reverence.

His lips quirk into a half-smile. "Next time, you better scream *my* name. If you don't"—his voice deepens, green eyes darkening to an emerald that borders on black— "there will be consequences."

I shiver at the tone of his voice—at the delicious promise lingering there that says I might like my consequences even if I'm slightly terrified to find out what they are.

He strokes his fingers over my wet core, two digits slipping inside easily while his thumb presses against my clit. I gasp, hips jolting.

He grins, eyes flashing. "How many times do you think I can make you come?" He cocks his head to the side. "You've already come once. Hmm? Three? Five? More?"

"I don't know," I gasp as he works his fingers in and out of me.

"God, do I love a challenge. You're one I look forward to conquering."

He rises up, mouth claiming mine even as his fingers work me. I feel like maybe I should be embarrassed by how wet I sound, but I realize this is Zav and I have nothing to be embarrassed about.

Another orgasm shudders through me all too easily and with Zav's mouth still on mine he swallows each sound I make.

"You're so fucking pretty when you come," he croons, lips grazing my neck. "You flush the prettiest shade of pink. Pink just might be my new favorite color."

With a groan, I give him a shove and he rolls onto the other side of the bed. Now that I know he's a vampire with freakish strength and healing abilities and who knows what else, I know that he's only rolled over because *he* wants to. He smiles at me, crossing his arms behind his head. It flexes his biceps, and I can't help but stare. I bite my lip when I get an eyeful of his cock pressing against his sweatpants. A guy in sweatpants is unrivaled.

"Can I?" My eyes dart to his, seeking permission.

"If I come the second you touch me, no judging."

I press my lips together in a futile effort to hide my smile. My heart leaps in my chest.

My hand finds him over his pants, palming his length.

Zavier hisses between his teeth, hips bucking. When I look back up at him, his eyes are closed and he's biting his lip, incisors poking out. My core flutters at the power I have over this man. Later, maybe I'll have the sanity to be horrified by how much his fangs turn me on, but now's not the time to question my mental well-being.

My fingers are shockingly steady as I pull down the top of his sweatpants and his boxer-briefs, revealing just the tip of his hard cock. I lick my lips in anticipation. I feel *greedy* for this man. Now that I've given in to this pull between us a boldness and rightness comes over me. Leaning over on all fours, I fully free him and stroke my hand up and down his shaft. His warm, smooth flesh is surprisingly velvety to the touch. A particular vein runs the length of his cock and in a trance, I trace it with my pointer finger.

He groans, crooking his arm over his eyes. "Jesus, fuck. Hottest fucking thing I've ever seen. I'm gonna come just watching you touch me." The words leave him in a stream.

Hesitantly, I lean forward and take just the tip of him in my mouth. I hum at the taste of him on my tongue as I suck away the pre-cum. His hands come down, needing something to hold onto, and his fingers fist in my sheets. He's muttering something under his breath, I think reciting the Hippocratic oath which is both random and honestly such a Zav thing to do.

I take him a bit further in my throat and laugh around his length when he stutters on his words.

I guess it's my laugh that does him in and he comes, shooting down my throat in a thick stream. I gag at the unexpectedness of it. Eyes watering, I let him go after I've swallowed every drop.

He meets my eyes, his face red with embarrassment. "Oops."

I laugh again and plant a kiss on his jawline. I can't stop the uncontrollable peals of it that are only cut off when I find myself thrown down on the mattress with his body looming above me.

"Are you laughing at me?"

"No," I giggle, unable to help myself.

"Liar." He kisses me. "I need to be in you."

My body warms with anticipation.

He pulls at my tank top, freeing my breasts. His mouth pops open and he just stares. "They're fucking perfect," he practically squeaks. "So round and the perfect size. Perfect for me." He bites his lip, making grabby hands and I can't help but laugh again.

I reach up, touching his cheek. "They're small."

"No, they're perfect," he repeats his earlier sentiment.

I bite my lip. "You can touch them."

"Can I?" His voice is higher than normal.

He doesn't wait for my response. He cups my breasts in his palms, testing the weight of them.

"So fucking perfect. Every part of you." His eyes meet mine while his thumbs roll against my pebbled nipples. "You were made for me, Celine. This is fated. *We* were fated and I'll thank the universe for giving you to me every single damn day."

Not only his words, but the reverence in which he looks at me, fills me with warmth.

He rids himself of his clothes and finagles me out of the confines of my tank top until we're both entirely naked. He's already fully hard again which seems impossible, but I remind myself this is Zav and he breaks all the rules.

"Do we need a condom?" I ask, my fingers grazing his jaw. "I don't know how this works."

He smirks, staring down at me. "I'm your first?"

I roll my eyes at his ridiculousness. "No."

He pouts. "You got my hopes up for nothing."

"I *meant* I've never exactly had sex with a vampire. I ... I'm not on birth control and I don't know about you, but I'm not ready for any human-vampire kids running around."

His bottom lip pouts even more. "But they'd be so cute."

"Zav, be serious."

With a sigh, he says, "Truthfully, human and vampire relations are rare, so I don't know for certain. There's not a lot of details on the matter."

"Drawer," I point. "Better safe than sorry."

He frowns, brow furrowing. "I don't want to know why you have condoms in your drawer."

"Because"—I mutter, answering him anyway— "I like to be prepared."

He leans over me and opens the drawer, pulling out the box. His body sags with a relieved sigh when he realizes they've never been opened.

Stupid, annoyingly hot possessive vampire. He opens the box and pulls out an entire strip. He rips off one and lays the rest of the row beside my head, giving them a little pat. "We'll be needing those shortly."

"Pretty sure you're getting seconds, are you?" I tease.

He growls, biting the crook of my neck. His fangs have receded for now. "I'm getting forever, love."

He rips open the packet with his teeth and pulls out the condom, rolling it down his length.

I glide my fingers down his chest to his stomach, tracing each rippling muscle along the way. His eyes flutter shut behind his glasses, fangs poking out again once more.

"Celine." His voice is a deep, rumbling growl. "Keep touching me like that and I'm going to embarrass myself all over again and that won't be fun for me or you."

"Sorry," I laugh, pulling my hand away from his smooth skin.

"Thank you." He nips my jaw with his teeth.

Hand on the base of his cock he guides it to my entrance, hovering there.

"Zav?"

His eyes flick up to mine, red hair falling delicately over his forehead.

"Sorry," he says, surprisingly earnest.

"Is something wrong?" I graze my fingers over his jaw.

He shakes his head. "No, I just ... I know you're about to ruin me."

He pushes inside me, just an inch at a time, and I relish in the sensation.

"Fuck," he groans, lips pressing to my neck when he's all the way inside. "Celine. This pussy is fucking *divine*."

"Zav?"

"Mhm?" he hums.

"Shut up and fuck me."

He pulls back enough to look down at me and I clench around his cock.

"So bossy." He grins, gently tucking my hair away from my face. "I like it."

I cry out with a small scream when he pulls out and thrusts in hard. His hands are firm on my hips, guiding me to meet each of his thrusts. The position he holds me in has his pelvis rubbing against my clit with each movement. The friction has my eyes rolling into the back of my head.

"Zav." My fingers scramble to find purchase on his body. Something to hold onto and keep me grounded to reality.

His green eyes glimmer behind his glasses. "Say it again, baby. Say my name."

"Zavier," I moan when his thumb finds my clit.

"Fuck. My name has never sounded so good."

I cry out when he pulls out, but in the next second he's flipped me over onto all fours and is slamming into me from behind.

A scream tears out of my throat and my arms go out from under me until my chest is pressed flush to the mattress.

One of his hands curves against my hip, the other pressing me down against the mattress.

"Look how good you take me," he murmurs. "This pussy was made for my cock. Nobody else will have you." *Thrust.* "Ever." *Thrust.* "Again." *Thrust.*

I whimper, unable to find words. I'm so close. It wouldn't take much.

The hand he has on my back slides around to my stomach and down, until his fingers find my clit, and he plays me expertly.

I come apart with a cry, legs shaking as my pussy squeezes his cock in waves.

When I finally come to, I'm on my back again with Zav grinning down at me.

"So fucking beautiful." He leans down, tongue swirling against first one nipple and then the next, making sure to give each equal attention.

"Zav," I whimper his name.

He has me screaming it a second later when he thrusts back into me. My back bows off the bed and he wraps his arms around me pulling me up until I'm practically sitting in his lap, and we're face to face.

I wrap my arms around his neck and pull on the chain resting against the hollow of his throat. His mouth finds mine, the kiss stealing my breath and any form of thought that I have left.

He cups my cheek, thumb swirling gently over the spot.

"I'm so lost in you," he confesses. "I'm not going to last much longer."

I entwine my fingers in the hair on the back of his neck. "Let go," I encourage. "I'm right here."

He groans, kissing me again as he thrusts into me at a steady pace. I hold onto his shoulders, beyond shocked when another orgasm overtakes me. Zav's right there with me this time, though. We cling to each other like if we don't, we might float away, lost to time and space.

Zav lowers me gently to the mattress, his body clinging to mine. He doesn't pull out of me right away. We lay there in silence as our breaths sync. I think this is the longest he's gone in my presence without talking.

My body is sated and exhausted, my lids struggling to stay open. I feel him wrap around my lower body like a koala and rest his head on my chest like my boobs are a pillow.

I drift off to sleep, only to be awakened sometime later by him kissing every part of my body.

I hate to admit it, but I could get used to this.

38

Kissing along the column of her throat, I hit the same angle inside her pussy that made her moan a second ago. Her cries of pleasure fuel the fire of my own impending orgasm. I want to hear every kind of whimper, moan, cry, and scream I can wring out of her.

When I woke this morning and saw her lying beside me, hair splayed out on the pillow and pouty lips parted in sleep, I couldn't help but crave the physical connection between us once more.

Thrusting into her, I have to hold back my fangs that so desperately want to bury themselves in her throat. She hasn't fully surrendered to the mate bond yet and I want to hear her say she wants this, wants me before we complete the irrevocable bond between us.

A familiar tightening in my abdomen warns me I don't have much longer, but I refuse to come without her release first.

"Come on, beautiful. Let me hear what I want to hear."

Taking up a bruising pace, I hammer into her as her nails scratch at my back. I want to keep her marks on me, but I know they'll be gone within the next few minutes with my accelerated healing.

Celine rides the wave of pleasure with me, both of us coming together like I wanted. I fill the condom with jets of hot cum.

"You know how to give a girl a good morning," Celine huffs out between deep breaths as she slows her racing heart. Her breasts heave with each heavy breath and I watch the small swells of them with rapt fascination. "Not that you let me sleep much." She rolls onto her side, hands tucked beneath her face. I frown, sad that she's tucked her boobs out of my sight.

She's right, though, once I had a taste of her perfect pussy it was game over. I wanted to worship every part of her body, and my cock wanted inside of her every minute it could be. It feels like I've been waiting forever to be with her like this, and I guess in a way I have. Every other experience in my past pales in comparison. No one can match the allure of your mate.

It doesn't help matters that vampire stamina is unmatched and her being my mate gives me an almost animalistic need to claim her over and over. Even now my cock is hardening against my thigh for round number ... I've lost count at this point.

"You loved every second of it." I lean over and kiss her sweaty forehead. She hums and closes her eyes curling up like a kitten. "How about you lay in bed a little longer and I'll make us breakfast, hmm?" The unintelligible noise she makes sounds like agreement to me, so I swing my body up and out of bed even though it's hard leaving her there.

Hearing movement behind the bedroom door Midnight must know someone is there and scratches at the wood with loud meows. Celine throws a pillow over her head to drown out the sound and I laugh because all I can see under the pile of blankets and pillow is a breast sticking out. I have half a mind to go over and lick it until her nipple pebbles, and she begs me to make her come once more.

I slip out of the room and fight not to trip over Midnight as he weaves between my legs on the way to the kitchen.

"Morning, buddy." Reaching down I grab the fluffy cat and give him a long stroke.

Setting him up with his food, I get to work making pancakes. It doesn't take long to finish our respective shortcake stacks, and I make sure to decorate hers extra pretty. Strawberries create eyes, chocolate chips make a smile, and whipped cream finishes it off with fangs for a perfect vampire smiley. I hold the plate out to Midnight for his approval, and he hops off the counter and rubs up on my leg.

Filling glasses with orange juice, I admire my work and head back to the bedroom. Breakfast in bed with my girl sounds perfect. We both worked up quite the appetite last night and if I'm lucky she'll let me have dessert.

From the sound of her heartbeat, she's fallen back asleep, and I creep into the room, setting our glasses and plates down on her desk before I wake her. I stifle a laugh at the blanket monster that is Celine. She's taken to building a pillow fort around herself to block out any light or sound and I'm disappointed to see she's covered up her stray boob.

Light bulb going off over my head, I sneak to the bottom of the bed and snake a hand under the covers. Grabbing her foot, I tickle the arch and it's not long before she's squealing and trying to yank it out of my grasp. She's no match for my strength and I pull her down further which makes her peek out from behind her cover.

"You need to wake up, sleepy head. Breakfast is ready."

Celine harumphs but I see the small smile on her face. Unearthing herself fully from her cave, she sits herself up and leans against the headboard. Half asleep she still looks fucking delectable, and I pass her plate over to her before settling myself.

"I was thinking, maybe I can convince you to move back in with me after last night." I try my luck, but I'm greeted with silence.

Looking at Celine, I see her frozen in place, fork held in the air but not touching the food. It's a comical freeze frame with her jaw unhinged and eyes wide in shock.

"Are you that wowed by my art? I'll pat myself on the back for that one." I do just as I say and continue to eat my pancakes.

"What is this?" Her tone is hard which has me wary.

"Pancakes?" I reply earnestly.

"I fucking know that." Celine's brown eyes meet mine and she finally lowers her fork. "This smiley face. I've seen it before." The cogs in her brain are spinning and for a second, I don't know what she's getting at. Then I understand.

I level her with an even-keeled look and say nothing else as she continues to work through it in her brain. I was going to tell her eventually. I thought she might even be proud of my work.

"It was you?" she asks it hesitantly like she doesn't want to believe it.

Setting my plate down, I cross my legs, interlocking my hands around my knee.

"You?" Celine repeats again to herself and sets her uneaten food on the side table. "Fucking say something, Zavier!"

"I don't know what you want me to say," I respond because I truly don't.

"You kill people!" she shouts and stands up while quickly wrapping the comforter around her nude body. "I didn't want to believe it was you when I started to suspect, but it is!"

"You've known I kill people."

"But not crazy serial killer murder spree killing people." She throws her hands in the air and grabs clothes out of her closet before stomping to the bathroom.

"Only the bad guys," I reason.

"Seriously?" Celine calls from the bathroom.

It's not like I wasn't going to tell her eventually but it's also not a natural conversation to have. Maybe it would've been better to tell her myself before she found out, so it came from me. It was careless to draw on her pancakes like that, but I can't help it that she makes me lose any sort of rational thought when she's near me.

Celine storms out of the bathroom, yanking a brush through her tangled hair. I want to cringe at the hair she's ripping in the process and brush the delicate strands myself, but I don't think she'd take too kindly to it at the moment.

"It's not just the killings, it's that you didn't trust me enough to tell me. I'm not an idiot. The puzzle started to come together that it was you and part of me has known this whole time but wanted *you* to be the one to confirm it." She looks heartbroken and it crushes me.

"I was going to tell you eventually, but learning I was a vampire, and your mate seemed like a lot to process on its own. Telling you I kill bad guys on the side for fun didn't seem like the best time."

She scoffs and levels me with a look.

Throwing the brush on the bed she leaves the room to quickly change and then grabs her purse from a coat rack by the front door. She shoves her feet into her boots and makes to the grab the door handle.

"Oh, hell no." I sprint over to her, and she jolts at the speed. "Where do you think you're going?" I bite out.

"I need space," she sighs, and I can see the hurt and confusion in her eyes. "Please, Zavier. This whole vampire and mate situation is a lot to take in and finding out the serial killer I've been investigating is actually my boyfriend takes the cake." Tears well in her eyes and she wipes them away angrily. "I'm not rejecting you, that's not what this is, but for right now I need to be away from you. Don't fucking follow." She holds up a finger that shakes. "I know you love to follow me everywhere but this time I'm telling you don't fucking do it."

"Celine." Her name leaves me in a sad whisper.

Fuck, this isn't how I wanted this to go. I don't know how I expected it to go, and if I'm honest with myself I hadn't given much thought to telling her anytime soon and I guess that's a poor reflection on myself.

"I just need space," she reiterates.

Watching her walk out the door is singlehandedly the most painful thing I've ever done.

39

Un-fucking-believable.

Does he think I'm a fool?

Zavier was the killer this whole time and he knew I was the detective investigating the cases. He came to one of the crime scenes for crying out loud.

It had seemed like it was impossible for one perp to kill so many people—especially the sprees that included ten or more people at a time. Killing one person is an exhausting endeavor on the human body let alone that many. It all makes sense that the murderer was never human now that I'm privy to supernatural beings.

Walking down the block with no real destination in mind, I cycle through endless thoughts in my head.

Anger and sadness are the two emotions spiraling through me the most. What hurts most of all is him not telling me.

I know revealing the murderer is him wouldn't have been easy. When I really think about it, the crime scenes are gruesome, and he might take it a bit too far with the theatrics, but he's only killing people that deserve it. Some of these criminals the police force can't even take down so he's doing the city a favor.

Zavier choosing to keep it a secret especially when he knew we were mates and growing closer is a stab to the heart though. I want our relationship to be based on honesty and sometimes that means hard truths.

I shiver and curse my stupidity when a breeze ruffles my shirt and I realize I forgot my jacket in my race to get out the door. It's a shock Zav didn't thrust it at me himself, but it goes to show how distracted we both were when I left.

Rays of sunlight stream between buildings and I realize it's still early in the morning. I lost all sense of time after he carried me to my room last night. Pigeons flitter by and walk along the sidewalk with me as silent companions aside from the occasional coo.

On a normal day, I wouldn't be out and about at this time, even with work. Zav waking me up for another round of sex this morning wasn't unwelcome though. Well, until everything dissolved when I saw that stupid smiley face on the pancakes and figured it out.

Even with my troubled thoughts, I still envision a future with Zavier which might be insane, or it could be the bond talking.

Cars honk even at this time of the morning as I mosey my way along to the river. I wonder what people could possibly be so pissed off at this time of the morning already. Did they also find out their vampire boyfriend was a serial killer?

I kick a stray rock in my path and watch it skip along the pavement. It stops right at a pair of booted feet and for a second I'm about to rip Zav a new one for following me. Then I scan up the body and quickly discover it's not him.

A cold, shivery feeling travels down my spine. The kind of fear that roots you into place even when every instinct is screaming at you to run from the predator in front of you.

Vampire.

And he mostly definitely doesn't want to chat with me.

He advances quickly, I know he could be in front of me in a millisecond, but he seems to like dragging it out.

I rest my hand on my pocket where the knife Zav gave me rests. Even in my upset state, I was smart enough to slip some sort of weapon in my pocket. There was even a moment when I thought I might have to use it to stab Zav if he followed me. Not that it would actually hurt him, and I'm fairly certain the sick fuck would enjoy it. I'm not sure how good the knife can do against a vampire but I'm not about to go down without fighting.

Slipping my fingers in my pocket and fingering the edge of it, I slash out as soon as the vampire is within distance. It doesn't do much, but it gives me a slight advantage when I turn to run.

I should've known better.

My luck isn't that good and another vampire advances on me from the other side. I have nowhere to go. I'm outmatched.

The new vampire strikes out with his arm, smacking me across the face.

I fall to the ground, my vision going black, and then there's nothing.

40

I pace around the apartment for as long as I can stand it, before I follow Celine. Her walking away distraught hurt more than I expected and there's was no way I can leave her alone for long. I'm taking a risk going after her and I want to respect her space, but anything can happen to her right now.

I understand her feelings on the whole matter, but still, how can she walk away? After last night it would be cruel to have a taste of her only to have it ripped away because of my mistake.

Midnight gives me a reassuring meow as I leave.

Outside, I follow the trail of her lingering scent. She wandered shockingly far in a short amount of time and with the constant breeze I'm glad I can still pick up the trail.

Her scent begins to grow fainter, and I panic at losing it. She can be as pissed at me as she wants that I'm following but I don't give a fuck. It's not safe right now. The constant rainy weather is proof enough of that.

A sudden jolt of terror zings through my chest and I *know*

it's her. It doesn't matter that we haven't completed the bond it's a feeling that's without a doubt sent from her.

"Celine!" I shout as I use my speed to get to her as fast as I can.

Within seconds I'm in the middle of a sidewalk where her scent stops. Glancing around frantically, I search and hope to spot a dark head of hair but there's no sign of her.

My boot crunches down on something and I look down to find the knife I gifted her laying on the pavement.

No. Please, no.

I grasp it and run my hand over the carved handle like it'll show me where she is.

I'm not the praying type and haven't believed in a higher god for a long time, but I start to pray to any being out there who will listen.

Please don't take her from me. Please keep her safe. Show me where the fuck she is.

I know something bad happened. This wouldn't be laying on the ground if she didn't try to use it, Celine wouldn't be the type to throw it away in anger at me. She might not realize it, but she's surprisingly sentimental.

Spinning in a circle, I further examine the area for any clues on where she might've gone.

Drowning out everything I take a deep breath and inhale a scent I initially missed.

Blood.

Vampire blood at that.

A few trickles almost invisible to the naked eye dot the sidewalk and upon closer examination the blade of the knife holds the scent as well. It's a musty, coppery smell that's tainted by the evil intent of its owner.

Good girl. She fought back.

Now that I know it's a vampire who took her, I see *red*.

It takes every one of my three-hundred years of life to keep me from lashing out on the humans and objects around me as agony rips through me. Knowing my mate has been taken feels like someone is trying to rip my body in half.

When I find her, no vampire will be immune from my wrath.

If she's dead ... no I can't think that way. I *refuse*.

I clench my fists and the humans walking past keep a wide berth like they know I'm a ticking time bomb.

Grabbing my phone from my pocket I shoot a quick text to **Death's Assistant** to meet me at the hotel. I'm going to need as many eyes looking out for Celine as I can get. I also dial the next person on my list.

"Hello?" Luna's voice rings across the line.

"Celine's been taken," I cut right to the chase.

Her gasp rattles in my ear. "What do you need from me? I'll help however I can."

After giving her a quick rundown of the situation, I ask her to keep her eyes and ears open for who could've taken Celine via her clients. She sees a lot of vampire traffic and will be a great help in that regard.

Rushing as fast as possible to the hotel, I formulate a plan on what to do.

No being in hell, heaven, or on Earth will keep me from finding my mate.

Whoever took her from me has no fucking idea the monster they've unleashed.

41

old.

Waking up in a daze, that's my immediate thought.

My body shivers against a hard, frigid surface.

What the hell? Am I stuffed in a refrigerator?

I blink and try to clear the haze from my brain, but a pounding in the side of my skull makes it hard to focus. I squeeze my eyes shut and try to blink them open again hoping that will help things come into better focus.

Gingerly touching my head at the source of the pain, a hiss rips out of my throat. Tender and throbbing I can feel the goose egg forming on my skull. My fingers come away wet, and I find both dried and fresh blood crusting my hair.

What the hell happened?

I rest a hand against the floor and push up to sitting as quickly as I dare with my head throbbing. It takes me a couple tries since the pain is so debilitating, but I manage to hoist up my torso. Cradling my head in my hands I drag my legs into a criss-cross to sit.

"Fuck me," I groan and once again the area around me blinks lazily to focus. It feels like my body has been put through a meat grinder. What did those vampires do with me after I was knocked out? It feels like they played hacky sack with my unconscious body.

Once I feel more in control, I scan my surroundings, but it's so dark and dank it's hard to make anything out.

Underneath my legs there's old stone flooring. I squint and see cell bars in front of my face. I run a finger along the metal and rust comes away.

My hearts beats rapidly in my chest as I realize the predicament I'm in. I have no clue where I am, presumably the vampire that kidnapped me is still around, and I'm a sitting duck. I might have training in taking down perps, but I'm still very much human against at least two vampires and my gut tells me there are more.

Will Zav come find me?

He has to. He's more tuned into me than anyone, and with his vampire senses and lack of patience it can't take him long to realize I've been taken. Knowing him, he probably started following me shortly after I left. I can't imagine he was far behind.

I try to calm my heart and take a few slow breaths. He's coming for me. I just have to be patient and figure out what's going on.

As my eyes slowly adjust, I try to make out what I can, but it's so dark I can't see much beyond my cell. The only light source is a few flickering candlelit flames set into sconces on the walls outside my cell. It smells old and musty. I have to wonder if we're somehow beneath the city. I don't think they would've taken me out of Chicago.

Hobbling to my feet, my muscles scream in protest and my entire body aches from the treatment I received in coming here. I'm sure the vamp knocked me out and threw me in here without much care.

I grip the bars of my cell and push and pull to test the strength. They're rusty but unfortunately still sturdy. One side of my cell is flush to the stone wall and the other is connected to another cell. The padlock on the door I could potentially pick if I had any kind of instrument, but at the moment I'm out of luck.

Mustering up a semblance of strength, I attempt to kick at my cell door, but it doesn't budge. A scream of frustration wells in my throat and I tilt my head toward the ceiling.

"Conserve your strength," a raspy voice echoes nearby.

I yelp at the unexpected sound and look toward the neighboring cell.

It's shrouded in shadow and at first, I think I'm going crazy hearing things in my head, but after staring, I see movement in the darkness.

"Hello?" I question warily.

A groan and chains scrape against the stone floor. A shadowy form starts to make itself apparent until a man drags himself over to our shared wall of bars.

At first, he keeps his head tilted down and I can't see his face. From what I can see, he has long dark hair which falls in a raggedy curtain. Dressed in a tunic like shirt and pants they look like they've seen much better days. Blood speckles stain the fabric and it's torn and holey in many places. I'm shocked it's staying on his body at all.

Long, elegant fingers clutch the bars in front of him. His nails are broken at odd angles and caked with dirt and dried blood. Where his skin is visible, I can tell he's emaciated and closely resembling skin and bones instead of a healthy human being.

How long has he been here? Who is he?

Something about him reminds me of a frightened animal and I remain silent, waiting for him to speak again. He lets out a long sigh and drops his arms to his sides where he leans now against the bars.

"Don't expel your energy unnecessarily," he finally croaks out, and I cringe a little at the growly rasp in his tone. It's the kind of sound when someone wakes up after sleeping for too long and they need to clear their throat.

"What's your name?" I can't help but ask.

The man is quiet for a while, and I sit with him in silence once more. I get the impression he doesn't talk much at all. Who knows how long he's been down here looking at the state he's in.

"Nobody has asked me that for quite a long time," he replies with pain behind his words.

"You don't have to tell me."

"Valen," he finally whispers after a moment.

"Hi, Valen. I'm Celine," I reply and his intake of breath when I say his name tells me it's been even longer since someone said his name.

"Celine," Valen parrots. "I'm sorry for what's about to happen to you."

"What do you mean?" I'm once again reminded of the situation I'm in. Valen distracted me temporarily.

His curtain of dark hair shifting, I finally get a glimpse at Valen's face. He keeps his eyes cast downward but candlelight dances across his features. In flickers I'm able to take in his heavily bearded jaw, aristocratic nose, and deep-set eyebrows. For someone so frail and sad looking he still gives off an air of power and maturity.

I'm also able to see the shiny, wrinkled skin of old scars littering his entire body. He's absolutely beautiful in a way I've never seen before—downright ethereal—but this poor man has been reduced to a shell of who he must've been.

"I've tried everything that's already run through your mind." Valen stops to cough after grating out the words. "There's no escaping them."

"Who's they and what are they going to do to me? Why are they targeting me?" I shiver at his words.

Valen looks up and I meet his eyes, so dark they almost look black. If the fire reflecting in them didn't show the slightest hue of brown, I'd believe they were leeched of all color. The devastation and hopelessness staring back at me show a broken man.

Blowing out a long breath, he slumps down even further.

"I don't know why they want you, specifically, but anyone else that's been down here hasn't lasted the night."

42

"**F**uck!" I shout and take ten years off the life of an old woman walking next to me.

I've searched the city endlessly for any clue as to where Celine's been taken and have come up with nothing. It's infuriating. I'm a vampire and yet none of my superhuman skills are helping me. Whoever took her, covered their tracks well and I haven't caught so much as a whiff of Celine or the offending vampire's scent save for the blood on the concrete where they nabbed her.

My contact and his crew have searched high and low to no avail. Luna hasn't heard anything either.

I feel the edges of madness tainting my thoughts, and it's getting harder and harder to keep my inner beast caged.

He wants his mate by his side and doesn't care who he has to take down to make that happen. My fangs split the skin on my lip for the hundredth time since I can't get them to stay up for long.

Fangboners should be reserved for Celine not for the absolute insanity I feel at her absence.

Pulling her sheathed knife out of my pocket I hold it against my mouth.

Where are you? I think as I stare at the deadly blade, willing it to give me some clue, any clue, to her location.

Tracing my steps one more time, I run through the path from the apartment to where she was taken. Her scent has long since blown away in the wind and the first time I realized it was gone I lost my shit. It was like nature erasing her presence. It's enough to drive me mad, but I have to keep my head, or I'll be useless in finding her.

I discover nothing new and hang my head in defeat. The longer she's gone the easier it is for her to get hurt.

Sensing my hunger levels rising to a dangerous amount, I head back to the apartment to down some blood before I set back out once more.

The walk there is a blur. I trudge into Celine's apartment because I can't stand being alone in mine right now.

"Hi, Midnight," I automatically greet my cat bestie, but freeze when he doesn't respond. Normally he'd trot right over and meow after a rub against my legs.

Still facing the door, I realize the light switch for the living room is turned on and I most definitely turned it off when I left.

Someone or something is here.

I don't hear any other heartbeat in the room, not that it means much, but I don't smell anyone either which is odd. Spinning abruptly on my heel I hiss and let my fangs down to threaten whatever's infiltrated my mate's space.

What I see leaves me shocked to the core.

A deceivingly beautiful creature I haven't seen in years sits at Celine's kitchen island. She holds Midnight hostage and strokes him like she's simply comforting the pet and not silently threatening him with her sharp nails so close to his throat.

His yellow eyes meet mine and I can tell he's scared shitless, wanting to jump out of her arms at the predatory aura she exudes. Animals can always sense intentions, and hers are never good.

Blood red nails that more closely resemble talons hold him to her in a grip tight enough to keep him from escaping but not enough to hurt him ... yet.

"Been a while hasn't it, Zavier?" Her hauntingly familiar voice rings through the air. "Did you miss me? I missed you terribly." Pouty lips turn down in a mock frown.

Black hair cascades in waves around a face that looks like it was sculpted out of pure marble. Supernaturally vibrant brown eyes are framed with thick lashes most women would pay a fortune for. Dressed in a flowy crimson top that matches her nails, she's just as lithe and graceful as she was the last time I saw her. Too bad she's nothing but a pretty face with a rotten interior.

"Wish I could say the same, bitch queen." The insult rolls right off my tongue. "Why are you in my fucking home?"

She clucks her tongue at me like she's scolding a child. "That kind of language is beneath you. I thought you'd be happy to see me." She strokes Midnight again and I resist the urge to rip him out of her arms. I remain rooted on the spot where I am in fear of her doing something rash.

If she hurts that cat she won't like the consequences.

"Now what pray tell would make you think that, Genevieve?" Feigning calm, I lean back against the front door and cross my arms over my chest.

Ignoring my comment, she continues, "This isn't your home by the way, is it? Breaking into a girl's apartment is naughty.

What does Celine think about it? Does she know you've been sneaking in for longer than she's aware of?"

As soon as she says Celine's name my fragile control breaks and I can't hold myself back. Blurring over and slamming my palms against the counter I lean in so we're almost nose to nose.

"Don't you dare say that name," I snarl, fangs snapping close to her neck. "How do you know her? What the fuck are you up to?"

I fight the red staining the edges of my vision. I'd love nothing more than the tear her to pieces, but while she holds my floofy friend and most likely knows Celine's location it's too much of a risk.

"Celine?" Holding Midnight like a baby she loves dearly, I tense when she flexes her wrist. "She didn't tell you we've met already?" Giggling in a way that grates on my eardrums she flutters her lashes at me. "Nothing's happened yet but we're due for a little girl talk." Genevieve flicks her wrist out to peek at the golden watch she dons. "Actually, I should be heading there soon. It's rude not to be timely."

Unable to hold myself back I jolt toward her, and she tightens her grip on Midnight causing him to yelp in pain.

"Genevieve," I grit out, instantly freezing.

Blood leaks down the side of my face and onto my chin when I bite down too hard with my fang.

She holds eye contact with me while she loosens her grip and gives Midnight one last pat before letting him go. He darts out of the room with a yowl to hide somewhere, and I sigh in relief. Not only is he my buddy, but he's very important to Celine, and I can't have him hurt under my watch. Celine already got taken and I won't let it happen to anyone else either of us loves.

"So jumpy over a simple creature. What happened to you?"

She clucks her tongue and leans over before I can stop her to lick the blood trail off my face.

She moans at the taste, eyes closing in ecstasy.

Books crash loudly onto the floor and wood splinters when I slam Genevieve against the bookshelf. I'll have to make that up to Celine later, but I'm disgusted at being violated in such a way. Now that Midnight is out of the room I can bleed information out of her.

Genevieve recovers quickly and shoves me back, slamming me against the opposite wall. Picture frames shatter and fall to the floor in a symphony of shards.

Fuck, I'm going to have a lot to clean up.

"Watch yourself, Zavier. If you don't want a hair harmed on your little human's head, you'll listen to me." Her eyes bore into mine and I see nothing of who she used to be. "If you're smart, you'll do exactly as I say."

She strokes a finger along my temple reverently and I attempt to push away when she hurls me back against the wall in warning. Standing down isn't in my nature but I hiss a warning around my fangs.

"Give me what I want, and she walks free." Genevieve sing-songs.

Crazy bitch.

"What is it you want?" I bite out.

Smiling she answers with one simple word.

"You."

43

Shivers wrack my body as I huddle in a ball in the corner of my cell.

Valen and I have fallen into a comfortable silence other than when I ask him a question and he answers in as few words as possible.

Valen is an interesting man. He's not very forthcoming about his history or why he's here, but I can tell he's been locked away for far longer than I can fathom. His existence hasn't seemed to have been kind but even with his broken soul, there's an air to him that feels old. Ancient even.

"You're a vampire, right?" I ask abruptly and his eyes dart to mine.

He hasn't explicitly said it but from context clues there's no other answer.

He replies with a tired, "Yes."

"How old are you?" Curiosity gets the better of me.

"You're bold for a human, aren't you?" He lets out a mirthless laugh. The gruffness in his tone has improved slightly but it still sounds like it's painful to speak.

"Eh, we're both down here and I'm probably next on the chopping block so there's room for boldness." Of course I'm hoping Zav will come, I don't doubt he's looking, but from what little Valen has said, it'll be hard to find us.

Chest rising and falling, he rolls his head to angle toward me.

"Much older than you can fathom, child." A strand of dirt crusted hair falls into his eye, and he doesn't make any move to touch it. How exhausted and hopeless he must feel.

"My boyfriend's three-hundred years old." I laugh at the statement as soon as it makes its way out of my mouth. "If you told me I'd be dating a vampire a few months ago I'd laugh in your face. On top of that, I'm a detective and it turns out he was the killer I was investigating the whole time on my case." Valen stays silent but I can tell he's listening. "He drives me insane, and our personalities couldn't be more opposite but despite all of that..." I trail off.

"You love him." Valen fills in the blank and internally I freak out for a second.

Do I love him?

Relatively speaking, Zavier and I haven't known each other all that long. Since day one I was drawn to him. Mates or not I'm positive that magnetism would've been there. I'll be damned if the mate bond dictates our relationship.

Cocky but sweet, handsome but devilish, he fills in the things I lack and vice versa. I haven't completely forgiven him for not being forthright about his actions, but I'm not mad anymore. Blame it on potential impending death but being away from him and envisioning a life without him driving me up the wall, is hard to imagine.

"I love him." I finally admit.

The realization is an exhilarating one and as soon as we're reunited—because we will be since I refuse to even contemplate the alternative—I'm telling him exactly that. He deserves to know that I feel as much for him as he does me.

"Have you ever been in love?" I ask Valen.

He's quiet for so long I worry I crossed a line and that he won't answer.

"No," he whispers. "But if I'm ever fortunate enough to find a love like the one you seem to have, it will have made all of this worth it." A cough sputters out of his chest and an idea pops in my head.

"Feed from me," I blurt out.

"What?" His voice is the loudest I've heard it.

"Feed from me. We can start building your strength so that we can bust out of here." I don't see any other options and he's in worse shape than I am. It's not my first choice to have a vampire that's not Zav feed from me, but it's life or death. If the resident vampire can ingest enough to give us an edge, we might have a chance. God knows I don't stand a chance against a load of vampires, but Valen? He might if he's strong enough. It's obvious to me they're keeping him weakened for a reason.

"We can't risk it," Valen says after a moment. "I haven't drank freely, let alone straight from a human, in a long time. Even with you having a mate, which would naturally repel me, I could kill you."

Pulling myself to his side so we're eye to eye, I plead with him.

"Please. It's the only chance we have." Sticking out my wrist I can see the hunger simmering in his brown eyes. "I would rather die trying to get free than to let them do whatever it is they plan with me."

Valen seems to have an internal struggle with himself. Just when I think he isn't going to do it, he grips my wrist gently with a withered hand. Fangs peek out from around his lip, and he shudders in anticipation of his meal. Lifting my wrist to his mouth he takes one last deep breath before striking.

This might be a horrible decision. I realize belatedly that as starving as he has to be, there's probably a good chance he could drain me.

The pain is sharp, and once my blood hits his tongue he seems to lose himself in it. A low groan hums against my skin. When I pull away on instinct, he grips it tighter, and I wince.

Greedy pulls feel odd as my blood leaves my body to sustain his. I might be crazy, but more color seems to flood his cheeks with each gulp.

In a show of great control, Valen pulls away and licks the last few drops of blood that remain from the puncture wounds. Releasing a large breath, he drops my arm with a pat.

"Thank you, Celine." His words are heavy with reverence, and I know we're starting to form a kinship no one else will ever fully understand.

Time passes and I lose track of how long I've been down here. Has it been hours, days, a week? Nobody comes for us, and I start to lose it with the constant drip of water against stone and the frigid temperature that has my teeth chattering. I'd rather be subject to Ava's ministrations than deal with this any longer. Don't even get me started on the pee bucket. Valen doesn't show any outward sign of discomfort, seeming used to the environment and whatever torture has been inflicted on him.

I've attempted to sleep multiple times and doze here and there but it's fitful and I constantly jerk awake at even the smallest sound. The musty air feels heavy in my lungs and my clothes are damp against my skin making it hard to get comfortable. I'm worried if I stay wet, I'll get sick but that's the least of my problems at the moment.

I've fed Valen off and on as time passes in the hopes of slowly increasing our odds of escape. He looks better each time, although I know he's going to need much more once we get out. The only caveat is I get weaker in turn.

I'm closing my eyes to try for sleep once again when a door slams against its hinges somewhere above us. Shooting up, I tuck myself in the shadows of my cell as much as I can hoping to observe our visitor.

Valen merely opens one brown eye and shuts it at the sound. So used to his miserable existence down here, it seems like the man can't be subjected to anything worse than he's already been through.

Heels tap along the floor in a rhythmic sound and draw ever closer with each breath I take. I squint to try and make out the figure, but can't see a thing even with being down here as long as I have, and my eyes adjusting.

A soft whistle echoes through the chamber, and though soft and lilting, it sounds more like a hymn of death.

"Poor little Celine. Caught in a cage like the pathetic rat she is."

Every muscle in my body tenses at the familiar voice.

Stopping in front of my cell, my eyes travel up from the knee length boots, tight pants, and blouse. Black hair, brown eyes, and a malicious smirk complete the picture that is Genevieve. Gone is the sobbing young woman from the station and here is an apex predator with her eyes on her next meal.

The dangerous glint in her eyes is terrifying to see and she must watch my perusal of her, reveling in the big reveal, because she flashes a fang.

Any words I might say are stuck in my throat.

So, it *was* her voice I heard before.

She was behind my kidnapping? Why?

"I can tell just from looking at you you're wondering, why me?" she says mockingly. Squatting down she watches with feline grace. "You have something that belongs to me."

My brows furrow, confusion sliding through me. "What could I possibly have that you want?" I spit out, finally finding some gumption within myself.

"Think about it." She wraps blood red nailed fingers around the bars and tilts her head to watch me work through it. Her smile is downright maniacal. It has me feeling extremely uneasy. "Come on, Celine, prove to me you're not a total dummy."

"Crazy cunt," Valen mutters from next to us. I momentarily forgot he existed with the Genevieve revelation.

"Ah, sweet and pathetically sad Valen," she mocks with an exaggerated pout and takes his insult in stride. "I'm not the one caged down here, now am I?" He doesn't grace her with a reply and instead covers his eyes with a thin forearm to block her out. "I'm going to have to tell your handler to treat you extra nice the next time they come for you," she titters gleefully.

Valen shivers at the statement, and I can't help but wonder what exactly he's down here for, and what they do to him.

"Back to you." Genevieve's soulless eyes bore into mine.

I sigh and think about it. Nothing comes to mind relating to my work or my day to day. She's a freaking vampire what is there that I could possibly have that she would want?

Wait.

I'm already cold, but it feels like a bucket of ice water drenches me with the realization of the *only* thing she could be talking about.

"Ah, you've figured it out. Took longer than it should've for a so-called detective." Tsking me with her fingers she stands with hands on her delicate hips. "If he doesn't heed my warning, bad things are going to happen to you and to him."

Does she have Zavier too?

Panic fills me. If she has Zavier then ... then no one is coming to help.

With dark promise in her eyes, she walks back up the stairs and the door slams shut with finality behind her.

44

t's been a week since I last saw Celine.

A. Whole. Fucking. Week.

One glance at me and anyone could tell I'm not right in the head. Well, I'm not on a good day, but especially so right now.

The absence of Celine is like a hole in my soul. I love her, and she belongs by my side. She's my mate for fuck's sake. Instead, she's been kidnapped by my psycho bitch of an ex who can't take no for an answer.

Genevieve promised to kill Celine slowly if I didn't accept her as my partner.

I'll be damned if that happens.

Genevieve has always wanted what she can't have. I met her not long after I was turned, and she coveted me from the start. With my vibrant red hair and inability to be contained, I stood out. Her brand of crazy loved mine and I'm ashamed to say we had a few decades together wreaking havoc. Once I gained full control of my bloodlust and primal tendencies, I wanted out.

I haven't seen her in at least fifty years. I suppose she's been watching me from the shadows, lusting after what she can't have, and once she got wind of Celine, she decided it was time to strike.

I tried following Genevieve after our run in at the apartment, but she vanished and somehow has dampened her scent.

Sitting back on the couch I feel Midnight jump into my lap. He's continued to prove himself as my emotional support pussy and cuddles with me when I'm here. I'm in and out since my primary focus is finding Celine, but sleep and feeding are necessary. I know Genevieve and she's psychotic but smart. She'll have powerful vampires helping her. I need to be at my full strength for when I do find Celine.

Midnight's rumbling purr grounds me and I plant a kiss on top of his head.

A loud bang on the front door scares him and he digs his claws in before jetting off at the jump scare. Not making any sign to move, I hope whatever human is out there will go away so I can rest before leaving again.

The obnoxious knocking continues, and I growl while heaving my body up.

"Celine! I hear you in there," Ava yells, voice desperate.

Great.

"Fuck you for ignoring my calls for the past week!" she continues to knock. "You called in sick, but you can't respond to me? I'm worried!"

Not being able to stand the ringing in my ears I walk over, and wrench open the door. Fist poised, about to knock again, Ava almost hits me in the face.

"Cel—oh Zavier." Stopping in shock but launching right back

into rage mode she pokes my chest. "Where's Celine?" She barges past me in a flurry of pink hair and heads for the bedroom, looking for her friend. "Do you have her locked up for a sex-a-thon and missing work?" A pillow gets thrown like Celine's hiding behind it.

How I wish it were that easy.

Unsuccessful in her hunt, she stands in front of me, hands on her hips, looking like an angry little fairy. Her poofy pink dress and flats make me chuckle before I remember why she's here.

"Where is she? It's not like her to fall off the face of the planet even for you." I can see how distraught she is.

Truth be told I've been so hyper focused on finding Celine I didn't even think about others that might be missing her. I sent an email to her captain, feigning illness, because I know how much Celine's job means to her, and I didn't want it to be jeopardized just because my crazy ex is holding her hostage somewhere.

I wrack my brain for what to tell Ava but can't come up with anything believable. She'll sniff a lie out in seconds. She's a bit of a blood-hound like that.

"Ava." I grip her shoulders. "Celine's been kidnapped." Immediately her eyes go wide and she tries to buck out of my hold.

"What? Kidnapped?" she screeches, eyes large and round with horror. "Why haven't you called the police?" I hold her steady and try to calm her down which is laughable since I'm certainly not calm myself.

"We can't go to the police," I say slowly, trying to make sure she takes in each word I say. "I can't tell you why, but you just have to trust me. I'm doing everything in my power to find her." Her light blue eyes fill with tears. "I swear Ava, I will get her back."

I loosen my grip, and she starts to pace the length of the room.

"You know how batshit you sound, right? My best friend got kidnapped a week ago, but we can't call the police? You, a man who she's been dating not long at all, is telling me to trust you to find her. For all I know, *you* could be behind her kidnapping." She throws her thin arms in the air. She pales, slapping a hand over her mouth. "Oh my God. You killed her, didn't you? And now you're going to kill me? Oh, this is bad. Real bad." She paces the room.

"I would never harm a hair on Celine's head, and you know that, Ava."

Midnight trots over to me and I pick him up to drape over my neck as a cat scarf. Ava watches the interaction and ceases her pacing.

Her bottom lip trembles with the threat of tears. "This is the kind of shit that ends up on Dateline. What aren't you telling me?" She takes a defiant power stance and stares me down.

"God, Ava I don't have time for this," I growl. If I could have a headache right now I would. She's so goddamn persistent.

"Make time for it, buster!" She pokes me in the chest—hard for a human. "You've got another thing coming if you don't think I'll go out and find her myself. I'll also tell the police like you should have from the beginning." With a harumph and flourish of her pink dress she makes for the door. "I'll make sure you're the first person they come looking for."

Closing the door before she can blink, she gives a wide-eyed stare.

"How'd you get over here so fast?"

"Listen," I sigh, knowing I'm about to tell yet another human my truth. It's weird to share this with people after so long of avoiding humans unless I'm killing them for their heinous acts. "You can't do that, because it'll be a death sentence for Celine." I guide her over to the couch and encourage her to sit. "She's been taken by vampires."

Ava purses her lips and blinks her owlish eyes at me. Then she bursts into raucous laughter.

"Oh my God, you're psycho! You definitely killed her or else I'm going insane. Maybe I hallucinated this whole thing," she mutters the last part to herself.

"Ava," I say her name carefully. "*I'm* a vampire." I flash my fangs at her to further prove my point, and a scream of fright rips out of the petite woman "We can't involve the cops because there's nothing they can do."

She holds a hand over her rapidly racing heart.

The surprise slowly wears off and she seems oddly calm. "Huh. That explains a lot. How you always seem to be everywhere and why you look like you." She gestures a hand at me. "Too hot for your own good."

I grin. "You think I'm hot?" I shake my head. Now is not the time to let my ego get the best of me. I need to focus on the most important thing and that's the fact that she's no longer freaking out. Apparently thinking I'm a murderer is a deal breaker, but a vampire is fine. "That's it?" My voice raises a few octaves. "You and Celine have something wrong with you that you both accepted that so easily." I'm baffled by this pair.

"Have you met you?" Ava sputters. "It makes too much sense and who am I to question the ways of the world. I've always thought there was more to it than we know."

A sense of relief comes over me that there's someone else that knows my secret. Maybe life won't be so isolating and lonely moving forward.

"I'm helping you look for her." Ava stands and hikes her purse up her shoulder.

"The hell you are," I sputter.

"Yes, the fuck I am." She goes toe to toe with me, hands on

her hips. She stands on her tiptoes, trying to give herself the illusion of more height.

"What does she see in you?" I bicker. "You're an argumentative energizer bunny."

"What does she see in *you*?" she retaliates. "Red hair, glasses, and a stupid necklace?"

"You take that back," I gasp in outrage. "Celine loves my chain. Especially when she grabs it so I fuck her harder." I stick my chin in the air.

Midnight's tongue darts out at her like he's defending my honor as well.

"Ew. I didn't need to know that." She plugs her ears with her fingers but fights a smile much like myself. "Fine." Ava sticks out a perfectly manicured hand. "So, I'm in?"

"I guess," I mumble and shake on it. "But you're playing by my rules and the first is to sit your ass down and listen."

I deal with her peppering of questions and give her the low down and she agrees to be on standby until I tell her otherwise. We can't go in guns blazing—or in my case fangs—we have to be smart about this.

Patient.

And that's really fucking hard.

45

Walking down the street the next evening as I try to sniff out any hint of Celine or Genevieve, my phone rings. After another long, unsuccessful day I answer it on instinct thinking it's one of my contacts with an update.

"Hello?" My greeting comes out gruff and tired.

"Make a decision, handsome?" Genevieve's voice croons from the other end.

This bitch.

My back goes ramrod straight and I can't help the growl that comes out of my chest. Looking at the phone screen I realize it's an unknown number. Subtly glancing around I check for her slimy self but don't see anything.

"Yes, in fact. After much consideration I've decided you can fuck off."

Genevieve isn't impressed by my answer. She huffs and I hear bracelets clink against each other as she adjusts the phone.

"You know what I'm capable of, Zavier. Don't fucking play with me. I'll rip your pretty little mate's head off without a second thought. I promise you, I'll do it."

"I'm not getting back together with you. Get it through your thick skull." A passing human gives a side glance at my aggressive tone, and I head over to stand in the shadows. "Where's Celine?"

"Wrong answer. I told you something would happen if you didn't fall in line and now, you'll see the consequences of your actions. Heed my warning again, next time I'm going for her life. I'm done playing nice." She ends the call, and I crush my cell in my hand.

Throwing the pieces down the alleyway, I scream out in frustration. Should I have antagonized her? Probably not, but it physically hurt me to lie and play her game. Now Celine will most likely suffer for my stupidity.

I have to find her. I *need* to find her.

My breath comes out in a heave, and I close my eyes in an attempt to keep the bloodlust at bay.

Nowadays, it comes on quick and rides me hard.

Without Celine, it's becoming harder and harder to pull myself back from my animalistic side. Whenever I sleep, I'm plagued with nightmares where she's tortured and killed in various ways at Genevieve's hand. Her scent has almost disappeared off her pillow and I fear the day it's gone entirely, I'll be lost.

This is getting me nowhere and I need to calm down before I do something stupid. I'm in no state to find her, wound up as I am. I need a distraction, and the perfect thing will be chess with Tom. For all I know he might have some good advice for me. Unlikely, but you can't blame a guy for hoping.

Last we talked, he was excited one of his granddaughters was having a baby. She's getting close to her due date, and he warned me our weekly chess game might be pushed because of it. But I don't think he'll mind if I drop in for a surprise match today.

Jogging the few blocks it takes me to get to the restaurant, I hop up the stairs and enter the building.

"Tom, ready for me to beat your ass at chess?" I sing-song in an attempt at positivity.

He's already sitting in his usual spot, and I head toward him. The place is quiet and devoid of customers since it's almost closing time, but I love that he's still doing his thing in the corner. Slightly grumpy he's still a hard worker and wants what's best for the restaurant.

"You don't know how much I need this." I blow out a breath.

It feels wrong to be playing a game when I should be looking for Celine, but I also know a visit with my friend will help me in the long run. I need to clear my head so I can think logically. I feel like I'm missing something.

I grab the board and set it on the table before plopping down in the seat across from him.

"You go first." I fold my hands on top of the table and look at my pieces.

Silence.

"I said you go first, you old coot," I raise my voice since he has "selective" hearing and wait for his move. "Do you need to turn up your hearing aids?"

Silence greets me once more.

"Tom." I finally look at him in exasperation and immediately wish I hadn't.

Tom is indeed sitting across from me, but his plaid shirt is coated in blood. Thick lines of it start from his neck and run down in crimson rivers to the floor. Blank eyes stare back at me, and his mouth is agape. I realize I don't hear any heartbeat. The only sound I hear now that I'm truly paying attention is the *drip, drip, drip* of his life source onto the wood paneled ground.

I should've smelled the blood. I should've known the second I walked in here. That's how distracted I am that I didn't even realize my friend, my only friend, was waiting here for me like a trussed turkey. A gift from Genevieve no doubt, to prove to me that she's not fucking around.

"Holy fuck. No." My chair thuds loudly as I run over to him.

Barely touching his arm, I jump back when his head quite literally falls off his neck and rolls across the floor with a sick thud. Blood trails behind it and I'll never get the image of his soulless eyes peering into mine while his body remains headless in his chair.

"Tom?" I squeak out, wishing away the horror in front of me. "No, no, no!"

I've killed thousands of people in my three hundred years. Some might say I have no soul, no moral compass. As a vampire who's to really say, but I'd like to think I do. Most humans that I've killed were those who deserved it. Tom most certainly did not deserve this.

My friend. One of the few friends I have left in this world.

Had. Fuck that hurts.

I clutch my chest as tears cascade down my cheeks.

He doesn't deserve this.

A kind old man who loves his family and is weeks away from meeting his new baby granddaughter. A man who is a staple in the city and whose loss will be felt seismically. The one small kernel of good that comes out of this is that he's reunited with the love of his life, but even that thought doesn't ease the roiling of my stomach.

I swipe my tears away when they trail down my cheeks.

Glancing back at his body, I spy a bloody stained piece of paper. It sits on his crudely cut neck, and I cringe while grabbing it. Gore has never bothered me before but knowing that this is Tom has bile climbing up my throat.

The scrawled handwriting on the paper makes me vibrate with fury.

She's next.
Love, G.

Paper crumples under my fist and I fucking lose it.

I refrain from tearing apart Tom's restaurant out of respect, but the urge to destroy something is very much there. My chest heaves and my vision turns fully crimson. This hasn't happened since my early days of being turned. It's like peering through a colored lens, the red swirls and floats wherever I look. I flex my fists, and my fangs make themselves known. I hiss around them knowing if I don't drink some blood soon it'll be bad news.

How fucking dare she?

First my mate, and now my best friend. Genevieve is begging for death. I'll take great pleasure in separating her spine from her body and stringing it up like a gory Christmas garland for all to see.

Celine says I'm not a monster, but right now, knowing all the things I want to do to Genevieve, I feel like one. I won't be able to rest until Celine is safely back in my arms.

If Genevieve thought this would be enough to get me to hand myself over to her, then she doesn't really know me at all.

Not wanting Tom to exist in this state any longer, I attempt to squelch my anger and give my friend the sendoff he deserves. I'm lucky none of his family members have seen him yet and can't have them finding this. Two of the workers are out cold in the back where thankfully, Genevieve didn't kill them, but they'll wake up with a nasty headache.

"Hey, buddy, I'm going to get you all cleaned up," I whisper brokenly, and set about my task.

Using stray tablecloths, I wrap Tom's body. Then I use a trash bag to cover him. It feels wrong and makes me furious all over again that this is what I have to do. Then I set about cleaning the blood up best I can and disposing of anything too far gone to keep.

Under the cover of night, I transport Tom's body to a funeral home and compel them to call the family tomorrow to tell them there was a tragic accident and the body can't be seen because of said accident. Suspicious? Yes, but they deserve a proper goodbye. No one should have to see their loved one like this. I'm used to this kind of carnage and even I'm upset by the sight of it. Thinking of how scared he must've been in his final moments fills me with rage all over again.

The last thing I compel them to do is to send all bills to me.

I leave the funeral home once I'm certain everything is taken care of, and I won't be remembered, and return to the restaurant. I look over my work to make sure nothing is out of place. Our chess board catches my eye, and I gulp at the pieces we'll never move against each other again. No more jokes cracked, no more shouting, and no more Tom.

My eyes narrow in, realizing a piece is missing. Weird.

I had known one day Tom would die and I'd go on living, but I never expected it to be like this.

A part of me crumbles and I get a peek into the human part of myself I thought I'd lost a long time ago.

46

'm once again sitting, eyes closed, in the dank corner of my cell, wondering how long I've been down here. Without much food, water, and proper rest, weakness is setting in. A few times I've woken up to bits of old bread and a tiny dish of water in front of my cell but it's not much at all. Valen sits in his typical spot shrouded in darkness. I still can't figure him out and he doesn't help with his one-word answers, but I feel bad for him.

We've tried to formulate a plan and different scenarios for escape, but I can tell he's nervous to hope. How many times has he attempted to get out to no avail? I've been feeding him along and I can tell he's getting stronger. His color is warmer, his cheeks a little pinker.

The familiar sound of a door slam echoes through the room and whoever is headed our way is on a war path. Aggressive footsteps thud and I don't have to wait long before I know who it is.

"Miss me?" Genevieve sits crisscross applesauce in front of my cell and flicks something at me. It bounces off the floor and rolls to my feet.

Fumbling with my hand in front of me I locate the item and hold it up to see what it is. Genevieve watches with a sadistic gleam in her eye, such a stark contrast to her vampiric beauty.

"A chess piece?" I feel the ridges and bumps of the queen piece.

She smirks, eyes flashing with danger. "I told Zavier what would happen if he didn't listen, and he's defied me at every turn. Something had to give." She shrugs like our conversation is trivial. "Maybe now he'll take me seriously."

My hand closes around the chess piece, my eyes narrowing in concentration.

Chess? Zav?

Tom!

Oh my God, Tom!

"Oh my God." I realize exactly what she's getting at. "What did you do?"

She purses her lips in a mocking form of a pout and makes a clucking sound like she's trying to console me when I know that's the furthest thing from the truth. "What I had to, Celine. I know your puny pathetic human brain can't understand, but Zavier is just playing hard to get. I needed to return the favor in kind." She smirks victoriously and brushes back an invisible strand of perfectly smooth hair.

"You hurt Tom?" I choke out in horror. A few flecks of dried blood flake off when I rub the chess piece and I fear she's done much more than that.

"I killed him," she confirms my fears. She giggles and it's like a knife to my heart. The sound is shrill, pure evil.

No!

I press my lips in a firm line, trying to keep my face as

LOVING A VAMPIRE IS TOTAL CHAOS   325

neutral as possible because I know a reaction is exactly what she's searching for, and I won't dare give her the satisfaction of receiving one.

Poor Zav, though.

I can't even imagine the pain he must be in losing his only friend. He must be falling apart between trying to find me and now this, that is if he's not stuck here too. Rage coils in my belly and a spark ignites, my temper getting the best of me.

"Fucking monster!" I throw the piece at her even though it's no real threat to an immortal like her. "Zav will never be with you. He loves *me*, and I'd rather die than let you use me as a pawn over him."

An animalistic sound comes out of Genevieve and before I can blink, she's inside my cell forcing me onto my back with a hand around my throat. She snarls and bares her fangs dangerously close to my fluttering pulse.

Fear holds me hostage. I know deep down that she could snap me like a twig, and I'd be dead before I knew it.

"You're nothing." Her teeth slash at my neck, but don't bite down. "Zavier would never settle for you when he can have me, a perfect being that matches him. You are *weak*. A pathetic waste of life source. You're *human*. No sane vampire wants to be mated to a fucking human. You are the cockroaches of this world. Do you understand me? Dirty and fucking useless."

A whimper slides past my lips before I can stop it as she squeezes my throat.

Stars flood my vision when she reopens my head wound by slamming my skull against the stone floor. She doesn't stop there though and drags her nails down the side of my face, leaving a bloody trail in her wake. The sting is sharp, and I know it'll likely scar with how deep the gouges are.

"I might not be able to kill you yet, because I'm not done getting what I need from you, but that doesn't mean I can't rough you up a bit." She stands and dangles me just above the floor. I claw at her tight grip, fighting for air. She laughs, the sound mocking and cruel. "Truly, how could Zavier ever want something as pathetic as you. I'm barely doing anything and you're *this* close to dying." She tilts her head at me in an unnerving, predatory way.

Just when I think I'm going to pass out, she drops me like a doll and I collapse, sputtering on the ground. My throat burns as I suck in a sharp lungful of air. A kick to my ribs steals what little air I've managed to take in.

"Leave her alone," Valen's deep voice grates from the side.

"What are you going to do about it? Stuck in a cage withering away, it's pathetic honestly." Genevieve walks away from me to taunt Valen. "And here I thought you were meant to be powerful." She reaches through the bars and grabs ahold of his cheeks, her nails digging in like she'd done with mine before throwing him away. "I'd think it was all a lie if I hadn't seen the proof with my own eyes."

Using this opportunity to my advantage while she's distracted, I crawl my way over to the door to my cell where it remains ajar from her entrance. My arms shake at the effort, but I keep dragging myself along. I will not die here. I will not let her be the reason for the end of my existence. If I go down, I'm going down with a fight. I've never balked at a challenge, so why should I now?

"Your time will come," Valen replies cryptically. "It's quite sad, you take to harming an innocent human simply because a man told you no." He flips back over to face the wall and dismisses Genevieve. I can practically see the smoke coming out of her ears.

Reaching a hand up to touch the lock, she speeds over and slaps me down. My knees scream in pain at the sudden contact with the stone beneath me, and she presses my forehead flush to the floor.

"Think you're slick? You and your new buddy here? I'm always a fucking step ahead. Remember that." Genevieve steps out of my cell and slams the door behind her before turning the lock.

More footsteps echo through the chamber and a deep voice calls from up above.

"Look at that, Valentine. Collection time." She doesn't spare us another glance and skips away back to wherever the fuck she lurks when she's not taunting us.

Before long, a bulky vampire I've never seen before drags Valen out of his cell. He doesn't put up a fight, but we lock eyes. The fear and shattered spirit in his gaze breaks my heart. I try to communicate that I'm here and it'll be okay. We're in this shitty situation together and I finally have the upper hand. His eyes widen slightly, and I nod to confirm I have a plan before he disappears. Well ... perhaps not a *plan* more of an idea of one, but it's better than nothing.

Genevieve probably thought my sad attempt at reaching the door was to leave, but I managed to place a small pebble in the lock. It was my hope that her own hubris would keep her from realizing what I was actually up to.

Testing my theory, I feel hope for the first time since I was taken when it opens at my push.

I breathe out a sigh of relief and shove my hands in my pockets for warmth. A crinkling catches my attention, and I pull out a wadded-up piece of paper. My brow wrinkles as I unfold it and a sob catches in my chest when I see it's a note from Zav. He must've stuck it in my pocket when he ripped off the sliver from his notebook at the police station.

You look hot as fuck in those jeans, sweet thing.

—Zav

Also known as Zav Daddy or Zaddy.

Despite my situation, a laugh rips out of me, and a tear catches on my jawline.

I kiss the note and put it back in my pocket.

I'm getting the hell out of here, and I'm taking Valen with me.

47

A pink explosion greets me when I walk into my apartment. Ava's taken up temporary residence in it since I refuse to sleep anywhere but in Celine's bed. Her apartment is also on the other side of town, so it made sense for her to camp here.

I've not been gone long, only popping over to Luna for a fresh blood supply and to check in with my contact, and she's already made herself at home. It's not like the apartment was ever really mine to begin with, so I don't mind.

Over the past few days Ava and I have poured over maps of the city and stayed in contact while we walked and drove the routes. She did the latter since I didn't want her in any danger, while I could reach places with my speed and strength that would be impossible for her. So far, our search hasn't provided any answers and we both grow antsier by the minute. The fact Celine's kidnapper has gotten the jump on my guys is unheard of. They're too good.

I feel my sanity floating away bit by bit, and Ava has given me more than one side glance of worry. I'd never hurt her, I know how important she is to Celine, plus she's grown on me, but I struggle with her presence. We're far more alike than I ever thought I'd admit. Celine has a good friend in Ava. The only time she isn't actively searching for Celine is when she's at work. But she's immediately back at it as soon as she's done.

As time keeps passing, we used the excuse of Celine's dad needing her because it didn't make sense to keep saying she was too sick for work.

"Where are we searching today?" Ava plops beside me on the couch with her Pad Thai.

I stretch out my legs and pull out my notebook. A multi-page list with more things crossed off than I'd like, details our agenda. I rattle off some names and Ava freezes. She drops her food none too gracefully on the table getting noodles on my paper. I growl at the sight of my now soiled paper.

"We are so stupid!" she shouts and hits her head with the palm of her hand. "I know exactly where we need to look. We're focusing on the wrong spot." Shoving one more mouthful of noodles in, she rushes around to grab her coat and shoes.

I follow after her, because she must be on to something to act this way, and to leave her food behind. Another thing I've learned about Ava is she takes her takeout food very seriously.

"The club!" Ava shouts as we run down the hallway. "I can't believe I didn't think of it sooner. Celine always thought Vex was so fishy. I thought she was just being paranoid, but it makes sense, right?" She doesn't wait for me to answer. "That has to be it."

I shake my head but follow her onto the elevator anyway. "I scoped it out multiple times. I didn't smell anything or find evidence otherwise. "

"We've only ever seen the public part of the club. Celine

tried to see into the back once but got stopped by the goons guarding the door. Remember the kidnapping and all that weirdness?" She crosses her arms over her chest. "Besides, you're the one that said her smell just vanished the day she was taken so I think you're being a little cocky and relying on your vampire mojo a little too much."

I shake my head, confused. "I thought that whole thing was resolved with Vex, and they found the body without any club connection?"

Ava turns to me with exasperation. And Celine thinks I'm the one without patience.

"We overheard suspicious things the first time we went there, and I know Celine didn't agree with the outcome of the case. It has to be the club. My spidey-senses are tingling, Zavier." She wiggles her fingers. "The woman she was in contact with was an odd one." Ava taps her heel in quick succession on the ground. "There was just something off-putting about her." She shivers at the memory.

"What woman?" I tilt my head, following her off the elevator. "Celine didn't mention a name."

"Oh, so she tells me things she doesn't tell you, huh?" She sticks her tongue out and I do it right back. "Genevieve was the name of the woman who reported her friend missing. But I'm not so sure now that they were really friends. Maybe it was a ruse to get close to Celine."

"You've got to be fucking kidding me." I'm seething at the dots that are slowly connecting. She met with Celine behind my back and with her scent being undetectable for some fucking reason I had been none the wiser.

Filling in Ava, she rages with me and for the first time in almost two weeks I have hope.

I just pray Celine is okay and in one piece when I get to her.

48

"Five hundred," I whisper.

I count five hundred seconds exactly before I attempt to leave my cell. While terrified to leave, I'm even more terrified to stay. Who knows how long before Genevieve snaps and takes me out. Sure, she has me for leverage over Zavier, but I know her fuse is short, and it wouldn't take much. Plus, what's stopping her from lying to him? She could chop me into little pieces and send me floating down the river tomorrow. I'm under no illusions that I'm making it out of this alive if I stay here.

All I can hope is the blood I've been slipping Valen is enough for him to give us a fighting chance. I can't do this without him.

My body protests with every move I make, and the bits of stale bread and water sips haven't sustained me. Not to mention I'm probably in need of a blood transfusion myself and running on fumes at this point. I use the metal bars to drag myself to a standing position and my legs shake like a newborn foal. I'm pissed at how shot my endurance is since I've been held and deprived for so long. Boxing is going to be a bitch to get used to again. Resting my forehead against the metal, I center myself and give a mental pep talk before proceeding.

My needy vampire is out there looking for me. Who's going to keep him out of trouble if I don't? He could also be trapped here like I am. Plus, my dad needs me. Save the day, Celine. It's what you're made for.

With renewed determination, I cringe at the squeaking of the door when I open it part way. I'm not sure who all is around and what they can hear. Hopefully Genevieve is long gone for the day.

Turned sideways, I slide through, not wanting to risk more noise than necessary. Valen's cell remains empty, but I spot a small item wrapped in cloth against the wall. I've seen flashes of him holding it when he thinks I don't notice. I'm not sure what it is, but it's clearly something of importance, so I snag it and pocket the bundle.

Multiple times I have to stop while climbing the stairs. From my stint down here, however long it's been, my endurance is shot. It's sad how quick it is to leave your body when you aren't consistently using it. It pisses me off that I'll have to hit the gym hard before I'm at full strength for work again.

Ugh. I'll probably be bedridden while I heal, and I know Zavier is the mother hen type.

I pant and wheeze like an out of breath whale. The air gets slightly warmer the higher I get, which is a relief, but also feels like needles against my skin after all this time. It went numb early on and to have feeling back is a double-edged sword. God I probably look and smell horrendous. My hair is greasy and matted. When I get out of here—because I will get out of here, I refuse to think about the alternative—I'm taking the longest shower ever.

There's a door at the top of the stairwell and it appears to be unlocked. Stupid vampires. Ever so gently I push and peer through the sliver of exposed hallway behind the door. At first glance it's silent and empty of life but that doesn't mean I'm letting my guard down.

I slip through and close the door behind me. Now in another creepy, hallway that's only slightly less musty, but more modern than the dungeon below, I get my bearings. There's a door at either end. I choose the right to head toward.

My footsteps are as quiet as I can make them and the closer I get to the door, the more I hear a slight whirring sound. I walk over and repeat the process of slowly opening the door to peer in. Thankfully, I chose the correct room and Valen lies strapped to a table. His arm is full of tubes that are pulling blood out and cycling it through the machine before depositing it into bags.

The coast is clear, so I approach him. His eyes are closed and at first I don't know if he's awake or not.

"Valen," I hiss as loud as I dare.

His eyes peel open slowly and widen at my appearance in his room.

"We're blowing this popsicle stand. Come on." I jerk my thumb over my shoulder and get to unplugging him from the tubes. I'm not a nurse, but it doesn't matter. Desperate times call for desperate measures.

He seems a little out of it from the collection, but I run over to a large storage fridge in the corner. Pleasantly surprised to find my hypothesis correct, I grab a few bags of blood and shove it at him to drink. Valen doesn't question me and quickly gulps them down. Hopefully it wasn't his blood because that's kind of weird, but I guess not any worse than drinking a random person's blood.

The puncture wounds on his arms heal before my very eyes and I'm reminded of how much *more* he is than me. Hopefully once we're out of here we can get to know each other like normal friends. Knowing Zav, though, he'll get jealous and need to supervise. Maybe I shouldn't tell him he bit me before Zav did.

We must look like an insane pair right now. Him with his long, limp hair and ratty old clothes. Crimson dripping down his chin and onto his bare feet. Me with my dirt and blood encrusted pale skin. My outfit isn't much better than his.

"Do you have any idea how to get out of here?" I whisper, peeking out the door to see if anyone has noticed our shenanigans.

"No," he answers, sounding stronger than ever before. "Whenever they bring me up, it's straight here and back down."

"Fuck. I guess we're winging it then." It's probably foolish to hope for a clean break but so far so good. "Let's go."

Valen grabs my hand and squeezes it.

"See you on the other side, Celine."

I hope he doesn't mean *the other side* like the afterlife.

I nod back at him and steel my resolve.

Valen and I step into the hallway and make it to the other side when the door opens. A vampire is just walking through and spots us in front of him with a face full of shock. Faster than I can track, the vampire's heart is ripped out of his chest and his head is knocked off his body.

I turn to Valen who holds the bloody heart and looks a little shell shocked himself at what he just did. It seems like he acted on instinct but I'm sure it's been a long time since he last felt strong enough to do that.

"Fuck," I mutter when I spot the handheld remote that's now flashing. A big red button has been pressed by the vampire just before he died and from the sounds of pounding footsteps, he's informed the cavalry of our escape. "We're fucked."

"This way." Valen grabs my arm in an attempt to keep me up to speed with him, but it's hard when my feet keep getting tangled up.

I'm panting and the urge to dry heave is overwhelming. He must get fed up with how slow I am because he hoists me up in his arms. Between my blood and the bags he consumed, I guess he's feeling well enough to carry me and I certainly won't complain if it gets us the hell out of here faster.

Careening down the hall so fast my hair blows around us, Valen blindly follows something. With his vampire senses fully functioning, I trust he knows what he's doing.

"Wait, we need to check for Zav," I panic, reminding Valen. I can't be for certain that Genevieve doesn't have him chained up somewhere around here too.

"I'd smell him if he were here. Now that I've tasted your blood, I can sense the connection." He calms me down and continues to navigate the maze of halls and doors.

Relief floods me. Zav isn't here, so hopefully that means he's safe. I can't contemplate the alternative.

My stomach rolls at the speed in which Valen's moving. He stops in front of a door and opens it, shoving me in. I'm in shock and realize I'm surrounded by cleaning supplies. I have no idea why he's done it and then hear the absolute chaos outside the door.

I peer out to see Valen going head-to-head with a few vampires. Even with his imprisonment, he's holding his own well, and I know having me to protect would've been too much. Whenever any of the vampires get close to the door, he slaughters them. It almost seems like a renewed sense of motivation has sparked inside of him.

One of the vampires manages to jump on his back like a feral raccoon and he shakes to dislodge them. They land a bite and tear a chunk out of his shoulder. Valen grunts in pain, and I know it hurts like a bitch, but he doesn't react otherwise. Getting a firm grip on the vampire's arms, he flips them over his head and stomps on their chest when they land. His bare foot quite literally goes through the vamp's chest.

What the fuck is Valen? I don't think he's your typical vampire that's for sure.

First wave of vampire goons down, Valen shows some fatigue and leans against the wall for reprieve. It won't be long before he burns through the blood he's consumed and then it's bad news for us. To make it this far and end up right where we started would be unfortunate.

I just want to get home to my grumpy cat and unhinged, sunshiney vampire. Ava was probably waiting to scold me, I needed to call my dad, and I'd be lucky if I still had a job at the end of this.

We're not left alone long before another group of vampires come bursting down the hallway. Valen weighs his options and swings the door open fully to grab me in his arms again before darting away, taking our chances elsewhere.

"I don't know how much longer I can keep this up," he huffs. "I should have conserved my energy back there, but I'm not used to having my strength back."

The maze of hallways and stairs makes it feel like some underground tunnel system. Where did it come from and what's it used for? Could it be solely for vampiric purposes or something else?

"We have to be close to getting out of here," I murmur,

losing a little more of my consciousness. Adrenaline is wearing off and I'm reminded of my weakened state.

Valen tightens his grip and shakes me a little.

"Stay awake, Celine. We're going to get out of here," he says it matter of fact, but I don't miss the shakiness to his voice.

"Well, well, well, what do we have here?"

Fuck.

49

Breaking every speeding law known to man, we manage to make it across town. Feeling rather spiteful, I formulate an idea as we approach the building.

"Uh, Zav." Ava grips her handle above her head. "You can slow down any time now."

I press my foot down hard on the gas.

"Zavier!" Ava slaps my arm as the building comes closer into view.

Thankfully, nobody else is right behind me in that particular moment, so I floor it. Glass shatters and bricks cascade around us as I careen through the front door of the building. I quickly turn and hold Ava against me to protect her from any harm. Our airbags deploy and Ava screams at the unexpected entrance. Since it's daylight, the club is closed, but now it's open for business at my say so.

"You crazy son of a bitch," Ava yells and I simply chuckle in response. "Give a girl some warning next time before you drive through a fucking building."

Celine's in here, I know it, and a locked door won't keep me from her. Since Ava threw out the idea I've felt it in my chest that this is where she is.

Pulling away, I tilt the broken rearview mirror so I can see myself. A strand of hair is slightly out of place, and I smooth it back where I want it to be. Meanwhile, Ava coughs and stares at me like I've grown a third eye. I knew she'd be okay. I wouldn't risk her safety. Plus, I drive like a pro.

I unfold my long legs from the car and scan the room. The car is totaled but hey it was worth it; I'll just buy a new one. Hell, I'll let Celine pick it out this time. Whatever she wants she'll get, as long as she's back in my arms.

Ava hurries to keep up with my brutal pace as I inspect the area, but my patience is non-existent. She goes to follow me when I head toward the door in the back of the room, but I hold out a hand.

"You're staying outside." I frown at her. "I don't want you involved in this when the cops show up."

"Are you kidding me? Celine is most likely down there, my best friend, and you're sequestering me to the sidelines?" she argues, stomping her foot like a petulant child. "We just crashed through the damn building. I'm an accomplice."

"We don't have time to argue, Ava. I can't risk you getting hurt if this is where she's held. I can compel everyone to not remember your involvement. There are probably vampires crawling everywhere and you won't be much help. Just a hinderance. It's just the facts," I reason with her, antsy to head inside. "Celine will never forgive me if something happens to you," I add, because I figure that more than anything else will help get through to her. "Just go across the street to the pottery place where you'll be safe. I'm sure they'll try to call the police.

and I'd rather have the least amount of collateral damage as possible so you can tell them the owners here have already called."

"Fine. As soon as you have Celine back you let me see her." Ava relents and doubles back to the store across the street.

That settled, I walk in with nothing but bloodshed and carnage on my mind.

50

"It would seem our two lab rats have escaped," Genevieve purrs. She clacks her long nails together like some stupid villain in an animated cartoon. I have to admit, thinking of her that way makes her a lot less scary.

I shiver in Valen's arms, and he grips me tighter. I thought we were making headway and now we've hit a huge roadblock in the form of this vampire bitch. She just won't go away.

"Move," Valen rumbles.

I applaud his bravery, but more vampires appear behind Genevieve, and I know we're well and truly fucked. Valen's expelled a lot of energy to kill the first round of them, and he was already in a weakened state despite the blood. And it's not like we're in a place where I can offer him more. Even if I could, I'm not sure if I'm in well enough shape to.

Wracking my brain in my half-asleep state, I try to come up with a plan to get out of this. Everything I think of ends in us dead or trapped back in the basement ... and then dead.

And I *really* don't want to die.

"You have to realize your little escape attempt has failed." Genevieve slowly walks closer to us and Valen steps back in turn.

The ultimate chess game. What would be our next move?

Her goons go to follow her, and she holds up a red nailed finger to point at me.

"Grab the girl."

"Over my dead body," Valen snarls and I grip his neck in fear at the approaching vampires.

Desperate hunger contorts their features in a grotesque way. Barely hanging on by a thread they seem to barely listen to Genevieve. All they see me as is a fresh body of blood.

"You wish. Too bad we still need you." She flicks a hand in my direction again and the vampires pursue.

Valen takes off back down the hall from where we came from, and it feels like each step we take is one further from escape. A whimper crawls out of my throat at the fact that we're going backwards, not forward, but I'm not one to give up. Even if it's getting harder to believe we're getting out of this alive.

At least if I die, I'll know I went out fighting for my escape.

Abruptly choosing a door and going inside, Valen breathes heavily and sets me against the wall to rest while he barricades the door. We seem to be in a storage room of sorts with filing cabinets which end up being perfect for securing us in.

"Are there any vents or secret doors in here?" I can't sit still for long, starting to feel around the room for just those things.

"Secret door," he snorts, rolling his eyes. "Doubt it." His eyes dart around, and the door starts to groan under the weight of the vampires trying to get in. He looks up and points. "Air vent, though."

I look up at it with a frown. "It's small." I eye his massive shoulders. "Can you fit?"

He swallows a lump in his throat. "Probably not."

"I won't leave you here." It's probably too noble of a state-ment to make in the face of imminent death, but I don't think I could live with myself to leave him behind. The banging gets louder, and I know with that many vampires on the other side it's only a matter of time before they find their way in. As if conjured by my thoughts a split appears in the door. "Can you get yourself up there? We have to at least try."

Valen purses his lips and nods. "We try," he concurs. He's tall enough that all he has to do is stand on a chair to rip the vent off the ceiling. "C'mere." He lifts me easily and gives me a boost into the vent. "Go, Celine. If I can't make it, promise you'll keep going."

I look down at him, my stomach churning at the thought of leaving him behind. "I'll bring help. My mate—"

He shakes his head. "Go."

A shrill scream that has to be from Genevive has me crawling on all fours through the vent in record time. I hum softly to try to keep my breaths even. I fucking hate spaces this small. But if it gets me to freedom I'll keep going.

The vent rattles as Valen joins me. "Fuck," he groans, drag-ging behind me. "I can't believe I'm saying this but thank God they've been starving me or I would never be able to squeeze through here."

We army crawl through the vent and I have the horrifying thought of what if I fart? Poor Valen.

There's another scream behind us and I'm not sure how far we've made it from the room, but I move a little faster.

Get out. I have to get out.

The vent groans and I freeze near the next opening. "Hold still," I whisper to Valen. "It's—"

My words are cut off when the vent gives way, falling from

the ceiling to crash below. The metal breaks around us and my body screams in pain from the fall.

"Celine," Valen says, my name laced with worry.

"I'm okay," I grunt out, all the air having been expelled from my lungs with the fall.

Valen shoves the debris aside and helps me to my feet. I'm unsteady and sway in place. He holds my shoulders to steady me. Grunts and cries of pain can be heard not too far away, but where we've landed the coast is clear. There's even a door at the end of the hall open for us like whoever came through it was on a mission and didn't have time to make sure it was shut.

Valen picks me up again and carries me through the open door and into the exact place I suspected we were being held beneath.

Vex.

Except the club is looking a little different at the moment. Bright rays of sunlight stream in through the front of the building where a car has driven through the doorway. A car I very much recognize as Zav's.

He came.

He found me.

If it weren't for the fact that Valen's holding me in his arms, I know my knees would give out on me now.

"Celine!" A female voice cries out in surprise.

I look toward that large open space where people on the street are gathered looking at the mess of the car in the building and find Ava running toward me, her hair a pink cape flowing behind her.

"Ava!" I whimper and Valen sets me down just in time for me to fall into my friend's arms. He watches, eyes wide as he takes us in, and then I watch him practically melt into the space around us and disappear.

What the fuck? Is he some kind of chameleon? Can he go invisible? I've never seen Zav do anything like that.

Worry clings to me, but I hope wherever he's off to that he'll be safe.

"You're okay," Ava sobs, holding my cheeks and taking me in. "I thought you'd be dead."

"How long have I been gone?" I ask her, squeezing her tight. I need to get out of here, but something tells me that Zavier's handling Genevieve and her goons and I needn't worry.

"About two weeks," she replies, smoothing my matted hair back. She makes a yuck face and says, "I'll schedule you for a hair appointment." She eyes my nails. "Better get nails done too." She seemingly shakes herself free from those thoughts and says, "I've been helping Zavier track you down. He couldn't smell you and..." She pauses, glowering at me. "When the fuck were going to tell me your boyfriend is a vampire? A vampire!" She shrieks and I hope no one on the streets can hear her over the sounds of traffic and the music blaring from Zav's wrecked sports car.

"He told you?"

Ava wipes away a tear from my face. "I mean, he kind of had to. I accused him of murdering you and I might've tossed some threats around."

I smile and hug my friend, a few more tears leaking out of my eyes. Ava can be a bit much at times, but I wouldn't have her any other way.

"I need to go find him." I grab her by the shoulders.

"Oh, no you don't, missy." She tightens her hold. "You got away from that psycho bitch, Genevieve, and you're not going back."

My lips part. "How did you know it was her?"

Ava rolls her eyes. "I pay attention. Duh. If it wasn't for me,

Zav would've never figured it out. For a redhead he's a bit of a dumb blond, don't you think?"

A laugh bubbles out of me. "A little," I admit. "Can you get me a blanket? Some water? I'm so thirsty."

Ava, oblivious to what I'm doing, nods and squeezes my shoulders. "I'll find some. Why don't you wait outside?"

"I'm okay here."

She gives me a funny look, like she can't figure out why I'd want to stay in the club, but shrugs and goes in search for what I've asked for.

As soon as her back is turned I sprint, well hobble, for the open door I just came through. I'm insane to be going back, I know that, but the need I feel to get to Zavier is indescribable. The tug has never been this strong before. He needs me. I know it.

It doesn't take me long to come upon the carnage I have no doubt he left in his wake. Bodies and limbs litter the long hall, growing in numbers the farther I go.

I round a corner and there he is.

Something inside me *knows* I should be trembling at the sight in front of me, but I'm not scared. I could never be scared of him.

His eyes are such a brilliant green behind his glasses that they're otherworldly. His mouth and most of his body is covered in blood and from his right hand hanging by the strands of her hair is Genevieve's decapitated head.

"Zav," I breathe out his name.

His body shakes with the thunderous breaths he takes.

"Zav," I say again. "I'm here. I'm here and I'm okay."

I can tell he's not fully with me. My guess would be that he's fighting his baser, vampire instincts at the moment. Taking out that many other vampires couldn't have been easy and if I were to guess, he's been hanging on by a thread up until now.

"Zavier," my voice breaks on his name. "Come back to me. I'm begging you. I'm right here. I'm safe. Please, baby."

When his pupils continue to stay enlarged, I worry not even I will be able to pull him back from this. I'm not afraid of him, though. I ignore the gore beneath my shoes and close the distance between us. He lets Genevieve's head drop and I try not to gag as my hand finds the back of his neck.

"Hey." I smile, seeing his eyes begin to return to normal at my touch. "There you are. I knew you'd find me." I wet my lips with my tongue, trying to keep my tears at bay. "I love you, Zav. I know I didn't say it before and I'm so sorry, but I want you to know now that I love you." Stroking the hair at the base of his neck I revel in him being in front of me.

Slowly, I feel him place his hands on my hips. "You ... I'm not imagining this am I?"

"No." I shake my head, sniffling. "I'm here, baby. I'm alive. Looks like I was trying to get out to find you and at the same time, you were coming for me. We really are mates, aren't we?"

His fingers stroke my cheeks gently like he's still trying to convince himself that I'm alive and in one piece.

"I love you," I say again. Now that I've said the words I want to keep saying them.

He presses his forehead to mine and closes his eyes. "Fuck, Celine. I've never been so scared in my entire life. I thought ... I couldn't survive it if I lost you. I love you, too. You are ... you're my soul. Without you there would be nothing left of me."

He moves in to kiss me and I cringe away. "Um ... maybe kiss me after you shower, hm? I wouldn't mind a shower first myself."

He seems to realize then that he's covered in blood. "Yeah, good ... that's a good idea."

I can tell he's still a little dazed, but he's returning and that's all that matters.

"Please, get me the hell out of here," I beg, and he does just that.

51

She's in my arms.

She's alive.

She's okay.

I keep repeating this mantra to help calm myself down. I went into a rage back there. I don't know if I've ever lost control like that in my entire existence, but I saw Genevieve and her posse and I fucking lost it. She took my *mate*. The one woman I've ever truly loved. I couldn't leave that unpunished and she knew that.

She fought back hard, I'll give her that, but she was no match for my lethal rage.

I clutch Celine tighter to me and breathe in her scent for the millionth time since she found me in the hall. I refused to let her go and told her as much. Since I had totaled my car, we were out of a ride, but I couldn't wait for a taxi to take us. Not as if any sane person would've taken us in our current state.

I ran us home faster than I ever have before, the people and city of Chicago a blur around us.

I turn the shower on to warm and gently peel her clothes off her body. They smell of mildew and urine and other things I don't want to think about. Like her blood.

My fingers tremble as I toss her clothes in a pile and mine join them. I'll burn them later.

I check the shower, finding it warm enough and tug Celine in with me. Immediately the water at our feet turns red as it swirls down the drain.

Celine nuzzles her nose against my bare chest, and I run my hands up and down her back.

She sniffles and I close my eyes, resting my chin on top of her head.

The horrors my girl has probably lived through ... I don't want to think about it.

"Turn around," I murmur and grab the purple loofah sitting on the shelf.

She obeys, reluctantly letting me go. I think we're both going to be needy for the foreseeable future.

Squirting berry scented soap onto the loofah, I get to work cleaning her from the neck all the way down to the tips of her toes. I take my time and gently scrub at stubborn grime. Each scrape, bruise, and scar I spot on her body I pepper with a kiss, trying to erase whatever memories cling to them.

She's here. She's safe.

I must be stuck in my thoughts longer than I think, because next thing I know, Celine is facing me with a look of understanding on her sweet face. She strokes my jaw with the back of her hand and holds my gaze to communicate silently we're here and we're okay.

Celine takes the loofah from my limp hand and begins to clean my chest. Her eyes are hyper-focused on my skin and getting rid of every bit of dirt and blood. She takes my glasses off my face and sets them outside the shower to rub at my face with a damp washcloth. Due to my shit eyesight things go blurry but I focus on the feeling of her cleaning me up.

Both of us naked and in close quarters it could easily be sexual, but this is more than that. It's coming home and reminding each other we made it through and we're together. The intimacy and closeness I feel with Celine in this moment is monumental.

I feel her tremble and open one eye to see her tears. Gathering her in my arms I lower us to the floor of the shower. She sobs into my chest, gut wrenching cries that I know she's been holding in for two long weeks. I periodically place kisses on her forehead, her chin, her eyes.

"I've got you, pretty girl." I rest my chin on top of her head and close my eyes as I lean against the shower wall. "The next time you want to fight, please don't tell me I can't follow," I beg.

That pulls a watery laugh from her. "I bet you followed anyway."

"I did," I concede. "But apparently I gave you too long of a head start."

She sniffles again. "I'm sorry about Tom. I know he meant a lot to you."

I stiffen and squeeze her tighter. "You know about Tom?"

"Genevieve brought me a chess piece. It had dried blood. It didn't take much to figure it out."

"My smart girl," I croon, kissing the corner of her mouth.

Her round brown eyes lock on mine. Even with my vision blurred it would be impossible not to miss the intensity in her gaze. She strokes her fingers lovingly over my cheek, down the slope of my nose, before finally tracing the curve of my mouth.

"I meant it, you know?"

"What?" I rub my face against her neck, and she gives me a gentle shove so I'm forced to look at her.

"That I love you." She presses a soft kiss to my lip. "You might be a little insane, and kill bad people, and show up everywhere I am but you're mine and I love you."

I thought I might never hear those words from her and now I fear I'll never get sick of them.

I clear my throat, suddenly thick with emotion. "It's been a long time since anyone's loved me."

She cups my cheeks in her hands. "Don't worry, I'll love you enough to make up for every time you felt unloved."

She leans in and kisses me and as much as I want to deepen it, make it more, I don't because I don't know exactly what kind of trauma she's been through, so I'll let her lead, and I'll follow. I'm perfectly fine with being on her leash. Kinky, but true.

When the water grows cold, I reach up and turn it off and stand with her in my arms, carrying her out of the bathroom and to her room. I lay her down on the bed and grab my glasses and wipe them dry before I turn toward the dresser to get her something to wear.

"Zav?" she says softly, and I look over my shoulder, groaning at the sight of her sprawled on the bed damp and naked. Her body is perfect and the divots in her hips call for me to place my hands there, but I'm a good boy and stay right where I am. Her well-being matters more to me than trying to be all over her.

I swallow hard. "Yes?"

"I ... I want you to..." She licks her lips and sits up, balancing on her knees. "I want our bond," she says finally. "I want to do whatever it is I need to so I can accept the mating bond."

My lips part and dammit if all the blood in my body doesn't go south straight to my dick.

Down boy. Now is not the time. I mean it. You're embarrassing me.

I move closer to her, and she reaches out, fingers gentle against my stomach. "I'm not ready for you to turn me—I assume you can turn me?" She waits for me to nod before she continues. "I want to keep my humanity a little longer. But this —" she wiggles her finger back and forth between us— "I want it now."

"Love," the endearment slips out in a lisp around my fang-boner. "Are you sure? You can't take it back once it's done."

She holds my eyes. "I know what I want, Zavier, and it's you. I'm tired of denying how I feel." Her hands slide up the back of my neck and I slip my arms around her, holding her to me. "I could've died and you ... you would've never known what you mean to me. I was so mad at you when I left, and I hate to think that would've been your last memory of me."

Tears fall anew and I wipe them away with my thumbs. I don't want to see her cry.

"Okay," I say softly.

"How does it work?" she asks, biting her lip. I want to pull that lip from her teeth and bite it myself, but I refrain.

"I need to drink from you, and you'll drink from me."

She arches a brow, lips curling in disgust. "Even though I'm still human?"

"Even though you're still human," I concur. "It won't taste like blood to you, though," I promise, smoothing an errant piece of hair behind her ear. "It ... your mate's blood is ... well, I've heard it's the best thing you'll ever taste. Nothing else compares."

She gives a tiny nod. "Okay. I'm ready."

Midnight, asleep on the pillow I normally use, opens one eye and gives a meow before he runs out the door like he knows what's about to happen and doesn't want to be privy to it. Smart pussy.

"Lie down, honey."

She does as I say. The pulse point at her throat races, tempting me to make my first bite there.

"We have to take turns," I tell her. "About five times to fully settle the bond in."

She nods. "Do it. I'm ready." She reaches up and touches my cheek again. "I love you," she says, like she wants to remind me how true it is.

I close my eyes, absorbing those words. No one has professed their love to me since my parents were alive. That's a long fucking time to go without any love. Sure, I had dalliances, but there was never any emotions involved. All said, I've had a lonely existence, but I'd do it all again, a million times over, to get to here—to get to her.

I lean down and kiss the spot on her neck. "Ready?" I ask.

"Y—"

She can't even get the full word out because I bite into her flesh and suck.

Fuck.

The stories I've heard are true. There's nothing in this universe comparable to the taste of Celine. I suck, trying to memorize the unique taste of her. It's unlike anything else I've ever had. Any word I think to describe it, honey or even vanilla, is too flat of a flavor for how full and alive she tastes.

I pull my mouth away from her neck and bite into my own wrist, offering it to her.

She holds my eyes as she grabs it and brings it to her lips.

"Don't be scared," I murmur when I see the fear reflected in her eyes.

She gives a tiny nod and sets her mouth on the wound I

created, sucking at my blood before the skin can heal. My head drops back, a moan ripping out of my throat.

She goes to pull away, but I shake my head. "More. You need more."

She obliges and sucks down some more of my blood before I switch and take from her again.

Back and forth we go, the bond between us growing stronger as we do. I feel her more fully and sense her emotions. Mates can't read each other's minds, but we can sense certain things like intentions.

When the drop comes, the full snapping of the bond, we both gasp in surprise.

It feels like a rubber band snapping into place and ricocheting from the force.

Celine blinks up at me. "That was..."

"I know." I kiss her, pulling her into my arms and beneath the covers. "Sleep," I encourage, kissing the top of her head.

Luckily, she's too tired to argue. She falls asleep with her head on my chest, her even breaths fanning across my abdomen.

"I'm never letting you go," I vow. "Never again. Not for anything."

Our peace is short-lived. It's less than an hour later when Ava shows up at the apartment, banging her hand against the door.

"You two better be in there. I looked for you everywhere at the scene and you both were just fucking gone."

I shift Celine to the side, and she groans. "Your ferocious pitbull of a friend is here."

"Pitbulls aren't ferocious," she retorts, stifling a yawn.

"Fine," I acquiesce. "Your dragon of a friend is here."

"You two better let me in or I'm going to scream. Three, two—"

"Let her in," Celine says.

I slip on a pair of boxer-briefs and I'm at the front door in less than a second. "Get in here tiny pink one," I grumble.

"Thank you." She steps around me, chin stuck haughtily in the air. "Rude of you to leave me at the scene of *your* crime. A car in a club and a bunch of bodies."

"Sorry about that." I rub my jaw, trying not to grin.

"I just want to check on Celine," she says.

The bedroom door opens and Celine steps out in a robe. "I'm sorry for sending you away," she says to her friend. "I needed to get to Zav."

"To bone, I can see that. God, I hate being single," she groans, dropping her head back. "But you're okay?" She crosses the space and hugs Celine.

"I will be," Celine answers, smiling at me over her friend's shoulder. "I have Zav." Ava pulls back to glare at her. "And you," she adds. "You're a given, Ava."

"And what? I'm not?" I point at myself. "That's not fair." I pick up my emotional support pussy from where he meows at my feet and settle him on my shoulders. "At least I'm someone's favorite around here."

Celine rolls her eyes at my antics and things, surprisingly, almost feel normal. I know deep down though it's going to be a while before she recovers from this. But I'll be there to support her in whatever ways she needs.

Ava takes a deep breath and squeezes Celine's hand. "Now that I know you're home and safe, I'll leave."

Celine tugs on her friend's wrist. "You could stay in Zav's apartment if you want, so you don't have to go across the city."

"It's okay." Ava tucks a pink piece of hair behind her ear. "I am going to need a new apartment soon, though. The lease is up in a month."

I scratch my chin. "My apartment is going to be vacant moving forward so it's yours if you want." Celine gives me a *look* —one that says, *excuse me sir what are you thinking saying that?* I send her one back that says *you're my mate and you're never getting rid of me now so deal with it.*

"Really?" Ava says in surprise.

"Rent's paid for the next year. It's yours if you want it."

"Zavvy!" she cries and runs over to me, throwing her arms around my middle. I grunt at the impact. For someone so tiny she's shockingly strong. "Thank you."

"Mhm." I pat the tiny human's head.

Pulling away, Ava says, "I'm going. For real this time."

I open the door and see her out, locking up once she's out.

Celine comes over and wraps her arms around me, curling her body into mine. "You're moving in, huh?"

I grin down at her. "I already have your heart. What difference does it make if we live in the same apartment?"

She sighs dramatically. "Excellent point, roomie."

I kiss her cheek. "I think I might prefer husband."

She throws her head back and laughs. "I already accepted your mate bond." She pats my stomach. "Let's wait a little while on marriage."

"But you will marry me one day?" I can't stop my smile.

"One day," she agrees.

"And have my babies?"

"Zav," she groans.

"They'd be the cutest babies you ever did see." I try to reason.

"Maybe," she muses and reaches up to adjust my glasses for me.

That maybe is going to be a yes.

She entwines our fingers. "Let's go back to bed."

I let her drag me along, grinning like a fool. Despite the hell the past few weeks have been, the future is looking pretty fucking bright.

We settle into the bed, and I spoon her from behind.

I kiss the skin beneath her ear. "You were worth the wait."

I sense her smile rather than see it. "Duh."

I pinch her side for that sassy comment, and she dissolves into giggles.

Never, in my centuries of existence, did I think I could be this happy but I'm really looking forward to conquering whatever comes next with my mate at my side.

EPILOGUE
THREE WEEKS LATER

"What the hell do you have in here, Ava?" I huff out a breath as I set down a cardboard box in what is now going to be Ava's apartment.

"Um..." She eyes the box. "I think that's my hair supplies."

"Of course it is." I attempt to catch my breath.

Zavier, show off that he is, comes in behind me and sets down a stack of three large boxes. Now that Ava knows about him, he isn't concerned about hiding his true nature.

"Zavvy?" Ava plants her hands on her hips. "I'm curious, how did you come to acquire an apartment right next to Celine?" She taps her foot. "Now that I know you better, something tells me it was by no normal means."

Zav shoots a shocked, wide-eyed gaze my way. "Uh..."

"I'm just saying," Ava goes on. "I find it highly doubtful that this place was vacant before you."

Zav's eyes turn apologetic, and he gives me a sheepish smile.

I gasp. "Zavier! Did you kill Cory?"

He thrusts his hands up quickly in a gesture of innocence. "It's not my fault, really. He talked shit about you, so I kind of punched him a little too hard and killed him. Total accident."

"Zav," I groan, very much doubting this was an accident.

He shrugs, smiling sheepishly. "Oops."

"You killed him. Like … in here." Ava points at the floor and he nods. "Fuck. Is this place haunted?"

"No," he answers quickly. "Everyone knows ghosts aren't real."

"But vampires are?" she retorts.

Watching them battle it out is highly amusing. Ava and Zavier are quite a lot alike. Both stubborn and tenacious to a fault.

A noise pulls my attention to the open doorway and my jaw drops.

"Valen!" I gasp.

I've since filled Zavier in on my cellmate and how I worried about him since I wasn't sure where he disappeared to or if he was even okay. Zavier had reached out to some of his vampire contacts, but no one knew anything about someone named Valen. But there he is looking a world better than he did the last time I saw him.

I still have so many questions about what was going on beneath Vex and the truth of why they held Valen captive, but they're questions I've told myself will have to wait. I need to heal—not just physically, but mentally, too. I've put in for an extended leave of absence from work. Working crime and murders is too much for me right now.

I take Valen in, noting that his skin color has turned to a warm olive tone and his hair has been trimmed. Longer on top, shorter on the sides. Face cleanly shaven and showcasing a chiseled jawline, he wears a pair of new jeans and a t-shirt with a jacket over the top.

"Hi," he says, voice gruff and raspy like he hasn't spoken in a while. "I'm sorry I left you."

"It's okay," I say, walking toward him. Tears burn my eyes. I'm so relieved to know he's okay. "Can I hug you?"

I don't wait for him to answer, just step around my mate and wrap my arms around the giant vampire.

"You saved me."

He pats my head awkwardly. "You saved yourself."

I let him go and step out. "I'm glad to see you alive and well. I've been worried."

"I needed some time on my own," he says. "But I think I'm going to stay in the city for a while. I'm looking for a place to stay."

"Oh," I gasp. "Maybe you could stay here with Ava?" I suggest. "She's looking for a roommate." Even though Zav has the place paid for, she says she doesn't want to live alone and solely be our third wheel.

"Wait, who is this?" Ava points at Valen. "I think there are a few things I haven't been filled in on."

"This is Valen. He was my cell buddy. He helped me get out."

Ava's mouth forms a perfect O. "Got it."

"Valen, this is Ava." I point between my friend and the vampire.

"Put 'er there, partner." Ava extends her hand to him.

Valen hesitates before taking it and then his eyes go wide. "I wondered," he whispers on a gasp. "But it is you."

Ava scrunches her nose. "Huh? What?"

Valen takes her in like he's seeing the sun rise for the first time.

The next words out of his mouth shock us all.

"You're my mate."

A note from Aura

We know you probably have some unanswered questions, so we're happy to announce that there's a second book coming for Ava and Valen! Stay tuned for more information!

-Love, Aura

ABOUT AURA

Aura Hayes is a bestie writing duo whose combined interest in paranormal and fantasy romance had them coming up with their own ideas and they're finally putting those ideas to paper. When they're not scheming about vampires, werewolves, and other lore you can find them with an iced coffee in one hand and their kindle in the other. Loving a Vampire is Total Chaos is their debut romance.

Printed in Dunstable, United Kingdom